RAVES FOR THE PREVIOUS
VALDEMAR ANTHOLOGIES:

"Fans of Lackey's epic Valdemar series will devour this superb anthology. Of the thirteen stories included, there is no weak link— an attribute exceedingly rare in collections of this sort. Highly recommended."
—*The Barnes and Noble Review*

"This high-quality anthology mixes pieces by experienced author and enthusiastic fans of editor Lackey's Valdemar. Valdemar fandom, especially, will revel in this sterling example of what such a mixture of fans' and pros' work can be. Engrossing even for newcomers to V...

PROPERTY OF
RANCHO MIRAGE PUBLIC LIBRARY
71100 HIGHWAY 111
RANCHO MIRAGE, CA 92270
(760)341-READ(7323)

DISCARD

"...provides each author's personal stamp on the story. Well written and fun, Valdemarites will especially appreciate the magic of this book." —*The Midwest Book Review*

the World

Changing the World

All-New Tales of Valdemar

Edited by
Mercedes Lackey

DAW BOOKS, INC.
DONALD A. WOLLHEIM, FOUNDER
375 Hudson Street, New York, NY 10014

ELIZABETH R. WOLLHEIM
SHEILA E. GILBERT
PUBLISHERS
http://www.dawbooks.com

Copyright © 2009 by Mercedes Lackey and Tekno Books.

All Rights Reserved.

Cover art by Jody A. Lee.

DAW Book Collectors No. 1494.

DAW Books are distributed by Penguin Group (USA).

All characters and events in this book are fictitious.
All resemblance to persons living or dead is coincidental.

If you purchase this book without a cover you should be aware that this book
may have been stolen property and reported as "unsold and destroyed" to the
publisher. In such case neither the author nor the publisher has received any
payment for this "stripped book."

The scanning, uploading and distribution of this book via the Internet or any
other means without the permission of the publisher is illegal, and punishable by
law. Please purchase only authorized electronic editions, and do not participate
in or encourage the electronic piracy of copyrighted materials. Your support of
the author's rights is appreciated.

First Printing, December 2009
1 2 3 4 5 6 7 8 9

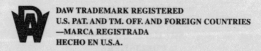

DAW TRADEMARK REGISTERED
U.S. PAT. AND TM. OFF. AND FOREIGN COUNTRIES
—MARCA REGISTRADA
HECHO EN U.S.A.

PRINTED IN THE U.S.A.

ACKNOWLEDGMENTS

"The One Left Behind," copyright © 2009 by Mercedes Lackey

"For Want of a Nail," copyright © 2009 by Rosemary Edghill and Denise McCune

"Softly Falling Snow," copyright © 2009 by Elizabeth A. Vaughan

"The Reluctant Herald," copyright © 2009 by Mickey Zucker Reichert

"A Storytelling of Crows," copyright © 2009 by Elisabeth Waters

"Waiting to Belong," copyright © 2009 by Kristin Schwengel

"The Last Part of the Way," copyright © 2009 by Brenda Cooper

"Midwinter Gifts," copyright © 2009 by Stephanie D. Shaver

"Wounded Bird," copyright © 2009 by Michael Z. Williamson

"Defending the Heart," copyright © 2009 by Kate Paulk

"Matters of the Heart," copyright © 2009 by Sarah A. Hoyt

"Nothing Better to Do," copyright © 2009 by Tanya Huff

"The Thief of Anvil's Close," copyright © 2009 by Fiona Patton

"Twice Blessed," copyright © 2009 by Judith Tarr

"Be Careful What You Wish For," copyright © 2009 by Nancy Asire

"Interview with a Companion," copyright © 2009 by Ben Ohlander

Contents

The One Left Behind
by Mercedes Lackey

Mercedes Lackey is a full-time writer and has published numerous novels, including the best-selling Heralds of Valdemar series. She is also a professional lyricist and licensed wild bird rehabilitator.

Marya was doing her shopping when the Heralds rode into the village, and the flash of white and sudden turning of heads in the corner of her vision made her stomach twist into an angry knot, her jaw tighten, and her fists clench. She knew what it was. Only one thing could be that white in the middle of a village in the middle of a rainy spring.

"Done," she said, cutting off her bargaining abruptly and leaving Druk Pelan, the egg seller, open-mouthed in astonishment. She shoved the coppers at him, took up her basket and the eggs, and strode quickly back toward her house at the east edge of the village without getting any of the other things she'd meant to buy.

The house, inherited from her mother, which had been her parents' before her, was really more of a cottage. They hadn't needed much space: the loft bed for her, the bedroom her mother had slept in once she inherited the place until the day she died, and one big room that served as kitchen and work space and held

1

her baskets of yarn and the big loom. So far as Marya knew, the cottage had been built around the loom; she couldn't imagine how some of the big beams had been brought in otherwise. The windows were all positioned to give the person sitting at the loom the best possible light, all day. The kitchen was almost more of an after-thought; more often than not, Marya, her mother, and her grandparents had eaten food cooked at the baker's or cold meats, raw vegetables, bread and cheese. Well she would have to make do with what she had, now.

The plain linen warp was half full of colorful woof threads now, with the cartoon beneath, for Marya was not just any weaver; she was a weaver of tapestries. So her mother and grandparents had been. People sent commissions to her from all over Valdemar, mostly from extremely wealthy households, for when you wanted to really impress people, there was nothing like an enor-mous tapestry hung against the wall. Ordinary arras hangings would do to keep down drafts, but a tapestry! That *meant* something.

This one was of some fancy family or other's coat of arms, a pair of stags fighting on their hind legs. Some tapestry weavers sent out for their cartoons or used im-ages that they kept carefully folded and put away. Up in the loft, there were stacks of those, some going back a hundred years or more. Her family had relied on such aids since they had begun weaving.

Not Marya. Marya drew her own. The sketch she'd been sent had been no bigger than her hand. The car-toon was twice the length of the loom, and that was only half of it. She'd flip it for the other half, the mirror image of the stag she was working on now, and carefully sew the two halves together for the finished whole. And an impressive backdrop to a head table that would be, too.

But she was not thinking of that. She was thinking of the Heralds in the village square and wondering angrily how long they were going to be in the village. Not long, she hoped. Because she had no intention of leaving her house while they were here, or she just might be tempted to—

She froze at the polite knock at her open door.

Surely not.

She turned slowly, but the reflection of white in the pots on the kitchen wall told her who it was before she actually finished the turn.

"Marya Bannod?" the older of the two Heralds asked.

She nodded curtly, unable to trust herself to speak.

"We'd like to ask for your hel—" he began.

She exploded. "Oh, you've a *lot* of nerve coming here and asking for *my* help!" she hissed, hands balled into fists at her side. "Whatever it is, you can damned well just go and take care of it yourselves, you with your great minds and fine ways! *Get off my stoop!"*

And she slammed the door in their astonished faces.

Then she let out a breath. That had felt good. Not as good as flinging some kitchen things at them, but good. Now they'd go away, and get on their white horses and—

There was another knock.

Surely not—

She opened it. They were still there.

Briefly, she entertained a fantasy of snatching up the beater from the loom and driving them down the street with it, cudgeling their heads and shoulders the whole time. But . . . no. These particular Heralds hadn't done her any harm.

Just Heralds in general.

"You're not wanted here," she said, folding her arms over her chest and glaring at them. "Get out."

"Perhaps you didn't—"

"You think I'm feebleminded?" she snapped. "I understood perfectly. You've got some sort of tangle. You think I can sort it out for you and save you some time and effort. *No.* I realize that you don't hear that very often. Perhaps you should; it would do you good. *No.* What part of *no* do you not understand?"

She slammed the door again. This time when the knock came, she didn't answer it. Instead, she went to her loom and began work on the tapestry, singing out the color changes as loud as she could to a tune of her own invention. It helped her concentrate, and it soothed her nerves a little.

She heard the sound of voices at her door; four of them. She sang louder. Eventually the talking stopped; then there were footsteps going away.

She kept working.

She didn't stop until it became too dark to distinguish between different shades of the same colors. By then her arms were weary, and her back was stiff. She didn't usually work that long at a stretch on the loom without taking breaks, but she had been so angry that she hadn't dared stop, or she was sure she would have smashed something.

She had started a fine pea soup with a ham bone in it this morning; it would be ready now. She'd wanted fresh bread to go with it but . . . oh well. She'd just have to bake her own bannocks or griddle cakes until the Heralds left. She was *not* leaving her house, and they couldn't make her.

The soup was perfect. She ladled herself out a bowl, set some tea to steep, and was about to sit down when—

There was another knock at the door, and her anger flared like lint caught in a fire. She snatched up her frying pan and stalked to the door, flinging it open. "I told you—"

"Now, now Marya—" The mayor of the village, Stefan Durst, held up both hands placatingly. "Don't go hitting me with that. I need the few wits I have left."

She snorted, but she let the hand with the pan in it fall to her side. "I suppose you'll be wanting to come in and explain to me why I need to do what their lordships think I should."

"Well . . . in a word, yes."

"You can come in. But I'm having my supper, and I'm not feeding you." She glared at him. "You eat better than I do."

Stefan just sighed and looked put-upon. She moved out of the way to let him in but closed the door firmly behind him, lest some Herald think he could sneak in when she wasn't looking.

She sat back down at her tiny table and began to eat her soup. Stefan looked about for some place to sit, and eventually he took the loom bench. Stefan, a balding, plump man with mouse-colored hair, looked down at his well-groomed, clean hands.

"Marya, they're Heralds," he said plaintively.

"I know they're Heralds," she snapped. "I'm neither blind nor feebleminded."

"They've got the Queen's mandate." There was a whine to his voice. He'd been whiny as a child, and he hadn't lost the habit.

"They can have the Queen's crown and underwear for all I care. I'm not helping them." She put her spoon in the empty bowl and glared at him again. "And you, of all people, should know why. What have Heralds *ever* done for me but make my life a misery?"

He moved his hands a little, helplessly. "Yes, but—"

"Do you have *any* idea what it was like to grow up without a father? To have every other child in this village mock me by telling me he'd run off to rid himself of me and mother? To watch my mother write letter after letter that was never answered, and go from hopeful to hopeless to bitter?" She'd held this pent up for too long. "And then, then, when a man from this village takes a shine to me, and there's talk of weddings, along comes *another* one of those damned white horses, and there am I left in the rain like my mother, and the letters start to say 'You wouldn't understand,' and then they stop coming altogether." The very words were bitter on her tongue. "At least I wasn't left pregnant and alone. Just alone."

She got up and washed the bowl and spoon in the sink.

"Well . . . that's what they're here about. Danet, that is."

She turned, slowly. He was twisting those too-clean hands together and staring at them. With guilt, she thought.

"What do you mean, they're here about Danet?" Her voice was dangerously soft.

"All I know is what they told me," he replied, cringing a little. "They're here about Danet, and they need your help. That's all."

"You can pick yourself off that bench and you can march yourself back to them, and you can tell them from me that Danet Stens can rot in hell for all I care, and there's an end to it!" She was unaware that she had picked up her sharpest kitchen knife and was holding it, until Stefan's eyes went to it, and he gave a little yelp. She slapped it down on the table. He jumped. She pointed with her chin. "The door's that way."

He took the hint and scuttled out.

She moved her chair closer to the fire and took up her knitting. It was soothing; she never did patterns and never had more than one color on the needles, although she would use up all the little ends of her weaving by making them into crazy-colored knitted blankets and scarves. After all the intricate pattern weaving she did during the day, it was restful to be doing something with no pattern and no counting except to cast on. She made smocklike sweaters out of rectangular shapes that needed only to be sewn together. In winter she could layer on as many of those as she liked to keep warm. It wasn't as if anyone cared what she looked like.

It wasn't as if she wanted anyone to. One heartbreak in a lifetime was enough.

Oh, she remembered Dan, all right. Handsome, witty, charming . . . everyone liked him, and she had been so flattered when he started to pay attention to her. Though her mother had eyed him with suspicion and disfavor whenever he showed up, she'd been absolutely and utterly sure that her mother was suspicious for no reason at all. Who wouldn't love Dan?

Oh, it was true that he didn't seem to do a lick of work, but why would he need to? He did what he did best for his father, bring in business to the little tavern with his ready stories and skill at games. He didn't get paid for that, of course, but that didn't matter. She was already doubling the family business with her weaving. Once it became widely known that she wasn't just copying old cartoons for her tapestries, that she was making original images, she'd be turning business away. He could do what she couldn't: flatter and please the customers, so she could concentrate on the weaving.

She had it all planned out in her mind.

And then, between one day and the next, he was gone.

There had been some talk about some thefts—she dismissed them out of hand, and then the whole village had been forced to do the same when letters came back telling how he had been carried off by a Companion to be a Herald. The whole village had been forced to admit that they'd misjudged him, and although she got her letters with some misgiving at first, still, she *was* getting letters. She was *not* replaying her mother's story all over again.

But then the letters began to change. It seemed as if every other line ended with ". . . but of course, you wouldn't understand." At first it made her anxious and bewildered. Then, as the tone grew more and more patronizing, it made her angry. "Then explain it!" she demanded, more than once. It wasn't as if she were stupid! If he thought she didn't understand, well, if he would just—

But the letters grew fewer and fewer and finally stopped altogether.

By that time, her feelings had turned as bitter as her mother's. She threw herself into her work. Her mother died in the middle of that winter, but at least Marya could congratulate herself that she'd had every possible comfort. Not even the mayor's wife had such a fine goosedown bed, pillows, and comforter. Not even the mayor was served such savory morsels when she could bring herself to eat. It was all that Marya could do for her when the bitter love had turned again to anguish in her mother's last illness, and she spent her last breaths weeping and calling for her lost lover.

Oh, how she hated the Heralds.

Her anger made the needles fly, and row after row of knitting grew beneath her hands. Stefan was an idiot. But then again, the entire village was Herald-mad. Probably all of Valdemar was Herald-mad. Little girls *and* boys made white stick horses and played at being Heralds. You found decorations of Heralds and Companions everywhere. There were more ornamental white horse heads than there were representations of the actual arms of Valdemar. The one and only commission she had ever turned down was for a tapestry of a Herald and Companion—the noble family of someone whose son had been Chosen. She had used the rather specious argument that she would never be able to get the Companion and the uniform white enough, and that the white wool would soon become dingy. They had countered that they would send her Companion mane and tail hair to make into yarn, hair that would never get dingy, because Companions literally shed dirt. She had replied (without attempting it) that Companion hair could not be made into yarn and that she could not in all good faith take on such a commission knowing that Herald and Companion would soon become a grayish yellow. She never heard from them again.

And I would starve to death before I—

There was a knock at the door.

She did not rush to get up. She put up her knitting, made sure the fire was burning cleanly, while another couple of knocks came, and only then did she get up to answer it. Stefan could just wait out there with the night insects biting him.

Serve him right if he was covered in welts tomorrow.

She opened the door, intending to tell him brusquely to be off and slam it in his face again. But it wasn't Stefan who was out there.

It was the two Heralds.

A moment of shock and rage held her rigid. And that was when the older of the two said the one thing that kept her from slamming the door in *their* faces.

"Danet Stens is not a Herald."

They sat stiffly side by side on her weaving bench. She sat stiffly in her chair, hands uncharacteristically idle.

But she was listening. And what she heard from the two Heralds—

"... as far as we can tell, he did not begin by deciding to impersonate a Herald," the older of the two—Herald Callan—was saying. "He sent back letters that he had been Chosen, we think, largely to cover up the thefts he'd committed here. But approximately a month later, he seems to have understood that if he actually put the full ruse into motion, he would have a free hand to do virtually anything."

She nodded, slowly. "But why keep on sending letters back?" she asked suspiciously.

"Until we find him, we can only speculate as to why," said the other, who had not yet given his name. "We have a lot of guesses—the most likely is to *keep* people from associating him with the thefts until enough time had passed that the losses were forgotten or at least the victims had given up on finding the thief."

She shook her head, puzzled. "I'd heard rumors of thefts but—you talk as if these were something large, and I certainly didn't hear anything about that—"

The Heralds exchanged a look. "I can't speak for the victims," the elder said, after a moment. "But . . . given the circumstances . . . I believe the items were purloined in a way that would have been very embarrassing to the victim if it had been made pub—"

That was when the younger interrupted. "He was sleeping with women—and one or two men—and making off with small valuables. Most of them were married."

Shocked for a moment, she sat there, blinking. She thought about some of her mother's comments. She thought some more about the curious silence that had followed Danet's disappearance. And still more about the times when he'd said he had something or other to do for his father . . .

"How did you—"

"When we began tracking him, we knew where he had come from, and we had an old list of things that had been reported as missing to the Guard," the younger said bluntly. "We've been interviewing the people who reported them stolen all day. Enough time has passed that when we told them that Danet is *not* a Herald, we usually got the truth out of them."

"Well, and the reports had generally come from the husband, but when we interviewed the wives . . ." Herald Callan blushed, visible even in the firelight. "Let's just say that they were less than happy. They were able to rationalize that he had taken the things to remember them by, when they each thought *she* were the only one. When we let it be known that this was far from the case . . ." He shook his head. "The spouses, of course, had no idea and had reported the items stolen independently. Most everyone assumed that it was a tinker or a gypsy or the like."

"We haven't enlightened the partners," the younger Herald said, with a quirk of his lips. "That would be adding insult to injury."

She unclenched her jaw. "I still don't see what this has to do with me," she replied stiffly.

They exchanged glances again. The elder cleared his throat awkwardly. "We were hoping you would come with us."

At this point, her emotions had been up and down so often her reaction was less rage and more incredulity. "You people are insane," she finally said, flatly. "Why in the name of everything considered holy would I want to do that?" Before they could answer her, she continued on. "I have a commission to finish. I have two more to start. This is how I pay for my food, my chopped wood, my wool. No one is going to give me these things."

She didn't mention that she had a very tidy sum tucked away safe and that if she wanted to, she could probably live on it for several years without taking another commission. In the first place, that was none of their business. In the second place, that was meant in case she became ill or injured or otherwise incapacitated. And in the third place, it was none of their *damn* business.

"And what makes you think I can or will do anything

more than you can?" She leveled the most evil glare she could manage at them.

"We thought because you knew him best—" Herald Callan began.

"Well, I didn't know he was sleeping with half the village women and stealing their valuables, and I didn't know that he never intended to marry me, so I obviously didn't know him very well, did I?" The bitterness in her words was so palpable that both of them winced. "Thank you for telling me the truth about him. You can leave now. No—wait—"

She got up and stalked to the little chest where she kept her few keepsakes and pulled out a bundle of letters. She didn't know why she had kept them instead of burning them. Maybe this was why. She thrust them at Callan. "Here. Maybe you can make out something you can use against him."

The Herald took the letters as gingerly as if they were on fire. "But . . . can you think of what he is likely to actually do? Anything? Anything at all? So far, all we have are complaints from what seem to be random isolated communities—that a Herald Danet comes through, makes a mess of things, and when he's gone, there are valuables missing. By the time we get the reports, he's long gone. This has been going on for two years now."

So, he'd been at it from the moment he'd left her. Oh, she should have known better. Really, she should have known better all along. He was years younger than she was. What handsome *young* man would ever have been truly interested in a dried up old spinster like her, anyway? It had seemed too good to be true, and so it was.

And that was when the final humiliating thing occurred to her.

Until either he had seduced one too many women, or the wrong woman, or someone was starting to make noise about missing items, he probably *had* intended to marry her. After all, she was making fine money. And she would have demanded very little of him. He could have gone right on sleeping with anyone he cared to, and she wouldn't have noticed. Or if she had, a few sweet words of contrition from him and she would have forgiven him. Over and over and over.

And meanwhile, he would have been living better than anyone in the village while continuing to do as little actual work as possible. As good as he had been at pulling the wool over her eyes, she'd have probably considered it her privilege to support him.

She went hot, then cold, then hot again with shame. Especially when she thought about how often she had daydreamed of the long winter nights they would spend together, cuddled up in each others' arms by the fire . . .

That was when it occurred to her that there was one thing she knew about him that they probably did not.

"If you can find his trail, it will end at a place where he intends to spend the winter," she said. "He won't travel in winter. He hates the cold, the rain, and the snow worse than a cat. That's all I know. You can get out of here now."

Reluctantly, they left.

Unfortunately, they did not take what they'd put into her head with them.

If it had been daylight, she could have lost herself in her weaving. Instead, she picked up her knitting; the needles flew at a furious pace, but they could not still her thoughts.

It had been bad enough when she had thought he had just gotten tired of her. When she had been left to wonder if she really *was* that dull, that stupid, truly unable to comprehend what being a Herald was all about.

It was worse now. She really had been stupid, but in an entirely different way. She'd been manipulated. Made a fool of. Now she knew the reason for the pitying glances she sometimes caught from some women in the village. All this time she'd thought it was pity for having been jilted.

Oh, no.

It was pity for being such a fatuous fool as to believe a handsome young man could *ever* want her. All those women that Danet Stens had slept with had felt the superior sort of pity that you do for someone who doesn't know she's living in a fool's dream.

Well, I got the last laugh, she thought bitterly. *Now all of them know they were played for fools too.* It didn't help.

Mother probably guessed. Or at least she guessed that Danet was only interested in the money I made.

That would be about right.

Finally, as the fire burned down, and the thoughts in her head would not stop buzzing about like angry hornets, she realized that she was not going to get any sleep, any sleep at all, without help.

She went to the cupboard and got out the little bottle the Healer had given her for her mother, to help her through the bad nights. She carefully measured out the right number of drops into a cup of lukewarm tea and drank it down. She had expected it to be bitter, but it had a kind of blossomy taste. Strange but pleasant. She went back to her chair and put away her knitting, noting sardonically that anger was good for one thing, at least. She'd finished the panel. She'd bind it off in the daylight and start another. Firelight was no good for binding off; you were asking for dropped stitches.

As she did every night, she carefully hung her clothing on the chair next to the bed, the bed that her grandparents, and then her mother, had slept in—though the mattress had been made new for her mother in her last year. She got into a flannel nightrail. The nights were turning cold now. Fall was not far off. If those damned

Heralds did their job properly, they'd find the wretch soon.

She got into the warm goosedown bed and wondered what he was doing right now. Probably getting into an equally warm goosedown bed with a pretty, plump woman who was someone else's wife. Not a thin, ugly stick like her.

She fell into strange confused dreams in which the Heralds and Danet chased each other around and around a copse of trees, until the snow fell and a trio of beautiful women came and carried him off on a flying sheep. All three of the women laughed and pointed at her as they flew away. She woke up feeling entirely out of sorts. For the first time that she could recall, ever, she was so very out of sorts that she didn't want to work on her tapestry.

Instead, she decided that she wasn't going to get any creative work done, she might as well give the place a thorough cleaning. She did have the very bad habit of leaving things she knew she would want later piled up next to her chair, beside the bed, or on the table. She hadn't organized the yarn since spring. For that matter, she hadn't done more than give the place a cursory sweep and dust since spring.

She spent the morning turning things inside out. The floor got a scrubbing, the mattress was turned, aired and the bed remade, the blankets all came down out of winter storage and got a good wash. Every surface got a scouring. She reorganized the yarn properly. She stacked all the rectangles of knitting in order on a little table beside the chair so she could finally sew them together. She went through her clothing, relegating a few things to be given away since they had shrunk or never actually fitted in the first place. She brought in all the dry blankets and laid them in lavender in the blanket chest at the foot of the bed. She looked at the number of knitted tunics she had and decided that her next project was going to be to use up the yarn ends in making another blanket.

By noon, the little cottage was clean, but her temper was still high. She decided that since the wretched Heralds hadn't let a closed door stop them from pestering her, she was going to finish her interrupted shopping. Serve them right if they turned up again and she wasn't there.

She was close-mouthed to the point of monosyllabic with the village merchants, but they were used to that. Usually it was because she was, in her mind, still back at her loom. It wasn't often that her temper was as frayed as it was today. But as she bought her bread and meat pies, her winter squash and her cut oats for porridge, her fruit and her soap and candles, she noticed that the shopkeepers were just as preoccupied as she was.

It was abundantly clear why. The entire village was abuzz with talk about Danet. And now, of course, *everyone* had suspected the worst of him. Even his own father, who held court in the taproom of his inn, holding forth about how his ne'er-do-well son had been a devil from the day he was born, and how no matter how hard he was beaten, all he did was shrug the punishment off and go and do what he liked.

This much, at least, Marya knew was a lie. Danet's father had never so much as laid a willowwand to his back. Everyone knew how Danet could charm his way out of any scrape he got into. But Innkeeper Stens brewed the only decent ale and beer to be had in the village and imported the only mead and wine, so no one wanted to nay-say him. And as for the innkeeper, well, he was making sure that memories were being "corrected" by pouring with a freer hand than usual and forgetting to charge now and again.

So the only one in the village today who wasn't singing the new song was Marya. And of course, everyone remembered that Danet was supposed to marry her. Looks both superior and pitying were cast on her, and plenty of curious ones too. But no one asked her anything. Perhaps they had already heard about the reception that Stefan and the Heralds themselves had gotten. Perhaps the black storm behind her eyes was more obvious than she had thought.

The upshot of it all was that she went back to her little cottage in the same temper that she had left it—and behind that temper was a sinking feeling. This was going to be a prime topic of conversation for the entire winter. And there was not one thing that she could do about it. Until something just as sensational took their minds off it, she'd be gawked at and talked about and whispered over until the thaw and hard work took peoples' minds off scandal.

She put her purchases away, put the eggs to boil, cleaned out a squash and tucked it into a corner of the fireplace to bake, then stood at her window and found that she was torn between wanting to sit down on the floor and bawl like a child, and wanting to break something. She and her family had always been odd ducks here—the only people whose income came from outside the village, and the only ones who made things that no one in the village could afford. They had always kept to themselves, and when Marya's father had gone off to be a Herald—

—and *had* he gone off to be a Herald, after all?—

That isolation had only increased.

She had reacted to the mocking as a child by throwing herself into the work—she did truly love the act and art of the weaving, the more intricate the better—and by going off somewhere no one would bother her and crying. This was often the dyeing shed; since the only way to get a big batch of a consistent color was to dye it yourself, that was what they did. Usually the shed was empty when a big tapestry was being made, so it was a good place to go to cry. Later, when she had mastered the craft of dyeing and was old enough to be trusted alone among all the boiling pots of dye and mordant baths, no one questioned why she wanted to take the job over. It was unpleasant in winter, hot in summer, and some of the dyes stank. Your hands turned colors, and it didn't wash off, it had to wear off. Her mother was just happy not to have to do it herself.

It looked as if the mocking—in adult form—was about to begin all over again.

Never had she so agreed with the philosopher's bitter observation, "The more I know of humanity, the more I appreciate my dog."

Maybe she should get a dog.

As she stood in the middle of the now neatly organized room and contemplated forcing herself to the loom, there was another tap on the door. More diffident this time.

She answered it.

Both Heralds stood there, the elder, Callan, holding out the packet of letters. "We wanted to return these," he said. "And thank you. They have been of incalculable help."

She made no move to take them. "You might as well keep them," she replied, her stomach twisting in knots that did not bode well for the squash baking at the fire. "I can't imagine how they helped you."

"We only got reports on what was happening as people sent them to Haven, which meant they weren't in order of when Danet was in the particular village," the second one—she still didn't know his name—explained. "By the time we got a report, people had forgotten when, exactly, he was there, as well. So there was confusion as to dates by the Guard, confusion as to dates by the victims. When we tried to plot his movement on the map, it didn't make any sense."

"But he very kindly dates his letters to you," Herald Callan pointed out wryly. "And although he doesn't necessarily mention the place he is in by name, he usually lets something slip that has let us identify it. *Now* we know where he was, when. His course of travel is quite clear. He's making his way south and west, by the easiest route."

She frowned. "He's not stupid. He can't be planning to carry on this scheme forever."

"We don't think so, either," Callan replied. "We think he intends to go to Rethewellan. His thefts by themselves have not been *very* large—the things he has taken have all been valuable, but not the sort of thing that someone would raise a huge hue and cry over. When he has defrauded people of money, it has not been large amounts. But impersonating a Herald, he has no expenses. People rush to give him food, shelter, anything he needs."

She nodded slowly. "So all those little bits are adding up to a right tidy sum."

"By the time he gets to Rethwellan, he'll have enough to—" Here Callan paused. "Well, I am not sure I know what he plans."

She thought it over for a moment, the same way that she thought over the design for a tapestry when it wasn't something straightforward, like the family arms. She let her mind go blank and waited for all the pieces to come together.

When they did, she was glad she didn't have anything breakable in her hand, for she would surely have thrown it.

"He's going to trick himself out like a rich man or a noble," she growled. "Then he will go looking for a woman with a lot of money, probably one older, or ugly. He'll be very clever about how he approaches her so that she never suspects what he wants. He'll make sure that in the end, it appears that she is courting him, rather than the other way around. He might marry her. He might just live off her, then disappear one day . . . and go find a new victim."

"Now you see why we want you to come with us," Callan replied. "You know how he thinks."

She opened her mouth to give him a sharp retort, but then the memory of her neighbors' pitying and smug faces rose up before her.

To have to face that for the next several weeks or months . . .

The tapestry she was working on would not be done before winter came and made it impossible to transport, and the owners were not expecting it before spring. She had no pets, no livestock, nothing that depended on her to care for it. She could just lock up the cottage and leave.

She had never been outside the village. Suddenly, she wanted to.

"All right," she growled. "But I won't be staying in any of your Herald shacks."

"We would never expect you to!" Callan said hastily. "They aren't build to hold more than two anyway. How soon can you leave?"

"No longer than it takes me to pack." She didn't need much, either. She wasn't some fancy lady that needed fuss and bows and scent. Just her clothing, her brush and her toothscrubber. She turned her back on them and went into the cottage. How hard was it to pack, after all? It wasn't as if she had clothing she had to go through. What she wore for every day was good enough.

To keep the Heralds busy while she packed, she took the squash out of the fireplace corner and set it in front of them with salt and pepper on the table. And even though she had never packed for an overnight trip before, it really was no great task to have everything in a neat bundle in a short period of time.

They weren't even finished eating by the time she was done. So she ate one of the meat pies, then put the rest of the food in her basket well wrapped up and put it next to her bundle.

To her surprise, without prompting, the Heralds cleaned up after themselves and washed all the dishes to boot.

"We'll get our things and the Companions," said the younger. And so they went off, leaving her to tidy what little there was left to do, and shut and lock the door. They didn't leave her waiting on her stoop long, either. They must not have unpacked their own bags. Long before she became impatient, they came riding up to her door, a pillion pad behind Callan.

Without a word, the younger got down, boosted her up behind Callan, and showed her how to hang on. He took her bundle and basket up and tied them up on top of his own bags, and they were off.

Being up on the back of an animal was a new sensation. It made her nervous at first, but after the first few paces she began to enjoy it. It was quite odd, being half again taller than she was used to. And the astonished looks that the villagers gave her as they rode through were altogether gratifying.

This might not be so bad, after all.

They stayed in inns, and not nasty ones, either. She'd heard about the nasty ones from some of her suppliers of dyes and the yarns and threads she couldn't get locally and from the merchants who carried away her commissioned tapestries. No, these were nice, tidy places where she wasn't afraid to sleep in the bed for fear of being carried off by vermin. The food was decent, not fancy, but she didn't particularly trust food that came all covered in sauces and spices and hiding inside crusts. She got her own small room. There was always a bathhouse.

The younger Herald—she finally learned his name the third day out—also made sure that she put her laundry with theirs. For the first time since she was a young child, she was fed by someone else, housed by someone else, waited on by someone else, taken care of by someone else. It was a way of life she suspected she could get used to very quickly.

She noticed that the Heralds "paid" for these stays with some form of paper scrip, and she finally wondered aloud how Danet was managing this without leaving some trail behind.

Sendar, the younger of the two, just shrugged. "They are not that difficult to forge; no one bothers because until now no one has ever tried to impersonate a Herald. All he had to do was get his hands on one, and if he is a decent copyist and could carve a copy of the Circle stamp, he could make as many as he liked. So many are turned in we'd never find the forgeries among the real ones."

She sniffed a little at that. It seemed rather too chancy a system to her.

She'd heard that riding was hard, that people were generally aching and sore when they weren't used to it. But maybe the people who had told her that were not used to working at a loom. She was a little stiff and sore, but it wasn't bad; then again, she was riding on a Companion—maybe they were different.

She began to pay attention to the Companions. Aside from their brilliantly white coats and blue eyes, a suspicion began to dawn on her. On the fifth evening, when Callan and Sendar had finished their plotting and planning over another nice, plain supper, she voiced it.

"Your Companions can't do anything a really good trained horse can't do," she said, perhaps a bit more tartly than she had intended.

Two sets of startled eyes met hers. "Well," she insisted,

"They can't. Or at least, a really good trained horse can make it look as if he's doing the same things. Five years ago, an animal trainer came through at Fair time, and his horse could do just about anything. Sit up like a dog, lie down, follow any command he gave it, count, add. I was watching, and he gave it signals, because I gave him a complicated sum, and the horse got it wrong just as he did. But Danet saw the same trainer. All he had to do was find a white horse trained that well, and get it to take signals from him, and there you go! Companion. Just keep painting the hooves silver when no one is watching, and plenty of white horses have blue eyes."

She thought a long moment more, while the truth of her words penetrated to them. "It makes me wonder now if he didn't plan this all along. Maybe he even had a horse ready for him when he ran off." That thought didn't help her at all; if anything, it made the deception even more bitter, because he clearly had never intended any of the things he'd promised her, and she'd had the wool pulled right over her eyes. But she wasn't one to lie to herself.

"If he planned that far ahead," Callan said, slowly, "Then he has surely planned for the moment when real Heralds confront him."

"He'll brazen it out long enough to buy himself some time, then bolt while you're dealing with all the people that think he is the real one and you are the imposters," she pointed out. "He doesn't need long."

There was silence. "This is why we asked you to come along," Callan said, ruefully. "You know how he might think, and you point out things that we would not consider—"

"Like trained horses?" She shrugged. "I hope you can work out some sort of plan to deal with this. I'm just a weaver." And with that, she took herself up the stairs to that extremely comfortable little room.

When she came back down in the morning to enjoy a truly fine breakfast, they still hadn't come up with much of a plan other than, "We are going to have to scout this out without him finding out we are Heralds."

"And what are you going to pose as?" she asked.

They both blinked. "We hadn't gotten that far," Sendar said.

She sighed and dug into a really outstanding slice of egg-and-bacon pie. "He won't have set up in a town. When he settles in for winter, he needs a small village so he can charm everyone in it. And the one or two who are suspicious will keep their mouths shut for fear of antagonizing their neighbors. That means everyone will know everyone else, and you cannot impersonate someone local."

"We could be peddlers—" Sendar began.

She laughed. "Where is your cart? Your packhorse? Do you know anything about the sorts of things that a peddler who visits a small village is likely to carry? Do you know the right prices? What a fair trade would be? I doubt that either of you knows the first thing about mending a pot, so posing as tinkers is not going to work either."

As they began to look nonplused and flustered, she helped herself to biscuits and butter. Finally she took pity on them. "Instead of trying to do something you don't know anything about, what *can* you do?"

They exchanged looks again. "We've never thought about it," Callan finally replied.

She bit back the reply of "Well, then start thinking about it!" and just left them to it.

They discussed it for far too long in her opinion, coming up with all sorts of things that were likely to fall apart the moment someone in the village asked a few questions. She was actually learning a lot about *them*, although they were probably utterly unaware of the fact. It became clear to her that neither of them had ever done what *she* would consider "work" in their lives. Which meant they were both from some highborn family or other, the sort of people who commissioned her tapestries.

Usually they managed to knock the legs out from under each others' schemes, which at least showed a modicum of good sense in her opinion. Once in a while she had to remind them of what life in a small village was like, how everyone knew everyone else, and how Danet, once he had ingratiated himself, would have the upper hand.

But finally it was Sendar who came up with something even she had to approve of.

"We make up a religion and become monks or priests of it," he said, finally. "Something humble, inoffensive. Vows of poverty, nonviolence, all that. We can crib things from any religion we care to, and it won't matter—no one can say we got it wrong because no one will recognize it, and we can exclaim about how wonderful it is that *our* god says the same as the *other* god if anyone notices the cribbing."

"Why would you be traveling?" she asked. "People will want to know."

"We're going from one remote chapter house in Valdemar to another in Rethwellan," Callan said with confidence. "I'm from up near the Iftel border, and I doubt your Danet will know anything about that area. We'll say we're from up there, and just make up another village in Rethwellan."

That seemed to be a good, sound plan to her, so she kept silent while they worked out the details of their new religion. Sendar did point out with some humor that it would be important that it didn't look attractive. The last thing they wanted to do was to create followers for a made-up religion. So aside from the vows of pov-

erty, abstinence, and chastity, they decided that complete
vegetarianism was probably going to be the most effective against country folk wanting to join up. She agreed.
"Country folk like our meat and cheese and eggs," she
said. "And in case you get some odd little fervent duck
who decides this is all very lovely anyway, make it a re-
quirement that the entire family join this religion before
any single member can."

"Ah, yes, the unity of the family is of the utmost importance," said Sendar, pulling a grave face. "Only when
the family is united can such serious matters be properly
decided."

They knew they were catching up to Danet when,
as they entered village after village, certain timid souls
would come up, quietly, as they sat at a meal. "Pardon,
Herald," the diffident speech would be begin, "But
I wonder if . . . well, this just didn't seem *right*, somehow . . . do you know of a Herald Danet?"

And thus would begin the revelations. Small things
mostly. Suspicion of taking a bribe. A girl's dazzled in-
fatuation with the white uniform taken advantage of.
Sometimes things gone missing. Occasionally, instead of
a quarrel being solved, having it fanned into a feud.

These things delayed them, though not, to Marya's
mind, intolerably, since she didn't have to do much but
listen and verify that no, Danet wasn't a real Herald and
yes, he'd taken similar advantage of most of the people in her own village. Free from the need to keep her
mouth shut over it, there was a certain relish in being
able to name names and reveal a great many indiscre-
tions. It felt a little like revenge, in a way.

And a strange thing began to happen. She found herself becoming the recipient of similar sad little stories.
Rather than confiding them to the Heralds, perhaps out
of embarrassment, people seemed much more comfortable telling their tales to someone who was just like

them, but whom they would never have to see again. A confluence of commonality and anonymity, perhaps. She began to take careful notes, turning them over to the Heralds at the end of the day. When Danet was found, would these things serve to determine his punishment?

She hoped so. His crimes against her were ... well, not crimes at all. Breach of promise? But there had never been any actual promise. He never stole anything from her but her happiness. But this was certainly a way in which she could exact revenge for that.

Each place they stopped and had to sort things out, Danet was "nearer" to them in time. He had been there two months ago ... a month ago ... a fortnight ...

It was clear he was not aware he was being followed, and it was time for the two Heralds to scout ahead in their guise of humble priests. They claimed they had also summoned help. How, she was not at all sure, since they hadn't sent any messages back that she had seen. But they wanted the people of Springdale to be convinced that Danet was a fraud first, so that he had no way to make them rise up against the real Heralds and whatever "help" was coming.

They left her behind in that village, still coaxing stories from people, and this time, having to do something new: She had to urge them *not* to follow in the false Herald's wake, and try to summon him to justice themselves.

"Think about what you would have said when he was among you," she pointed out. "The bastard has a charm that is almost magical. When he is around you, he can talk you into thinking almost anything he wants. You like him and want to believe him. If you go after him, all that will happen is that he will turn the people of Springdale against you—you'll be the outsiders, and outnumbered, and he will easily persuade them that you are, for one reason or another, disgruntled over his judgments. Sore losers."

Somehow she managed to persuade them. She wasn't quite sure how, because she had not been very diplomatic about it.

Actually, "not very diplomatic" was an understatement. She'd been her usual blunt self. She usually sat them down at a table near the fire in the inn and ordered beer for them. After all, why not? The king was paying for it. Then she began with, "Don't be an idiot," and ended with, "I know because he did it to me." Some people started off a little bristly, but when it become clear that she wasn't being personal, eventually they ended up nodding their heads and going away, if not satisfied, at least prepared to allow the real Heralds to handle it. It might have been her powers of persuasion, but she was more inclined to think it was the beer.

When the two Heralds returned nearly a week later, she knew from their guarded expressions that they had discovered just how powerful Danet's charm was.

"We found him; he went off the road to a smaller village, but we finally found him. He has definitely begun entrenching himself, and they all consider themselves *privileged* to be hosting him over the winter," Callan told her, over a gloomy dinner. "I must apologize to you, Marya. I thought you were exaggerating his ability to charm people. If anything, it is more potent than you described. There might even be some form of Gift at operation here; I don't have the ability to tell."

"Or he has simply gotten better with practice," she replied, dismissing the whole notion of these nebulous "Gifts" with a wave of her hand. "Tell me what he's done."

As Callan and Sendar talked, she listened carefully. It was clear that neither of them had any idea how to counter Danet's hold over an entire village. An enormous part of that hold was the white horse that he, or someone at least, had trained. The animal was amazing.

It did things that neither man had thought possible for an "ordinary" horse.

"Clearly it's not *ordinary* at all, it's an exceptionally intelligent and well-trained horse—which means it can almost do as much as an exceptionally well-trained dog," she said tartly. "He probably paid a pretty sum for it. So, the problem is, he has these people wrapped around his fingers, they'll look at his fancied-up horse and not see any differences between it and your Companions, and you don't know how to prove to these people what's what without—what?"

"We can't force a Truth Spell on anyone who's not been brought up in judgment," Sendar said gloomily. "Right now it's our word against his. And they think he's a Herald."

"Had you considered kidnapping?" she asked.

They both blanched. "Breaking the law is not an option," Callan replied faintly.

She shrugged. "All right. Then I might have a plan."

They rode into town and headed straight for the inn where Danet was holding court. He looked startled to see two real Heralds, but the expression didn't last long and quickly turned to his usual self-confidence.

He has the high ground here, and he knows it.

His expression slipped when she slid down off from behind Callan, however. He went absolutely blank.

"Hello, Danet," she said pleasantly. "I see that you have convinced all these people that you are really a Herald. I wonder if they would still believe that if they knew you had taken Elise Garen's silver locket. After you slept with her, of course. And you 'borrowed' over forty coppers from Tulera that you never intended to repay." She went down the list, adding, sadly, all too frequently "After you slept with her, of course," and paid close attention to the faces of some of the

women around him. Doubt was creeping in. Not much,
but—

"Of course, you must be a Herald now," she went
on, doing her best to sound perfectly calm and even.
"Because look, you have the uniform, just like Herald
Callan and Herald Sendar. And you have the Companion . . ." Now she turned to where the rather lovely white
horse was peacefully standing, quite untethered, a few
feet away. She had to admit he had managed a rather
good imitation of a Companion. If you didn't look too
closely. "Of course you do." She took a few steps nearer.
"Or . . . do you?"

Before anyone could move to prevent her, she dashed
forward. As she had expected, the horse was too well
trained to shy away, although it did throw up its head in
surprise and snort.

She lunged, and the hand she had held concealed in
the folds of her dress slapped the flank of the horse, the
wad of rags saturated with dark walnut dye leaving a
huge brown smear on its white hide.

"Of course, everyone knows that Companions are
white because dirt and all just evaporates right off
them," she continued as Danet and his little knot of admirers stared in shock. "So, to be fair, I should do the
same to the others. With the same dye, so you can't claim
that I've used something different on them."

She turned and wiped the dye off on the other two,
creating identical swaths of stain on their satiny hides.
"Now, let's just see—oh, look."

The two Companions had gotten a look of curious *concentration* on their faces the moment the rags
touched them. And the dye was already fading!

Within moments it was gone, and their coats were as
pristine as they had been before. Meanwhile the large,
ugly brown stain remained on the flank of the oblivious
horse.

"Goodness me," she said sweetly. "It looks as if your Companion is a fake, Danet. And if your Companion is a fake—what does that make you?"

Danet looked wildly about for help, but his former admirers were backing away from him with expressions ranging from doubt to accusation. She had a fair notion that the accusatory ones were the women he had already slept with.

Herald Callan stepped forward and clamped one hand on Danet Stens's shoulder.

"Danet Stens, I am taking you into custody to answer to one hundred and seventeen counts of theft, thirty-five counts of fraud, three counts of breach of promise . . ."

Danet could only stand there, looking stunned.

The Guards had arrived just as the Heralds had said they would, and they took Danet into custody. They did not take the horse. Marya put a claim on it, and since no one seemed willing to contest her for it, she got it. She immediately dyed all the blue tack a nondescript brown. She thought about further dyeing the horse, and decided to turn the streak into a patch, adding another couple just to make it look more natural. And significantly less like a Companion.

With Callan and Sendar to escort her back home, she got the hang of riding a real horse fairly quickly. And they could actually have conversations, riding three abreast, better than they had when she'd been pillion. She talked, for the first time, about her father. How devastated her mother had been when her letters were never answered. How miserable her childhood had been. They were troubled, apologetic, and on the whole their reaction came as close to satisfying her as much as anything ever would.

She was grudgingly coming to the conclusion that Heralds *might* not be so bad, when they reached Silvergate just as the first hard frost hit. By that time she was glad to see her own cottage again. She made arrangements with innkeeper Stens to board her horse with him. She had plans for that horse. She had decided that she liked travel. She had it in mind that from now on, she just might deliver her tapestries herself, now and again.

She had just gotten the cottage opened up, warmed by the fire, and fit to live in again when—

There was a knock at the door.

She opened it. Callan and Sendar were there . . . with a wooden dispatch box.

"When you told us about your father, well, it didn't sound right," Callan said without preamble. "So we sent off to Haven to find out what we could. And . . . there is no other way to put this: What you and your mother always believed was a lie."

She felt as if she had been slapped, and Sendar quickly added, "Not what you are thinking! He *was* Chosen to be a Herald. But he never abandoned you. Not willingly. Here—" He thrust the box at her. "Here are all the letters he tried to send, which your grandmother turned back. He was never allowed to contact your mother. He tried, but he was also in training, and he couldn't leave Haven and the Collegium until the Midwinter celebrations and the holidays, and then—"

"Then it was too late. He got sick. A lot of people got sick that year. And he died." Callan shook his head, sorrowfully. "The Collegium tried to contact your mother one last time, but they were turned away again."

Marya blinked, too stunned to actually feel anything yet. Finally, she stammered, "Come in," and took the box to the table.

There she took out all the letters, all the wonderful, loving, and then increasingly desperate letters, and read them carefully. That was when she knew, suddenly, exactly why her grandparents had done what they had.

Marya's mother had been doing the bulk of the weaving. Marya herself was showing early promise even as a toddler. But if they left to join their husband and father—

Rage filled her one last time, a terrible rage that swept through her—

And then exploded into tears.

She wept for her mother, herself, and the father she had never known. She wept for the bitter, selfish old man and woman who had kept their daughter miserable in order to keep her. She wept, first on Callan's shoulder and then on Sendar's, until she couldn't weep any more, and allowed herself to be led to her bed, where she fell asleep fully clothed and awoke in the morning feeling— empty. The anger was gone.

What was going to take its place, she didn't know. But the anger had been washed away on the tide of tears.

She reread the letters, knowing that she would do so many more times to come, reread them with a heart open to what was in them. And as she put the last of them back in the box, there was a knock at the door.

It was Callan and Sendar again, this time loaded down with all the shopping she would need for the next week and more. "We thought it was the least we could do," Sendar said cheerfully. "We'll be going back to Haven, but we wanted to thank you. We never could have managed without you."

"You certainly could not have, you highborn babies," she said, tartly, but with a bit of a smile. "No more notion of what common people are like than the man in the moon. And thank you, thank you very much. But you can do me one more favor. Since that's your direction."

"Certainly," Callan nodded. "We owe you a very great deal, still."

"Take this message to Lord Poul Haveland in Haven." She held out the folded paper. "I'll be taking that commission he wanted me to do after all. And I would be obliged if some of that Companion hair could be sent along in the spring so the creature can be the *proper* white and not a fraud."

And if the Herald in that tapestry looked something like her misty memories of her father . . . well. That would not be bad, either.

For Want of a Nail

by Rosemary Edghill
and Denise McCune

Rosemary Edghill has been a frequent contributor to the Valdemar anthologies since selling her first novel in 1987, writing everything from Regency romances to science fiction to alternate history to mysteries. Between writing gigs, she's held the usual selection of weird writer jobs and can truthfully state that she once killed vampires for money. She has collaborated with Marion Zimmer Bradley (*Shadow's Gate*), Andre Norton (*Carolus Rex*), and Mercedes Lackey (*Bedlam's Bard* and the forthcoming *Shadow Grail*). In the opinion of her dogs, she spends far too much time on Wikipedia. Her virtual home can be found at *http://www.sff.net/PEOPLE/ELUKI/* (Her last name—despite the efforts of editors, reviewers, publishing houses, her webmaster, and occasionally her own fingers—is not spelled Edgehill.)

Denise McCune has been writing since she was eleven—which was (coincidentally?) right around the time she fell in love with Valdemar. She has worked in the social networking industry for nearly a decade, and not having enough to do writing novels and short stories, she decided to launch Dreamwidth, an open source social networking, content management, and personal publishing platform. Denise lives in Baltimore, Maryland, where her hobbies include knitting, writing, and staying up too late writing code.

Navar was an ordinary man. A soldier, and a good one, rising from common foot soldier in the Baron's levy to sergeant of his company, but his true gift was to go from here to there unseen; and so Captain Harleth had used his talents for scouting, for the Barony of Valdemar was beset on every side by enemies. Not those that came by day, for all knew that the Eastern Empire was at peace, but those that came by night, for the Iron Throne ruled by fear and blood and dark magic, so that no man might call his soul his own.

In later years, many claimed to have known Baron Kordas Valdemar's mind, to have plotted with him for their exodus into the unknown West. Navar was not one whose status gave him entry into the councils of the good and the great, but he thought that such words were no more than idle tavern talk, the speech of men who wished to be seen as greater than they were. True enough that Soferu, who wore the Wolf Crown and sat upon the Iron Throne, was but a man. True as well that he was not a man like any other, for lust for power ran as hot as magery in Soferu's veins, and so the Iron Throne was an iron boot upon men's necks, and an iron collar about men's throats, and an iron chain about men's minds, and only a fool would sow treason farther than he must.

And Baron Valdemar had been no fool.

Only he, and Juuso Beltran, whose line had served Valdemar's as seneschal since the lands had first come into Valdemar's hands, and Terilee, Valdemar's lady, brave and bright as a swordblade, had known all Lord Valdemar's heart and mind. The three of them had warded their plans with subtle spells (so Navar heard later, and this tale he was moved to credit)—not wards that would draw the attention of the Hellhound Mages of the Imperium, but layer upon layer of subtle shields of misdirection, a deception as artful as a swirl of autumn leaves concealing a doe from the hunter's bow.

Of the journey to freedom itself, Navar knew as much as any man, for a scout's skills were as vital as a mage's when one must make one's way through lands first hostile, then unknown. They brought with them not merely the household troops that a barony was permitted to arm and muster, but nearly all who dwelt within Valdemar's bounds—all save for the baron's eldest son. Lord Dethwyn, fostered as was the custom at Soferu's court as hostage against his father's obedience, would have willingly ascended to his father's honors across his father's grave were he granted the slightest chance. When Valdemar's second son Restil came of age, he was meant to join his brother at the Wolf Court. It was not unknown for the sons of inconvenient nobles to perish at court so that their fathers' lands might return to the emperor's gift, and it was—perhaps—the thought of losing both his sons as much as anything else that caused the baron to move when he did.

It was the work of a year—hard travel, and sometimes terrifying; through the empire, then (by stealth and misdirection) across the kingdom of Hardorn, and at last into the western lands, which Hardorn did not claim—that brought them to haven. And Haven it was in truth, the city that they built upon the banks of the river that Valdemar named for his lady. Some had died on that journey, but their numbers were greater at the end of it than at the beginning, for the rumor that their fellowship journeyed to a freedom beyond the persecution of the Empire had spread, and those who did not join them in the first days of their exodus followed them in the sennights and moonturns that followed. To all who came seeking asylum, Valdemar—now King Valdemar—granted it, for the work of building a kingdom was the work of many hands.

For Valdemar now ruled a kingdom. The lands Baron Valdemar could now claim as his own were vaster by far than those that he had once ruled at the emperor's pleasure, and he ruled now at no man's pleasure save his own. And just as Valdemar's lands had grown, so had the army grown into a great force of many companies, many captains, many sergeants, and Harleth now styled general over them all.

That growth was the reason Navar was now uneasy.

The days in which Navar had known every man and woman with whom he served were long gone—had been gone since before they had come to rest in their Haven. Thirty years ago, when he had been new come to the baron's levy, he had known everyone his duties brought him near, both holder and servant alike. He had been able to measure the hearts and minds of all who sought to command him. Any soldier knew that just as there were good orders and sensible orders, there were bad orders and senseless orders, and it was a good soldier's duty to evaluate each given order to see where it fell. He had seen countless lives saved by a swift-witted sergeant playing sunstruck at precisely the right time, and he had kept his own list (in his mind, never written where agents of the Iron Throne might see, for no one would think to look within the thoughts of a common sergeant, and Navar played the fool better than most when there was need) of those whose orders he himself would "lose" for precisely long enough to ease their disaster.

In Baron Valdemar's holdings, that had been possible. In King Valdemar's country, it would not be possible for long. In the moonturns since they had settled here, many men and women had stepped forward to take places of service, and that was well and good, for the tally of things to be done to create their safe haven was so great that no one man could oversee them all. King Valdemar could direct their work from long before sunup to long past sundown and still not make every decision that must be made.

Thus far all of them had proven to have hearts as good and as kind as King Valdemar himself. But how long, Navar wondered, before someone with honeyed words and subtle magic stepped forward to cloak a desire for power in a promise that his actions were in Valdemar's best interests? Had they made this long and frightful journey only to stand vulnerable at the end to one who would seek to rebuild the empire with themself at its head? King Valdemar was a good and honest man and would likely raise young Restil to the same values, but—after him?

How long until Valdemar's people had to flee tyranny once again?

Navar kept his suspicions quiet, for lessons learned in the shadow of the Iron Throne would take longer than a single year of flight and a few moonturns of safe haven to fade away. They had reached their new home in autumn and suffered through their first winter scrabbling to feed and shelter themselves, for provisions ran as low as spirits ran high. But if nothing else, there was good timber and good grazing in plenty, and what began as a bedraggled city of camp tents in the first weeks of autumn was a crude (though growing) settlement of wooden huts by spring. Stakes and stone cairns marked the location of future streets and roads, so that the building could progress in an orderly fashion. All through the fall and winter, those who could be spared from the labor of building and hunting had ridden out to map and explore, for the new kingdom of Valdemar was an unknown place. Navar had been among them, for no longer was he Baron Valdemar's only scout, nor yet one of a dozen. Four score served in the King's Army who had once been the baron's huntsmen, or his spearmen, or common farmers, and (as all the army) they wore, not the uniform of the baron's guard, but ordinary clothes, with nothing to mark them out save a gray brassard worn upon their left arms. Yet both caution and weather dictated that the scouts did not go far from Haven.

When the snow was gone, and Navar's labor was no longer needed to help put the first crop into the fields, Captain Arwulf—he who had charge of the scouts now that they numbered a whole company of men and women—summoned Navar and asked him to command an expedition to scout the great forest to the western edge of the lands Valdemar's people had claimed. "See what we can use there," Captain Arwulf said, "and if there are any people who have claimed that land. I'll send a mapmaker with you. We need to know more about our neighbors."

It was a mark of King Valdemar's new teachings—for he had chosen as the motto of his kingdom the words "No one way is the true way"—that Navar felt that he might refuse this order did he think it was a task beyond his ability; and true it was that never had he commanded men and women in the field, though he was well liked by his fellow soldiers. Navar's skills had always been set to tasks where he must only command himself. Yet it was a needful task and one he did not think beyond his ability, and so he asked merely to choose those who would accompany him. And to this request Captain Arwulf made no demur, saying only that there was no better mapmaker than the one he had already chosen.

Almost did Navar reconsider his audacity at accepting such a great undertaking when, on the very day he and his dozen chosen soldiers were to depart, he first met young Doladan. The lad seemed to him hardly older than Prince Restil, and he frankly admitted—after he'd fallen off his mule while attempting to adjust his cloak, greet Navar, and repack his saddlebags all at the same time—that he'd never held sword or bow in his life. In the old Valdemar, he'd been the Master Gardener's chief assistant, and when several of Navar's soldiers dared to laugh at this admission, he pointed out hotly that the baronial gardens had covered several hundred acres, and without detailed mappings of what was planted where—and what *should* be planted where—the gardens would have been a wilderness.

"I wouldn't be so high and mighty if I were you," Doladan said fiercely. "If Mistress Karilgrass weren't here now to tell everyone what plants were safe to eat, you louts would have had a leaner winter than you did."

"True enough," Navar said, for the beginning of a journey was no time to set a grudge. "We've all become more than we were in the last year and more. And if you'll oblige me by learning a bit of swordwork, why, Torimund and Felara here will learn a bit of gardening."

Doladan, Navar realized, was quite beautiful when he laughed.

They followed the river north and west, for rivers were natural roads, and any threat to come to Haven would come more swiftly along the water road. At each stop, Doladan sketched tirelessly, filling page after page with detailed notes, and taking samples of plants and leaves as well.

Navar had hoped to be back in Haven by high summer, but the expedition took longer than he had planned, for the forest proved to be dark and dangerous, full of twisted creatures. When Torimund died, Doladan said angrily that that the name of the forest should be "pelagir," a word that meant "danger" in one of the Old Tongues, and Pelagiris Forest it became: Forest of Dangers. But if Torimund was the first casualty of the journey, he wasn't the last: they lost six of their twelve soldiers before they won their way home again with the first frost nipping at their heels.

When he and his company staggered back into Haven with the maps and surveys they had paid for with the lives of half their comrades, Navar was shocked to see that the settlement he'd left—crude wooden huts and houses—had been transformed through equal application of magecraft and sweat to a city that rivaled—

Well, perhaps not High Ashuel, the Eastern Empire's capital. But certainly one of the smaller cities in the empire they had left behind them.

And, well, King Valdemar and Queen Terilee and Lord Beltran, now King Valdemar's Chancellor, were all mages, and mages could work miracles overnight where mere men would require moonturns of backbreaking work. But Haven now was larger than Navar had ever thought it could be—and as much stone as wood.

"I am so glad to get home," Doladan said. He gestured at the young city before them. "And only look, Nav! Walls—and roofs—and floors! And neither of us had to build any of them! We'll sleep warmer this winter than last, I'll wager."

"If we can find our own roofs by first snow," Senard grumbled from behind them. "I hope they've built barracks as well as all these houses."

"I hope they've built a tavern!" Rusama chimed in. She glanced across the stubble of the fields. "Good harvest means good beer."

Navar let their chatter wash over him as he brooded on the sight before him. Seeing Haven flourishing so impossibly, Navar realized his greatest fear had never been for some future that he would not live to see but of a present that he most certainly would: if this fragile new kingdom grew past the ability of the great and the good to watch over it, who would defend it from Soferu's plots? Hardorn had ever been the empire's enemy. It would be a great coup for the Iron Throne to gain a foot-hold on Hardorn's western border.

He feared that day had already come. Who was governing the city? Who was making sure that the right decisions were being made?

No matter what else might happen in Haven, Harleth and Arwulf were competent soldiers, and so there were sentry riders set beyond the far bounds of the town. One of them came to direct Navar's little company to the new stables and barracks and to tell Navar where he could find Captain Arwulf. He'd hoped to make his report there and be released from his duties, for it was Doladan's report that King Valdemar would wish to hear, not his. But Arwulf had merely grunted when he presented himself and told him that General Harleth would want to see him at the palace.

"Not a patch on what it's going to be," Arwulf said. "But well enough for now. Praise the All that Valdemar's prayers were answered."

"Prayers?" Doladan asked, his eyes bright and shining as he drank in all the changes that their moonturns away from Haven had wrought.

"You'll see," Arwulf said.

Haven had been no more than a mean scrabble of lean-to shelters and tattered tents when Navar had ridden out. Now, though the air was filled with the scent of new-cut timber and the buildings that greeted their eyes as they walked in the direction Arwulf had indicated were all sharp and raw and new, they were sturdy and well-made. Perhaps Master Rilbard had built the sawmill that he'd talked of all the winter, for Navar could think of no other means by which so much good cut timber could have been procured in so short a time. There were even sturdy plank walkways edging the wide packed-earth streets, and that would be a great boon come the rains. The air was filled with the sound of hammering and sawing—and with the laughter and song of children as well. When Haven was being designed, on the dark days of winter when little else could be done but plan and wait for spring, parks and playing grounds had been thought as necessary to Haven as common gardens and proper drainage.

Soon enough they reached the far end of the city and what would someday be the royal palace.

For now, the palace barely deserved the name, though it was grand enough, considering their circumstances: a three-storied manor house of mage-cured wood rivaling, if not the baronial palace Valdemar had left behind, then certainly a manor house of one of his more prosperous underlords. It stood in the middle of a vast open parkland upon the banks of the river Terilee, its fields straddling the river and stretching away to forest left yet uncleared. Beyond it, where gardens might otherwise have stood, stonemasons had outlined the footings of what Navar could tell would become the permanent palace, and many workers were coming and going in good cheer. It was a busy place, full of industry, with children watching the goings-on with interest.

Navar could see several horses standing free in the fields on the river's far banks, their coats brilliant white and shining in the autumn sun. He wondered if wild horses had been found by another scouting party, tamed, and brought back for breeding stock. His group had seen nothing of the sort on their travels, either in the northern valley or in the heart of the forest that had tried so hard to claim their lives with its menace, but Captain Arwulf had surely sent others in directions other than to the west.

General Harleth, when found, proved to be one of the men hauling stone for the palace's foundation, stripped

bare to the waist and sweating even in the cooler air
of late fall. One of the bright-shining horses was linger-
ing nearby, watching the proceedings with what Navar
would swear was an assessing look on its face, and Navar
revised his earlier thought uneasily. This was surely no
new-tamed wild horse—its every line spoke of quality
and breeding. Navar had friends among Valdemar's os-
tlers, and in his many visits to the former-baronial stables he had never seen horses with such a glow to them.

When he gained Harleth's attention, Navar gave his
report upon the spot as tersely as possible, for he could
feel Doladan vibrating beside him with excitement.
Doladan had learned some measure of grace during
their travels, but his ebullience was undimmed.

Before Doladan could move to spread out his pages
of sketchings on a stone-wall-in-progress to show them
off, Harleth snickered at some thought Navar could not
guess and clapped Doladan on the back. "Come," he
said, shifting his gaze to Navar to include him in the invitation. "The king and queen and the Heralds' Council
are eager to hear your report."

The phrasing made Navar wince inwardly, for Harleth had never before seemed the type of man to take it
upon himself to speak for the baron-turned-king. Heralds' Council? Had the worst of Navar's fears come to
pass, and King Valdemar been influenced into letting power pass from his control so quickly? And who,
of the men and women who had been moving to secure
their position in Valdemar's new kingdom, had been
named to such a governing council, and how had Valdemar judged them worthy? How could any man be satisfied that he had properly taken the measure of another
without resorting to the same mind-magic coercion the
empire had used so freely and King Valdemar had de-
cried so fiercely? Had King Valdemar set principle aside
for expedience?

Have we fallen so far, so quickly?

Doladan either did not notice or did not think General Harleth's words troublesome, for he simply fell into step beside Harleth as the general reached for his discarded tunic and set out for the manor house. Navar would have chosen rather to wash and change his travel-stained clothes before showing himself before the king, but Harleth seemed to see no reason for delay. He led them straight to where King Valdemar and Queen Terilee were holding court, and the moment their small party stepped into the salon, Valdemar rose and held out his hands. "Welcome back!" he said, in his warm and booming voice that always inspired such trust and confidence in those who heard it. "We had feared you lost!"

"Not lost," Navar said, his mind unquiet, looking around to see who was in the room. He recognized but half of the two dozen men and women present, and his heart sank further at the sight of so many, for how could so many have fairly been judged? It seemed frighteningly likely that Valdemar had chosen but one or two or five, and they had filled his court with their own partisans, for of those he recognized, half were those he would not think to name to any council he would be comfortable obeying, and he could name at least as many more who he would have thought should be present and weren't.

Juuso Beltran was there, of course, now King's Chancellor, and young Prince Restil, now entering his fifteenth year, and those were to be expected. But so was Mistress Emolde, who had been wetnurse to both Restil and Dethwyn, his elder brother. Lorton, one of Valdemar's journeyman-mages, was present, but not Blydel or Imryn, the others. Mistress Karilgrass, the chief gardener and Doladan's old master, was present, but Captain Arwulf was not.

It was not that Navar thought all of those present were poor choices. How could he? He did not know them all.

Yet it seemed that these people were King Valdemar's chosen Council. How could so many who had joined the exodus as it proceeded have risen to such power?

"Tell us everything," King Valdemar urged. "What of your travels? Is the danger containable?"

And that was a curious thing to hear from the King, for Navar had mentioned the loss of his men and women to General Harleth, but he had not had time to speak of it here. Perhaps King Valdemar had been able to intuit the danger from the fact that their return had been so delayed.

Or perhaps King Valdemar was listening to his mind even now.

Navar blanked his face and did all he could to bury his thoughts, reporting briefly on what they had found. In contrast to Navar's taciturnity, Doladan chattered so energetically it seemed he scarce drew a breath. His maps were passed from hand to hand, and each man and woman who saw them had some thoughtful thing to contribute. Lorton pointed out a range of hills that might prove to contain iron for mining; a woman whose name Navar did not know spoke of the possibility that the valley to the north might be suitable for a farming settlement in another year or several. Navar could fault none of the questions or observations made, but neither could he shake the sense of unease that surrounded him like a cloak's mantle.

He listened carefully, and he watched even more carefully, for since the day that Captain Harleth had taken him from the ranks of Valdemar's household guard and set him the task of going forth and gathering information—not spying, never that, for spying was quite another matter than simply walking over the land and seeing what was to be seen—Navar had been able to see all before him and remember what he saw. And as he watched Doladan's speech before Valdemar's new

Council, Navar saw a great riddle lying at the Council's heart.

It was not merely that they spoke of sharing Doladan's report with those absent, for any might do that, or that they spoke names he did not know, for even now he did not know all the inhabitants of Haven. It was that they spoke of these others as if they were present now. Again and again he heard, "Ardatha says—" or, "Kyrith thinks—" and whoever they were—for those names, too, were strange to him—they were obviously held in high regard, for their advice was always heeded.

Doladan would have willingly talked the sun out of the sky, so on fire was he to tell of all he had seen and learned, but at last King Valdemar broke off with a rueful laugh. "But Ardatha tells me I am being very rude to keep you standing and talking, when you are undoubtedly tired and thirsty and wish for nothing more than a hot meal and a clean bed. I am certain Juuso can see you lodged. Be certain, though, that we hope to hear more of your journey."

Even the most informal court was a court nonetheless. Navar said nothing as he and Doladan followed Lord Beltran from the salon, but when the doors had closed behind the three of them, he cleared his throat.

"Meaning no disrespect, but I'd as soon go back to barracks. I'd be more comfortable there than in a palace."

Lord Beltran did not answer immediately. He seemed to be listening to words Navar could not hear, and whatever they were, he found them amusing. "Indeed, there have been many changes in Haven since you left us. I hope you will find them to your liking."

And if I do not? Navar wondered. "We'd thought the western lands were empty," he said carefully. "It's good to see we've found friends here. I saw their horses, I think, as I walked through the park."

To his surprise and consternation, Lord Beltran threw back his head and roared with laughter. "Horses!" he said, when he could draw breath again. "Oh, they have the look of horses—I grant you that—but the Companions are the answer to a prayer."

"Aren't they horses?" Doladan asked, before Navar could make some polite demur to get the two of them out of there. Whatever madness had taken the new kingdom for its nursery, Chancellor Beltran was obviously its nurserymaid.

Lord Beltran clapped Doladan on the shoulder, and Navar bristled with the helpless need to protect one who had become dearer than self in the past moonturns. "Come," the King's Chancellor said. "Let us share a cup of wine—or a stoup of new ale—and I shall tell you both of how fortune and all the good gods have smiled upon our kingdom."

The ale was good—and Beltran was no fool, for he provided bread and cheese as well. The food and drink went down Navar's throat with more ease than the tale he was told.

Their band of refugees had grown to twice its original size during their flight from the Eastern Empire. During Navar's absence, the kingdom of Valdemar had grown again, for Valdemar's legend had taken root, and all knew that the new king meant his land to be a haven of freedom tempered by law—one that would fall equally upon the shoulders of high and low, mage and commoner. Navar had heard the inevitable problems whispered about: that not merely law-abiding exiles and fugitives would flock to Valdemar's banner, but every stormcrow and wolfshead and gallowglass that Velgarth held, men and women who would make of their refuge a sanctuary for lawlessness and depravity. In fact, many such had attempted to join them, seeking protection from well-deserved justice—only to find that they had leaped from the cooking pot into the cook-stove itself. And so, one spring night, when a new band of refugees had arrived, petitioning to become citizens of Valdemar, King Valdemar had prayed to all the gods and goddesses that his kingdom would be saved for all time from corruption such as he and his people had fled, so that Valdemar would never fear to be a haven for the innocent nor a judge of the wicked.

His prayer had been answered—so Lord Beltran would have it—by the appearance (from a copse of woodland in the palace park) of a shining creature in the shape of a horse—save that its hooves were of shining silver and its eyes of deepest blue. These horses—or, as Lord Beltran would style them, Companions (for there were now nearly twenty of the creatures in Valdemar)—were able to speak directly into the minds of their Chosen, though not directly to any other. They were as smart as any man or woman but infinitely wiser and more good.

"I should like to see one," Doladan said yearningly.

"And Kyrith is eager to meet you as well," Lord Beltran said, smiling, "but without a Companion of your own, what conversations you might have would be more than a little one-sided. Tomorrow we will go to Companion's Field and speak to him."

Doladan opened his mouth to reply, and Navar feared that his next words would be a request for a "Companion" of his own. Already Navar's heart was troubled enough, for it seemed to him that he had never seen Lord Beltran, as Baron's Seneschal or King's Chancellor, look so much at his ease, as if a great burden had been lifted from him. He spoke up quickly, saying they had kept Lord Beltran from his duties long enough and would be on their way.

*   *   *

"You all but dragged me out of there by the hair," Doladan complained, once they were in the open air once more.

Navar looked about himself. Several of the white horses were in sight, but none close enough to hear. "I wonder how it is you lived to grow up," he said with a sigh. "The king surrounds himself with an outlandish court—Lord Beltran tells a tale of otherworldly guardians in horse shape who come in answer to the king's prayers and that can speak into the minds of the folk? It is but a small step from speaking to overshadowing— and we have but Lord Beltran's word that these beasts are good and wise."

"But—King Valdemar is a great mage!" Doladan sputtered, nearly skipping in his agitation and his need to keep up with Navar's long strides.

"There is no mage so great that he may not meet a greater one," Navar said grimly.

The barracks had been half built even before they'd left, as dormitory buildings were the quickest and most efficient way of getting Haven's population out of tents and under roofs, but they weren't the cheeriest lodgings to be had. Navar was spared that this night, for on his way back there—Doladan at his heels—he spied proof that Haven had become a city in truth: a tavern.

There was not yet a royal mint established, or any coin circulated, but the tavernkeeper was willing to take Navar's signed chit in payment. The "Journey's End" had all they might have found elsewhere, and one thing more.

Gossip.

This was not the only tavern in Haven—Navar was surprised to discover there were four—but it was the oldest by three moonturns, and the largest, and the nearest to the new palace. Men and women came here to drink beer and cider, to get a hot meal, and to exchange the news of the day.

That news was as grim as the news that Lord Beltran had relayed. Word of these "Companions" were on everyone's lips, from those who wished to be Chosen themselves to those who simply wished to give thanks that King Valdemar's prayers had been answered. None had anything less than full praise to deliver for these Companions' supposed wisdom and goodness, which merely raised Navar's suspicions further. One hallmark of life, learned through painful lessons: There was naught so good that someone would not despise it. For none to speak ill of these Companions spoke less of the quality of Valdemar's prayers and more to Navar's worst fears.

Doladan sought to discuss what they had learned, but Navar bade him hold his tongue, for he had already decided. This Haven had turned to nightmare, and Navar would not remain to be overshadowed in turn. They would leave at first light, he and Doladan, and make their way up the river Terilee until they could find a suitable place to winter, where they would be sheltered from forest's dangers. Come spring, they would continue pressing west, or perhaps south, until they found another settlement—one that bent knee to neither Iron Throne nor white spirit-horses.

He outlined his plans to Doladan in a quiet voice, masked by the sound of revelry in the tavern as drunken men grew more drunken, and Doladan looked as though he held back protest. Navar kept his eyes moving around them, looking for any signs that someone was paying more attention to them than he should. "I'll slip out after we've retired and find a storehouse to provision us," Navar said, while trying to decide if the barmaid was showing too much interest in their bowed-head conference.

:I do so wish you wouldn't.:

"It's the only way we can be sure to have sufficient

supplies for a winter," Navar said, trying to bite back his anger that Doladan would question him. Hadn't he proven his ability to plan and execute a long journey already? "We don't know how harsh the winters of this land will be."

Doladan ducked his head. "Can't we stay here and see what will happen? What if these—these Companions aren't a sign of something bad? What if they're exactly what people say they are?"

"You never suffered beneath the boot of the Iron Throne." Navar dropped his voice even further. "I have seen what power drives men to do, and I tell you: Freedom is sweet. I will not fall beneath a madman's subjugation a second time."

Navar brought Doladan back to their room and impressed upon him the urgency of remaining where he was, then dressed himself in his darkest clothes and smeared ash from the firepit across his cheeks and forehead as though he had simply failed to bathe after a day's long labor. It was well past midnight when all in the tavern's front room had finally retired for the evening and he could slide noiselessly through the tavern's doors.

The night was clear and cold, and the moon was barely a sliver. After years of scouting, it was second nature for Navar to remain in the shadows where an onlooker's eyes might pass him by. He wished he had had more time to learn the lay of the city, for the only storehouse whose location he could be sure of was the one that served Valdemar's army, and that was perilously close to the palace grounds. But every instinct was telling him to be gone by sun's rising, and that meant he could spare no time creeping from door to door until he found somewhere with sufficient wealth to serve their needs.

And besides, he had served Baron Valdemar for

thirty loyal years. True, he had been well-paid for them all, but he did not think Valdemar would begrudge him the cost of what he would take as a parting gift, while his conscience would not let him steal from another.

The army's storehouse was locked, of course, and Navar spent a moment praying to all the good gods that it was not locked by magecraft, for he no longer had the tools King Valdemar had betimes equipped him with for defeating the mage-lock of an enemy. His luck was with him, though, and so he knelt before the lock to work at it with two scraps of wire he had brought with him for that very purpose.

:You are the stubbornest man I have ever encountered.:

Navar's nerves were well-hardened against shock, and so he did not leap in fright to hear someone speak to him, merely turned his head to see whether he was at swordspoint or whether he had a chance of winning free. It was no man who spoke to him, though. At least, not in his ears. As he rose slowly to his feet, he saw one of the spirit-horses staring at him, near to the turning that would lead to the palace, and he would have sworn it beckoned him to come near.

And was that not proof of sorcery or mind-magic being applied? For Navar found himself following, without thought to his own safety: through the streets, across the grounds of the palace, over the bridge to the fields beyond, without struggling against the witchery—

Another voice sounded, different than the first. *:He thinks we're bewitching him. He doesn't realize his heart truly wants him to follow.:*

:Is he still being stubborn?: Yet another voice this time, and Navar realized that they were sounding not in his ears, but in his mind. The realization made panic rise in his throat, for to hear voices in the mind meant sorcery, and sorcery meant that he was far too late—

:Silence, all of you. You're frightening him. Navar, this is no sorcery. You have the ability to hear us all; it is a skill, nothing more.:

:Tell him—:

The spirit-horse that had led him stamped its foot as yet another voice interjected, and all of a sudden Navar's mind was silence again. He looked around, startled to find that he had crossed the bridge across the River Terilee, into the field beyond, into the copse of trees that waited there.

:This is Companion's Field,: the voice that had bade the others to silence said. Looking at the spirit-horse that had led him, Navar realized it must belong to the voice, or the voice belong to it. He was certain enough of it that when the voice continued, it seemed in response to that new understanding. *:And yes, I am Ardatha, King Valdemar's Companion. And I have led you here because we can't let you go running off until you're satisfied that we are no demons, nor pawns of some great sorcerer, and Valdemar is not overshadowed by some other mage. We need you. Valdemar needs you. King and kingdom alike.:*

"And I am to believe that?" Navar said, his voice rough. Well he knew that a man's anger was a blade set at his own throat, yet he could not keep himself from feeling it. He thought of Doladan, awaiting him in their bed at the tavern—Doladan, who trusted too quickly and too easily. He thought of the hope that he might live in freedom and under law, a hope that had kindled from a fragile spark to a great blaze over so many moonturns—

:It is for this hope that we have come,: Ardatha said.

"To crush it," Navar growled, for he had discovered that it was far more painful to have a dream destroyed than to live without dreams at all.

:No. Never.: And though Ardatha's face was a horse's

face, in his mind Navar could feel the Companion's emotions as if he could see them on Ardatha's face: horror, and disgust, and anger, and an utter repudiation of the thought of tricking King Valdemar into a tyrannous rule.

Navar desperately wanted to believe. And he knew that faces and voices could lie.

But for the first time since he had discovered that Valdemar had become infested by mind-controlling spirit-beasts, it occurred to him to wonder: If these "Companions" *were*, in fact, the answer to King Valdemar's prayer to keep his kingdom free of tyranny and corruption, just how were they going to go about it?

:We Choose,: Ardatha said. *:And those we Choose are good men and good women, who will govern, and lead, and administer the laws of Valdemar wisely.:*

"That's all?" Navar asked after a moment. "You just pick people?" It didn't seem like much.

He had the sense that Ardatha was clearing his throat in mild rebuke, though he could not say how he came to have that sense. *:We Choose,:* Ardatha corrected. *:And we advise our Chosen, speaking to them mind-to-mind, as I am to you, though you are the first who can hear all of us. Each whom we Choose has some Gift of Magery, though perhaps so small that it has never been noticed before. To be Chosen is a great responsibility.:*

"You haven't Chosen me, have you?" Navar asked in alarm. If he could hear Ardatha . . .

The silvery laughter of a dozen Companions filled his mind, until Ardatha stamped his hoof. *:I have Chosen Kordas, and our bond shall endure until one of us dies. You and I merely speak together through your Gift of Mindspeech, as I hope to persuade what is surely the stubbornest man in all Valdemar not to leave.:*

"You could tell the king to order me to stay," Navar said.

:I could ask Kordas to ask you,: Ardatha corrected.
*:He would not compel you to remain against your will.
Nor will I. Nor will any of those who have been Chosen
compel you to stay: Prince Restil, or Herald Beltran, or
Herald Peralas. They will but ask. As do I.:*

Peralas, Navar recalled, was General Harleth's milk-
name. He thought of the Herald's Council and its unlikely membership.

It seemed to him—standing here in the freezing dark,
beside a horse that was far more than a horse—that this
was no more than a dream. But Valdemar itself was a
dream—the best dream the hearts of men could hold,
rather than the uneasy nightmare of oppression and tyranny they had fled. He thought of the Pelagiris Forest,
and he knew there would be no sanctuary for him and
for Doladan there. And a man might live rough for one
moonturn or even a dozen, but in the end, all that might
be found in a solitary life in the wilderness was starva-
tion and an early death. Worth it to die in freedom.

Foolishness if he fled merely from shadows in his own
mind.

"I am nothing and no one," he said at last. "I can
hardly threaten your plans for Valdemar."

Ardatha seemed to sigh in exasperation. *:Hardly,:* the
Companion said. *:But you can make them a reality—if
you have the courage.:*

"Courage?" Navar asked. His voice was hard, for no
one had ever questioned his courage.

*:Not even a . . . oh, what did you call us? 'Mind-
controlling spirit-beast infesting Valdemar and tricking
Kordas—poor simple-minded Kordas!—into placing his
people under a tyrannous rule.':* The voice in Navar's
mind was a new one. Somehow as feminine as Ardatha's
was masculine. It belonged to the white horse—the
Companion—who walked from the stand of woods behind Ardatha and stood at his side. *:If you believe that*

King Valdemar is so weak and foolish, it's a wonder you followed him all this way,: the new Companion added.

"I believed," Navar said simply.

:Then believe in him still,: the new Companion said, more gently now. *:Help him. He needs good men. And yes—stubborn ones.:*

"To do what?" Navar asked roughly, taking a step toward her.

:What is right,: she answered. *:Always—only—what is right.:*

Her words were feast after famine, water in the desert. In the east, the baron had been accounted a good man, but to keep his people safe, he had been forced to turn a blind eye to injustices done outside his own borders. So many times in his service to the barony Navar had been forced to balance what was right against what was safe—or politic—or possible—and the actions he had taken had caused him to armor his heart so that he could deafen himself to its promptings.

The reality was so simple, now that he could see it. He had lived so long in that chambered silence that he had nearly succumbed to the greatest folly of all: of believing in evil and refusing to believe in good.

He had believed in Valdemar's dream when it had seemed dangerous and impossible. He would believe now.

He took a last step forward and reached out his hand. The not-horse placed her soft muzzle into it. *:My name is Tisarand, Navar. I would Choose you for my Companion, if you would have a mind-controlling spirit-beast.:*

It was as if the sound of her name had unlocked a floodgate within his own mind. His answer—promise and agreement and avowal—came faster than he could form words, conscious choice and automatic answer all at once. Navar took another step forward, wrapping his arms around her neck and burying his face in her silken mane. His body shook with reaction—he had come so close to stealing away into the night thinking Valdemar had been taken over by monsters! Not monsters at all, but something far greater.

Hope.

:I might have gone after you to bring you back,: Tisarand said. *:And I would have disliked that very much. We have a great deal of work to do here, Navar.:*

"Yes," Navar said. "Yes, we do." He took a deep breath. "And the first thing we have to do is get back to the tavern before Doladan comes looking for me. He's a man of many gifts—including that of getting hopelessly lost within a few yards of his own doorway."

Tisarand's mirth sounded like silver bells within his mind, and Navar's voice sounded strange in his own ears. It was a moment before he recognized the new note in it.

It was joy.

Softly Falling Snow
by *Elizabeth A. Vaughan*

Elizabeth A. Vaughan writes fantasy romance; her most recent novel is *White Star*, part of the Star series. At the present, she is owned by three incredibly spoiled cats and lives in the Northwest Territory, on the outskirts of the Black Swamp, along Mad Anthony's Trail on the banks of the Maumee River.

"I believe that is the last issue before us today?" Queen Elspeth the Peacemaker kept her face composed as she rose stiffly from her seat, thus cutting off the possibility of further discussion. Her knees creaked as she straightened up. She'd had more than enough for one day. "The council is adjourned. My thanks, my lords."

Chairs scraped back as the councilors rose and bowed as she swept out of the room, the full skirts of her Royal Whites brushing the floor.

As Queen's Own, Lancir had the privilege of accompanying her back to her chambers. He extended his arm, and she placed her fingers lightly on his wrist, as custom dictated.

"The private audiences now, I believe." Elspeth tried to make her voice regretful, but Lancir had her measure. He arched an eyebrow as they walked toward her chambers.

"Only one, Your Majesty. For some reason, not many seek a private audience with you during this season."

"True enough. And those that do, don't linger." Elspeth agreed. "Refreshing, how they get straight to the point."

"I am sure," he said dryly. "I'll have one of the Herald trainees escort Lord Wolke to you."

She gave him an impish look, and he quirked an eyebrow at her. A few paces before her door, he stopped, and bowed.

The guards opened the doors on her approach, and they also bowed as she moved past. She nodded to them both as she stepped into her antechamber, only to meet with a flock of bright songbirds. Or so it seemed to her. Her handmaidens, all daughters and wives of her councilors, were fluttering about, dressed in all the colors of the rainbow. She towered over most of them, like the thin old stick she was. Some days it made her feel as plain as a pin to wear her plain Royal Whites, with the black trim of mourning.

Her Companion stirred in the back of her mind and sent an image of a mink, the black tip of its tail twitching.

Elspeth sent back a pulse of laughter. She might not have mind-speech, but they'd communicated very well this way for all the many years since she'd been Chosen. She wondered if her dear one was warm enough.

The feeling of a warm blanket draped over her shoulders, and she knew that all was well. She turned her attention back to the room and the chorus of voices that resounded around her.

"You can't, Your Majesty!"

"Don't go out there, you'll catch your death."

"It's snowing!" one of the youngest cried out, and the flock circled and wheeled around the room to press their faces to the windows, looking out over her private gardens.

Meredith, her maid of many years, stood nearby. "I've your boots warming by the fire," she said quietly. "Do you need assistance?"

Elspeth gave her a grateful nod. "Yes, please." It wasn't easy to admit that she needed some help with dressing, but Meredith understood and made no fuss.

Elspeth sank onto one of the chairs closest to the hearth and drew her petticoats and skirt up. Meredith knelt down and gently eased off her slippers. "Don't linger too long, Your Majesty," she said softly. "There's a formal court dinner tonight."

"I'll remember," Elspeth said with a smile.

Meredith gave her a knowing look as she laced up the boots, but she said nothing more. She just helped Elspeth with her heavy winter white cloak, the hood lined with white fur. She retrieved the matching white furred muff for her hands.

Elspeth smiled at her. "Warm as toast."

"Mind you stay that way," Meredith whispered, with the ease of an old friend. "I'll send out tea for you and your guest."

Elspeth turned to the garden door, smiled blandly at her protesting women, and stepped outside. She closed the door firmly behind her and took a deep breath of cold air.

Silence, blessed silence. The cold air stung at her flushed cheeks, and she took another breath, watching the vapor rise.

Her private garden lay deep in a blanket of snow. The trees were frosted like cakes, and the ground sparkled as if diamond dust had been blown over the crust of white.

Her spirits lifted after a morning spent in an overheated council chamber. Oh, how she loved winter.

A path had been stamped out, and she followed its curve as it angled away from the door. Her skirts brushed along, swishing against the edges of the path. There, in what was normally a rose bower, sat two benches opposite each other, a brazier set between, filled with glowing coals. The rosebushes, cut back for the season, protruded from the snow like thin black fingers.

She settled on one with a sigh of pleasure and looked about at the trees. The sky was a pale blue, with just a few clouds that promised more snow later on. But for now, there was only the occasional fat fluffy flake falling to rest on the fur of her muff.

The snow made everything look different. Perfect, with the covering of white and the glint of ice. Cold and lovely. Her Herald-Mages had offered to set up a warm shelter or cast a warming spell on the benches, but she had refused. They didn't seem to understand that the entire point was to be cold.

Well, that and keeping these private audiences short and sweet. No one lingered with petitions and political maneuvering in this kind of weather. Elspeth had been too long on the throne to actually chuckle, but she smiled inside.

Two pages approached, bundled up and carrying a tray and a small table. She offered them thanks as they set the table down and poured her a large mug of tea. She slipped her bare hands out of her muff and carefully took the hot mug in her hands, enjoying the warmth.

"Please let the Queen's Own know that I am ready," Elspeth smiled at the pages.

The two young lads bowed slowly, then ran off down the path to the door. Elspeth sipped her tea, enjoying the white perfection of the cold stillness.

She heard the door open, and one of the Herald trainees appeared, with Lord Wolke in tow. The trainee hadn't bothered with a cloak, and he walked briskly toward her. She plastered on her court smile, setting her mug down on the bench next to her.

"Your Majesty." The trainee looked so serious and so very young as he bowed. But all the trainees looked younger to her every day. "Lord Wolke."

Lord Wolke bowed as well, his cloak wrapped tight around his body. Such a handsome young man, with charming manners, or so she'd been told.

Elspeth smiled as the trainee left them alone. "Sit, Lord Wolke. May I pour you some tea?"

"That would be most welcome, Your Majesty," he sat on the stone bench gingerly, as if afraid he'd freeze off something valuable. "You honor me."

"Not really, I'm afraid." She handed him his mug and then refreshed her own. "This is an 'honor' my court avoids at all costs. I can't seem to convince them of the loveliness of the garden after a snow. Even my Companion prefers a warm stable." Elspeth cast her mind in that direction, to be met with a sleepy, comfortable response.

"Their loss is my gain, Your Majesty." He flashed her a smile. Oh, yes, there was charm there indeed. No wonder half her ladies had lost their heads over him.

"Aren't you nice," she laughed lightly. "I've always loved to come out into a clear, cold day and enjoy the sun. I am so glad you could join me."

Wolke shifted his weight on the bench and tried to adjust his knees so they wouldn't come into contact with the brazier. "I've been at court for some time, Your Majesty."

"Yes," She picked up her mug and gave him that same smile. "Without a summons or invitation. Let us discuss that, my lord."

Elspeth watched as young Wolke retreated down the path, moving as fast as dignity allowed.

The afternoon shadows had lengthened in the garden, and thin clouds had moved in. The snow had turned a pale bluish color, the tree branches blacker in contrast. The lights from the window cast a glow over the drifts in front of the windows. Night would fall soon enough. Still, she sat, deep in her furs and white leathers, and stared into the glowing coals of the brazier.

The pages approached again with more fuel and tea. She watched as they fed the coals and filled her mug.

"I do not wish to be disturbed. I will come in when I am ready." Elspeth said, and they bowed, and ran off, back to the warmth of the palace.

They probably thought her mad or eccentric. Lancir understood, as did some of the older members of her council. They knew it wasn't so much the cold or the snow that drew her out of the warm palace.

Snow meant that armies were not moving to mass at the border to threaten Valdemar. The cold kept feuding lords at their hearths. Bandits did not attack settlements or raid the herds of cattle, since any fool could track the transgressors in the snow.

Ice cloaked the roads and paths in treacherous footing. Rivers froze, the ice uncertain. Various religious holidays and celebrations kept people busy with other tasks, rather than killing their neighbors. The lack of daylight concealed the world, keeping those with malice inside, their lights burning bright.

They might plan and plot, connive and ponder, but they stayed within.

Winter was peace made manifest.

She dreaded spring. Oh, not the warmth or the violets with their lovely scent. It was a joy to watch the garden come alive again. Small green leaves and delicate flowers emerged from the soil almost overnight. But the land wasn't the only thing astir.

The fragile network of agreements that she'd built

over her reign always trembled under the strain of spring. She could already see problems looming . . . she stared at the fire and wondered if she'd have the strength to deal with it all.

She heard the door open and the crunch of footsteps on the path. Her eyes weren't what they used to be, but she recognized the stride of the man coming toward her, his scarlet uniform a stark contrast to the snow. As he grew closer, she could see his face, one that still stirred her heart after all these years.

He approached and then made a formal bow with a flourish of his hand. "Your Majesty," he said, as he knelt in the snow, his tone a mocking one. "The Queen's Own has asked that I inquire as to your welfare."

"Bard Kyran," Elspeth glanced toward the door. "I take it, then, that they can see us from the windows?"

"Why else would I be on my knee in the snow, beloved?" Kyran looked up, his eyes twinkling. "Some of the younger handmaidens are pressed to the farthest window, watching to see if I can convince you to come in and get warm."

Those eyes . . . she'd fallen for those eyes so many years ago, those eyes that seemed to glow for her and her alone. The years had not dulled their sparkle. "Sit with me for a moment," she said, gesturing to the bench so that the watchers knew she had given her permission.

"You've a formal court dinner this night," Kyran reminded her as he rose with grace and settled on the bench. "Ah. Still warm from young Wolke's ass." He held his hands over the brazier and rubbed them together. "He blew through the chamber without a word or a nod to anyone. Are we rid of him then?"

"Yes," she tucked her hand back into her fur muff. "I sent him back to his lands. Young fool."

"The ladies of the court will be crushed. He'd charmed almost all of them."

"Idiot," Elspeth growled. "To think he thought he could claim a position on my council. I should have boxed his ears."

"Now, there would be something to sing about," Kyran chuckled. "Gather now, my children, for you should truly hear, of the night that Elspeth Peacemaker, boxed young Wolke's ears . . ." He raised his eyebrows. "There's still time. I doubt he's left the palace yet."

She stared at him, a sudden sorrow welling up in her chest.

He frowned, concerned. "Elspeth?"

"Was it worth it, beloved?" She choked out, tears beyond her control filling her eyes. She clamped down on the pain to protect her sleeping Companion.

Understanding filled his face. "Oh, my love, what brought this on?"

"I don't know," Elspeth closed her eyes, letting the tears fall. "I woke this morning, and I felt so tired. So very tired. I do not think I can bear the spring, Kyran. I just wanted to lie there, in my warm bed, with my soft pillows, and sleep forever."

"Elspeth," Kyran whispered.

"No," Elspeth blinked her eyes, not daring to lift a hand to wipe the tears away. "Since the day I took the throne, I've fought, argued, beguiled, and struggled to keep the peace." She looked away from him, up to the snow-covered trees. "I turned from you, my love, to marry a man I didn't love, for the sake of an alliance."

"Elspeth," Kyran grew somber. "So long ago . . ."

"Even after his death, I used my mourning as a political tool, fending off other offers of marriage, playing them off against each other." Elspeth held herself still on the bench, not moving a hand or making a gesture that would give the watchers any information. "And then Darvi . . . my son. My beautiful boy. Dead." Her voice caught in her throat, and for a moment, they sat in silence and shared pain. She looked down at her muff, where a few tears were clinging to the hairs of the fur, small diamonds against the white.

"Which brings to mind a bit of gossip from the city." Kyran's voice was rough. "Seems that one of the crafts-men of the city recently died. In his will, he took advantage of that new law of yours."

"The one about the statuary?" Elspeth choked out, all too willing to change the subject.

"That's the one. Seems he was fair well off, being of a thrifty bent. He's endowed a statue of himself, to be built in the city, and provided for its upkeep." Kyran cleared his throat. "Has the nobility in a bit of a snit."

"How so?" Elspeth asked. "I placed no limits on—"

"Well, the dead gentleman has apparently snagged one of the busiest crossroads in the city. So very soon, there's to be erected a statue with a water fountain, for any and all to drink from. And not just humans—there's a lower font for animals."

Elspeth knew Kyran well. She titled her head and waited for it.

"Well, it seems our craftsman is fairly short of frame and rather round. And bald. I understand he was well known for his cheerful countenance. So in among the heros of the realm and the proud members of the noble bloodlines, he will stand, smiling happily, holding the tools of his trade. Much to the horror of the noble lords and ladies." He laughed, that easy laugh she loved so well.

"I should have named you Laureate," she watched as a few flakes settled in his thinning hair.

"Me?" He widened his eyes in mock horror. "Wear a coronet, and attend all those interminable council meetings?" He shook his head. "And have the entire court and kingdom speculate on our relationship? Elspeth, it would not have worked. Besides, I have had all that I wanted." He drew a deep breath. "Do you remember?" His voice was low, a gentle caress. "Your first formal court dance?"

Elspeth nodded. "I was so nervous. Father and Mother and the entire court watching me. You walked over, held out your hand and asked me to dance, a dashing young Bard-trainee. How could I resist?"

Kyran laughed. "I was so startled when you took my hand and let me draw you onto the dance floor. A Bard-trainee, and not an ounce of noble blood in my veins. I thought all the lords and ladies would have brain storms, they were so enraged."

"It was a lovely dance," Elspeth said.

"It was, and my last for quite some time. I was hustled out of there and informed in no uncertain terms that just Was Not Done." Kyran's laughter echoed off the stone walls. "And well and truly punished by the Bardic Council—fifty copies of 'My Lady's Eyes'. Do you know how many lines that song has? Add in the instrumental parts . . ." Kyran shook his head. "I thought the cramp in my hand would be with me until the end of my days." He focused on her again. "Then I got your note."

"I couldn't believe they punished you," Elspeth rolled her eyes. "For a dance!"

"'Meet me in the Collegium Library'," Kyran quoted. "You apologized—you! Standing there, in your grays, cursing the Bardic Council. I think I fell in love right then and there, with your dark hair and flashing eyes and the scent of violets . . ." Kyran tilted his head back, so very serious as he looked up into the trees. "Why is it that we remember the pain of our lives more than the joy?"

Her breath caught in her throat. "I don't know, beloved."

"Then know this, Elspeth, Queen of Valdemar and my love," Kyran's voice was low and strong. She hung on every word, as he intended, no doubt. "Valdemar has been at peace since your father's time, and you are the reason. Everything you have done, everything you have suffered, has been worth every moment. Your people are safe and prosperous, your kingdom secure."

Elspeth shrugged. "I worry that it will end on my death. I worry that my grandson will not be able to—"

"Randale will be fine," Kyran said firmly. "You'd worry a wart off your hand." He spread his hands over the coals. "Do you suppose your father worried that you'd ruin the kingdom?"

"I doubt that," Elspeth snapped. "He knew that I'd always put Valdemar first above all else."

"Would Randi do less?" Kyran asked.

Elspeth caught her breath, then scowled. "Do you have to be so . . . so . . ."

"Irritating? Aggravating?" Kyran smirked. "Rational? Accurate?"

Elspeth growled, trying to stay angry, but he just gave her that innocent carefree look. "It's why you love me," he assured her.

"I suppose . . ." Elspeth said.

"Well, that and my lute." Kyran wagged his eyebrows.

Elspeth laughed out loud. "Your lute's not quite as in tune as it once was, my love. Any more than my sagging breasts and wrinkled skin."

"Alas, time's passage takes its toll. Still, it's ever yours to command. And finger. And fondle, if your majesty so desires. And as to your breasts—"

"Enough," Elspeth snorted. "I cry mercy."

"Then I cry enough melancholy, my love." Kyran said. "All the years, all the pain and the joy—I would not change a thing for fear I'd change what lies between us."

The tears started again, but not with sorrow. "I love you."

"And I, you." Kyran said. "And on the morning when you do not wake, I'll not be far behind."

Elspeth's heart leaped in her throat, but then common sense intervened. "You're freezing."

"I am. Come. You've a court dinner and even Queen Elspeth the Peacemaker had best not anger the cooks." Kyran stood and offered his arm.

She stood, stepped close to him.

"You still smell like violets," Kyran whispered. He held out his arm.

Elspeth placed her hand on his wrist, stroking his cold skin with her fingers tips. As they started down the path, Kyran flipped his hand, and for a brief, sweet moment their fingers intertwined, before returning to their proper places.

"Meredith is on duty in my inner chamber tonight," she offered the bit of information with a sly look.

"Really?" Kyran arched an eyebrow at her. "Meredith likes me. If an old worn out Bard were to appear at your chamber door late at night, she'd open it and none the wiser."

"True," Elspeth said. "I'd even welcome an old, worn-out Bard to my chamber, away from prying eyes and whispering tongues."

Figures moved in the glow behind the windows. As they grew closer, the door opened, letting warm air wash over them.

"I'll let you strum my lute," Kyran whispered as he bowed her into the room, eyes bright.

Joy rose in her heart as Elspeth laughed.

The Reluctant Herald

by Mickey Zucker Reichert

Mickey Zucker Reichert is a pediatrician, parent to multitudes (at least it seems like that many), bird wrangler, goat roper, dog trainer, cat herder, horse rider, and fish feeder who has learned (the hard way) not to let macaws remove contact lenses. Also she is the author of twenty-two novels (including the *Renshai*, *Nightfall*, *Barakhai*, and *Bifrost* series), one illustrated novella, and fifty plus short stories. Mickey's age is a mathematically guarded secret: the square root of 8649 minus the hypotenuse of an isosceles right triangle with a side length of 33.941126.

Lubonne's wooden sword cut through the ice-grained air of early spring, and his feet stamped evergreen needles deeper into the muck. Sharp, brown burrs clung to his britches and the hem of his tunic, prickling through the fabric as he moved. His bandy legs switched directions with sharp precision, their shortness belying their strength and speed. His relatively long arms supplied a reach that never failed to surprise opponents. The practice blade skipped around his homely features: his eyes small and pallid, his nose broad and overarching, his mouth thin lipped but wide. Mouse-brown hair, cut short, framed his features, unwanted curls fluffing it at the back.

A voice interrupted Lubonne's solitary practice. :*Hello there.*: It left an impression of femininity and strength, yet it felt strangely ephemeral, as if he sensed rather than heard it.

Lubonne hid his startlement behind a feigned-deliberate sword stroke. It bothered him that while he practiced martial maneuvers, he had allowed someone to sneak so close through his defenses. He had heard stories of fey and magical creatures inhabiting these and other woodlands, tales of spirits and drakes, of humans taking beast-form and -nature, yet none of them involved friendly voices shocking through a young man's mind in broad daylight. Keeping the mock weapon raised, he glanced around the clearing.

As usual, Lubonne squinted, the sun painful in his too-light eyes. Trees and shrubbery flashed through his vision as he turned, then something brilliant white seized his full attention. It was large and horse-shaped, its fore-lock and mane snagged with the same type of burrs that clung to his clothing. One enormous blue eye, nearly as pallid as his own, studied him. His gaze went immediately to its back, where no rider or saddle perched, not even a dirt-smudge to suggest one ever had. It wore no bridle or halter, either.

Lubonne lowered his sword. "What's this?" He had seen only one animal this magnificent: the stallion Herald Walthin rode whenever he came to town. *Has something happened to Walthin?* Suddenly alarmed, he called out sharply, "Herald Walthin! Are you all right?"

:*Walthin has decent hearing, but I doubt your voice will carry all the way to Valdemar.*:

Lubonne went utterly still, his next shout frozen on his lips.

The voice in Lubonne's head recited the answers to questions he had not yet thought to ask. :*Yes, a white horselike creature is speaking to you. No, there's no other human around. Yes, I'm speaking directly into your mind.*: It paused, apparently hoping he would take his turn.

Lubonne found himself still incapable of action, except to pinch himself through the fabric of his britches, where his buttock met his right leg. He idly wondered where this convention had originated and how it had become cliché. Surely, a man could dream he had pinched himself, a detail far less shocking and strange than what faced him at the moment.

The creature seemed to read his mind. *:Oh, and don't risk injuring your backside. You're not dreaming, Lubonne.*:

That finally jarred his jaw loose, though Lubonne asked the least important of the myriad questions now bounding through his mind. "How do you know my name?"

The animal studied Lubonne. *:Why do you ask? Is it a deep dark secret?*:

"Of . . . of course not. I just . . . don't have the . . . um . . . pleasure of . . . of your . . ." Lubonne looked around, wondering if someone was playing a cruel joke. His brothers probably crouched, snickering, behind a nearby bush.

:Carthea.: The beast bowed, one long leg extended forward, the other curled beneath its broad chest. Lubonne could no longer convince himself that the voice came from any other source. *:I'm your Companion.*:

"Well, yes. At the moment, I suppose you are," Lubonne managed to sputter out, marveling at how stupid he suddenly seemed to have become. *What does one say to a talking horse?*

:Your Companion,: she repeated. *:With a capital "C".*:

"Oh." *Still stupid.* Lubonne pinched himself again, with the same result. *Even if I am dreaming, I can at least try to act like I have something more substantial than rocks in my head.* Discovering no more words, he left the conversation to the Companion again.

The beast stomped a snowy hoof. :*This is the part where you squeal, "Oh, I've always dreamed of the chance to become a Herald of Valdemar, leap joyfully upon my back, and take a smooth and magical journey to the Collegium to train."*:

"It is?" *Gah! I still sound like a total moron.* Lubonne shook his head, trying to clear it.

:*It is.*: Carthea bobbed her head once, forcefully and with finality.

At last, Lubonne discovered his wits. And his tongue. He bowed, as if to royalty. "No, thank you."

The Companion merely stared. :*What do you mean, "No, thank you?"*:

Now who sounds like a moron? "I wasn't aware that 'no, thank you' required explanation. I appreciate your generous offer, but I decline it. While you are an inarguably beautiful animal with clear, amazing abilities, I have no wish to ride to Valdemar, to attend a Collegium, nor to become a Herald."

Carthea planted all four feet in the mud left by the spring-melted snow. :*You can't refuse. I've Chosen you.*:

Lubonne waved and started to turn. "I'll forget it, if you will. Just go and choose someone else. Who will be the wiser?"

:*It doesn't work that way.*:

Lubonne sighed and reluctantly looked back. Real or dream, he hated to disappoint what seemed like a wonderful and decent animal. "Listen, Carthea. My answer is 'no,' and I won't change my mind. I have the perfect life here. I'm the third son of wealthy parents. My older brothers inherit the land and the responsibilities that go with it. I get money and no duties, free to spend it as I please. I'm engaged to an exquisite woman. My life is happy, and I have no intention of changing it." With that, he turned on his heel and left, intending to walk out of Carthea's life forever.

*   *   *

Lubonne never looked behind him as he strode toward
the village, the wooden sword tucked rakishly into his
belt. His route took him from forest to beaten path to
cobbles; and it was not until he reached the latter that
he heard the steady clop of hoofbeats behind him. He
stepped to the side and stopped, making room for the
rider to pass him. But, the instant he went still, the noise
ceased as well. *I've got horses on the mind.* Lubonne
continued on his way. With his first new step, the hollow,
unmistakable sound of hoof on stone resumed.

Lubonne whirled to find himself nose to nose with
Carthea. She studied him curiously through one eye,
neck gracefully arched, head tipped. "Perhaps I didn't
make myself entirely clear—"

Carthea raised her well-muscled neck and snorted.
:*You did.*:

Lubonne glanced around to make certain no one
could hear him talking to a horse. Seeing no one all the
way to the edge of the village, he continued, "Then why
are you still with me?"

:*Because you are mine, Chosen One. And I am yours.
We are a team, bonded until—*:

"No!" Lubonne waved his hands in broad gestures. "We are not a team. We are . . . barely nodding
acquaintances."

:*Ride me.*:

The temptation was great. Lubonne had known how
to ride a horse as long as he could remember, most often bareback and on boyish whim. He suspected he had
molded the shape of his buttocks from Old Rinny's
back. He knew a great animal when he saw one, and
Carthea's conformation impressed him mightily. He
could imagine the powerful legs bunching beneath him,
the silky mane stroking his face, the thrill of its wild gallop, the closest thing to human flight. "I certainly will not

ride you. You've already told me you'd carry me off to Valdemar."

:*Yes!*:

"Well, I'm not going to Valdemar. Or anywhere. I'm happy here. It's home."

:*Home is where your heart is. And, I, Dear One, am your heart.*:

Lubonne rolled his eyes, sighing. "No, ma'am. I'm pretty sure my heart is that familiar beating thing lodged firmly in my chest." He started back down the road toward his parents' mansion. "Please. The sooner you leave me be, the sooner you find your rightful partner." Without another glance, deliberately deaf to the drum of hoofbeats, he headed toward home.

And Carthea followed.

A nudge awakened Lubonne with an abruptness that sent him leaping from his bed. Blankets tangled around his legs. His foot mired on a misplaced bedsheet, and he tumbled to the wooden floor. The familiar sights and smells of his bedroom surrounded him, but those seemed to disappear as he focused on the one oddity: a furry white head shoved through his only window. Carthea stared at him, head cocked, twin puffs of breath smoking in the cold air.

"What the hell are you doing?" Lubonne scrambled to his feet and attempted to wrap the blankets around himself. In the process, he wrenched a corner from directly under his foot and wound up sprawled on the floor a second time.

:*I'm sorry,*: Carthea sent. :*Did I wake you?*:

In a whirl of surprise, anger, and uncertainty; feeling awkward as a toddler, Lubonne resorted to sarcasm. "No, no. I'm still asleep. I'm thoroughly accustomed to massive animal heads popping through the window to shove me onto the floor." He rose more carefully and twisted the blankets around his half-naked body. He could barely comprehend the discomfort he felt beneath her stare. Surely a mare, even one intelligent enough to speak, had no intention of judging or worrying about a human's exposed privates.

:*You don't have to mock me. I can read your moods, you know.*: Only then, Lubonne realized that she had sent him more than just words. He read a mixture of emotions radiating from Carthea as well. She was clearly young, little more than a filly, uncertain, and definitively frustrated. :*And you don't have to talk at me. You're quite capable of Mindspeech.*:

I am? Lubonne shook the thought aside. *Of course, I'm not. I've never heard Herald Walthin or his stallion. I've certainly never mastered reading what any woman is thinking.*

:*That's because you've only just met me.*:

Lubonne squawked and covered his head, as if this might protect his mind from the Companion's intrusion. "Get out of my mind!"

:*You have other Gifts, too. Strong ones, in fact. You'd just never realize them without a Companion to enhance them.*:

"No, no, no!" Lubonne wrapped both arms around his head, trapping the blankets in place with his elbows. "Stop enhancing me. Quit bothering me. Go away!"

:*But—*:

Lubonne would hear nothing more. *"Go away!"*

The horsy head retreated from the window and disappeared into the night. Lubonne replaced his sheets, respread his blankets, and tried to get back to sleep.

Servants, decorators, and cooks filled the mansion, and Lubonne escaped into the stable as quickly as decorum allowed. Though excited about his upcoming engagement party, Lubonne withered under the constant flurry of questions. He had no opinion on the menu, saw no need to add flourishes to the already spectacular décor. He had selected his suit weeks ago. What others wore did not interest him; he would not refuse a friend fresh from a spar, sweating profusely and swathed in filthy rags.

To Lubonne's relief, the groomsman, Vannath, had his bay mare saddled and bridled. Smiling, he stirred the star on her muzzle, revealing pink skin beneath the spot of white fur. Idly, he wondered if Carthea's hide was pink throughout and swiftly banished the thought. He wanted nothing to do with the creature who named herself his Companion. "Ready for a ride, Rinny?"

"All ready, Master Lubonne," Vannath replied.

Giddy with anticipation, Lubonne joked, "Why, Rinny, old girl. Your voice has deepened. You sound positively masculine."

Vannath chuckled dutifully. "I knew you'd want to get away from that, sir." He gestured vaguely toward the manse. "Engagement party preparations." He shook his grizzled head. "It's no fit place for man or beast."

Lubonne agreed. "Wall-to-wall womenfolk. They actually seem to enjoy it." He stepped into the left stirrup and swung his right leg over Rinny's red-brown back to settle into the weathered saddle. "Well, I'm off to find Honoria. Better make sure she's still crazy enough to agree to marry me before we seal the engagement." He walked the sturdy bay from the stables and into the late-morning light.

Vannath's voice chased him. "Good luck, Master Lubonne."

With a backward wave of acknowledgment, Lubonne trotted across the grounds. He dared not look at the mansion, hoping no one recognized him from behind and demanded his return. He rode, unaccosted, to the gate and bent for the latch. Years of practice allowed him to swing it open and closed without dismounting, the latches bent and battered from all the previous efforts of himself and his three brothers. A perfectly measured push sent it swinging back into place, and he heard the satisfying clang of its proper falling and engagement. *No dismount necessary this time.* He mentally applauded himself. *Yes.*

Rinny stood placidly and patiently while he worked. Accustomed to the brothers' antics, she took loud noises, fidgeting riders, and waving sticks and swords in stride.

:*Insecurity is not a crime.*: Carthea's voice came out of nowhere.

Lubonne nearly crawled out of his skin. Instinctively, he whirled, only to find the Companion just off Rinny's left flank. "What?"

Carthea stepped out fully from behind the neighboring smithy. :*Some of our most heroic and gifted Heralds initially believed themselves unworthy.*:

"I'm not insecure."

Every eye in the street went suddenly to Lubonne, reminding him he was no longer alone. He waved cheerily to a friend headed for the tavern and tipped his hat toward the smith's young wife. Carthea had said he could use Mindspeak, and this seemed the perfect time to try it. He focused heavily on each word. :*I . . . AM . . . NOT . . . INSECURE!*:

Carthea shook her head, falling into lockstep with Rinny. :*Stop shouting. I heard you the first time.*: She timed her steps to the bay's, so that it sounded as if one giant horse walked the cobbled street instead of two smaller ones.

Lubonne reined toward the woodland path, preferring to take the back route to Honoria's home over trying to explain the presence of the Companion to every passerby. He could imagine getting stopped every few steps as someone new admired the white mare and questioned him about her presence. He tried to put together mental words without the emphasis, wondering how much thought the creature could read. *:I'm sure I told you to go away.:*

:You did.:

:But you're still here.:

That being self-evident, it scarcely needed acknowledging; but Carthea obliged him. *:I am.:*

:Why?: It surprised Lubonne how easily Rinny accepted the presence of a strange horse. Usually, such a meeting would result in sniffling, sharp whinnied challenges, sometimes even a bit of mock battle.

:Because, Chosen One, you are my heartmate, my soulmate, my lifemate.:

Lubonne suppressed a scream. As they moved from cobbled road to wooded dirt, he returned to regular speech. It felt more natural. "Exactly how many times, and in how many ways, do I have to say 'no'? Find another heartmate, Carthea. I'm not it."

:But you are.:

"I'm not."

:And you have to undergo your Herald training.:

"I don't."

:You must come—:

"I mustn't."

Carthea pulled up directly in front of Rinny, perpendicular to the path, and the bay pranced to a stop. *:You can do this, Lubonne. You really can.:*

Lubonne sighed. Drawing Rinny to the left, he walked around the living road block. "I told you, I'm not insecure. I *know* I can do it. I've got decent weapons training, and I'm a damn-sight smarter than Herald Walthin, bless his kindly heart."

Carthea followed, drawing abreast of Rinny again. A quaver entered her sending. *: All right. Perhaps it's me who's insecure, then. I'm only three years old.:*

Lubonne looked at Carthea. "Three years . . . you're just a baby." A fluttering wave of guilt and empathy passed through him, and his patience softened. He felt abruptly sorry for the persistent creature.

:You take that back.: Carthea's lips tightened, and her wide nostrils flared. *:I'm not a baby! I'm big enough and strong enough to carry a grown man.:*

"I'm sorry," Lubonne said sincerely. He had not intended to offend her. "Look, Carthea. I'm just not the heroic type, all right? I'm a bit spoiled, somewhat of a gadabout, and satisfied with my life the way it is. If I didn't wear this face . . ." He waved a hand in front of his homely features, "I'd probably be a carouser, like my little brother. As it is, I'm lucky to have my beautiful Honoria." He could not help smiling.

Emotion clearly crept through in his voice or thoughts. *:You love her, this Honoria.:*

"I do." Lubonne sat back as the trees bounced by them, unnoticed. "We're getting engaged, officially, tonight. We're having a party."

Carthea tipped her head toward him. *:And what, exactly, is wrong with your face?:*

Lubonne stared at the Companion. "My nose is . . . well, like a second head."

:I don't see anything wrong with your nose.:

"Of course not. You're a horse. Your nose *is* your head."

:Hey!:

"I'm not being mean. It's what a horse is supposed to look like. On a horse, a giant honker is sweet and soft, it's ideal." Lubonne had come to grips with his appearance long ago. "I have a nickname: Hawknose. My brothers call me Beaky. I'm cursed with pale, squinty little eyes, too, that only make the nose more obvious; and I've never found a way to tame this crazy hair."

:Me, either.: Carthea tossed her matted, burr-filled mane.

"Ah, but a simple grooming will make yours shine like the stars. Brushing just makes my hair fluffy."

Carthea rolled back the eye on the side of her head toward Rinny to look directly at Lubonne. Her ear went with it, pressed nearly flat to her head, while the other cupped forward to catch upcoming sounds. *:Why quibble over features? All humans look essentially alike to me on the outside. It's the inside that matters; and your insides, my Chosen, are the insides of a Herald.:*

Lubonne's small eyes ratcheted to slits. "That sounds ... utterly disgusting."

Carthea raised her head as if to trumpet out a whinny; but no sound emerged. *:I'm not talking about your bowels, Beloved Idiot. I mean your soul. It's gorgeous ... :* The words came with a wash of love bordering on awe. *:And you're more Gifted than I initially guessed. Look how quickly you picked up Mindspeak.:*

The Companion's words gave Lubonne pause, but only for a moment. *Just call me Hawknose Gorgeoussoul, a Collegium trainee.* It all seemed a ridiculous fantasy. "Look, Carthea. Those sound like lovely compliments, aside from the 'idiot' part. It's not a matter of whether I'm capable of becoming a Herald; I'll take your word that I am. It's just that ... I'm happy with my current life. I want to live it out fully and completely. And I made a lifelong promise to Honoria."

Carthea's gait went stiff. She clearly wished to say something, and a hint of an unidentified emotion that seemed rough and unkind slipped through the mental contact. However, she remained silent.

Rinny did not need guiding to take the left fork toward Honoria's family home.

"Do you understand?" For the first time, Lubonne

actually wondered what Carthea might have been thinking, what cruel words she had kept to herself.

:Responsibility. Heroic devotion.: Carthea seemed to be thinking aloud. *:These are the virtues, and the curse, of a Herald.:* She bobbed her head. *:I understand.:*

Lubonne heaved a sigh of relief. "Then you'll leave me alone?"

Carthea melted into the woodland shadows, but the mental contact left a lasting impression.

Lubonne scarcely dared to believe that, this time, it might actually, finally, be over.

A private, sunny picnic with Honoria drove all thought and concern about the Companion from Lubonne's mind. Their engagement felt so right, so normal, as opposed to the odd conversations he had shared with the magnificent horselike creature moments earlier. Though barely a day's ride away, the country of Valdemar seemed like another world in another time, and its self-named city even more so. Lubonne could almost convince himself that Carthea had merely appeared to him in a series of weird and consecutive dreams.

It took most of the afternoon for Honoria to pick out her dress, the process every bit as tedious as the decoration of the feasting hall. Blurry-eyed and bored within the hour, Lubonne found himself saying the same flattering words over and over until they sounded insincere even to himself. Then Honoria's sisters combed and cut and perfumed the couple's hair until Lubonne thought he could stand it no more. In the end, he looked exactly the same, at least to his own eyes, but he complimented the girls to the sun and beyond just to get them to finish.

Dusk darkened the horizon by the time Honoria's parents and sisters rode off in their small, family carriage. They lived a modest life, their fortune more meager than Lubonne's own. Honoria planned to use Lubonne's inheritance to fix up the small piece of soupy land that served as her dowry. Then he would secure a guarding job in the city to support her and their forthcoming family.

Honoria perched delicately behind the saddle while sure, steady Rinny picked her quiet way across the packed earth roadways through the forest.

"Must we go this way, my darling Hawk?" Honoria asked sweetly. "I'm afraid things falling from the trees might muss my hair."

The thought had occurred to Lubonne, but he still worried about the need to explain Carthea. The Companion had left him to his own devices since he had chased her away that morning, but she had a habit of turning up inconveniently. Lubonne removed his coat and held it over Honoria's head with one hand, the other clutching Rinny's reins. "Here. Use this."

Honoria looked up. "I don't want your coat stained, either. I want a perfect entrance." Nevertheless, she took the coat in both hands and held it over her hair to protect it from the wind, leaves, and elements.

"Perfect entrance, eh? Then I'll have to walk in backward," Lubonne quipped. "Or this nose will precede us and spoil everything." He expected Honoria to laugh, but she did not.

Instead, she muttered, "At least our children won't have to worry about it."

Lubonne's brow furrowed as he tried to make sense of the comment. "About what, my darling?"

At his back, Lubonne felt Honoria stiffen. "Nothing."

Nothing? Lubonne frowned, wondering what she had intended to say. "Our children will have your stunning beauty. No one will even notice the size of their noses. But even should one inherit my beak, it's not such a bad thing. I've done well enough with it." He reached back to pat her hand. "I'm blessed enough to have you as my future wife."

Honoria gripped his hand. Released on one side, the coat flapped over her. "My darling, Hawk."

Rinny bunched beneath them; but, accustomed to boys' play, she did not shy at the noises the wind made of his coat. Honoria let go of Lubonne's hand to grab up both sides of his coat again, and the fluttering sounds ceased. Soon, however, Rinny's walk slowed to a crawl as she navigated jutting roots, rocks, and pocks in the makeshift roadway.

As the earthern path met the cobbled one, Lubonne pulled Rinny up to wait for two servants to assist a cousin's family from their coach. As the cousins headed for the house and a groomsman led their horse and vehicle away, Lubonne reined Rinny at the gate.

Vannath took the bay's reins, while a servant Lubonne did not recognize helped Honoria dismount. Apparently brought in by one of the hires, the young, handsome man seemed to enjoy his duty a bit too much. He cradled Honoria in his arms as he carried, more than assisted, his grin containing a hint of interested leer. "My lady, you shouldn't ride in a gown like that. Horse hair doesn't become anyone, and the stench of the beasts is hardly perfume." Without so much as a glance toward Lubonne, he held out the young lord's coat.

Lubonne accepted it curiously. "What's your name, groomsman?"

The young man finally spared Lubonne a haughty glance. "Haralt, sir. And I'm not a groomsman. I'm a server. I'm just helping until my job comes up."

Lubonne pursed his already thin lips into a taut line. "Well, Haralt. You may place my bride on the ground now. Last I checked, she did have feet, small and delicate though they are."

Honoria giggled coquettishly as Haralt obeyed. "Yes,

sir." Turning on a heel, the servant walked stiffly back toward the house, while Vannath took Rinny to the stable.

Lubonne crooked a brow, uncertain how to feel about the exchange. "Do you know that man?"

"Of course I do. A friend of my family. He's sweet, really."

"Sweet, maybe." Lubonne pulled on his coat absently. He watched the man's back as he headed up the walkway, fine blond hair splashing over muscular shoulders. "But he certainly took a few liberties."

Honoria hit Lubonne's arm in mock irritation, then set to work preening her dress and hair back into proper order. "Oh, please. Don't be so priggish. You're not going to be the kind of husband who lords over me and bridles every time a man looks in my direction, are you?"

"That was hardly looking in your direction."

She hit him again, a bit harder. "You're going to have to get used to it. When you marry an attractive woman, men are going to stare."

Stare, yes. Lubonne knew better than to contradict Honoria aloud. *But I don't expect them to carry off my bride.* He shook his head at his own concern. *I love her; she loves me. I won't let the antics of a poorly trained servant distract me from our own party.* He took Honoria's arm, reveling in the silken touch of her skin. "You smell lovely."

"Not like horse sweat?" Honoria pulled at the back of her gown.

"Nothing like horse sweat." Lubonne took a deliberate sniff. "A nose like mine never lies. You carry the delightful scent of Honoria, freshly laundered lace, wind, and that fragrance your younger sister spilled on your head." *And even if you did smell like Rinny, I love the smell of sweet old Rinny.*

Servants met them at the door, fussing with collars, brushing off bits of twig, leaf, and horse hair. One stepped forward to announce loudly through the din of conversation, "Presenting Master Lubonne and his lady, Honoria."

The talking ceased, as if choked; and silence fell over the ballroom. The clapping began in one corner, where Lubonne's parents stood and swiftly spread in a wave that morphed into thunderous applause. Honoria curtsied gracefully, then started up the marble staircase that arched over a balcony and into the ballroom below. Head high, grinning at his bride-to-be, Lubonne climbed proudly at her side.

A noise behind him caught Lubonne's attention, and it took force of will to remain focused on Honoria and the crowd below them. Then, suddenly, someone cursed, and the hollow sound of hoof falls on marble clattered through the chamber. Grin wilting, Lubonne whirled. Carthea marched up the steps at their heels, looking for all the world as if she belonged there.

"What are you doing?" Lubonne shouted before he could think to hold his tongue. "What the hell are you doing?!" Only then, he thought of Mindspeak. *:Mother throws a fit when Father's dogs come in the house!:*

The light of every torch and candle seemed drawn to Carthea, and her burnished white coat gleamed so brightly that Lubonne found himself squinting again. Someone had combed the burrs from her mane and forelock, and it fell around her neck in glossy waves. Her pale eyes looked as gentle and innocent as an infant's.

Murmurs rose from the crowd. Then, before Lubonne could think to stop her, Honoria gasped in utter delight and hurled herself at him. "Oh, thank you, thank you, my darling Hawk. She's beautiful!"

Honoria's warmth stunned him. They had embraced before, but she had always felt woodenly reluctant, shy and demure.

"No woman has ever had a more wonderful engagement gift." Releasing him, Honoria caught Carthea
around the neck.

Carthea took two careful backward steps, teetering
on stairs designed for human paces. *:Get her off me!:*

Honoria's grip tightened, and she buried her face in
the smooth white fur.

"No, Honoria. You don't understand." Lubonne
lunged for his betrothed as Carthea's balance wavered.
"You know I'd give you the moon and stars, if they were
mine to give. But they're not, and neither is—"

Honoria was not listening. Lubonne could see
Carthea's delicate hooves slipping. The sounds of the
crowd grew louder.

"Honoria!" Lubonne grabbed her as Carthea wheeled.
She struck Honoria's a glancing blow and sending her
staggering breathlessly into Lubonne's arms. Carthea
sprang the length of the stairs, toward the door. For an
instant, she hovered in midair, a massive yet strangely
agile bird in flight. Then, she landed on the parquet,
scrambled helplessly for a moment, somehow caught
her footing, then raced for the still-open door. She disappeared through it in a flash of snowy white, leaving
the attendants ashenfaced and slackjawed.

"My horse!" Honoria wailed, loud enough for the
whole assemblage to hear her. "My magnificent, perfect
engagement present." She buried her face in Lubonne's
coat.

Lubonne could do nothing but hold her and curse
the Companion who seemed hellbent on ruining his
life. "Honoria, please. If you want a horse, I'll find you
the finest my money can buy. But that one does not
belong to me. Do you hear? She's not mine to give
you."

"I . . . don't . . . want . . ." she sobbed. " . . . any horse.
I . . . want . . . that one."

Lubonne had never seen his beloved like this. "Honoria, please. We'll talk about this after the party."

"No, no!" Honoria refused consolation. She pulled away from Lubbone, rubbing tenderly beneath her bosom where the hoof had grazed her. "Is no one in this hall man enough to catch her for me?" Her gaze roved over the gathering to land directly on the servant who had helped her from Rinny's back.

Now impeccably dressed in caterer's livery, balancing a loaded silver tray, Haralt looked tall, lean, and remarkably muscled. Fine blond curls swept from chiseled features: his forehead uncreased, his chin heroically squared, and his nose flawless. Placing his burden on a nearby table, he bowed prettily and gazed up at Honoria. "I'd be honored to assist, my lady." Without another word, he headed up the stairs, edged around the bridal pair, and strode through the open door.

Scattered and hesitant applause followed Haralt's action. Honoria clamped her hands together and watched him leave. "Isn't he wonderful?" She continued to rub absently beneath her breasts, oblivious to a smudge the hoof had left there.

Lubonne could think of no appropriate reply. "Sure. Wonderful." He placed his hand on hers, stopping it. "Are you all right? Do you need to see a healer?"

Honoria let her hand fall into Lubonne's. "I'm fine. She barely hit me."

Lubonne wanted to drop the whole matter but needed to say one more thing. "You know, even if he finds her, he'll have to let her go. She doesn't belong to him or to us."

Honoria straightened her dress and plastered a smile back on her face. "For now, let's just enjoy our party."

And enjoy they did. Lubonne did not awaken until nearly midday, and he did not attempt to visit Honoria until the following day. He found her out, though no one could say where. And though she returned that night after his visit, when he came for her the next morning, she had gone away again.

Preparing for the wedding, Lubonne tried to convince himself, but doubts plagued him. He could not forget the way his betrothed had sought assistance from the selfsame servant who had swept her so majestically off of Rinny's back. He could see any woman falling prey to Haralt's striking appearance. A beautiful woman like Honoria deserved a beautiful man; yet Lubonne knew she loved him. No mere servant, no random pretty face, could steal her away from him, and Honoria deserved a better life than Haralt could possibly give her.

Alone with his thoughts, Lubonne walked the edge of the forest, headed for his favorite river bank. There, he could lose himself in the bird calls, the rustling of the wind through reeds, and the occasional plop of fish and frogs in the water. Whenever he paused there to skip stones and revel in the sunlight, happy boyhood memories invariably swept away his adult worries.

A faint call touched Lubonne's mind. *:Help me!:*

Lubonne stiffened, turning. Only one creature could communicate with him in this way. "Carthea?" He had not seen her since the party, either. "Where are you?"

He received no direct reply, just a repeat of the indistinct, soft call. *:Help me, Chosen. I need you.:*

Lubonne focused on mental words, this time deliberately shouting. *:WHERE . . . ARE . . . YOU?:*

A flood of relief accompanied the next communication, apparently over finally reaching him. He wondered for how long she had been calling him. *:The clearing where we first met. Hurry!:*

Lubonne hesitated. He could run back home, get Rinny and a weapon, and gallop back nearly as quickly as he could run straight to the clearing. In the end, he chose the shorter distance, running as fast as his bowed legs would carry him. *:I'm coming.:* Though it took no breath to answer, Lubonne found himself too focused on movement to concentrate on Mindspeaking. *:What's wrong? What's happening?:*

Carthea gave him only, *:Come see.:* Then, it seemed as if a wall had closed between their minds.

:Carthea!: Lubonne called. *:Carthea!:*

He got no answer.

He dodged between trunks, vaulted deadfalls, trying to save a few paces and hoping he did not corner himself and have to backtrack for his efforts. Brush tore at his tunic, and prickles scored his legs. *:Carthea, answer me.:* A vine entangled his ankles, and he tumbled into a bush. *Damn!*

He got nothing in return but the vague wonder of why it mattered. He was not a future Herald; he was not Carthea's heartmate. He could not be. Yet she had done nothing worse than try to convince him. She had the same good soul she sensed in him, and he would not leave her in danger, especially if he might, indirectly, have caused it. He tore his way through the bush, ignoring the scratches and jabs that tore clothing and flesh alike. *:Answer me, Carthea!:* He staggered free.

Now, Lubonne could hear faint voices, punctuated by a boisterous whinny, the type horses use to call to lost herd companions. He quickened his pace, bursting breathlessly into the clearing.

Carthea was there, her coat dark with sweat and striped with filth. She held her head low, a rope winched around her neck, and bloody foam bubbled around a hard steel bit. More ropes circled each fetlock, the feathery hair shaved off by movement against them. A crude wooden saddle lay strapped to her back; and a tight rope bridle bit deeply into her cheeks. Gaze fixed on the Companion and her plight, Lubonne barely noticed the five humans who shared the clearing. Iron stakes, deeply

pounded, held the ropes enwrapping Carthea's hind fet-
locks. Men struggled with the two in front, holding her
splay-legged and, essentially, helpless. A third forced her
head down, preventing her from rearing.

Fire boiled through Lubonne's veins at the image
of this proud and intelligent creature trussed up like
the main course at a banquet. He opened his mouth to
shout, then saw the other two humans in the clearing.
A man and a woman oversaw the process, holding one
another's hand. Lubonne recognized them at once, Haralt and Honoria; and no words emerged. His mouth just
kept silently opening, wider and wider, until he thought
his jaw might touch the ground.

Honoria ran to Lubonne. "Darling, you've ruined the
surprise."

Lubonne doubted it was possible for him to be any
more surprised. "Let her go," he managed, the words
strangely soft-spoken but still firm and controlled. He
had intended to scream them.

Honoria took his arm, snuggling against him. "We're
breaking her for you, my darling Hawk. For us."

For once, Honoria's touch failed to move him. "No.
I don't want this." Lubonne looked at the three men
straining at the ropes. "Let her go." He wanted to attack, to chase them all away from Carthea. How could
anyone condone this cruelty?

Honoria ran a hand along his cheek. "It's not what it
looks like, my darling. We're not hurting her."

Haralt finally spoke. "Master Lubonne, she's worthless as she is, but an exceedingly valuable horse once we
break her. Sometimes—"

Lubonne snapped. "I don't want her broken; I want
her whole." He shook off Honoria. "She's perfect as she
is, and I order you to release her."

"—sometimes the process looks harsh, but I assure
you it's necessary to—"

This time, Honoria cut him off. "Forget it, Haralt. It's not going to happen." She turned to Lubonne, and her whole demeanor seemed to change. Where she had once seemed demure and dewy-eyed, she became as callous as any huntsman. "It could have worked out perfectly for all of us." She shook her head, frowning. "You would have had your bit of land and your gorgeous, fawning wife despite your . . ." She made a gesture to indicate his face.

Haralt turned positively green. "Honoria, what are you doing?"

She persisted, undaunted. "I would have had my handsome lover, and our children . . ." She poked Lubonne. " . . . *your* children . . . could they have been more stunning?"

Lubonne gritted his teeth as it all became clear. Honoria had never loved him; she had wanted only his status and his money, which she intended to use to make a home for them. Then, while he was out, she would entertain Haralt, pass off his offspring as legitimately Lubonne's, and live out her life in secretive happiness.

Honoria threw up her hands, as if Lubonne were the one who had just exposed a cruel scheme. "And we all would have lived happily, contented, if you hadn't put an animal over your love for me."

Torn between screaming and crying, between attacking and running, Lubonne stood his ground. He continued to speak gently, his tone flat to hide his building rage. "I could say the same for you, that you put your love for an animal . . ." Lubonne turned his gaze directly on Haralt, " . . . over me. But, then, I would be granting this conniving servant the same status as Carthea, and he does not deserve it."

Haralt drew himself up, clearly affronted. He did not speak, however, nor dare to approach.

"Let her go!" Lubonne roared, fists clenching and

unclenching. He wished he had brought a weapon; even the wooden one he used for practice would suffice.

Honoria grinned wickedly, then started to laugh. "By what authority do you command this, Hawknose? You've admitted in front of an entire ballroom that you have no claim to this animal. You don't own her. We have as much right to her as you. More so, because she is now in our possession."

She was right, Lubonne knew, and his heart sank. He looked at Carthea, forcing himself to examine only her sweet, long-lashed eyes. If he took in the entire picture again, he could not have retained his composure. *:With my help, can you break free?:*

:I . . . don't think so.: Carthea dropped her head further. *:I've tried. They're strong, and I'm exhausted.:*

It's up to me. Lubonne studied Honoria, wondering what had seemed so special about her in the past. Where once she had seemed flawless, he now discovered a million faults. Her external beauty seemed worthless, her gray eyes as welcoming as a rusty steel trap. "What do you want her for anyway?"

Honoria glanced at Haralt, who seemed suddenly engrossed in his own boots. "As Haralt said, she's a valuable animal." She headed back toward the servant.

"Once she's broken," Lubonne reminded, watching Honoria leave. He had never before noticed how she waddled when she walked. *Which will never happen.* "How's that going so far?"

Carthea snorted, pale eyes like brimstone.

"We'll break her," Honoria promised. "No matter how long it takes."

"Or," Lubonne suggested, suddenly thoughtful. "You could sell her."

Honoria shrugged. "We'll have to now. We'll need that money to fix up the land, build a house."

Lubonne had heard those plans before, many times.

But, always in the past, "we" had included him. Now, he felt certain, Honoria referred to Haralt.

:*You knew all the time, didn't you?*: Lubonne accused his Companion.

:*Knew what?*:

:*Knew what kind of person I had affianced myself to. Knew she didn't really love me, that she would hurt me badly.*:

Carthea snorted again. :*I knew.*:

:*Why didn't you save yourself this trouble and pain? Why didn't you just tell me?*:

Carthea rolled the one eye he could see. Her ears pricked forward. :*You know why.*:

:*I do?*: And, suddenly, Lubonne realized, he did. *I wouldn't have believed it. I would have thought she was lying to get me to join her.*

Though he made no attempt to Mindspeak the thought, Carthea apparently received it. She bobbed her wise, white head once before the man holding the rope jerked it still.

At the violence of the movement, anger flared anew. *I was so busy chasing fake love, I didn't see the real thing when it thrust its huge, fuzzy head through my bedroom window.* Lubonne turned his attention to Haralt and Honoria, driving all trace of malice from his tone and his features. "How much?"

"What?" The word was clearly startled from Haralt's mouth.

Honoria had more experience in matters of finance. "You want to buy her from us?"

"Yes."

Honoria's smile broadened, and Lubonne wondered why he had never before noticed how dingy her teeth looked, the meanness in her grin. "It would cost you . . . your inheritance."

"Sold!" Lubonne said, before she could change her

mind or think to ask for more. He had no wish nor need to reduce the deal to writing. Honoria had four witnesses to corroborate her claim, and he had no intention of dishonoring his word. He claimed the ropes from each man in turn. Carthea remained utterly still while he unwound each rope, removed the offending bridle, and tossed the makeshift saddle to the ground.

:I'm not going to fall off, am I?:

Carthea turned him a withering look.

Using a deadfall for a step, Lubonne clambered upon his Companion, a Herald trainee astride his heartmate and bound for Collegium. "Tell my parents the money is yours. And that I've gone to Valdemar."

Carthea bounded over a copse of berries in one smooth leap and settled onto the packed earth, forest road. *:Home for your things?:*

:And spoil this grand exit for a few possessions?: Lubonne made a broad gesture in the general direction of Valdmar. *:I have my future and my Heartmate. What more do I need?:*

:What more, indeed.: Carthea agreed.

A Storytelling of Crows

by *Elisabeth Waters*

Elisabeth Waters sold her first short story in 1980 to Marion Zimmer Bradley for *The Keeper's Price*, the first of the Darkover anthologies. She continues to sell short stories to a variety of anthologies and magazines. Her first novel, a fantasy called *Changing Fate,* was awarded the 1989 Gryphon Award. She is now working on a sequel to it, in addition to short story writing and editing the annual *Sword & Sorceress* anthology. She has also worked as a supernumerary with the San Francisco Opera, where she appeared in *La Gioconda, Manon Lescaut, Madama Butterfly, Khovanschina, Das Rheingold, Werther*, and *Idomeneo*.

The horse wasn't the first animal to come to Maia calling for help, but it was the first one with a human on its back. Not that Maia noticed the human at first. She sat in a clearing in the Forest of Sorrows, avoiding her older brother. She was listening to the chatter of the crows while working on the fletching of the arrows that she made and her brother sold to support them. Then the voices of the crows changed, warning her of strangers in the forest. This was followed by the sound of something large stumbling through the trees and then the sight of a white horse with an arrow protruding from a hind leg and a pile of arrow-studded red and white rags on his back.

:Help my Chosen!: His voice was very clear in Maia's head; he spoke as if he expected a human to hear and understand him.

Maia been able to hear—and converse with—animals as long as she could remember, but this mental voice wasn't like that of any animal she had encountered before. It sounded more like a human, which made her wary. Shortly after the death of her parents three years ago, the people of their village suddenly and inexplicably didn't like her any more—and her brother had never liked her. Now she avoided people whenever possible. Living at the edge of Sorrows helped; she could retreat into the forest and be left alone.

Still, whatever this was, he was in distress, so she dropped the arrows and moved to his side.

"Help your chosen what?" she asked him.

:My Herald. Her name is Samina. I am Clyton.:

"Let's get this arrow out of you, Clyton," Maia said, "and then perhaps you can get closer to the ground so I can get her down without dropping her." She looked at the arrow in his leg and frowned. "This looks like one of mine," she remarked, grasping it firmly below the fletching and pulling it straight out. The horse cried out in pain, and Maia stared in horror at the arrow she was holding. It *was* one of hers, but the last time she had seen it the shaft had simply been sharpened to a point. Since then somebody had added metal barbs to the tip, and it had not slid out as she expected it to. Instead, it had ripped a chunk out of Clyton's leg.

"I am *so* sorry," she gasped. "It didn't have barbs when I saw it last!" She snatched up a cloth she used to wrap supplies in and pressed it against his leg to stop the bleeding.

:It's not that bad,: Clyton said, although she suspected

him of being less than truthful. :*At least we're far enough into Sorrows that the bandits aren't likely to track us here.:*

"Probably not," Maia agreed. "My brother won't even come in here." Still keeping pressure on the leg, she twisted to look at the woman on his back, who had at least four arrows in her. "Bandits?" she asked. "There are usually no bandits anywhere near here."

:*There are now,:* Clyton said grimly. Suddenly she found herself looking through his eyes. She recognized the road leading to her family's farm, not that it was much of a farm since her parents had died and her brother had sold all the animals and stopped working the land.

As Clyton and his Herald approached the farm, men fired arrows—all of them barbed—from the trees on both sides of the road and then moved into the road to surround horse and rider. She saw her brother's face clearly for a moment as he reached to grab the left side of Clyton's reins, but then everything blurred as Clyton put on a seemingly impossible burst of speed and broke out of the trap.

Maia blinked and found herself back in the present and seeing through her own eyes again. "Was that real?" she asked. "What I just saw, I mean."

:*Yes. That's what happened to us. You obviously have Mindspeech if you can pick it up from me like that.:*

Maia lifted the cloth carefully and looked at his leg. The bleeding had almost stopped. "I think you'll be all right for the moment if you don't try to move much," she said. "I'll just have to lift Samina down as carefully as I can and hope for the best. I can see four arrows in her back—do you know if there are any more?"

:*I don't think so, but check before you try to move her. And be* careful *removing the arrows!:*

"Don't worry," Maia assured him; "I learned my lesson with the one in your leg!"

:*Better my leg than her body,*: Clyton sighed.

Maia felt around Samina's body to check for additional arrows, but she didn't find any more. She wriggled her arm and shoulder between Samina's body and the saddle, took most of the woman's weight, and went to the ground in something between a slide and a fall. At least Samina landed on top of her, and none of the arrows hit the ground. Maia positioned the Herald carefully so that the arrows were still pointing away from the ground. "I'll need to cut them out very carefully," she murmured, looking around for the knife she used to trim arrow shafts.

:*There should be a medical kit attached to my saddle.*:

"That would help," Maia agreed, moving to examine the saddle. An impressive variety of items was attached to snaffles on the skirting. "It might be more to the point to ask what's *not* attached to your saddle," she remarked as she searched for and finally found the medical kit. In addition to a clean knife, there was a needle and thread to sew the wounds and cloths to bandage it after she was done. There was also a jar of something Clyton said should be put on the wounds to help clean them, and a powder that could be made into a tea to lower the fever that Samina was undoubtedly going to have. At the moment she was still unconscious, which made cutting out the arrows and cleaning and sewing her wounds easier, but Maia could feel Clyton worrying about Samina's lack of responsiveness. She could see that the woman had lost a lot of blood.

But there was nothing she could do about that, so she unsaddled Clyton and put the saddle on a fallen log.

The crows came swooping toward her, calling that her brother was home and looking for her. The vision of her brother working with the bandits flashed back instantly, filling her sight. *My brother is a bandit. No wonder the villagers hate us.* She shuddered. "I can't go back," she said to herself. "He'll know that I know."

:What are you talking about? Who will know that you know what?:

"You can't understand the crows?" she asked. "They said that my brother wants me."

:Maybe he could help us?: Clyton asked hopefully.

"He was the one who tried to grab your reins," Maia informed him, "so I really doubt it."

:Your brother is a bandit?:

"He attacked you," Maia pointed out. "Even if he wasn't working with the bandits, he doesn't like animals, and he's not all that fond of me. He doesn't like work, either." She frowned, considering her brother's past behavior. "He's always taken the easy way—I just didn't realize how bad it had gotten."

:It's not just bad,: Clyton pointed out, *:It's getting cold—and dark. You're not dressed to stay out all night, and the bandits got our pack mules and all of our supplies except what I was carrying. We need to get to the Waystation.:*

"You're very smart for a horse—"

:I am not a horse. I am a Companion.:

"—but you don't have hands. With your leg injured, you can't move around much, and Samina can't be moved at all. Can you tell me how to find the Waystation?"

:Unless you can see in the dark, it doesn't matter what I can tell you!: He sounded exasperated.

"I'm *trying* to help here!" she snapped back. "And *I* don't have to see in the dark as long as I have friends who can." The crows retreated to the tree branches as an owl floated silently out of the darkening sky to perch on the log next to Clyton's saddle.

:It's worth a try, I suppose,: Clyton sighed. *:If I show you the path to the Waystation, can you show it to the owl?:*

"We can try," she said, mentally linking with both of them. It was a struggle, because the Companion and the owl saw things differently, but finally she was satisfied that she and the owl knew the way. She pulled out her fire starter, gathered twigs, and started a fire near Samina. She walked quickly around the edges of the clearing to get dead branches to keep it going. "Can you add the branches to the fire as it starts to burn low?" she asked. "We need to keep Samina warm until I can get back with blankets—there are some at the Waystation, right?"

Clyton nodded, looking subdued. He didn't need to say anything; Maia knew he was in pain and worried about his Chosen.

"I'll be back as quickly as I can," she promised. "In the meantime," she continued, "since you don't have hands, I'll leave you with someone who does." She sent out a mental call, and a few moments later a raccoon poked his head cautiously into the clearing. "Dexter," she said, "this is Clyton, and the lady is Samina." She handed Dexter a clean cloth. "Could you wet this in the stream and use it to cool her forehead, please? Also, if the bandages start to come loose, fix them, all right?"

Dexter assured her he would take care of her new friends. Maia looked at Clyton to see if he could hear Dexter, but apparently he couldn't.

She prayed to whatever gods might be listening all the way to the Waystation and back.

When she returned, staggering under a load that was as much as she could possibly carry, the moon was high, and the clearing was bright with its silvery light. Samina was awake and fretting, despite Clyton's attempts to calm her. "I need my arrows," she insisted.

"I should think you'd had enough arrows for one day," Maia remarked. Samina tried to twist to face her, with a notable lack of success.

"I need my arrows!" she repeated desperately. "They're in a case attached to my saddle."

"Where else?" Maia asked ironically.

"I'm already getting delirious—I have to send the message while I still can!" Samina insisted. "I woke up and saw a *raccoon* nursing me."

"Relax," Maia said soothingly. "If all you saw is Dexter, you're not hallucinating yet."

"Dexter?"

"The raccoon. I had to leave for a while, and he has hands—in fact, he's quite dexterous." She ignored Samina's look of disbelief. "I'll find your arrows for you." She went to where she had left the saddle. Clyton limped over to join her and shoved at a cylindrical case with his nose. She unfastened it from the saddle and took it to Samina.

"Thank you." Samina opened the case and removed three arrows. One had a green band and the other two had yellow bands. With shaking hands Samina bent several of the barbs on the fletching of each arrow and tied the arrows together so that they didn't interfere with the patterns in the fletching. "Clyton," she said, "These need to go to the Healing Temple—you know the one."

"Clyton can't take them," Maia said. "He was shot, too; didn't you notice that he's walking on only three legs?"

Samina buried her face in her hands and moaned.

"Does he have to be the one to take them?" Maia asked. "Or will they be enough of a message if they just get there?"

"They'll be enough by themselves, but how else can we get them there? Can you take them?"

Maia shook her head. "I know a faster way. Clyton," she asked, "exactly where is this temple?"

"You can hear my Companion?" Samina asked in astonishment.

"Yes," Maia said. "He says I've got Mindspeech." A view of a road and the temple at the end filled her vision. She passed it on to the nearest group of crows. "Do you know this place?" she asked them. "Can you find it?"

About a dozen crows spiraled down out of the trees to perch in front of her, assuring her that they knew exactly where to go. "Take the arrows then," she told them, "and make certain that nobody on the ground sees them. I recognized my brother, but I don't know who his friends are or where they live. Fly safely."

One of the crows grabbed the arrows, and they took off clustered together. Even knowing that the arrows were there, Maia couldn't see them.

Maia didn't know how many days passed before the crows returned with a healer. Clyton's leg was obviously hurting, and Samina, despite Maia's—and Dexter's— best efforts, became feverish and delirious. Maia collected several bruises trying to care for her. She wondered, when she had a moment to think, if she would have done a better job if she actually *knew* anything about healing. "Just keep her alive till the Healer gets here," she told herself. "That's what matters."

Finally she heard the chatter of crows escorting the healer. A woman in green robes arrived in the clearing riding double with another person dressed in white and riding a white horse, presumably another Herald and Companion.

The crows were all talking at once, telling her all about their adventure, but Maia was too tired to care. As soon as she finished telling the Healer what little she knew and what little she had done and explaining to the new Herald what she knew about the attack, she fell asleep and didn't wake for days. By then the military units had rounded up her brother and his fellow bandits and taken them away for trial. The Healer explained that Maia would not be needed for the trial as she had not been present during the attack.

"I guess I'd sound pretty silly telling a judge that I saw the attack hours later through the eyes of a horse," Maia told Samina later. Samina was recovering, but the Healer didn't want her to move yet, so she encouraged Maia to sit and talk to her. Clyton was doing better also, but he still wasn't up to galloping at top speed while carrying a rider, so they were still camping in the safety of Sorrows. It was a much more comfortable camp now; someone had brought three mules and a load of actual camping supplies, so they were no longer making do with what Maia had been able to scrounge from the Waystation.

Samina looked sharply at her. "You can see through Clyton's eyes?"

"Only when he wants to show me something," Maia clarified, "but when he does, I can see what he saw."

"And you can communicate with the raccoon . . ."

"His name is Dexter," Maia said.

" . . . and the crows. Anything else?"

Maia shrugged. "I can understand pretty much anything that wants to talk to me. Why?"

Samina smiled. "It's one of the Gifts. We Heralds call it Mindspeech. It appears that you have a strong aptitude for it." She paused, and then asked, "Could you hear your brother?"

Maia shook her head. "Just animals. And Clyton. I didn't even know that my brother wasn't supporting us by selling the arrows I made, the way he told me. He was using them to rob people." She frowned in thought. "Does that mean that my arrows aren't good enough to sell?"

"I though they were very effective," Samina said dryly. "They certainly made an impression on me." Her face was straight, but Maia could tell that she was joking.

"Several impressions," Maia agreed, keeping her face straight and as innocent as possible. "But I didn't put the barbs on them," she added quickly. "Did Clyton tell you that?"

"He did," Samina reassured her. "He also said that you saved my life."

"It was the least I could do, after having made the arrows that nearly killed you." Maia shrugged off the praise and returned to her original subject. "I notice that you carry arrows. If my arrows *are* good enough, can the Heralds use a fletcher?"

"I'm sure we can find a place for you." Samina smiled. "Are you saying that you want to go back to Haven with us?"

"Can Dexter and any of the crows who want to come with me?"

"I don't see why not," Samina said. "I've brought back stranger things from my travels. Are you really certain that you want to leave your home?"

Maia nodded. "I wasn't raised alone in the forest; that happened after my parents died and my brother antagonized all our neighbors. I didn't know why everyone suddenly hated him—and me—but now that I do, I think it will be better for everyone if I leave here."

"Then you can come with us as soon as Clyton and I can travel," Samina said.

The Healer had done some work on Clyton, and he was walking normally now. It looked as though the flesh Maia had accidentally gouged out of his leg was going to heal completely without so much as a scar.

The crows were still telling stories of their trip to the temple; they had been ever since their return. They appeared to regard it as a great adventure.

Samina smiled as she watched Maia listen to them. "What are they saying?" she asked.

"They're telling stories," Maia said. "It's hard to sort out and put into words."

"Did you know that there are two name for a flock of crows?" Samina asked.

"No," Maia admitted. "Most of the villagers called them a nuisance, but I never thought of them that way."

"They're often called a 'murder of crows,' but yours saved my life, so that's not right for them." Samina grinned. "These are obviously the other kind: a 'story-telling of crows'."

"I do talk with them a lot," Maia admitted, "and they certainly talk back."

"You know," Samina said. "I think you're wasted as a fletcher—not that you aren't good at it," she added hastily, "but there are more good fletchers than there are people with Animal Mindspeech."

"So you think I should do something else?" Maia asked uncertainly. "What?"

Samina smiled and took Maia's hand. "There's a Temple in Haven that would kill to have you—if all its priests weren't such gentle and peaceful souls."

"There's a *temple* that would want me?" Maia said in astonishment. "What kind of temple is that?"

"The Temple of Thenoth, the Lord of the Beasts."

:It does *sound like your kind of place.:* Dexter's mental voice was encouraging. Maia started laughing.

"Yes," she agreed, "that does sound like a place I could fit in."

Waiting To Belong

by Kristin Schwengel

Kristin Schwengel's work has appeared in two of the
previous Valdemar short story anthologies, among others. She and her husband live near Milwaukee, Wiscon-
sin, and recently adopted a gray-and-black tabby kitten
named (what else?) Gandalf. Kristin divides her time
between an administrative job, a growing career as a
massage therapist, and writing and other pastimes.

When the Companion had come to Breyburn, folk had
gathered in the square, though no one had raised any
summoning cry. Nearly the whole of the town was there
to see who would be Chosen when the dazzling white
horse trotted into the square, gleaming harness-bells jin-
gling and dancing in the late afternoon light.

Not that anyone truly doubted for whom the Companion had come on Search. No one was surprised to
see Teo standing to the front of the crowd, framed by
his family, staring at the Companion with a dumbstruck,
delirious smile. His joy shone from every fiber of his being, so strong Shia could have sworn that she felt it too,
rippling through her in waves.

Shia had turned her gaze away at the last moment
before the Companion brushed its (no, *her*) soft nose
against Teo's, incandescent blue eyes meeting guileless

brown even as their minds spoke. To Shia, it had seemed too intimate a moment to be observed—never mind that the rest of the town was staring avidly. *She* could not watch it.

Afterward, there had been an evening of well-wishing, of jokes and congratulations, and the occasional hearty "We always knew you'd make a Herald someday! Surprised they waited till you reached fifteen winters to send a Companion out for you, lad!"

And then they had gone, Teo and his Companion, off to Haven and his new life with the Heralds. Shia had held a baffling empty ache deep in her heart, taking small breaths to control it as she (and the rest of the town) watched them canter off the next morning. Teo's face was flushed with the excitement, his unruly hair bouncing in time with his Companion's long strides. She had watched only until he was far enough down the Old Quarry Road that she wouldn't be thought rude, then had fled to the stillness and sanctuary of her herb room.

It was there that Calli Stadres found her, her head bent over the table while she stared unseeing at the plants and herb mixtures before her, one foot and ankle twined anxiously around the leg of her tall stool.

"He looked back."

Shia's head jerked upright, and she stared at her visitor through the wispy blonde strands of hair that fell over her forehead. Not many years older than Shia, Calli was wife to one of the town's wealthiest merchants and already had a young daughter toddling beside her, clinging to her mother's skirts.

"His parents waved, as though he had turned to look for them, but he didn't wave back. I don't think he even saw them."

Shia reached out to a pile of dried seed-pods from the edge of the table, trying to still the unexplainable trembling in her hand. Calli watched the younger girl work, savoring the quiet coolness of the room and the crisp herbal scents around them.

"Why could you not say something to him? He is still Teo, after all."

Shia glanced over at Calli, then returned her attention to the dried seeds as she carefully separated them from their husks for storage. The silence between them drifted a little longer, then she shrugged.

"A Herald's place is in Haven. A Herald belongs to Valdemar, to the Crown, to the people." She hunched one shoulder, as if hiding behind it. "After my mother's death, the town allowed me to take her place as herbalist. I belong in Breyburn."

Calli frowned. "There is no law that says otherwise, yet I think you are wrong. Thirteen was too young for you to be tied to such responsibilities, no matter how much you wanted to earn your keep. Surely there has to be more for you."

"It does no good to dwell on it," Shia responded at last. "It is as it is. Here, rub these together until they crack open for me." She held out a handful of the dried pods to Calli, who looked at them for a moment, then giggled like a much younger girl.

"You're just trying to make me *useful*, aren't you?"

Shia only smiled, her hand still outstretched.

Of course, Teo came back to Breyburn, but only briefly, not even every Midwinter over the several years of his training. When he did, his time was taken up with his family, with the townsfolk at large, with the town council, and with the other Herald or Heralds he was usually in company with. And, of course, his Companion.

He was never there just as Teo, not anymore. He was Teo the Herald trainee, Teo the journeyman-Herald, soon to be Teo the Herald. He even looked like someone else in the gray clothing, especially when he suddenly grew several inches from one summer to the next Midwinter.

Unsure of how to approach this new person who looked so different and yet should be so familiar, Shia chose to retreat, keeping to herself in the solitude that had been hers since her mother's death barely two years before Teo's Choosing. If she was there at all when Teo came back to the town, she stayed to the rear of the crowd of townsfolk, ducking her head so her hair fell over eyes. She never noticed the concerned blue gaze of Teo's Companion following her, nor did she see Teo's eyes wandering restlessly over the faces when all were gathered together.

"Shia! Sheeeee-aaah!" Up on the mountainside, far from the town walls, where the winds sighed and roared by turns in the deep firs, there was no way that Shia should have heard a child's thin cry. But hear it she did, in her head as much as her ears, and with that impossible sound came another impossible thing—a bone-deep knowledge that something was very wrong in Breyburn. She grabbed the last of her herb packs (how was it they were full already? what had she been gathering while her mind had been wandering who knows where?) and sprinted to where she had tethered her shaggy mare, stowing the pack and freeing the horse almost in the same motion. Without thinking, she reached up and broke off a small branch of one of the overhanging firs, tucking it and its three cones between the straps of the secured packs. She pulled herself up into the saddle and kneed the dun into the fastest trot she could safely take on the uneven mountain paths, letting the mare choose her steps as the early spring mountain-fog started to coalesce around them.

The knot in the pit of her stomach took on more solidity as she approached the town, although the urgency faded. She reined in the mare while she was still hidden beyond the treeline, looking down on the cleared lands of the townsfolk, and her guts churned. Smoke coiled upward from somewhere near the center of town, dark and thick, and the smell of it as it drifted towards her was wrong, wet and musty. She could see broken staves of wood near the main gate, and a few of the town guard nervously standing at attention beside the gate. Whatever it was had come and gone again, leaving the town in uneasy quiet as the day slipped towards evening. She kicked the mare to a canter, angling from the forest to ride onto the Old Quarry Road far enough down that the edgy guardsmen would recognize her well in advance as she approached—or would at least know Mirri's stocky body and rough coloring.

The relief on Guardsman Fellan's face as she rode up would have been amusing, were it not for the worry and fear that haunted the corners of his eyes.

"Bandits," he said, before she even pulled up the mare. "Surprised, we were, and they seemed to know where to strike hardest. They knew who to hit, more'n what the usual raiders we've seen would know. Cap'n was first, then Sergeant. The merchants, too, they attacked and robbed, and then they were gone, quick as they came."

"Dead or injured?"

"Four, five dead maybe, dozen or more injured. M'lady Stadres has got 'em all down to the chapel—they fired the inn."

Shia swallowed, her heart quailing at the thought of that many injuries. Her mother had only known the basics of herbcraft and had often scolded her daughter for being an indifferent student. Apprehension of the severity of wounds she might face filled her, and despair clawed at her, tightening her stomach and freezing her blood in her veins. When the guardsman looked up at her, question in his eyes, she gave herself a mental shake. Healer she might not be, but she was the closest thing to one that the town had. She would have to do.

She nodded at the guards and angled Mirri down to the square, to the house across from the town's one inn. As she neared it, she could see that the smoke was still drifting from the inn in slow coils, now held lower to the ground by the weight of the late afternoon fog that had started to roll down from the mountaintop. The building wouldn't be lost, though, she thought. The rainy season was only just over, and the timbers hadn't yet dried out, so they had been slow to catch and even then had smoldered rather than burned outright. It looked as though the townsmen had been quick enough to set up a water chain from the cisterns, and as she rode past, she could hear voices from the side of the building, assessing the damage.

She slowed Mirri as they approached the Stadres household. It was the only house in town large and elaborate enough to boast a chapel dedicated to Kernos, and the Stadres family were certainly the only ones wealthy enough to build one. Calli Stadres stood at the front door, her young daughter clutching her hand.

"I told you she would hear me!" Pira cried in triumph before her mother hushed her. Calli's eyes met Shia's in question, and Shia gave the tiniest of nods before dismounting. The impossibility of Shia hearing Pira's voice was something that they would think about later—but Shia suspected that it would not be more than a few winters before Breyburn would have another white visitor.

"How many? How bad?" Shia started unloading her herb packs, glad that Calli had always been sensible. She was sure that most merchant's wives Calli's age would have been in hysterics, instead of calmly gathering the wounded into their own homes for care.

"Captain Nolan and two others were dead before

the bandits left, but I think Sergeant Dara will be well soon enough. Several of the guardsmen can only have their pain eased, I think, but most of the others have lesser wounds. Twelve injured guardsmen, including the worst."

Shia sucked in her breath. With three deaths, that was more than half of the town guard unable to act. No wonder those who remained were bewildered and uncertain. She handed two packs to Calli and swung the others over her shoulder, absently tucking the fir branch she had brought into the lamp bracket beside the door before she realized that she had harvested a silver pine, the tree of Kernos' protection. She whispered a brief petition for the god's hands to hold all those whose wounds she was about to tend, then followed Calli inside the house.

"And the others? The men at the gates said some of the merchants were attacked." She reached out her hand to touch Calli's arm as they hurried down the hall to the chapel. "Your husband? Is he—"

Calli's breath hitched, but she kept walking. "Injured, but not the worst. Master Widthan may not last the night, though, nor Josette. And Master Riordan is gone."

"Lord Corus will need to be informed, although I don't know that he'll be able to send any men from Torhold—the muster to Karse has spread his forces thin," Shia said faintly. "He will need to send word to Haven, to the Heralds. His Majesty must also know of these new attacks, especially if they are organized. It might be they had help from Karse. Either way, if they met with what they deem success, they will be back. And Herald-Trainee Teo must be told of his father's death." She hoped her voice didn't sound too strangled. Well, if it did, let Calli think that it was fear of more bandit raids that stole her breath. Even three years later, the strange empty ache that had blossomed as she watched him ride down the Old Quarry Road still swelled within her whenever she thought of him. "Take me to Sergeant Dara, first, then I'll see the worst of the rest."

For Shia, the next candlemarks passed in a blur of treating the wounded, moving from one injured person to the next. Thankfully, Calli was for the most part accurate in her assessment of the severity of injuries. Sergeant Dara had been knocked unconscious, but her other wounds were minor. She regained her senses while Shia was applying healing poultices to the cut that laced across her leg, and it was clear that she was in full possession of those senses. She began directing the remaining guard, propped up in her cot, the captain's sword bared across her knees. She even dictated a message that two of the merchants' sons would take down the mountain roads to Torhold on the fastest of the town's horses.

Calli Stadres proved a surprisingly capable pair of hands assisting Shia, readily learning how to mix the basic poultices and clean and dress the lesser injuries. And if, between one patient and the next, she always walked down the hall to stand for a few moments at the door to the room where her husband slept, bandages swathed around his head and shoulder, Shia could hardly blame her.

When they had finished tending the last injured merchant, Shia was pleased with her work. She even thought that her herbs might be able to bring around a few of those that Calli had thought would not last. Josette, the innkeeper, she was sure, would make it, although she herself wouldn't be able to take credit for that. The old woman was just too stubborn to, as she put it, "let 'em put paid to me if'n I wouldn't let 'em put paid to my inn." She had grumbled and complained about the damage to the inn while Shia had "fussed" over her, but she had finally accepted the sleep tea and let her body get to the more important business of healing.

Shia was glad, though, that she had been gathering

in the area of the mountain where she had been, at that height, several of the best wild plants for bleeding injuries developed a higher potency. And today she had harvested an inordinate amount of those plants, more than she ever needed for the normal injuries of the remote mountain town. This was not the first time, however, that she had harvested without thinking about it. Every so often she would gather herbs in a daze, seeming neither to hear what was around her nor even to see what she was doing. She had learned to trust it, those rare occasions, for what she gathered in those moments was always used—like the time when she and her mother had gone to harvest feverdraw, and she had found her basket full of the elm bark they used in tinctures and teas for throat ailments, and that winter a coughing illness had stricken the town.

"Pira, stop twirling about like that! You'll make me too dizzy to think!" Calli Stadres laughed as her daughter danced in the shaft of sunlight that lanced across the sunroom, her outstretched hands scattering tiny bits of seed-fluff that floated and glinted in the air around her. Her mother turned back to the worktable, reaching one hand around to rub her lower back. "Some days, I don't know how I'll ever keep up with two—" Her voice cut off when she saw Shia's face, and she lunged forward to take the mortar and pestle from the young woman's hands before she dropped them.

"Shia, what is it? What's wrong? Are you well?"

Shia leaned forward until her head rested on the cool stone slab laid across the top of the table, trying to calm the roiling in her stomach.

"I . . . am well," she managed. "Captain Dara . . ." her voice trailed off as another wave of *something* that felt like pain and anger hit her. Then, as soon as it had come, the feeling fled, replaced by the same surety of wrongness that she had felt up on the mountain when the town was first attacked. She pushed her hair out of her face and met Calli's worried eyes.

"I think the troop has been ambushed."

"How do you . . . ?" Calli's eyes widened when Shia only shrugged, and she glanced over at Pira. The young girl had stopped twirling but just stood in the sunbeam, looking at her mother in confusion. Calli took in a slow breath of relief that her daughter had not been affected, then nodded slightly.

"I'll check the bandage kits while you rub the powders for the poultices. We've set so many supplies aside from caring for the traders that we shouldn't need to prepare too much new."

By the time Captain Dara brought the wounded of her small troop back to the room in the Stadres household that had served as a makeshift infirmary since the first attack, Calli and Shia had prepared enough that they were immediately able to care for the worst of the injuries. This time, at least, none were life-threatening.

Shia unwrapped the hasty field bandages and held Lieutenant Fellan's arm tightly, trying to keep from jarring his newly realigned shoulder as she attempted to match up the shattered bones of his forearm. "You seem to have had the worst of it of all the group," she murmured. He had already bitten his lip to bleeding on the ride back to the town, and her liquor-laced herbal concoction for pain had barely started to take the edge off.

"Don't know how they do it," he muttered hazily. "They dance around the town when there's traders, then slink off into nowhere. Traders're coming 'round less, too. If'n we can't stop 'em, it'll be a thin winter. Cap'n Dara's good, but she's only one." He grunted as Shia made a last shift of his wrist, then settled to a drugged sleep as the herbs deepened their effects. Letting his arm rest on the splint on the low table beside them, Shia closed her hands lightly over the break, trying to sense if anything still was out of place beneath the skin. Her fingers tingled slightly, feeling the heat of injury spreading up from his flesh, and she held her hand there for a longer moment, as though she could force the angry heat to subside and the bone to knit together.

Binding the lieutenant's arm securely to the slats of her splint, Shia glanced over to where she could see the captain standing and talking to Calli and one of the other injured guardsman. Lord Corus had sent his approval for Dara's field promotion to captain as soon as he had learned of the first attack, but as they had suspected, Torhold had not been able to spare any militia to pursue the bandits. Even Torhold's Healer had only given a half-day's visit to check on Breyburn's injured. He had come a day or two after the first attack, glanced at the dead who were about to be buried, briefly examined those who were not yet back to their activities, then returned to Torhold, saying only, "The girl's mother must have had good skills to teach her that well, for all that no one knew where she'd come from."

Accepting that they were on their own, the townsfolk had resolutely taken matters into their own hands. Dara had taken any and all volunteers from the townsfolk or the shepherd and small farm families outside the town, training up some to join the town guard, others to simply learn how to stay alive if the bandits came back into the town. And come back they had, though none of their raids had the impact of the first. Rather, they picked away at the town and the trader caravans, making trade sporadic and shattering the cycles of the town's summer. The season was half over, but it felt as though it had barely begun, for few of the townsfolk had been able to work as they usually did.

Captain Dara held out her arm to Shia, wincing just the slightest bit as she dabbed the sharp cleansing ointment over the edges of the wound. "It's been months now, and we can't find the bastard," she said. "That's what bothers me. He runs aground as soon as we get close. We've picked off his band and found most of his hidey-holes, enough that I don't think he'll be back soon, but he keeps slinking off. Bad enough that they've been coming back all summer, but if he has time now to go back to wherever he came from and find more men, he'll be back as soon as the rains are done next spring."

Shia sighed as she put down the cleansing pad and reached for her bowl. "Lieutenant Fellan is right. You're only one. You need to take more care for yourself until Lord Corus can approve your new militia. No one else has the training, experience, or personality to lead the guard. Torhold can't spare anyone now, any more than they could when Captain Nolan was killed in the first raid."

"My young men—and the two girls—are doing well enough, especially since Fellan's arm healed up so quick and he was able to help with the training again. They did well enough to take on an ex-merc bandit who thought to control the trade routes down from the quarry and the tin mines. We've stopped him for this year, at least." Despite her frustration, the new captain's satisfaction with her troop was palpable.

Holding the edges of the wound together, Shia applied her poultice and started wrapping bandages, her fingers tracing along the length of the wound beneath the fabric, feeling the heat from the angry gash. An absent part of her attention drifted down to the injured flesh, almost willing the healing to happen. She didn't notice the startled way the captain's eyes flicked up to her, so absorbed was she in considering the importance of Captain Dara's success or failure. If they had indeed done enough damage to the surprisingly well-organized bandits to keep them from attacking for the last moon of the summer, the harvest and preparations for winter and the spring rains could go back to normal. Or normal enough to make do.

"At least the sheep and the goats have already been brought back down to the town green," she said at last. "And the traders won't fear to bring the grain supplies up here now, so we'll be able to winter the animals well enough."

The captain nodded, her eyes considering the young woman seated beside her. "We should think about increasing the grain stores this year, just in case. How are your harvests coming? Josette says her bones are telling her that it'll be a long winter and a hard rainy season."

Shia smiled fondly. "No one would ever dare suggest that Josette's bones are telling her that she's too old to spar with the youngsters. Calli and Pira have helped me gather, though, and Calli is allowing me to experiment with growing some plants in the sunny room next to the chapel. It's close enough to the kitchen fires that I think it will stay warm enough to keep some of the hardier stock alive all winter."

She didn't add that she thought that Josette's bones were right, and that she had already prepared for a long and hard season away from the mountain's wild herbs.

Drawn by some unnameable call, Shia opened the side door off the Stadres' kitchens and glanced out over the garden. As she expected, the rain was pouring down, creating lakes and rivers where in summer there were plant beds and paths. No sane creature stirred out of doors during the unpredictable flash rains, yet here she was, somehow knowing that she needed to be somewhere other than tucked securely in Calli's tiny spare room, where she had spent the winter tending her experimental plants. Tugging her cloak up around her ears, she darted out through the sheeting rain and splashed

around to the front of the house, finding a spot just under the eaves that was a little less wet. Not knowing why
she was standing there, she stared down the main road
for long, cold minutes, until she saw movement that was
not falling rain coming towards her from the edge of her
vision.

Mud-spattered, worn out, he was everything a Companion on Search shouldn't be—nothing like the gaily
caparisoned mare who had come for Teo. He was so
drenched, it was impossible to tell where the lathered
sweat ended and the cold rain staining his coat began.
He didn't even look white anymore, just a muddy dark
gray. Yet he was unmistakably what he was—even to the
bells on the soaked harness, though their ring could not
be heard above the rain pounding on the roofs.

This time, Shia was the only one who stood in the
square, rain running in rivulets down her face. Light
glowed out of the windows around the square, and she
suddenly hoped that no one was even looking out to see
this bedraggled colt slogging through the fetlock-deep
mud.

And then he was standing before her, his sodden
nose brushing her cheek, his glorious, impossibly blue
eyes swallowing hers.

:I'm sorry you had to wait so long for me, Chosen.:

Tears mingled with the rain on her face, streaming
warm with cold, and Shia collapsed heedless to her
knees in the muck, weeping out the agonizing emptiness
of the last four years.

The Companion—Eodan, she knew without words—
folded his forelegs and lay in the mud beside her, curv-
ing his neck around to draw her slight form against his
steaming side, his warmth seeping into her bone chill.

*:I came as soon as the King's Own Companion said
I was ready—although he warned me about the spring
rains in Breyburn.:* There was a note of self-deprecating

amusement in his rich MindVoice. *:You will learn that patience is not natural to me.:*

"What about Pira? She's Gifted, I'm sure, so shouldn't you be for her . . ." Shia finally managed to get words past the rawness in her throat.

:Her Companion is more patient than I—Pira is still a little too young to begin the training. You, my Chosen, should never have had to start this late.: There was a strange note of regret coloring his MindVoice as it echoed in Shia's head. *:It would have been different if—:* he cut off his thought, then abruptly changed the subject, nudging gently against her shoulder.

:Come, Chosen, it's a good thing you'll soon be wearing Trainee Grays, for those leggings are unsalvageable.:

Shia gave no response to his jest, lost in the wonder of Eodan's presence, and yet baffled by the forlorn ache still within her, deeper than the presence of Eodan beside her—even part of her—could reach. Without words, she knew that Eodan knew, and regretted, that it was there inside her, that dull pain, that lost feeling of incompletion.

:Trust me, Chosen. You will understand soon. When we are in Haven, I think.:

Shia turned to stare at him in disbelief, astonished at her own courage in thinking to argue with a Companion. "In Haven? What about Breyburn? I can't just up and leave them—and it's folly to go anywhere during the flash-rain season."

Eodan shook his head at her, and only now did she finally hear the jingle of his harness bells beneath the drum of the falling rain. *:Chosen, you have been patient enough for two, but now that I am finally with you, this will be my time to practice it myself.:*

The Last Part of the Way

by *Brenda Cooper*

Brenda Cooper has published over thirty short stories
in various magazines and anthologies. Her books include *The Silver Ship and the Sea* and *Reading the
Wind*. She is a technology professional, a futurist, and
a writer living in the Pacific Northwest with three dogs
and two other humans. She blogs and tweets and all
that stuff; stop by www.brenda-cooper.com and visit.

Three riders passed beneath trees shrugging fall color
into the wind. Each time a gust spurted through, cold and
edged in winter, it plucked gold and orange and brown
leaves and sent them to tangle in the riders' hair and
crunch under the hooves of their mounts. The redheads,
Rhiannon and Dionne, would have been impossible to
tell apart except that Rhiannon wore flamboyant Bardic
red and Dionne a soft and subdued Healer green. The
women shared the same red hair, bright blue eyes, slender figures, and the same deep laugh lines. They rode
similar horses: big sturdy bays with wide white blazes
and patient, alert walks. One of the horses had white
socks and the other didn't. Between them, a much
younger man named Lioran sat easily on the back of a
white Companion, Mila. Everything about Mila was neat
and trimmed and nearly perfect, while her Herald wore

his long black hair unkempt, had stains on the knees of his white uniform, and a sad silence on his face.

Dionne and Rhiannon had been riding circuit twenty-five years now and were too old to keep peace on the borders or fight teenaged toughs. But even usually peaceful towns needed healing and song, so they were sent around the easy middle of Valdemar, far from border skirmishes and the beasts of the Pelagir Hills and the intrigues of Haven. The twins were often assigned a young Bard or Healer who needed a safe year or two to gain confidence. But they'd never before been asked to take a Herald along. A mudslide had buried his family, and in fact his whole town; everyone he knew. The news had come to him right after he was given his Whites, right after he'd packed his belongings onto his Companion for a trip home to the small town of Golden Hill.

After two weeks, Dionne despaired of helping him. She watched Lioran's face as Rhiannon's musical voice chided him, "There will be things you can do, even in Shelter's End."

His voice came out gloomy. "There won't be anyone under forty there."

"You'll be there," Dionne responded, allowing only a bit of the disdain she felt into her voice. No one said you had to like a patient, or even a Herald. "We go where we're needed, and don't whine if we don't like it."

"I wish we could just go past. I don't want to stop in a retirement town, or a town at all. I want the woods."

Rhiannon looked as though she wanted to skin him, but all she said was, "The wind's chill. We'd better find a place to make camp. We don't really want to ride in on them at night, anyway."

"How about right here?" he asked.

"How about you and Mila find someplace a little more sheltered?" Rhiannon countered, the impatience in her voice enough to make Dionne wince, although

Lioran didn't bother to react. Mila cast both women a baleful look, turning her head slightly side to side, watching each of them with her bright blue eyes. Although Dionne had no Mindspeech, she imagined Mila's thoughts going something like, "He's young. He's hurt. He'll come around." Dionne grinned back at her, wishing for a way to tell the Companion how much she appreciated her patience. And how much she wished she had more of it handy. The boy got on her nerves.

Silence sat heavy on the group for half a mark. Dionne was about to give up and pick a place herself when Lioran pointed to a rather nice spot on a hill above the trail, in a copse of trees sturdy enough to shelter people and animals from most of the wind. Dionne rubbed her cold hands together as she waited for her sister's nod.

It was almost full dark by the time they fed and brushed and watered the animals, and gathered enough fuel to start a small fire. Lioran did his share, silent and sullen, but without actual complaint. After they finished, the twins settled near the fire, stretching their fingers wide and close to the warm yellow-orange flames. Lioran didn't sit beside them. He climbed up on Mila's bare back, and looking out into the woods, he said, "Me and Mila are heading off. We'll be back in an hour or two." He didn't wait for acknowledgement but simply faded into the trees and the darkness, his dirty Whites and Mila's clean white outline the last thing they saw disappearing into darkness. If tonight was like every other night, when he came back, he'd look soft and sad.

Rhiannon sighed. "It's too bad he's not a kid. Then I could just tell him to snap out of it. I know he's hurt, but all this pouting and whining is unbecoming in a Herald."

"In anybody."

"I sure hate him going off like that."

"He's a full Herald; he's supposed to be watching over old women."

Rhiannon arched an eyebrow.

"Well, that's what most would think." Dionne flexed her fingers and added another handful of small sticks to the fire. "Hard not to see him as a kid, even if we were younger when we got our uniforms. This is our last chance to get him out of his depression—we're due back in Haven in two weeks."

"So how do you think Shelter's End is going to help?"

Dionne shook her head. "It's not Shelter's End itself. I mean, it's a good town, and they always need help from a strong back. I hope that will get past his head and engage his heart." She sighed heavily, shifting her weight to ease her aching back. "I haven't been able to do it."

"So what makes you think anybody else can? He's skittish and hard."

Dionne added a log to the fire and watched the sparks do a sky-dance in the wind. "Well, one of my old teachers is there. Melony. She helped us all out of funks, and that's what he seems to need. I mean, it seems like he stopped being an adult in full Whites the minute he learned his parents died, and became a spoiled kid. I haven't been able to reach him; whatever's broken in him isn't physical, or even really in his emotions. It's like his very self is cracked. I bet Melony has some ideas. I'm going to ask her for advice. Don't you remember how she helped Jon after he broke his hand and Yvette after that merc in town roughed her up?"

"Maybe. I was pretty dazzled by the Collegium."

"Melony taught me salves and teas in my first two years there. Everybody loved her so much she got awarded Teacher of the Year three times in a row."

"She's still alive?"

"She was last time we came through."

"Five years ago? I think I remember her. Gray hair?"

Dionne play-slapped at Rhiannon. "That describes the whole town."

"Sorry. I don't remember everything."

"Yeah, well maybe age is getting in the way of your memory."

"Already?" Rhiannon laughed. "We're not gray yet."

"I pulled out two gray hairs yesterday." She looked toward the trees Lioran had disappeared through. "We should think about what we're doing next."

Rhiannon sighed. "I'm not ready to stop performing yet. But I hope your friend's alive to help. Old age and experience beats smarts."

Dionne let out a short, bitter laugh. "Then we should have succeeded by now."

"We're *not* old."

"Tell that to my fingers." Truth tell, it was Rhiannon she worried about, even though she showed no interest in even slowing down. As a Healer, Dionne would be fine even with the beginnings of arthritis, which was, truthfully, a bit noticeable on a cold morning of late. But old hands did real damage to a Bard. A Healer could speed the body's natural response to damage, but there wasn't much Dionne, or anybody else, could do about old age. And Rhiannon was stubborn as an old mule. She liked to take charge of everything. Queen of the Road. It made Dionne smile.

Sure enough, Rhiannon had a pronouncement about the topic. "We're not ready for Shelter's End yet." And that would be the end of that. Rhiannon reached into her pocket and pulled out a hand-carved wooden flute. She started playing, and Dionne settled in to listen, content for the moment to just be with her sister and pleased that the unhappy Herald had taken himself off somewhere else. They'd both be older tomorrow, and they could worry about being older then.

Lioran, true to form, returned after about an hour. He looked as bad as Dionne expected him to, his face thin and drawn, his skin so pale he might be the child of a ghost. It was all she could do not to wince as Mila picked her way carefully through camp and stopped at a good place to drop her tack. Lioran took good, if quick, care of his Companion. Then he lay down on his rumpled bedroll, plumped his coat up to be a pillow, pulled his thick woolen blanket close up around his ears, and turned away from them all.

Mila took the first watch. Rhiannon gave Dionne a resigned look, with a small smile attached. When Dionne nodded, Rhiannon picked up her flute and blew the first soft notes of a lullaby. Dionne followed, and so the two women sang together, Rhiannon's trained voice, the stronger, washing over Dionne until she, too, felt sleepy and content. They sang five songs and then the same five songs again, looking over at the back of the shivering, silent Herald from time to time. His breathing finally regulated into sleep. Rhiannon carefully packed her flute, and the women began to get ready to sleep themselves.

Dionne nestled closest to the fire, listening to the faint sounds of the warm coals and the stomp of the horse's feet. Wind brushed branches together above her head. She imagined finding Melony the next day, making little lists in her head of all the things she had to tell her old mentor.

She must have eventually gone to sleep since Rhiannon's soft hiss woke her.

Dionne opened her eyes, careful not to make a sound or change her breathing until she knew more. If it was Rhiannon's watch, it must be the middle of the night. A light fog threaded through the trees above her and dampened her cold cheeks and nose. The thud of at least five horses, maybe seven, went by on the road below. The flash of a torch blinded her to the details of the riders. Gruff voices called out, "Hurry," and "Quiet, now," although clearly no one in the party really believed they needed to be quiet. They had thick accents and gruff voices. Undoubtedly from somewhere else and, if allowed to pass, not likely to come back this way.

There were too many to confront. Maybe fifteen years ago, but now? Dionne's blood pounded through her as she held still, ready to leap up and grab her staff if the horses called attention to them. Or worse, if Lioran woke up and decided to play hero. The sounds faded slowly. Still, Dionne and Rhiannon held their tongues, listening until all they could hear was the night wind and an owl hooting mournfully in a tree above them. "Bandits," Rhiannon whispered. "Not good. Riding away from where we're going."

"And they sounded proud of themselves."

Mila must agree with them. She was already nosing Lioran up, her blue eyes wide with worry. Rhiannon covered the coals with dirt while Dionne and Lioran saddled up. They were on the road in short order. Mila's tossing head made Dionne ask Lioran, "What does she know?"

"Something bad's happened." His eyes looked big in his pale face, his expression hard to make out in the meager light thrown by the stars overhead. "There's death, and fear. She can feel it, but she can't tell what it is . . . what happened. In Shelter's End." His voice sounded high and a bit squeaky. "I'm the only Herald around."

In spite of their hurry, they started the horses at a fast walk before moving into a slow canter. It was too dark to allow them a full run. Mila pranced, keeping a close eye on the road ahead and behind, herding them toward town. Dionne glanced over at Rhiannon to see her eyes narrowed with worry, a combination of fear and fierceness playing across her features.

By the time they could see the town, dawn had started

kissing the horizon. Gray light illuminated the two long streets full of small houses beside a placid, thin river. Nothing appeared to have been burned. No dead bodies littered the streets.

Hooves clattered as they trotted from the dirt trail onto the stone road. When they stopped, they heard the horses 'hard-blowing breath and above that the sound of voices and tears and a low mournful wailing from one of the close-in houses.

Two men stepped out from behind a tree, both gray haired, one stooped and slow while the other still moved well. The slower one had on a torn red shirt. An old Bard, then. The stronger man wore no telltale colors, although that meant little. He smiled grimly as he neared them, looking to Lioren. "Glad to see you. I'm Jared." He nodded toward the house they'd clearly been guarding. "In there. Ask them to send someone out to walk your horses cool."

And this was where Lioran should be taking control of the situation. Dionne swallowed and let a beat of time go by. Rhiannon ran out of patience first, dismounting and handing her reins to the man. "I'm Rhiannon, and this is my sister, Dionne." She glanced at the Herald, her look driving him from Mila's back. "And this is Lioran."

The man gave the threesome a puzzled look but jerked his head toward the house. "They need you in there." He nodded toward Dionne, who was untying her healing bag from the back of Ladystar's saddle. "Especially you."

Dionne made it inside first. A great room full of seats, including extra ones pulled in as for an impromptu meeting. Most of the chairs were full. Shovels and staffs lined the near wall; makeshift and true weapons alike. The conversation stopped, although a woman sobbed softly in the back, where five people had been laid out, blood from wounds staining a thin green rug. At least fifteen other faces turned toward her, and then Rhiannon and Lioran came in behind her and the group's attention fell on Lioran.

Dionne headed straight for the back where two old Healers bent over the patients. She knelt beside them. "Can I help?"

"Her." One of the women pointed and went right back to work on a set of deep cuts she'd just finished stitching.

Dionne bent over a shattered wrist, taking a deep breath to ground herself.

Behind her, Rhiannon asked, "What happened?"

Dionne focused on the splintered bone under her palms, whispering, "Hold still," to the tearful woman she sat beside. "What's your name?"

"Leidra."

"Okay, Leidra, this shouldn't hurt much."

"I know." As Dionne drew the earth's energy to help her work, snatches of the story drifted at her from the lips of old men and woman. "They were strangers. Not from near here."

"They burned Smiley's farm before they came here, and who knows what else."

"They didn't expect us to fight them."

"Well, we didn't, not at first."

"They didn't respect who we are!" Petulant, a woman, her voice shaky.

"Were," someone else snapped, then continued, "We stood our ground, quiet like, wanting our lives more than our stuff, but then they started in on us, saying they were looking for treasure."

The warmth Dionne had built up in her hands flowed into the woman in front of her. She focused so hard that for a minute she didn't hear or feel anything but her patient's need. Only when she'd done all that she could did she listen again to the conversation. " . . . died, then we fought them. Old Ray . . . he's the one outside . . . he stabbed one of their horses in the butt with a pitchfork."

Someone actually laughed. Good. Laughter almost always had healing properties, no matter how ironic or pained. Dionne looked for the next patient, and one of the other two Healers directed her to a man who couldn't move his leg. She started feeling along it, starting at the foot and working up.

"But then they knocked him down. That got Cherie all mad, and she started throwing stones."

And, of course, Dionne could fill in the rest. Even though they were old and frail, they had all done their turns in the salle during training, and a few of them would have been on the front lines of various wars and skirmishes. Even though Heralds didn't tend to retire in Shelter's End, the assortment of older Bards who didn't want to teach and retired Healers who wanted the outdoors instead of the noisiness of the city included its own strengths. Melony was that way. She'd been offered a permanent place in Haven. Her answer had been that she'd spent forty years there, and now she was just darn well going to relax and be an old woman.

Melony! Where was she? Her patient groaned, and Dionne returned to the job at hand. Whatever had led him to choose this place for the end of his days, he'd come near them now. Blunt force—probably a fall—had shattered his hip, and he'd have to be really tough to make it out of this alive. The injury under her hands was simply insult added onto the deeper challenges of old age. But she could encourage his body to increase the flow of blood and help it feel less pain. After that, it would be pretty much up to him and how much he still wanted to live. She bent to her task, spending most of her awareness drawing and feeding energy, her lips spilling soft good wishes for the man under her hands, her eyes watching his cragged and lined face and his light green eyes. He stared at the ceiling, barely moving.

His breathing slowed and regulated. His skin began to regain color. His heartbeat was a thin thread. Rest would do him more good than she could now. Her knees hurt from kneeling on the thin rug, and her back screamed that she'd better stretch or find a Healer for herself. As she sat up straight and raised her arms, she came a little more aware of the room around her. There were fewer people; some must have gone off to bed or something. She hadn't heard the door open or felt the fall chill enter the room. Rhiannon held a teapot in one hand, conferring in low tones with two women. Lioran stood against a wall, an impassive look on his face. Surely he should be outside?

"Where did everyone go?" she asked.

Rhiannon glanced over at her, met her eyes, and the look in them sent a cold fear to settle into Dionne's chest. "What's wrong?"

"They're digging graves for the dead." Rhiannon put the teapot down on the top of the great cast iron stove and crossed the room, pulling Dionne up and holding her. "Your friend, Melony, she's the first one they actually killed. She got mad when they knocked down the guy you just finished working on. She told the leader off, and they made an example of her."

It couldn't be true. Melony should have died of old age, not violence.

Not after being the best teacher for three years running.

Violence shouldn't happen to old women.

What an irrational thought.

She was a Healer. So was Melony. They knew the world was unfair. But still, Melony's face swam in Dionne's imagination as she slumped into her twin's arms, grateful as always for Rhiannon. She swayed, held up by her sister, feeling as if everyone left in the room was watching them. Rhiannon brushed the hair from her face and whispered, "I'm sorry."

"I know."

Rhiannon, of course, knew what to say next, how to drag her into the present and focus her. "They killed two others, and one more fell and cracked his head. They're all outside digging graves together."

Dionne shivered, the room suddenly cold and her skin clammy. She swallowed. It wasn't as though she hadn't seen and felt death. But she'd so wanted Melony's help! She glanced toward Lioran, to find him watching her closely, his narrow, pale face a closed book, his eyes almost afraid. "I should go help them dig." She kept her gaze on Lioran. "We all should." Although people from nearby towns bartered for singing and healing with strong backs, she hadn't seen any. This near the end of harvest, there might not be any. They were the three ablest hands left here, and Lioran was the strongest by far in spite of being slight of frame.

The look he gave her was deep with resentment, almost like hatred. It couldn't be hatred. People with hatred in their hearts didn't get Chosen, but it was it was an emotion as dark as his eyes and his hair and as unfocused as her own pain. He stalked to the door, threw it open, and headed outside without so much as a word. Dionne took a step to follow him, but Rhiannon's arm shot out and stopped her. "Not after all that work you just did." For emphasis, she glanced down at the old man Dionne had just finished with. She led Dionne to an empty overstuffed chair. "You'll be wanted when they're ready to bury her. These people are used to digging graves, if usually for different reasons than this. It's probably familiar salve to their wounds."

"But Lioran?"

"Can hang himself for all I care." Rhiannon shook

her head. "I don't mean that. He's just gotten under my skin. Besides, Mila won't let him. Hang himself, I mean. If he doesn't go off into a blue funk, he might even be useful to the diggers."

He was already in a blue funk. Before Dionne could get even one word out, Rhiannon had covered her with an extra coat, kissed the top if her head, and turned back to the stove and the teapot. No use talking to the Red-headed Queen of any Situation when she was in this mood.

Her next conscious thought was to wonder how the room had gotten so warm. It smelled like black tea and flowers. Rhiannon was humming a soft ditty about working she often sang when they were setting up or taking down camp. Dionne blinked and looked around, her eyes starting out on Rhiannon, who held out a steaming cup. Dionne took the cup, warm in her hands. She sipped, the tea so pungent it opened her sinuses and made room for fresh thoughts in her full head.

Memories came back. Melony. Murder. The bandits.

Maybe she should have skipped the tea. The wounded still lay in the back of the room. One of the two Healers leaned back against the wall with her eyes closed, soft snores indicating she slept. A tired old woman who'd just done too much. She would look like that soon, herself. She and her sister were both getting old.

From the change in angle of the light slanting through the windows, she'd slept at least two marks, maybe more. Funny how it felt like moments. She took another sip of tea and choked some words past the lump in her throat. "Are they done?"

"Soon. That's why I got you up."

"Hmmmph." Dionne handed her the empty tea cup and walked over to the wounded. They still slept, a typical outcome of healing. They all breathed normally, and Dionne adjusted a pillow here and a blanket or coat there before she went to the privy to clean up and wash her face. The cold water did only a little to help her feel refreshed. Surely it was just because she'd spent so much energy healing, but Melony's death weighed on her mood like a stone, so heavy it was impossible to drag up a welcoming smile as a woman bundled in a warm coat and handmade sheeps-wool scarf came in the door. "Is the Healer here? Dionne?"

"I'm here."

"Ylia." The way the woman said her name had a bit of singsong in it. "We'd like you to come out, to say something before we bury them all."

Dionne shouldered into her coat, sure she didn't want to go stand graveside and say nice pretty things. She was too tired.

She and Rhiannon followed Ylia to the four graves. Either Rhiannon had told them about her relationship with Melony or someone had remembered, since although the other three were finished, they'd saved the work of throwing the first earth onto Melony's body for Dionne. The simple gesture made the last few steps to the graves even harder to take.

She stood in front of Melony's coffin. The lid was still open, the familiar, beloved face marred by a cut cheek and a bruised lip. With her life gone, her mentor appeared simply slight and thin, wispy. Dionne felt thinner herself, as if some of her soul followed Melony, as if her past had begun to die.

Lioran and Rhiannon stood behind her, close enough for Dionne to hear their breathing. The same man who had taken their reins this morning—Jared—climbed down into the grave and closed the lid of the coffin, hiding Melony from the world.

The faces standing graveside were lined with spider webs of dignity and pain, some of the men with settling jowls or bald heads, most of the women shaped more like boxes than urns, slow and broad, a few thin and reedy, all bone and skin. As a group, the primary expressions they wore were resignation and hope. Dionne tried to look hopeful, to be the Healer she was, but all she could manage was a lighter despair than she'd started with. The afternoon was like molasses, time moving slow and everything exaggerated.

She knelt down and took a fistful of rich, damp earth. A week of relentless rains had stopped a few days ago. Even though the surface of the earth had dried in the previous day's wind, the bottom of the grave was damp, dark mud.

As soon as she stood, she started talking, not saying anything at all like what she usually said at graves. Not comforting. "Life is not fair. It unfairly plucked this wonderful woman too early, and for doing what she always did. Helping people. I came here to get help from her; she has helped me all my life when I needed it. Oh, I haven't seen her for years, but that's partly because she helped me grow up."

Rhiannon came and stood beside Dionne, like a pillar. It gave Dionne the strength to continue. "This year I needed her, and she's not here." A tear fell down her face. She let it go. "Healers cry. That's something Melony taught me. If we don't cry, we die inside, a little bit every day. So when we need to, we cry."

And then she was sobbing, great piles of breath backing up in her throat and bursting out, her nose and eyes running like streams. She threw the dirt before she couldn't see any more; then she knelt down by the grave, Rhiannon next to her.

Head bowed, she heard other fistfuls of dirt thudding into the hole. Murmured prayers accompanied each throw. One and another and another.

"Thank you."

"Speed on your journey."

"I'll always remember the blackberry jam."

"Goodbye, and who am I going to weave with now? I'll miss you so."

"Pass well."

In time, the wet sloppy sounds stopped.

Rhiannon elbowed her gently.

Dionne looked up in time to see Lioran throw his own fistful of mud. A tear streaked down his cheek as well, and then another, the most genuine emotion Dionne had ever seen on his face. He was doing the one thing she hadn't seen him do since she met him. Crying.

She started to push herself up, but Rhiannon held her down. "Finish your own grief."

But her grief had lightened a little. She glanced back at the coffin, smeared and splattered with mud and prayers. "Thank you," she whispered. "You did find a way to help."

Almost everyone went back to their violated houses, and even Rhiannon followed, murmuring something about making more hot tea. Dionne stayed graveside, standing in the chilling breeze while leaves blew around her feet. Lioran came to stand beside her. His eyes were red and sore, his cheeks puffy and pink, his hands covered in mud, his Whites dirty beyond saving. He put an arm around her and pulled her close to him, the two of them standing in silence for a long time. She felt warmer with him there. Finally he whispered, "You'll remember her. I remember my mom every day. I remember the way she bit her tongue when she cut potatoes for dinner and how her voice lilted when she called Jackie, our farm dog. I remember my little sister calling me a wimp and a bookworm and then asking for help with numbers." His voice had lost the whine. "I remember my dad the day I was Chosen, looking like the best and worst thing ever had all happened to him at once and wishing me well." He swallowed. "That's where I go at night, to remember them. I'm so afraid that I'll go back to town and get busy and forget the little things, and then they'll really be dead."

Dionne looked down at the fresh earth. "She's dead. I will forget the details, because I'm not dead, and I have a job to do. But that doesn't change the beauty of her life or make what she gave me any less."

"I have work, too."

"Yes." More silence, and then Dionne whispered, "Thank you for telling me about them."

"Thank you for singing to me," he said. "I'll tell Rhiannon that, too."

Two days later, they started their return journey to Haven. There, they'd tell their tales and see if there was a way to get help for Shelter's End, maybe some guards or a few young families. They'd encourage the Crown to send out a hunting party to find the bandits and clean up after them. Ylia and Jared accompanied them to be witnesses, riding horses borrowed from a farm in a nearby town. Haven was stretched—it was always stretched—and Dionne expected that only a little could be offered. But they'd give whatever was possible.

Dionne cracked her sore knuckles and told her back there were a few more years of riding left. Shelter's End was worth keeping, maybe a place they'd go themselves, although not for a while.

On the first night away from town, Lioran picked a campsite without being asked. He did go off with Mila, bare-backed and silent, but on his return he didn't roll away from them all and stare out into the night.

He sat beside them at the fire, Ylia and Jared on one side, Lioran between Rhiannon and Dionne on the far side. When Rhiannon started to sing, he joined in. Dionne had never heard his voice. It was rich and full, and confident.

Midwinter Gifts

by *Stephanie D. Shaver*

Stephanie Shaver works in the online gaming industry, where she has donned the hat of writer, game
designer, programmer, level designer, and webmaster at various points in her career. Like most people
who work by day and write by whenever, her free
time is notoriously elusive. She can be found online
at *sdshaver.com* and other virtual hives of scum and
villainy. Offline, she is either hiking with the smirking
entity she calls "The Guy" or on the couch with cats
and a laptop stacked atop her, recovering from the
aforementioned hiking trail.

"This is madness," Lelia said.

"This?" Her twin, Lyle, looked over his shoulder at
the Haven marketplace, packed with people engaged in
the mindless, happy activities that swirled about at this
time of year. "It's just the Midwinter Market."

She punched his shoulder, a futile gesture as they
were both bundled up against the cold; she in mittens
and a coat, he in riding leathers and a heavy white cloak.
Lyle's Companion, Rivan, stood off to one side, saddled
and ready to go. Five years as a Field Herald had whit-
tled Lyle down—punching him felt like punching a tree.
He grinned at her pitiful attempt to bruise.

"You're such a mooncalf sometimes," she muttered, sweeping her bangs back under her cap so she could fix him with a full glower.

"I was being—what d'ya call it? 'Funny'?"

She only frowned. Anyone who knew the two would have been amused (or greatly alarmed) by their role reversal. She—solemn as a priest, he smirking like a page who'd filched cream cakes off the queen's table.

They were in a snug side street off the market, one of the few not accommodating the overflow of stalls and hawkers. A few minutes ago she'd been happily browsing jewelry in her Scarlets, which was probably how he'd spotted her. Usually she wore plainer clothes, but she'd hoped formal regalia would drum up a little Midwinter work.

Work had found her, all right. And it wore Whites.

"They realize I'm a Bard?" she said. "Not a Herald?"

"That's the point."

"They also know that I will likely foul this up?"

"You don't even know what 'this' is."

"Even more likely!"

"Lelia." He reached out and touched her shoulder, gracing her with a beatific smile that had reassured more than a few Valdemarans in its time. "You're going to do fine."

She narrowed her eyes. "Did you suggest me?"

Lyle cocked his head. "Actually, no."

"Well, if *you* didn't—"

Something nuzzled the back of her neck, and she shrieked, leaping forward. Lyle grabbed her shoulders and gently turned her around to face the Companion waiting there. The Companion inclined his head and bent his knee in an equine bow.

:Be polite to Vehs,: Lyle Mindspoke to her.

:Vehs? Companion to Herald Wil?: she thought back, sweating with the effort. Their twin-bond was not the

stuff of legend. If they hadn't been touching she wouldn't have been able to MindSpeak to him at all.

:Yes.:

Lelia's heart sank. Of course it would be *him*. The network of Heralds only went so far. Wil, Lyle's senior on Circuit training. Wil, who probably only knew one Bard—her. Wil, the Herald she'd been obsessed with years ago. Just the memory of the way she'd romanticized him made her ears burn.

She tried to reassure herself. *But you grew up. You stopped wearing that stupid necklace he gave you. You got over it.* She straightened her spine. *You're a Master Bard now.*

Suddenly Lyle hugged her, disrupting her train of thought. "Love you!"

She sagged against him, letting some of her anxiety drain out. "Stay safe," she muttered. "Remember that if you die on the job, I will eulogize you in a five-part cycle with at least two flute solos."

He chuckled. "By the way, I told Mama and Papa you'd come with me next year for Midwinter."

She drew back, horrified. "You didn't."

He grinned.

"Lyle—Midwinter is about earning *money* for a Bard—"

His face grew stern. "When was the last time you visited, Lelia?"

She sputtered, unable to say anything but, "I can't afford it!"

"We'll figure something out." Lyle winked, then gestured to Vehs, who had presented a stirrup. "Up you get!"

She ignored his offer of help, despite Vehs's mountainlike build. She didn't so much mount as *scale* him. He whickered and turned. At the last possible moment, Lelia twisted round and said to Lyle, "I'm staying in your room. Hope you don't mind."

His face fell. *"What?"*

She squeezed Vehs gently. He took her lead and leaped forward, moving off into the crowds. The last she heard from Lyle was: "Lelia! If you burn down the Herald's wing—"

Vehs chuckled in his Chosen's head.

Wil leaned against a post in the Companions' stable and thought back, *:What?:*

:I have been part of something sneaky. Mine is an evil chuckle.: He demonstrated it again.

:Oh.: Wil rubbed his brow. *:For the record—:*

:Yes, yes. It's a terrible idea. Understood, Chosen.:

Vehs chuckled again.

Wil paced. He was not alone in the stable—another Herald, the official who would be signing off on this "mission," stood nearby with hands clasped behind his back. Always still. Always composed.

Not Wil. He kicked up hay- and grain-dust as he paced between the deepening shadows of late afternoon. He wanted another solution, but no ideas were forthcoming.

He took a step, gray winter sunlight sliding over him, and the next put him in shadow. Another step, and—

His gut wrenched as his Gift triggered.

—body on the floor and a woman in jewelry standing over it, two knives at her waist, one in her hand, the tip bloody as she smiled and raised it—

He came back to himself on his knees, clutching his head. Over on the other side of the stable, the other Herald asked, "Are you all right?"

"Fine," Wil said, climbing to his feet and brushing off his knees. "Sir, I don't know if this—"

"Wait for her to get here," the Herald said. "Then we'll decide if it's a bad idea."

I could swear he's been talking to Vehs, Wil thought sourly.

As if cued, Vehs said, *:We're coming through the Herald's Gate.:*

Wil walked over to stand beside the senior Herald. He folded his arms across his chest, and watched as the red-clad rider drew closer.

Vehs stopped a few feet away from the big open building of Companions' stables.

Oh, Lelia thought when she saw who stood next to Wil. She dropped to her feet and executed a deep curtsy, sweeping off her cap. "M'lord Herald," she said.

Queen's Own Talamir inclined his head slightly.

"Herald Wil," she said to the other, dropping another curtsy, albeit more shallow. A fierce joy welled, unbidden, inside her. She did her best to squash it.

I am a Master Bard! I am a Master Bard! she reminded her galloping heart.

Wil grunted a hello.

"How much did Lyle tell you?" Talamir asked her. His voice had a faint quaver, but his gaze was direct and difficult to meet. Even if he hadn't been spooky as a haunted castle, being under the eye of a Herald *this* high gave Lelia the quakes.

"Nothing," she said honestly. "Just that the Heraldic Circle's interested in enlisting a Bard for something delicate." Her voice dropped in volume as she finished the sentence, glancing about nervously. She had to presume that the Heralds had chosen the stables for a reason, but it still felt awfully open.

"It's safe," Wil said blandly, addressing her concern. "The Companions are keeping an eye out."

Lelia nodded.

"Lyle vouched for you as trustworthy," Talamir commented.

Lyle, you mooncalf, Lelia thought furiously.

"He—" Talamir indicated Wil with a nod "—has reason to get inside the mansion of a lord in Haven without anyone knowing a Herald is there. And I have it on good authority that the lord's wife is seeking a musician for her Midwinter parties."

Lelia pursed her lips. Suddenly, this didn't sound so bad.

"Discretion would be required," Talamir said. *"Who* placed you there would have to remain confidential. This is a potentially volatile situation."

She nodded. "Discretion. Understood."

"Do you?" Wil asked, fixing her with a look. His tone caused a flicker of irritation to rise inside her, and when she met him gaze for gaze she saw in his face something she hadn't anticipated: deep distrust.

Not skeptical, not suspicious—he didn't *trust* her.

The joy of reunion died, leaving behind a wealth of annoyance.

"I've performed for the queen," she replied coolly, and had to suppress a smirk when he blinked in obvious surprise. *Didn't know about that, did you?* she thought. "M'lord Talamir, would you say I did so with grace?"

"Indeed," the Queen's Own murmured.

"Also," she continued, "it's been a while since I wore my Rusts, but I'm sure Dean Arissa would vouch for me." *Assuming she's forgotten about that incident with the chirra and the inkwell.*

"Well, Herald," Talamir said to Wil, "it's either this or try to get in as a servant."

Wil massaged his forehead, grimacing. "I guess . . . we'll try this."

"Very well." Talamir rubbed his hands together lightly. "I will make the arrangements. Do you have a handler?"

"Maresa Applegate," Lelia replied promptly.

"I shall make your arrangements with her, then. I leave you two to the rest." He walked off abruptly, without further farewell.

When Wil finally bothered to look at Lelia, he did so with a sad, sober expression. It made her own smile fade a little.

"I'm glad to see you," she said, and hugged him.

Women confused Wil.

He never felt comfortable around them unless they were younger than fifteen or older than dirt. Or married. Or saddled with babies.

None of which described Lelia. When she'd been younger, she'd been—well, manageable didn't cover it, but it had been *different*.

Now, though . . .

He patted her back awkwardly as she hugged him and felt relieved when she disengaged. Not that it hadn't been a nice hug—her coat hung open, and he'd shed his due to the warmth of the heated stables. Her body squished comfortably in the right places. Her height had also put her hair right under his nose, giving him a whiff of honey and cinnamon.

And so it went around the women-who-confused-Wil. They hugged him, or said they were glad to see him, and his response always felt *wrong*.

He decided to focus on what he knew: being a Herald.

"I'm staying at the Companion's Bell," he said, "as Attikas Goldenoak."

"What else can you tell me about this—whatever it is?"

He briefly thought about explaining it to her. *Well, Lelia, I've been having stomach-lurching visions of a horrible murder, but there's no hard evidence aside from a brigand's confession and a handful of gems. In fact, the only solution the supposedly brilliant Queen's Own could come up with was dropping me in the lord's home and "letting my Gift do its work."*

No. No, the only thing worse than this so-called plan was trying to explain it to someone. "The less, the better," he said.

She rolled her eyes. "You won't pass for an entertainer, you know."

"That's just one problem with this plan."

:*It's* not *a problem,*: Vehs said stubbornly. :You *just don't want to come up with a solution.*:

"Assistant?" Wil hazarded, trying to mollify his Companion.

"The Whites might give you away."

"Conveniently, I wouldn't be wearing them."

She widened her eyes innocently. "The Queen lets you take them off?"

Wil felt his cheeks burn. Was she being funny or making fun of him? She was smiling. What did it mean?

She nodded to herself. "I have an idea. You have a weapon?"

He gave her a disgusted look.

"One you can wear to a party without looking like an idiot?"

"Yes."

"Excellent. On that note—"

"Going to tell me *why*?"

She cocked her head. "Oh, I think the less you know, the better."

Vehs chuckled gleefully.

:*Glad you're amused,*: Wil thought sourly at him.

"I need to collect some things," she said. "See you at the Bell in the morning?"

"Sure," he mumbled.

"Have a good night, Herald." She waved and wandered off, whistling as she went.

Wil directed his attention to Vehs.

:*It* was *funny,*: Vehs said.

Wil stalked off in a direction opposite hers. Not the

fastest route off the Palace-Collegia complex, but at least it guaranteed he'd be alone.

Vehs drew up beside him.

Mostly alone, Wil thought.

:Talamir thinks she's capable,: Vehs said. *:And Lyle is a Herald.:*

:I'd be happier if she were, too.:

:But then she wouldn't be a Bard. And then you wouldn't be able to get onto the Count's grounds.: Vehs's amusement sparkled like barleywine.

Wil looked in the direction the Bard had gone. *:She has matured. I mean, physically. She has—um—:*

:Womanly assets.:

Wil flushed, remembering the brief but warm hug. *:I wasn't looking—okay, I was. But that wasn't—exactly—:*

:She's a woman now.:

:But she's still Lelia.: He found distinct comfort in that bit of curmudgeonry.

Vehs bumped him from behind. *:This is your problem, you know. You only have faith in me and other Heralds.:*

:That's because I like breathing.:

:There are worse things than dying.:

:Like what?:

:Never truly living?:

Wil guffawed. *:What philosopher's memoir did you dredge that from?:*

Vehs would not be deterred. *:Just because someone doesn't wear White—:*

:I'll think about it,: Wil replied, annoyed. Vehs went silent.

But Wil knew the Bard, and what she was capable of. And that worried him.

Wil thought he'd been poleaxed by another vision when the countess swept in. But his gut remained quiescent, and no invisible force drove him to his knees. They were here, now.

"I am Countess Chantil of Tindale," she said. Three attendants accompanied her: two ladies and the stiff-collared butler who had fetched her.

"I'm Master Bard Lelia." Lelia dropped a curtsy and skillfully elbowed Wil at the same time. He bowed hastily. "This is my bodyguard, Attikas."

Chantil's brows crept upward. "Bodyguard? Really! Admirers following you home, Bard?"

Lelia smiled blandly. "Something like that."

Bodyguard. That had been Lelia's plan yesterday morning when Wil'd walked downstairs and found her waiting. Wil had (grudgingly) admitted it wasn't a bad idea. A visit to the Midwinter Market had yielded proper clothes, and his long-knife completed the ensemble. No one expected him to dance, sing, or even speak—just look grim. Something he excelled at.

Chantil gestured. "This way." She swept off down a hallway, retinue trailing.

Wastes no time, Wil thought.

"You'll be playing in the grand hall," Chantil said, walking so briskly Wil thought her heeled shoes would crack the marble floors. "Any needs you have, please speak to my steward, Einan." She gestured to the man Wil had taken for a butler.

She wheeled suddenly, causing her voluminous raw silk skirts to spin. "I would appreciate it if you kept things—" She coughed delicately into her satin-gloved hand. "—*cheerful* and *understated.* Nothing *morose,* please."

A glint lit in Lelia's eye. Wil immediately knew that had been the wrong thing for the countess to say. He hoped that Lelia's retaliation would be discreet enough to not get her position here terminated.

:Focus on your job, Chosen. Let the Bard do hers.:

:If she performs a protracted sing-along of "The Vigil That Never Ends".....:

Vehs snickered.

"As I stated before," Lelia said, reemploying that graceful curtsey she'd used earlier, "I am well experienced at performing for clientele of your caliber, Countess. And might I say what an *honor* it is to be here. Your happiness is my first priority."

These seemed to be the words the Countess wanted to hear. "Oh, you Bards." Her eyes flitted to Wil, and her smile soured a trifle. "Surely, it's quite safe here—"

"It's a matter of my peace of mind," Lelia said firmly. "And now, since you have me performing this very eve, I find it necessary to test the acoustics of the chamber."

Chantil's smile didn't quite play true. "If you need anything, the kitchens are that way." She gestured toward a wing of the mansion. "Or find Einan or Marjori. They can assist you." She gave Wil a final cursory glance and then sashayed off, minions in tow.

Lelia set herself up on a chair, gittern in lap. Wil stood about, feeling awkward and unnecessary, until she said, "You know, I think the countess is right. I should be quite safe here. Be a dear and fetch me some water?"

When he didn't move, she gave him a curious look, then broke into a laugh and shooed him. "Go on."

As he started forward, she called, "Don't get lost."

His confusion lasted to the door—and then her hints sunk in. Getting lost was *exactly* what he needed to do. He plunged into the depths of the mansion.

As a trainee, he'd been taught that ForeSight wasn't all flashes of the future—that his uncanny "gut instinct" stemmed from it. And that doubt proved particularly toxic to someone with his Gift, because it muddled its messages.

He tried to listen to his gut now as he passed oaken doors with brass knobs and double doors with inlaid glass leading out to the atrium. He navigated twisty corridors, noted alcoves with busts of former Tindale lords in them, and passed a door with gryphons carved on it. He saw cozy windowseats with curtains both drawn and down, flower petals strewn across the cushions.

He tried, but eventually he had to admit defeat and return to the Bard, empty-handed.

Midwinter Vigil wasn't for four more nights, but you couldn't tell that by the press of revelers at the mansion. Lelia thought her sets were well received, although they sounded contrived to her ears. No one listened to her, anyway. She was little more than a musical bauble at parties like this.

Maresa had worked out an excellent contract, not just in payment, but also in the number of breaks Lelia got. It gave her ample time to lurk and mingle while Wil went on endless "errands" to fetch her water and tidbits. The countess's entourage avoided her, but the servers were happy to talk.

The characteristics of a Bard were curiosity as deep as the sky and enough charm to coax secrets from a stone. By the end of the night Lelia had a pretty good idea why Wil was here.

"So," she said, once they were back at the Bell and could safely shed their coats and personas, "I talked to some servants tonight."

Wil's eyes narrowed.

"Andris is the countess' fourth husband. Did you know that?"

His face went blank, and she thought, *Ah ha!*

"The count's *awfully* young," she continued. "Seemed impressionable to me. Vulnerable, too."

"Lelia."

"I hear her last three husbands all died under questionable—"

"*Stop.*"

She held the sentence's ending hostage, meeting and holding his gaze.

"It's not a game, Lelia," he said quietly.

"And I *told* you I *know* that and you *act* like I *don't!*" She shook her head at him, hoisting her heavy pack of books and notes. "Good night," she muttered, and stomped off to trudge through the cold.

Wil rubbed his forehead.

"I can't do this," he said at last.

:*You can!:* Vehs protested.

:*No. I can't.:* Wil unbuckled his belt and slipped his weapon loop off. :*The stories are right. Talamir's halfway to the Havens. Only a simpleton would have assigned me to do this with—her.:*

:*Chosen.:* Vehs's mind-voice was flat serious. :*That isn't it at all.:*

:*Vehs, I* can't—:

:*Shut up!:*

Wil rocked on his heels, feeling as if he'd been slapped.

:*Ever since you spoiled that brigand's ambush, this is all I've heard! Endless whining about how you* can't *and this isn't your* forte. *You're a Herald. It's* all *your job!:*

Wil sat, stunned into silence. He'd never known Vehs to be this—direct.

:*You* are the one *Herald with ForeSight having these visions. You* are the one *who stopped the brigand, interrogated him under Truth Spell, and learned of the danger to Andris. And yes, you are the one who will uncover enough evidence to take to the queen so we can keep Chantil from murdering her fourth husband! And do you know why?:*

:*Why?:* Wil asked meekly.

:Because you are my Chosen, *dammit, and I didn't Choose an idiot!:*

A long silence followed, and then, *:And neither did Rolan.:*

Wil slumped. *:I'm sorry. I just—I don't—:* He carefully rephrased the thought. *:I feel like a fish out of water.:*

:Talamir gave you gills. Use them.:

Wil touched his neck, confused.

:The Bard, Chosen.:

:What? No. No no no—:

:She learned a lot in one night. She is far more social than you. She fits in where you do not. If you haven't completely offended her, she might even help you.:

Vehs retreated then, leaving Wil alone with his thoughts.

He crawled into bed, but it didn't want him. He tossed and turned, thoughts churning. Ages later, he gave a resigned sigh.

Vehs is going to be insufferable, he thought.

With that realization, Wil finally slept.

Lelia had neither a smile nor a good afternoon for Wil the next day. Wil tried to strike up conversation, and every time she either walked faster or intercepted a street vendor, cutting him off.

Oh, sure, when I want *to apologize . . . ,* he thought, irritated.

Once at the mansion, she immediately set up and started playing. He stood mutely by, finally wandering off when she muttered, "Water."

He wandered the hallways and corridors, trying to feel whatever his Gift relayed. Past an alcove, past a cupboard, past the door with the twin gryphons carved on it, and—

He stepped back to stare at the door. Hunger pangs, or something else? That *door . . .*

It opened.

He jumped, face to face with Einan, Chantil's toady.

"Are you lost, sir?" he asked.

"Uh—yes. Sorry. Privy?"

Einan pointed. Wil thanked him and hurried off.

The Bard's silence lasted even after her performance, and when they marched back to the Bell, she walked past the front entry.

"Hey—" he called.

She looked back, glaring coldly. She hadn't yet stopped.

Wil winced. He pointed to the Bell. "I want to talk. Please."

She slowed, then turned—and came back.

:*Nicely done, Chosen,*: Vehs said.

Upstairs, she sat down on the edge of the bed and said nothing.

Wil started pacing.

"I—" *Can't believe I'm saying this* "—need your help," he said.

She cocked her head.

"Somehow, I need to get around that mansion without anyone interrupting." Wil stopped long enough to meet her gaze. "Can you help?"

"I . . . can." She pursed her lips. "Have you heard about Salia?"

"What?"

"Chantil's former maid. One of her trusted circle. A week after the Tindales came to Haven for Midwinter Festival, Chantil ousted her for stealing." Lelia pulled her knees to her chest and rested her chin on top. "Einan, Marjori, and Ylora—that's the third one—won't talk about her, but the *others*—" She chuckled. "Oh, 'twas just *scandalous*."

"Okay. Interesting, but—" He stopped. "Wait. What was she accused of stealing?"

"Silver, jewelry. A couple of necklaces and brooches."

:The brigand's mysterious employer paid him in gems,: Wil thought, excited.

:You think Chantil took them off her own jewelry to pay the brigand and then blamed it on Salia?:

:And I have to wonder if she melted those settings down or hid them to reset later. How smart do you think she is?:

:Or how arrogant.:

Wil thought of the gryphon-door room, and his gut twinged. *:Exactly.:*

"Did Chantil report her to the Guard?" Wil asked.

"Curious you should ask!" Lelia's eyes sparkled. "Chantil never demanded the jewelry back, never brought charges against her. She didn't even do the ousting—gave all the dirty work to Einan or Marjori, depending on who you ask. Chantil said she didn't want to *see* Salia again."

Wil's brows lifted. "Well."

Lelia nodded. "Mull on that. I'll try to think of a suitable distraction."

He frowned. "Like what?"

She stood in the doorway and looked back over her shoulder. "The less you know," she said, winked, and stepped out.

Lelia timed her announcement for when the grand hall was at its fullest.

She stilled her strings, rose, and cleared her throat. With full Bardic projection, she said, "Attention!"

The volume died down. Heads turned. A few stray threads of conversations continued, but not for long.

"As some of you are aware," she said, "I am the composer and original performer of 'Today, I Ride'." She arched a brow. "Or, as some of you call it, 'That Sendar Song'." A murmur of recognition—and a few chuckles—

rolled through the crowd. "Well, tomorrow I will perform the song—" She lifted the other brow. "—*for the last time.*"

A collective gasp went through the room. Wil remained stoic.

"I ask that if you all wish to hear it *for the last time*—from its creator—that you be here tomorrow three candlemarks before midnight." She bowed deeply. "Thank you."

A wild clamor followed. The outraged look from Chantil warmed Lelia's heart. The entourage fluttered and muttered, looking just as distraught as their lady. Lelia had just swiped all the attention, and Chantil could do nothing about it.

If you're smart, you'll pretend you suggested it, M'lady, Lelia thought.

Back at the Bell and once again safe from prying eyes and ears, she said, "Sendar's song is a little less than a quarter candlemark in its full, unedited form. I can get you half if I include one of the parodies."

"There are *parodies*?"

"Oh, yes. My personal favorite is 'Today, I Lunch'." She giggled. "It's very respectful."

"Right."

"Nothing I haven't done before. So. Many. *Times*. I'm sick of it, to be honest."

"The wages of fame."

Her lips twitched. "Eh. Got me in to see the queen. I assume it's how Talamir knew me and why Chantil jumped to hire me." She took a deep breath. "Speaking of Her Haughtiness . . . I'll use my Gift. No one will leave that room."

"The *whole* room under Bardic Gift?"

"I'm not *that* good. But Chantil and Andris will be my focus. With them pinned, no one's going to leave."

"Might . . . actually work."

"Good." She stood up. "Tomorrow, then."

"Tomorrow," he agreed.

Lelia had her hand on the door to the Herald's wing when she heard the hiss of something swinging through the air.

Having spent years being hammered on by a large and skilled ex-captain of the Karsite army had its merits: when Lelia heard things hissing toward her, her first instinct was to duck. She dropped her weight, shed her packs, and rolled off to the side. She sprung up again, facing whatever had been swinging at where she'd been standing.

She saw a nothing that was something—black clothes, black gloves, black hood and half-mask. The black-clad nothing lunged at her with what looking like a club, taking another two-handed strike at her face. Lelia stumbled backward, opened her mouth, and screamed with full Bardic Gift, *"Stop!"*

Her attacker staggered in place.

Lelia jumped forward and landed with bone-crunching force on her assailant's foot.

A *clunk* followed the howl as the club dropped. Lelia crouched and came up swinging the discarded weapon; her assailant's ribs cracked like greenwood.

The figure issued an ear-piercing shriek, turned—and ran.

"Oh, no!" Lelia yelled, brandishing her new weapon. "Get back here you ba—guh!"

Her own pack fouled her. One moment she was on her feet, the next she sprawled on the pathway, tangled in books and leather, the club bouncing merrily away. The sound of footfalls receded. By the time she regained her feet, she was alone.

"Gods *damn* it," she whispered.

Somehow, she made it up to Lyle's room and lit the

hearth with shaking hands. The warm familiarity of her brother's quarters kept her from curling up into a hysterical sobbing ball. She locked and barred every window and door, shivering despite the warmth of the fire.

Wil heard a knock early the next morning. He stumbled out of bed to find the Bard on the other side of his door. "You look—"

"Got attacked," she said wearily. "Couldn't sleep."

"What?"

She told him with monosyllabic sentences and a demonstrative stomp. She showed him the short, lead-weighted stick of wood she'd turned on her attacker's ribs. She hadn't seen a face. But she also hadn't told anyone.

She did, however, tell him *where* she'd been staying.

"The *Herald's* wing?" He struggled to keep his voice level.

She blinked. "Everyone knows Lyle's my brother."

:I, uh, forgot to mention that's where she was staying, didn't I?: Vehs managed to sound sheepish.

:You're worse than me at being sneaky,: Wil thought.

"Why didn't you come and *get* me?" he asked her.

"Very wary after near-death experience. Long walk. No magic horse."

"Lelia!"

"'Sokay. Not hurt." Her eyes drifted shut. "Need sleep. Just a candlemark. Here okay?" Her eyes opened again, pleading.

He pointed to the bed. "Go."

She patted his cheek. "Good Herald."

The Bard curled up on his bed, dragging the covers over her. Snores drifted up from her a moment later.

Wil picked up the club. His gut twisted.

"Hellfires," he muttered.

*   *   *

Wil scanned the crowd, feeling a rising level of annoyance and frustration as he watched the countess dance gaily to Lelia's composition. Not a sign of pain or a limp.

The room was packed, stifling with heat despite it being (nearly) the middle of winter. The only reason Wil spotted the countess was that she'd dressed like a peacock that had been doused in rainbow-hued pitch and set ablaze, a gesture he took to be overcompensation for Lelia stealing her glory.

Lelia gestured him over and whispered, "Time now."

He nodded. "I'll get you that right away, ma'am," he said as he straightened, turned, and strode off.

"Ladies and gentlelords!" Lelia's voice boomed over the crowd, rolling out like a banner. "Who wants to hear a story about Valdemar's greatest king?"

Wil breathed more freely when he got into the corridor and away from the crush of people and the roaring cheers. Servants jostled past, babbling about whats-hername and the Sendar-song. Someday, he realized, he would need to ask her to play it for him.

The wide corridor beyond the great hall and kitchens echoed, utterly deserted. He tried to be quiet, but the farther he went, the more urgently his Gift nudged him, twisting his gut into harder and tighter knots. The need to *get there* overwhelmed the lesser need to be silent.

He turned a corner. His destination—possibly his *destiny*—came into view. A terrible notion slid over him—what if the door was locked?

Then I will break it down, he thought grimly.

He touched the doorknob. It turned with a *click*, opening on a room lit by a single lantern. A wan, familiar face floated in the inky darkness. Something metal gleamed.

Wil's insides gave one final, painful, all-too-familiar lurch—

Not now!

Knife. Blood. Silver settings, empty of gems. Crossbow. Wait—crosswhat?

As Wil staggered under the weight of Foresight, he heard the *snick* of a quarrel being fired.

The enraptured audience stood motionless before Lelia as she stretched her Gift, her attention utterly focused on the count, the countess, and her entourage of—

Where's Einan? Lelia thought.

Her fingers continued strumming even as her thoughts turned frantic.

Where is he?

Einan fired the crossbow cradled in his arms just as Wil's vision drove him to his knees. The bolt slammed into the wood paneling behind him, raining splinters into his hair.

Wil drew his long-knife. Einan swore and struggled to rise from the settee he'd been reclining on. Wil tackled him to the floor and, on a wild guess, punched him in the ribs.

The bones yielded easily. Einan screamed.

Handy Gift, Foresight.

"Heyla," Wil said, at a loss for words. "That wasn't very nice."

Einan's lips pulled back, showing his teeth. "You—displease—*her*." He coughed, then drew himself up, and spat at Wil.

Wil flinched and jerked back for just a second—all the time the steward needed. A dirk appeared in his hand from a holster on his wrist.

"Chantil!" he shrieked, and rammed it into his own throat.

Blood painted the walls and Wil. Einan expired, gurgling his lady's name.

*   *   *

"His *neck?*" Lelia said, toying with a silvery pendant dangling about her own throat.

Wil nodded from the edge of his bed—the real one, in *his* room in the Heraldic wing.

"Einan was Chantil's childhood friend. Low-class family. Couldn't marry her, so became her steward." Wil rubbed his eyes. He'd been debriefing for candlemarks since last night. Sleep had not been possible. "We found journals and . . . madness doesn't begin to cover half of it. Pages about how much he adored Chantil, how perfect she was, how the people who served her didn't deserve her. Including her husbands." He pointed at her. "You, too."

Lelia grimaced.

"He followed you home every night. Palace Guards keep records of visitors, but since he was the Tindale steward, no one questioned him being there. Einan was convinced you were a Herald in disguise."

She gaped. "What?"

"The irony is really not lost on us."

"What?"

"You were staying in the Heraldic wing."

"But—*everyone* knows—"

"Not everyone, it seems."

"Oh."

Wil rubbed his face. "Found the jewelry under the floorboards of Einan's bedroom. Empty settings. Chantil was flabbergasted."

"Would have loved to see that."

"Heh."

"In retrospect, she's not that bad a person." Lelia shrugged. "Still a snob, but—not a murderer."

Wil nodded. "Sometimes, people aren't what they appear to be."

:Oh?: Vehs said dryly. *:What philosopher's memoir did you dredge* that *from?:*

:*Hush, you.*:

Wil yawned, his eyes drooping. "Tired. Sorry."

"Don't apologize for doing your job." She stood. "So, what next?"

" 'Nother Circuit, probably. Work's never done."

She smiled. "Valdemar first."

"Yeah."

She bent forward and kissed his forehead. "I spoke to Valdemar. She said to sleep. It's her Midwinter gift to you."

He cracked a smile. "Thanks."

"No problem. Goodbye."

"Good night," he yawned back.

Before he dropped off, Wil thought it nice when she kissed him.

Lelia sang a word, the sound echoing across Companion's Field.

A white form broke off from the herd and trotted toward where she waited at the fence, an apple in her outstretched hand.

"Midwinter gift for you," she said as Vehs delicately nipped the fruit from her palm. The Companion chewed, then bent and touched his nose to the pack at her feet.

"The stories call," she said. "Evendim, if it matters. Rumors of half-hawk men there." She stood up on tiptoe and kissed his cheek. "Keep him safe."

Vehs shook his mane and stamped his hoof. A gesture of frustration? It didn't matter anyway, even if it was. She had songs to sing.

The Companion watched her as she walked through the frosty grass toward the gates, whistling as she went.

Wil hummed to himself on his way to Lyle's quarters. He lifted his fist to knock—

:*She left,*: Vehs interrupted.

Wil froze. *:What?:*

Vehs told him.

:This time of year?: Wil thought.

:Madness, I know.:

:Wait—you and the Bard—talk?:

:Of course not. She talked to me. And I'm the one who suggested her, remember?: Vehs's mental voice danced with amusement. *:Jealous?:*

Wil thought that a very stupid question, and expressed as much.

:In other news,: Vehs said when he was done, *:Kyril wants to meet about your next Circuit.:*

:Where?: Evendim, perhaps?

:Sorrows. The barbarians. . . . : Softly, Vehs added, *:I'm sorry.:*

Wil shook himself. *:Eh? What for?:* He shrugged. *:I go where the Crown wills.:*

Wil walked in silence down the stairs, rubbing his forehead lightly as he went.

Wounded Bird
By Michael Z. Williamson

Michael Z. Williamson was born in the UK and raised in
Canada and the US. A twenty-four-year veteran of the
US Army and US Air Force combat engineers, he is
married to a reserve Army combat photographer who
is a civilian graphic artist. They have too many cats and
two children who have learned how to fight anything,
including zombies, from the age of four.

Women only wore dresses in Mirr. Riga had compro-
mised with a knee-length tunic of wine silk with crim-
son and silver embroidery and beading over her trews.
It stuck out in vivid contrast to the somber blacks and
whites of the natives. She acceded somewhat to their law
and wore a kerchief over her flaxen hair, but her warrior's braid hung below, rather than loose under a long
headdress like the locals.

Not that it mattered to anyone but her. Father and
Erki knew her, and the locals would never regard her
as anything other than a girl. She saw how the locals
treated women: as servants.

Jesrin, for example, serving her minted tea, was lean
and healthy looking and seemed rather bright. She'd
never develop as anything here, though. She was un-
numbered and unlettered and probably not much of a

cook, just a serving girl. Riga would have liked to talk to her at least, but she'd have to go to the kitchen to do so. Women didn't talk in front of men. Even if Riga might, Jesrin certainly wouldn't. Riga thought about the kitchen, but that was a concession she didn't want to make. She was not a servant. She was a trader and a warrior.

Jesrin moved on with more tea for the Amar, the local trading lord. She hesitated around his gesticulating arms, then moved to pour. He changed his motion just in time to catch the spout of the samovar and deliver a big splash of liquid to the lush woolen rug the men sat on.

"Clumsy wench!"

Riga twitched as Amar Rabas backhanded Jesrin. The blow was hard enough to stagger her, but she flailed through contortions to avoid dropping the silver tea set. Riga could only imagine the penalty if the girl did that.

A moment later she wasn't sure she could imagine. The slight girl shrieked as her ankle twisted, but she laid the tray down carefully on the marble flagstones behind her. Not a drop spilled.

However, Rabas drew a heavy cord from somewhere and laid into her, the knotted end thunking heavily right through her thick clothes. The girl writhed and twitched, but she let out only whimpers. Presumably crying was punishable, too.

Father gave Riga a warning glance, and she nodded once, her face blank, while inside she burned with rage. It was not their business to interfere, though he obviously didn't like it either. Riga's brother Erki fought to keep his own temper. He was three years younger, though, only fourteen. What a lesson on foreign cultures for him.

It was worse for her because Riga was a trained warrior. Had the Amar swung at her like that, she'd have broken his arm and then sliced his throat. And, of course, been beaten to death or hanged for her trouble. It just drove home that fighting was not always the answer.

It also drove home that she despised this southern city and its culture. In the week they'd been here, the Amar had escalated his hospitality, gifts, and praise every day. He'd also escalated his brutality and rudeness to his servants and his own hires.

She knew she had to calm down, so she looked around their setting again. The walls were faced in gleaming marble. Wrought iron and bronze rails, hooks, and mountings adorned the stairs and walls. The doors, posts, and lintels were carved elaborately, some of them with scenes that made her blush. Apparently, denied other outlets for their energy, it went into suggestive figures.

While the small fleet of five ships—both of theirs and three others belonging to distant cousins—were being packed with valuable spices, silk, and teas, Riga really wasn't sure it was morally worth it. Mirr was pretty. Mirr was also a filthy dump as far as attitudes, decency, and anything beyond decadently carved stone and flowers went.

"Amar Rabas," Father interrupted diplomatically. When the man looked up from his flogging, he continued, "We are grateful for your hospitality. It is time to retire to our inn for the day. I hope to see you again tomorrow, as we prepare to leave."

The Amar rose, and the girl crawled to her knees and bowed low. He glanced at her, snapped, "Get to the kitchen," then turned back to his guests. "Of course, Gunde. May I host you for dinner tomorrow? A feast in farewell before you eat ship rations?"

"My son and I would be honored," Father said. Of course, Riga was only a daughter and was not mentioned here, any more than a dog would be.

They bowed all around and departed, as the girl scurried limping away, taking the tray and towel with her.

Once outside and out of earshot, Riga muttered, "I think I'd prefer ship biscuits and salted meat to hospitality such as his."

"They are not a nice people," Father agreed. "But we need the trading stop. If we could transport only across the lake back home and stay solvent, I'd do that. We need proper trading voyages now and then, though. It's also good learning for you two."

"We need to learn that some people are pure evil?" Erki asked.

"The Amar is brutal even by our warrior standards," Father said, "but he is not evil. At least their trade is honest, and tariffs fair. They've held off Miklamar's encroachments so far. If you want evil, you remember the refugees fleeing that murderous thug."

"I do," Erki said as he rubbed his stubby thumb. So did Riga. She vividly remembered him losing half that thumb when the two youths had had to be warriors and guides for those refugees.

"Tonight is our last night in the inn," Father said. "We'll remain aboard ship, under tent, until we leave."

"Oh, good," Riga said. "I prefer our tent to their opulence. It's friendlier." Nothing about this city was friendly except the other traders and embassies. Of course, they weren't of this city. Riga wore heavy clothes despite the mild weather but no sword. Erki and Father carried swords. They were her protectors. Her status: none. At home she wore her cat-jeweled sword, and no one would be silly enough to ask if she knew its use.

The feast was not a happy event. It could have been, but . . .

Riga had no complaints about the food. She didn't like being behind a curtain at a second, remote table set up for women, where she ate with the wives and servants. She didn't like getting what were basically the leavings from the men. The entertainment would be better if she could actually see it, rather than just hear hints of it past the curtain. The food was wonderful, though, redolent with spices and rich and savory. The manner took getting used to. One formed rice into balls, or tore pieces of bread, and just reached in to scoop up the saucy mess.

Even at the women's table, there was a hierarchy. The senior wife sat at the far end. Her two junior wives flanked her, and the wives and concubine of two other guests sat down from there. Riga guessed her position at a table end was of some status, and two daughters flanked her. Between were the servants.

A warm, sweet smell seemed to indicate dessert, or at least a dessert. There'd been two so far. Jesrin served the men, then came through to serve the women.

As she leaned past Riga to put down a platter of pastry, her layered gown slipped, revealing some shoulder.

Riga almost recoiled in horror at what she glimpsed. That delicate shoulder was a mass of blood blisters, bruises and welts. Their color indicated they were healing, but he'd laid into this girl horribly.

Steeling herself, she said nothing, made no acknowledgement—servants weren't people here—and ate quietly. The food was good. It would have been twice as good if she'd been granted the courtesy of eating with the men. She reminded herself that her own people regarded her as a warrior. No insults here could change that.

Of course, Father had asked that she diplomatically not discuss any of her "manly" skills. While she knew weaving and a little of spinning, she knew much more of boatkeeping and lading, numbers, letters, horse care, and maneuver. The women chatted amiably about textiles and art, and Riga just nodded and smiled.

Jesrin slipped back through a few minutes later, came over, and discreetly handed Riga a slip of parchment, which Riga just as discreetly opened in her lap and read.

"We are staying here tonight. Your room will be across the hall from mine—GundeFather."

If there was one thing Riga didn't want to do, it was stay here, beneath her status. She momentarily raged inside.

It wasn't just being treated as an inferior. It was that it didn't matter what her status was, didn't matter her skills. She could run the business herself if need be. She lacked Father's decades, but she had a grounding in all the basics and plenty of her own travels and deals and war. But here, just being born female meant that she was beneath a horse, even beneath a dog, and wouldn't even be treated with contempt. She just wouldn't be treated at all. The offered hospitality was for Father and Erki, not her. Her room was a mere courtesy to Father, otherwise they'd stick her in a hole with the servants, she was sure.

After that, she withdrew completely from the conversation and just steamed silently, until Jesrin led her up the marble stairs, long after the men had retreated, to a frilly, dainty, girly room. It was very lavish, of course. See how well the Amar treats even a daughter of a trader?

"If you need," Jesrin said, "That cord will ring a bell below. I'll hurry right up."

"You won't sleep yourself?" Riga asked.

Jesrin seemed confused by Riga's accent, or perhaps the question itself.

"Of course, I'll wake up. It's my duty to serve. If I'm not available, then Aysa will come."

"Thank you, though I'll be fine. You've been so gracious."

Jesrin replied with a demure bow. "Thank you, all I do is on behalf of my lord."

Riga couldn't wait, so asked, "Jesrin, would you like

me to look at your shoulder? I may have a salve that will help."

"Oh, Miss Riga, you are gracious, no. The house-mistress is taking care of it. I will be fine." The poor girl seemed embarrassed and ashamed just to discuss it.

Girl. Jesrin was easily a year older than Riga's seventeen. Yet Riga was a woman among her people, able to run her household, sign contracts, travel freely or as mistress of a mission. Jesrin seemed younger, frailer, helpless. She could manage any number of chores, but she had no voice, was illiterate, a glorified pet. Riga could give orders to laborers and warriors. Jesrin wouldn't know how even if she could.

With nothing else to offer, Riga said, "Then I shall retire. I hope to see you in the morning, and please rest. You've made me most comfortable, thank you."

"A blessing on you." Jesrin bowed and withdrew with what looked like a happy smile. It made Riga shudder.

The next morning, Riga awoke to sun peeking through chiseled piercework in the shutters. The weather was wonderfully mild. The bed was silken over feathers, with a very fine cotton sheet.

Riga would gladly give it all up to keep her status.

A breakfast of fruit and pastry sat on a tray near the door. She snagged a couple of fat strawberries and a roll, partly to quiet her stomach and partly to be polite to Jesrin and the other servants. She didn't care what the Amar thought and was pretty sure he wouldn't even ask how she'd fared. She rebraided her hair, threw a scarf over it to appease local customs, and opened the door.

No one was around, so she crept across and tapped on what she hoped was Father's door. She could hear his voice, and Erki's, and that brightened her mood a lot.

He swung the door open and said, "Welcome, Daughter! I'm sure you're dreading returning to the *Sea Fox*."

"Oh, yes, very much, Father." *Please get me out of here now*, her mind and face said.

Once downstairs, she stood back while Father, Erki, and the Amar exchanged bows. She wasn't expected to participate, for which she was glad.

A few minutes later they were striding down the broad, dusty street toward the port.

Erki said, "I'll be glad to eat normal food. I got sick of the rich, fancy stuff very quickly."

"I enjoyed the food. Not the company. I wish I could have. Jesrin seems like a nice girl," she said.

"She does. He sent her to my room an hour after bed last night," Father admitted.

"Oh, Father, you *didn't!*" she exclaimed.

"Of course I didn't," he replied with a grimace and shiver. "Gods, she's barely older than you, girl. Ugh." He cringed again. "I bade her sit and talk for a while, gave her some medicine for the pain and some herbs to help heal. They don't do that here, either. Herbs are the work of the devils. She wasn't easy to convince, but I promised her I'd never mention it. Then I made her sleep on the divan. She seemed both grateful and put upon."

Riga wasn't sure she parsed that, but no matter. "Thank you," she replied.

"For what? Not bedding a child? I need no thanks for that." He sounded annoyed.

"I wish we could help her. Buy her, perhaps?"

Father leaned up and back and met her eyes.

"I know you mean well, but no. Her looks make her highly prized."

"You could ask," she said. "I have my share to pledge against the cost."

He sighed and looked uncomfortable.

"Riga, His Beneficent Excellency was struck by your stature and eyes. He offered me a sack of saffron and your weight in gold for your hand for his son."

Riga choked and stared wide-eyed. Great gods. That was more than both their ships were worth. They might do that gross business in five years.

Feeling nervous ripples, she asked, "And you told him ... ?"

"I said you were to be betrothed to a wealthy merchant in our lands, but his offer was most generous and thoughtful. I thanked him for the compliment he paid me as a father and merchant."

Seeing her sunken expression, he added, "Riga, she's got good food, a warm bed and shelter. Her lot as a free peasant would be no better in this desert. It would be worse. You can't save everyone. Remember the birds? And the rabbit?"

Yes, she'd tried to save injured animals when younger.

"You stewed them," she said accusingly.

"I only stewed them after you tried to save them and they died. They were meant for the pot anyway."

"I didn't appreciate it at the time," she said.

Erki said, "If a Kossaki treated a woman like that, he'd be driven from town in disgrace. It's a strange place. You should have been treated better, Riga. I'm sorry."

"It keeps me humble," she said, trying for self-deprecating humor. Few places gave women the status the Kossaki had. This place, though ...

"Well, tonight we sleep in linen and wool and fur," Father said. "We have dried goat and fish, berries and nuts. I'll see about a stew."

Erki said, "Let me, Father? I'll be glad to make us some real food." He leaned over and added, "And I promise not to cook any stray pets you find, Riga."

She stuck her tongue out. "You cook. I have to help tally the goods, the tariffs and the port fees. Then Father can sign it and pretend I'm just a dumb girl."

"I'll pretend nothing," he said. "They can assume whatever they wish."

Under the sail tent, Riga couldn't sleep. The contrast between the beauty and the evil just seemed to make the evil that much more horrifying.

The girl had been beaten for the slightest of errors, because it "embarrassed" her owner. Then she'd been sent to whore for a guest, while still full of welts and crippling bruises. That was considered redemption here . . . for the Amar.

That thought decided it for her. Riga rolled her quilt off carefully, slipped to the deck, and felt for her boots.

In minutes, she was dressed for her mission, and in a way no woman should dare dress in this city. That made it both joyous and sobering. She could wind up dead for what she planned, even if she didn't succeed.

Erki was still and undisturbed, and she figured to leave him there. He was handsome even asleep, and she smiled. Then she realized there was one thing she needed him for, if nothing else.

She touched him on the shoulder, and his eyes snapped open.

She held a finger to her lips in a shhh! and beckoned him to join her.

He slipped his feet out and fumbled for clothes and gear. He was always twitchy and energetic, but at least he was silent about it.

He seemed excited, probably because he knew she was up to something. Would he be agreeable when he found out what, though? He matched her choice of dull fighting clothes. When she pointed, he grabbed his sword without hesitation.

A few minutes later, they shimmied over the gunwale and onto the beach. None of the crew were awake or had noticed. Some of them were still in rooms in town, in fact, and would only return in time to push off, she hoped. If they were late . . .

Erki whispered, "What are we doing?"

"We're going to rescue that servant girl, Jesrin."

"You haven't discussed this with Father, have you?" he asked at once.

Damn the boy.

"No," she admitted. "This is my plan."

"He'll thrash us both," Erki said. "How will that help her?"

"He'll thrash us because we deserve it," she said. "That girl got far more than that."

"I didn't say I wouldn't help you," he said. "But how do we keep her from being found?"

With that first part agreed, she started creeping across the beach. "She only has to keep out of sight in our ship. The fleet leaves in the morning. With luck, they won't even start looking this way by then."

"If they do, Father might just give us to them. We'll be endangering everyone."

"Really. I thought we were warriors and nations quivered at our mention," she said with contemptuous sarcasm.

"Not as much as they did long past," Erki said. "Look, I'm still with you."

"Good, then stop trying to argue me out of it," she said, because he was right. What she proposed was dangerous, foolish, and could start a war.

She also knew it was the right thing to do.

"I swore my Warrior's Oath to protect the weak," she said. "And I didn't swear that it stopped at the edge of our lands."

The beach was convenient. The docks proper had activity at all hours, but just a few dozen yards away, few people were about. Only small fishing vessels and the shallow-draft Kossaki trade and warships used the beach. Even when trading, the Kossaki ported like raiders, ready to dart away in moments.

The two youths flitted through from shadow to shadow. Their boots were soft-soled leather. Their dull clothes disappeared into the night. Riga had no sword, but she did have her *seachs* knife.

She planned to not need it. That would mean their mission had failed. It was the principle, though. Besides, if she did get caught, she wanted them to know she was a warrior.

It also helped her cope with the knowledge that if discovered, she would at the least be publicly beaten with canes and heavily fined. Or rather, Father would be fined. At worst . . .

In far less time than she remembered, they were at the outer wall of the Amar's residence. The building ran around three sides of a courtyard.

"I know her room is on the left . . ." Riga said.

"Second window from the far end, down that alley."

She cocked an eyebrow.

"How do you know?"

Erki blushed even in the dark, stuttered, and then said, "She's very pretty. I watched her go there."

She had to smile.

"That's fine. Good lad." She left it at that. "Lead the way."

"Right there," he pointed.

She really hoped he was right. She also hoped that Jesrin was there. If the Amar had her in his bed . . . or even if she was just doing scullery work . . . of course, either would let them return, knowing they'd tried.

Or, more likely, cause me to escalate until we do have a war, Riga thought. She had no illusions about her diplomacy or temper.

The shutter opened to the fourth pea-sized pebble.

Once Jesrin understood their gestures, her eyes grew

a foot wide, and she shook her head in horror. They gestured again, come down, come with us. Riga even held up the spare cloak for emphasis.

It took long minutes, while occasional flickers of lamplight in other windows indicated early risers, up to bake breakfast or reach the tide, before the girl nodded assent.

Erki tossed up a coil of thin, strong silk rope, and it took more minutes to explain she should loop it around the center post of the window and run it back down.

Riga was worried if Jesrin was strong enough to slide down a rope rather than fall, but she managed well enough, though clearly stiff from some beating or other. She bumped the wall and scuffed loose some plaster, which made Riga cringe. Perhaps she was being too cautious. There was no indication anyone else had noticed. She was thankful they didn't like dogs here. Dogs would have heard and smelled them long before.

The seconds were hours long as Jesrin slipped down the slender rope. Her layered dress was not practical and would be abraded to shreds before she reached the ground.

Then she slipped and fell. Erki and Riga both rushed forward and caught her, and she convulsed in agony at their hands on her beaten back. The fall had scraped her knuckles and forehead, and she leaned over in the dust and vomited, twitched, lay still for a moment, then twitched again as she woke up. Through it all, she barely uttered a sound.

Erki snatched the rope down as Riga gingerly helped her to her feet. With the shutters ajar and the rope recovered, there was no obvious sign of departure. But it was early, and Father would awaken soon himself. They had to move.

The girl meekly donned the offered hood and tied the cloak around her neck, wincing as even that weight touched her abused flesh. She'd pass as Kossaki from a distance, but her underdress was clearly servant class, and her poise was as submissive as Riga's was challenging. Still, that shouldn't matter.

"This way," Riga said, and led the way. A moment later, Erki grabbed her shoulder and stepped in front.

Oh. Right. Male must lead. She flushed in anger, embarrassment, and frustration. Still, that's why she'd asked him along, and he was doing his part well, the stout boy.

They were five streets away when a watchman came around the corner, right into their faces.

"Who are you?" he asked. Riga could puzzle out the words, but she couldn't speak. Had Erki paid attention to their lessons?

And then she knew why she loved her brother, annoying as he could be. He stepped forward, as he did for any problem, and showed no reluctance.

"Harad of the Kossaki," he lied, "and my sisters. I return to my uncle's ship."

"It is very late." The man spoke simply for them, but his tone made it clear he wanted an explanation.

"My sister took sick and had to stay with friends. We are lucky your gods saw fit to make her healthy in time."

It was very rude to look at a woman's face here, but this man was an official. He looked as if he was considering doing so, and he stared at their feet.

She's wearing sandals, not boots, Riga realized. Explain them as locally supplied? But she couldn't talk, and would Erki grasp it?

Under her cloak, she gripped the hilt of her *seachs*. In about five heartbeats, he was going to find out why she was called "Sworddancer," even if all she had was a knife.

He looked at Erki again, said, "A blessing on you," and turned away.

Riga exhaled. Jesrin whimpered. Erki didn't twitch at all, and he led the way forward.

It was definitely near dawn, and gray, as they reached the beach.

Jesrin spoke at last. "We go on your ship?"

"Yes, quickly," Riga said, gripped her elbow carefully—it might be bruised—and hurried her along.

Some crew were about, securing the ships for sea. The tents would be down soon, then hoisted back up as sails. Luckily, no one paid much attention to three youths.

Erki bounded catlike over the gunwale and pulled at Jesrin's hands as Riga shoved at her hips. The girl winced. Beaten there, too. But it took practice or help to board the outward curve of a *kanr*.

In the dim twilight, Father was visible at the stern, checking the steering oar and ballast. Before he turned, Riga shoved Jesrin down behind a pair of barrels.

"Erki," she said, and stood as he threw a heavy, smelly tarp atop the girl.

He stood and whispered, "Don't move at all until I say so."

Father came back, moving easily around netted crates and barrels. He didn't look or act his age, and the ship was his domain.

"Where have you been?" he demanded crossly.

"I took a last look at the tiled market to the south," she said. "It's so pretty." She tried hard to make that sound honest. It was something she might have done ... four years before. Would Father catch that?

"You'll have cleaning duty until I say otherwise. Both of you," he replied. He looked relieved and annoyed but not angry.

"Sorry, Father," she said.

"Yes, Father," Erki agreed.

"Stow the ropes, help with the sail bindings, and get

ready to depart. We have a good wind to speed us north by west."

"At once," she agreed. Good. Shortly they'd be away from this beautiful hell.

The incoming tide made the ship sway and bob, and the wind and the poles inched them down the sand. All at once they shifted, dragged, shifted again, and *Sea Fox* was back in her realm. The crew jumped to the oars and sculled for deeper water. They were free peasants, hired and paid, and Riga would bet them against any slave rowers. As free men they'd also fight for their master and their pay. Yet another reason the Kossaki traded unmolested.

The ships were just forming up in line to head out to sea, when a bright yellow harbor boat headed for them, with a toot of a brass horn. They all stopped their departure, keeping station in the lapping waves to avoid beaching again.

The boat drew alongside, and some official or other in gleaming white silk accepted a hand aboard. Behind him was the watchman from the night before, and Riga's nerves rippled cold.

"May I help you?" Father asked. "I believe our tariffs are in order." He held out a leather book with a stamped sheet from the revenue agent. He'd paid the tariff Riga had calculated and tossed in ten percent as "a gift for the temple," which meant for the agent's pocket. All should be in order. Though Riga knew that was not the issue in question.

"My apologies for disturbing you," the man said with mock politeness. "The Amar sends his regards and his sadness at losing a fine servant girl."

"We brought no servant girl," Father said. "The only woman on my ships is my daughter. Grom has his wife and girl child aboard his ship. Ranuldr has his wife and two daughters."

Erki stood alongside Riga. They'd had the same lesson, that to stand firm was better than to cower. Here they were side by side, and would the guard know, or mention it if he did?

Erki had changed clothes, so he would not be apparent at once. Would the man recognize Riga, though? But no local man should look at a woman. He'd seen her earlier, but had he "seen" her? She was also in shipboard trews and tunic now, leaning on a rigging hook as if it were a spear. She stared back at him, trying to look quizzical and faintly bored. He studied her, but it was all pretense. He really hadn't noticed the women. There'd been no real reason to at the time, and he wouldn't admit so now. Riga didn't blame him, knowing how the Amar might respond.

He looked hard at Erki, but without the cloak and in light, the boy looked more a man. He also didn't show any expression at all, though she could sense the nervous shivers.

"She was with a young boy last night. What about your boys?"

"Only Erki here," Father said. "He was on watch last night. I expect your own shore patrol will remember him. There are a number of other young men, though it depends on what you mean by 'boy.'"

Was Father lying as a matter of course, to get this over with? Or did he know and was covering for them? His words were unbothered.

The watchman looked Erki over but didn't finger him. Good so far.

The official asked, "Which girl was sick and stayed in town?"

"Not mine," Father said. "I suppose it could have

been Ranuld's eldest girl. She's fifteen. All ours are accounted for, though, we're not missing any."

Of course they weren't missing any. Father was deliberately misunderstanding. *My people are in order. Do you believe your own are not?*

"All your women are as they should be?" They looked uncomfortable. The Kossaki ships had canvas weather shields at the rear, and little privacy. It was understood that one didn't stare or annoy a woman even bathing or changing, but that was certainly not understood here. The very subject made them cringe and shy away. Inside, Riga grinned. They were going to back off, right now.

"There are few enough that I can count to six," Father said with a grin. Riga twitched. Would he insist on seeing them all?

"I will inspect your cargo and your manifest then, as a courtesy."

Riga grimaced as Father said, "If you wish." Everyone knew something was up at this point. They were all just pretending it wasn't.

He started at the bow, peering through the nets and checking the crates for stamps and seals. All were as they should be, and of course he knew that. He moved slowly back to a pile of barrels staked down, containing figs, tea, and spices. Past the mast and the bundles of sail lashed to the spar.

Father said, "I don't wish to rush you, but we have five ships and tide to keep. We've always dealt in good faith."

"I'll just work my way back and be done, then," the official said, with a false frown.

"Be quick about it. I feel sorry for the Amar, but I have my own dramas, and I don't share mine with the help."

Was Father trying to cause the man to search in detail? That comment flustered him, and he checked a barrel's number very carefully.

"You might want to check under that tarp. It's a prime place to stash an escaped servant girl. I don't find my own daughter enough trouble, so I try to pick one up in every port."

Clutching his tally board, the man strode forward again in a careful, dignified fashion, swung over into his boat, and indicated to the rowers to leave.

He turned back, looked at Father and said, "Thank you for your help."

"You are most welcome. I hope the Amar finds this girl and that she hasn't fallen among those who would shame her or him. I cherish his hospitality and trade."

"I will tell him," the official said, beckoning the guard to join him as he sat down on a thwart. "Good travels to you, and a blessing."

"A blessing on you, and the Amar, and your king," Father said.

As they rowed away, he turned and ordered, "Pick up the speed. We're not earning money to row like a holiday ship." He seemed quite relaxed and good natured.

Riga wanted to run back and check under the tarp. She knew Jesrin was alive, though, and silence was a good thing. It might be night before she could come out. It might even be five days and port before she admitted the girl's presence. She had silly notions of sneaking her ashore with a few coins somewhere she could find good work, though she knew the girl, like any injured creature, would need support for a bit.

She stood her post, and helped tighten the sail as they gained room to maneuver, and the five ships spread into a longer line for travel.

They cleared the headland and entered open ocean, the deeper swells swaying *Sea Fox*, twisting and torquing her. She was designed for that, though, and surged across the waves.

Father came past, checking the rigging. "How's the servant girl?" he asked quite casually.

Riga knew better than to lie. "Alive and quiet," she said at once.

"This is the same servant girl we discussed, I assume."

"Yes, she is. Jesrin. Badly bruised in body and spirit."

"Damn it, Daughter, this is worse than an injured goose. You can't save every helpless creature in the world! Especially at a risk of war."

"Of course not," she said.

Then she smiled at him, a challenging smile that would yield a flogging in Mirr, and perhaps start a duel in Kossaki lands. It was the smile of a merchant and warrior among her peers.

"But I can save this one."

Defending the Heart
By Kate Paulk

Kate Paulk pretends to be a mild mannered software quality analyst by day and allows her true evil author nature through for the short time between finishing with the day job and falling over. She lives in semirural Pennsylvania with her husband, two bossy cats, and her imagination. The last is the hardest to live with. Her latest short story sale, "Night Shifted," is in DAW's anthology, *Better Off Undead*.

"What are you doing to That Damn Kitten?" Jem asked from under the tree, his voice laced with laughter.

Ree lay stretched out on a tree branch almost too small to support his weight. With his toe claws dug in, he stretched his hand as far as he could toward a kitten maybe ten weeks old who, in the way of his kind, kept just out of reach and fluffed its white and gray fur into a big dandelion puff while emitting ceaseless, plangent meows.

Because Ree was a hobgoblin, changed in the magic storms into something with cat claws, cat eyes, and the brown fur and tail of a rat, he heard the kitten's cries in a range humans couldn't hear. Besides, the kitten's mother, That Other Damn Cat, had been adding her own increased-range pleas to Ree to save her baby.

Damn kitten. Ree stretched his hand to the cower-
ing furball, who, of course, retreated farther out of the
way. There was only so far Ree could stretch and he'd be
cursed if he was going any further on the frail end of the
branch. He tried to make the peculiar chirping sound
That Other Damn Cat used to call her kittens.

Beneath the tree, Jem laughed. He'd grown a lot over
the last year—was now the height of a man and had
blond fuzz on his upper lip. His voice was changing, too,
to adult man ranges. Just thinking about it made Ree's
heart turn in him.

He'd been just a hobgoblin, like other hobgoblins.
Sometimes he'd been more animal than human. He
thought if he'd not found Jem, if Jem hadn't been so
convinced Ree was human, in time Ree might have forgotten he was human, himself. He might have become
one of the wild hobgoblins—a beast and nothing more.

But he'd saved Jem's life, and Jem . . . Ree liked
to think it was love, or some form of it, and that they
would be together their whole lives. But they'd met really young. Though neither was that sure of his age—
not exactly—they'd been thirteen or fourteen. That had
been two summers ago, and now Jem was changing.

Ree knew, from when he'd been a human among
humans, that when young men changed, a lot of things
changed about them. Not just their appearance and their
voices, but their manner, their ways, and sometimes their
hearts too. As for Ree . . . who knew what happened to
hobgoblins? He didn't think he would change much.

Looking away from Jem, he turned back to concentrate on the kitten in a storm of flustered mother-cat-
like meowing. Or at least he hoped it was mother-cat
like. *I'm probably telling the poor thing I want to eat it,*
he thought.

Jem's laughter wasn't helping. Oh, Ree imagined he
looked very funny, but all the same, if one of the green

apples festooning the tree had been within range, he'd have flung it at Jem's head.

Even so, the kitten didn't seem put off by the laughter. It looked at Ree with big, rounded eyes, as Ree continued what he hoped were his reassurances of fish and milk for the kitten back at home. For a while it looked as though it would back up yet further, then suddenly it seemed to make up its mind and charged forward, needle-like claws extended. It ran lightning-fast along the branch and leaped atop Ree, bracing itself with claws in the space between Ree's neck and his shoulders.

Ree's involuntary shriek only caused the claws to dig in further, and Jem said, now sounding concerned, "Come on down. That branch is too thin for you."

"I'm coming, I'm coming," Ree said, shuffling back uncertainly. What did Jem think, exactly? That he wanted to set up a treehouse up here?

Just at that moment there was a crack like thunder, and the branch moved beneath him. On the ground, Jem jumped out of the way and yelled, "Ree, be careful."

But it was too late for Ree to do anything short of growing wings, and that he'd missed when the changes had come.

The branch didn't break, it just peeled off the tree, Ree and all. His world tilted down, and then he was holding onto the branch and there were other branches flying past him as he fell. He tried to grab onto the passing branches with hands and feet, all the while trying to secure the kitten with yet another hand.

Even as That Damn Kitten dug its claws hard into the securing hand, it occurred to Ree that it might have been a good idea to have been caught near an octopus when the changes came. Failing wings, he could have used another complement of limbs.

He landed on the ground, still atop the branch. The force of impact jarred his brain and made him dizzy. Jem was there, trying to help him up. Jem was taller than Ree by a full head now, but the look in his eyes was the same as it had been two years ago, when he'd decided to cast his lot in with Ree and that they'd stay together come what may. "Are you all right?"

Jem's gaze was balm to Ree's heart. He brought the screaming kitten down off his shoulders and put up a hand to prevent Jem reaching for it. "Don't touch it. That Damn Kitten is full of needles." He put it carefully on the ground, where it ran to rub on That Other Damn Cat, who hovered nearby and who gave Ree a reproachful glance.

Ree sucked on the claw wounds on his fingers. "Gee, I rescue her baby and she glares at me. You'd think she'd treat me like a hero."

Jem sidled close, smiling but only half joking. "I think you're a hero. Isn't that enough for you?"

"Well . . . it just might be, if only—" He stopped. He stopped because having raised his head, he'd caught sight of something against the sky. But it was a good thing he stopped, because what could he tell Jem? *If only I weren't sure you'd grow past and away from me and forget all that lay between us?*

"What is it?" Ree never could hide anything from Jem: the younger boy caught his expressions before anyone else would.

Ree pointed. "See smoke, up there? It's not cooking fires. It's darker, and it doesn't look right. I think it's a house burning. And look, there's another one farther off. That means soldiers." His chest and stomach tightened. Soldiers meant trouble. He didn't know if it was the Empire coming back to make sure everyone paid their taxes and to take away the boys who were old enough to be in the army, or if it was one of the bandit lords they'd heard about.

It didn't matter. Either would kill him, just as they'd

kill the wild hobgoblins that haunted the forest. That was the law, and maybe it was right. After all, who knew what would happen to Ree when Jem grew up and moved into the world of men and left Ree behind, alone with the beasts?

If there were soldiers coming, Garrad had to know. He was the farmer here—an irritable old man whose temper protected a heart big enough to take in a city waif and a hobgoblin when Ree and Jem had arrived two winters ago.

If they hadn't found Garrad just in time and if he hadn't been willing to shelter them on his farm, Jem would have died of a horrible persistent cough he'd caught after they'd left Jacona. To be sure, Garrad would probably have died too, as he'd injured himself in a fall and been unable to get up and look after himself. But all the same, even in that situation, Ree knew most humans would have turned him out. Garrad taking to Jem was easy. Jem looked enough like him he might have been his grandson. Taking to Ree, though . . . what human in his right mind would want to offer shelter to a creature part rat, part cat and part human?

Now Ree and Jem ran to find him. Jem had the advantage over Ree, his legs having gotten much longer, loping over a cluck of chicks pecking at the dirt and barely avoiding a head on collision with one of the goats. Ree followed behind, his claws digging into the dirt, the farm animals scampering away from his path.

Garrad was in the barn with the cows. When the boys had come, there had been two cows and an old horse and not much else. But Ree and Jem had had to kill some of the wild hobgoblins to defend the farm. It wasn't something they talked about. They just did it. They patrolled the forest and kept the bad or stupid hobgoblins away and killed the ones who wouldn't obey.

The hobgoblin furs fetched handsome prices, as did the herbs and mushrooms they gathered in the forest where villagers from the nearby hamlet of Three Rivers were afraid to go. Now they had four milk cows, an unruly herd of goats, and a donkey. The donkey had come straying in from the forest, arrived from who knew where. She was a yearling, wounded and weak. Perhaps Jem had thought she was like him, because he'd nursed her to health, and now he harnessed her to the cart he took down to the village once a week to sell milk and cheese and herbs.

Garrad looked like a prosperous farmer, in clothes they'd had made from bought cloth and not homespun. And they looked like a prosperous farmer's grandsons. In all except Ree's unfortunate modifications.

"Granddad," Jem shouted as he came into the dim, cooler barn, which smelled of clean animals and fresh milk.

Garrad was sitting on the milking stool, milking one of the cows. White liquid splashed into a tin bucket. He looked up and frowned at them. He always frowned, but Ree had learned to read the expressions, and this one was alarm. "What is it?" His hand reached for the stick that rested near him. Jem had carved it to help Garrad walk when they'd arrived, but now it was used mostly as a pointing tool and a weapon. "What happened?"

They told him. The smoke. Soldiers. Garrad's thin, hawkish face grew grim. "Well, then," he said. "If they're coming they will come. There ain't much we can do, is there? Not like we can pack up the farm, the animals, and those damn cats and all and hide out of their way."

"I can go to the forest," Ree said. He'd deliberately hung back, in the shadows of the barn, behind Jem a bit and out of Garrad's line of sight. "And stay there, you know? It might make it easier for you." Easier surely, if the soldiers didn't think they were harboring a wild hobgoblin, which was as much a capital crime as being a hobgoblin. Not that Ree had ever quite understood how it could be a crime when he'd had no control over it.

Garrad snorted and turned back to his milking, his movement so jerky that the cow shifted her back leg and gave a low, surprised moo. "You cutting out on your family, boy?" Garrad said, as he gentled the cow. "Yeah, you might have to hide when the soldiers come, but not in the forest. Stay nearby, boy, we might need you. Or don't you care?"

There were no words to say how much Ree cared, so he simply said, "All right," and went to muck out the goats.

Peering through the narrow air slits high up in the barn let Ree see Garrad leaning on his walking stick so he looked as helpless and inoffensive as a cranky old man could, and Jem pretended to support him all the way across the field. Ree didn't think it would help.

It had taken the soldiers three days to get to the farm, and each day smoke pillars had risen up from the valley bringing with them a smell of unclean smoke. When he climbed the trees near the farm, Ree knew the soldiers were burning out places. And the column in which they moved grew, with long lines of people tied up behind the soldiers. Slaves or prisoners, didn't matter which. Even children were tied up and dragged along, little ones, barely able to walk.

Garrad snapped at Ree when Ree couldn't eat and said they would be all right. But it seemed to Ree no better than a magic incantation, and everyone knew magic wasn't much good anymore.

Jem and Garrad approached the soldiers—Garrad doing his best to limp, Jem supporting him solicitously. The leader of the soldiers didn't dismount. He stayed atop his big gray mare, glaring down at them like a man who knows a put-on when he sees it.

He looked like one of those big mean bastards, built solid, like Garrad's outhouse, and he sized up Jem and Garrad like a trader checking furs. Or—and the older memory made Ree swallow and wipe his hands on his pants—like some of Ree's mother's customers when they looked at him, back when he'd still been human. Before she'd shooed him away to avoid his being sold to some of those that preferred boys.

The commander's metal armor glinted in the sun. About half of his soldiers had the same armor, the others a mix of metal and leather, but all of them had swords, and some of them had long bows. They weren't Imperial soldiers—those all had metal armor—but they moved like men who'd worked together and knew their strength.

The big one grinned at Jem, licked his lips, and then looked at Garrad. Before he could say anything, a different man rode into Ree's view. This one wasn't a soldier. He was dressed like Ree's idea of a lord, only he didn't have a sword. Instead, he had a big leather bag, and he held a rolled paper in his hand.

"Is this the farm of Garrad Lenar's son?" He spoke as if he smelled something bad, all thin and whiny.

Garrad nodded. "It's my place. And you'd be?"

The man sniffed. "We represent the Grand Duke Parleon, who owns this land."

"Really?" Garrad leaned forward on his cane. "Last I heard it belonged to the Emperor. Emperor Melles, so I heard."

A few of the soldiers looked at each other. They must not have expected to hear anything about the Emperor here.

"Times have changed," said the unarmored man. "My Lord Parleon holds here." He unrolled his paper and glared at Jem. "According to the records, you have no dependents."

Garrad shrugged. "That paper of yours is a bit out of date. My boy in the Imperial Army, he sent me his son to look after me." He nodded to Jem. "He's a good lad. A bit sickly for soldiering, what with the hacking cough and all, but he helps."

Jem was skinny enough, but he couldn't disguise his height. He couldn't fake a cough, either. Jem was no good at lying.

The next thing the man said was all about taxes and fines and things, but it sounded to Ree more like he was looking to plunder as much as he could and was trying to claim as much wealth as the soldiers could carry off. It made no sense. In Jacona, the merchants and shopkeepers might complain about Imperial taxes, but Ree had never heard of their taking a man's whole living.

Ree remembered all the people tied up behind the soldiers and wondered if this Grand Duke just wanted to control everyone so he could have his own friends take the land and live off it without working for it, like the bandit lords the traders talked about. He must be dressing it in all this talk of tax.

Garrad didn't look happy about it. Jem held his head down, so Ree couldn't see his expression. When the long list finished, the old man grunted. "Go get them snow bear furs out of the barn, lad."

Jem left Garrad leaning on his stick and rushed into the barn. He didn't talk, just picked up the three cured furs and carried them off.

"Snow bears?"

"Hobgoblin critters," the old man said with a shrug. "They look sort of like bears, and they come down off the forests each winter since the magic storms."

The soldiers and the official looked startled when they saw the sparkling white fur piled high in Jem's arms.

"Pretty, ain't they?" Garrad grinned. "Fit for a king, I'd reckon."

The official ran one hand over the fur. "How . . . how many do you have?"

"We got three over from last winter," Garrad told him. "You want to go hunting 'em, forest's right there. We only ever see 'em in winter, and you can't tell they're there till they attack. Something magic in the fur, I reckon."

The official frowned. "And you kill them."

Garrad snorted. "One of them comes at you, you kill it or it kills you. Ain't saying it's easy, now."

A few of the soldiers chuckled. Ree supposed they understood.

The man must have decided, because he nodded, then said, "That will suffice. Take the furs and secure them. The boy joins us. He'll be trained and fight in my Lord's service."

Garrad's hands clenched tight, and his breath caught. "He's weakly. Sick. You'll be the death of him."

But the officer ran an eye over Jem and grinned. "Strong enough for what he needs to do."

Ree felt sick.

Jem caught the old man's hands in his. "It's all right, Granddad."

Garrad's eyes shut tight. "I lost one boy to the Imperials, son. I ain't losing you too."

"You're not losing me, Granddad." Jem hugged Garrad and whispered something Ree couldn't hear. "It'll be okay." He turned to face the big bastard. "Can I get changed? And what can I bring with me?" His voice didn't waver at all.

Ree stayed in the barn, trying to be as brave as Jem, until he heard Garrad say, "They're gone, son. Ain't gonna be back in a while, I reckon, not with as much as they've got to carry back to their damned Grand Duke fellow."

He looked worse than Ree felt, all gray and much older than he'd been this morning. Even though Ree didn't like to touch the old man—it was just wrong, him not being human—he couldn't help wrapping him in a hug before they went back to the chores. "I'm sorry, Granddad. I wish—" He shook his head. There wasn't anything they could do. He wished for Jem back. He wished for his humanity back. He wished . . .

They didn't eat much that night, and Ree didn't think Garrad slept any better than he did. He kept thinking of Jem and what might be happening to Jem, and his thoughts made him wake with his claws out and dug into the mattress.

Jem had said Garrad wouldn't be losing him. Were those just pretty words like *it will be all right?*

Two days later, Ree saw smoke from Three Rivers. Wrong smoke. The smoke of something burning. Once he was through with the milking, he told Garrad, "I'm going down to the village to see if they could use any help." He managed a crooked kind of a smile. "Don't worry, Granddad. No one's going to see me unless I want them to—I'll go through the forest," and hurried out before the old man could object.

Ree had to do something. He couldn't stand just waiting and hoping the soldiers never came back and yet hoping Jem did, somehow.

The forest was so familiar it hurt. Ree had run through here with Jem so many times he knew every tree and every meandering pathway. He noted the deer paths, the signs that there were more this summer than last, which meant they might get more antlers this fall, and maybe carve some needles and other tools from them. There were plenty of burrows, too, foxes and rabbits and other animals. It seemed as though everything was recovering from the horrible year af-

ter the change circles and starting to live like normal
again.

Everything but the people.

Or maybe it was normal for soldiers to come taking
away people's children and burning down their homes.
Ree didn't know, but he didn't think it could be right.
Who would plow the fields and raise the animals and do
all the things the cities needed but didn't have space to
do themselves? This Grand Duke must be very greedy
or very stupid. Maybe both.

Three Rivers village wasn't there anymore. Ree
stood at the edge of the forest looking down at what
had been a neat little cluster of homes on the tongue of
land where two rivers joined to become a third. There
was only smoldering ruins. His nose twitched and his
eyes stung.

It was far, far too quiet, as though everything else was
scared by the smoke. Ree was scared too, but somehow
he found himself running toward the ruins, his toe claws
digging into soil and hummocky grass and his chest
aching.

Not a single house stood. Vegetable gardens wilted
from the heat, and all the village animals were gone,
either taken by soldiers or run away from the burning.
There were bodies in the street, charred things that Ree
couldn't recognize and didn't want to. He shuddered.
He should never have come. Had Jem seen this done?
He couldn't think Jem would have helped. But if Jem
stayed with them long enough . . . His heart felt cold and
shrunken within him, like a small thing, trying to hide.

Around him cooling timbers creaked and settled. The
smoke was now more charred wood than charred meat,
and he was glad for that. He shuddered again, and his
stomach lurched toward his throat. The hazy air stung
his eyes and made them burn and tear.

Someone whimpered.

Ree followed the sound to one of the ruined houses. He edged toward it. It had been a big house. The thatched roof was gone, and the walls had fallen in on themselves in a tangle of wood and sun-dried brick, all of it charred and stark. The cellar doors, heavy wooden things with metal strapping, were still intact although the wood was badly burned.

Someone was crying in the cellar.

Ree hauled the doors open and scurried down into the dark, ashy-smelling air below. He could see the mess of everything that had fallen in from the house, but there was a small clear space, and a girl of about six huddled by the wall. She was trying to cry quietly and not really succeeding.

"They've gone," Ree said softly. "You're safe now."

She looked up, staring at him. Soot smeared her face, and her eyes were wide and full of fear. "You . . . you're old Garrad's goblin."

"Yep." Ree didn't go into the town, ever, only watched from the cover of the forest when Jem was there, but people had caught glimpses of him, and people always talked. "You think he'd keep something dangerous?"

Just as the kitten had, she watched him with big eyes, trying to decide if he was dangerous. He thought of the burned bundles in the street and of Jem taken away by the people who'd done this, and he wasn't sure he couldn't be very dangerous. He had to do something, but what?

"Mama put me here so the soldiers . . . Mama . . ." She cried, big wrenching sobs.

Ree sighed and picked her up. She didn't weigh much, and he'd carried Jem before, and he was stronger than someone his size should be, but he'd hurt if he had to carry her far. She buried her face in his shirt and kept right on crying.

*   *   *

In the end, Those Damn Kittens calmed the girl down.
Three of them had crept into her lap, purring and tum-
bling, and she'd calmed enough, watching them, to tell
Ree and Garrad her story.

She was the youngest child of the village mayor, and
named Amelie like her mother. Mama had put her in
the cellar because she thought her being so pretty might
tempt the soldiers. But the soldiers had taken everyone
and burned everything, and Mama . . . She'd eaten some
stew, petted Those Damn Kittens, and finally fallen into
an exhausted sleep.

Ree and Garrad had gotten her into a makeshift bed
under the eaves, then come back to sit by the fire.

"All of 'em?" Garrad asked softly.

Ree nodded. "Jem—" He said. His hands clenched,
his claws extending and digging into his palms. "He saw
it. He'll see it. He'll get used—"

The old man nodded, and sighed. "I don't know what
to do, son." He closed his eyes. "Seems like no matter
which way we turn, there's damn soldiers in the way."

"Yeah." Ree might be able to survive in the forest, but
not as a person. Here he belonged. He'd helped make
that chair and the matching one where he sat. There was
new plaster in the bedroom that he'd put on, and the
roof was weathertight because of the many times he'd
been up there fitting new shingles and looking for ones
too old and dried out to use any more. His humanity was
tied to these and to Jem in the kitchen, cooking, and to
Garrad making jokes about teaching Jem to shave because he couldn't call both of them Fur Face.

Why didn't one of the bad hobgoblins like the snow
bears go after the soldiers and kill them all, and let Jem
escape back home.

But that wasn't right. If they were grabbing boys like
Jem, that meant a lot of the soldiers were boys like Jem.

And besides, if there was one thing Ree knew, all the way from Jacona, before the changes, it was that you didn't sit around waiting for someone to solve your problems for you.

That reminded him of the way hobgoblins were hunted, how much they scared people in the city, where they had guards and soldiers to protect them. Wouldn't people out here be even more scared of creatures like him?

"Granddad? You remember when we arrived here?"

Garrad looked away from the fire and gave him a sharp look. It had to irk the old man to remember how helpless he'd been.

"You were scared of me, because I'm a hobgoblin, right? And you couldn't stop me." He remembered Garrad's frightened eyes.

A little life crept back into the old man's face. "I remember all right."

"How scary do you think a hobgoblin could be? At night?"

Garrad laughed, that short, harsh bark of a laugh that seemed to dare the world to argue with him. "Pretty damn scary, I reckon."

Ree crept toward the soldiers' camp, his heart and chest tighter than a miser's pocket. His fur prickled with every hint of breeze. He moved by animal instinct. Stealthily. He'd never thought there'd be a day when he'd thank the Little Gods for being part cat and part rat.

He'd taken off his clothes and hidden them in the forest not far from where the soldiers camped. This was just himself and his claws. And a lantern, to use later.

One of the soldiers walked past, boots stomping within inches of Ree's face. He held his breath until the man moved on before he inched forward again. Every sound he made seemed unnaturally loud, every rustle

of grass and trickle of dirt like an avalanche. His breath
was like thunder to his ears. But the soldiers didn't hear
him and didn't see him.

He found Jem lying pale faced and exhausted,
wrapped in a thin blanket. Ree guessed they worked the
boys hard, but there was no excuse for the big bruise
darkening one side of his face and the way he lay huddled as if afraid. He wasn't the only boy like that, and
the soldiers must have been scared they'd run away, because they tied all the boys up at night, the same as their
prisoners.

Soil and grass slid under Ree's stomach and tickled
his nose. Just as well it was night, because he could see
much better than any human. He hoped he could scare
them so they ran all the way back to their fancy Grand
Duke and never, ever came back.

Ree slid his way to Jem and up alongside him. Carefully, he started to untie Jem's hands. The way Jem
started when he woke, and bit back a scream, made Ree
choke on anger.

"Ree?" Jem barely breathed his name. "They'll kill
you!"

"We're leaving. We all are." When he'd decided that,
Ree didn't know, but he wasn't leaving anyone for those
bastards. Not even if he had to kill again. He gestured
with his head. "Can you get them free?"

Jem nodded. His lips went tight, and his eyes narrowed.
He looked so like Garrad that Ree's eyes burned.

"Good. Warn them about me."

"What are you going to do?"

Ree grinned. "What do you think? Big, terrifying
hobgoblin come to eat them for dinner."

Ree shielded the lamp before he lit it. It was one of the
old ones from when there was magic, with glass behind
the metal shutters and a lighter that you pushed to make

a spark. There wasn't any magic in the lamp, but it had taken a mage to make the lighter.

The click of the lighter seemed awfully loud.

None of the soldiers heard it.

Ree wiped his hands on his fur. He was sweating, and his skin prickled. He had to scare the soldiers so much they left their captives where they were.

He cupped his hands to his mouth and let out a hollow roar that could have come from one of the snow bears.

Soldiers stumbled up and moved a bit like bees, only with torches and weapons and looking for something to kill.

Ree caught the handle of the lantern with his claws and raced to the next place he'd chosen: a cluster of boulders not far from the woods. He let loose a second roar before he'd come to a stop, then darted back into the woods to get to his third place.

Another roar sounded, this one from the other side of the soldiers. Ree's heart jumped in his chest, then he grinned. Jem must have decided to help.

The ruin of an old building was Ree's stage; all that was left of it was half a wall that he could stand on. He hung the lantern and unshielded the side he needed, then stepped into its light. The effect on the soldiers was better than he'd dared to hope: They cringed from his hugely magnified shadow.

A whole chorus of roars erupted, some of them—to Ree, anyway—sounding like they came from little children.

Ree breathed in deeply and bellowed, making his voice big. "Begone! This is my territory!"

He didn't expect them to break and run right then, but they did. Maybe the shadows from the rest of the ruins made him look scarier, or maybe it was all the howls and roars coming from everywhere around the camp.

There were a few screams, too, men, not women or boys. Ree dropped back out of the light and shielded the lantern and tried to ignore the way his stomach knotted up. If some of the people who'd been chased out of their homes and . . . hurt wanted to pay back some, well, it wasn't any business of his.

He leaned against the ruined wall, shuddering. This wasn't over, not by a long way.

A shape loomed out of the shadows. A meaty hand grabbed for Ree's throat. He ducked aside, gulping. It was the big one, the commander.

Ree's lips drew back in a snarl, and he launched himself at the soldier. The man wasn't in his armor, just a shirt and pants, but he had a sword in his right hand. That wouldn't matter if Ree was right up close.

He caught the man's shoulders, digging his claws in while he arched his back so he could get his legs up and use the toe claws where it would hurt most.

The big bastard made a sound that might have been a scream, and Ree heard metal hit stone. His nose wrinkled at the man's smell of sour beer and worse. His toe claws got a grip, dug in.

The man grabbed at Ree's chest, trying to pull him away. That let Ree use his right hand to dig his claws into the man's eyes, his throat.

The big man's choking scream died to a horrible gurgling noise, and he pitched forward.

Ree scrambled to pull away from him and bit back a yelp when he found the man's sword the hard way. His feet might be tougher than a human's, but they weren't horn.

He stumbled away from the wall and loose stone and collapsed, gasping. His foot stung.

"There he is!"

Ree half-scrambled upright before he realized it was Jem's voice. A moment later, boys—or maybe young men, Ree wasn't sure—surrounded him, caring nothing for his fur or for anything but that he was hurt and that he'd freed them. The chatter while they unshielded the lamp and bandaged him made him want to be sick. He hadn't thought it would be that bad.

"They'll come back," he said when the young men quieted down a little. "Maybe not those ones, but others."

"Those won't be back." Jem sounded grimly amused. "They dropped all their weapons."

People gathered now, women and children and some older men who Ree guessed weren't fit enough to be put into the army. They weren't scared of him, and they weren't treating him like some kind of wild animal.

"What happens when others come, then?" Ree demanded. "More of them, because of the terrible army of hobgoblins that chased those away." It didn't matter that the "terrible army" was a handful of youngsters making noises. That wasn't what the Grand Duke would hear.

Instead of fixing things, he'd made them worse.

Jem frowned, but he looked stubborn and determined, not angry. "We've got their stuff. All of it. We can fix things so we can keep them away." He smiled. "You'll help, Ree, right? You'll be the fearsome hobgoblin king for us?"

"I'll help." He couldn't say anything else, really, not when he'd made sure there'd be trouble. "Granddad's going to complain, but I guess we can feed everyone until stuff can be rebuilt." Ree bit his lip. "Maybe make walls out of the places they burned, and traps and things."

"We'll manage." Jem said with a nod. "Come on. Let's go home."

It wouldn't be easy, Ree thought. Boys who were just about old enough to be men, frightened women and children who'd lost everything they knew . . . No one was complaining, though. Maybe they were just glad to be alive, as he and Jem had been that first night after escaping Jacona. It hadn't mattered then that they had nothing except each other.

Now they had something to protect, something to fight for, but they still had each other. Ree caught Jem's determined look, and Jem smiled. "We'll look after them, Ree. Like we look after each other."

Jem looked like a man. Like a young Garrad. Men protected and helped those in need. Men cleaved to their friends and their promises.

"Yeah," Ree said, his heart suddenly easy despite the danger ahead. "Yeah, we will."

Matters of the Heart
by Sarah A. Hoyt

Sarah A. Hoyt was born in Portugal, a mishap she hastened to correct as soon as she came of age. She lives in Colorado with her husband, her two sons, and a varying horde of cats. She has published a Shakespearean fantasy trilogy, Three Musketeers mystery novels, as well as any number of short stories in magazines ranging from *Isaac Asimov's Science Fiction Magazine* to *Dreams of Decadence*. Forthcoming novels include *Darkship Thieves* and more Three Musketeers mystery novels. She currently lives with her family in Colorado.

"Hello the house!"

Ree jumped when the unfamiliar voice bellowed outside the farm gates. As a hobgoblin, having got himself mixed up with a cat and a rat during Change Circle, he was proscribed in most places. Here, too, though the people who lived near Garrad's farm had gotten used to him and didn't fear him. In fact, since he'd helped them escape the soldiers who had come last summer and burned most of the farms around here, Ree had no fear of being seen. Except by strangers.

He dropped the shovel he'd been using to muck out the goat stalls and, pushing aside the goats, walked out of the stall, locked it, then walked out of the barn and across the farmyard, to where he could get a view of the gate.

Last week's snow coated the ground in a thin, brittle shell that crackled under the new boots that hid Ree's nonhuman feet. The air had a cold, dry taste tinged with the smell of wood fires; that meant it was going to stay below freezing even if the sun was out. Ree's breath steamed, and he wrapped his arms close around his body.

The new wall protecting the farm was about seven feet tall, too tall to see past—it was taller than Jem and topped with sharp bits of stone and metal—but the iron gate the village ironmonger had done for them, in gratitude, was big enough to let the donkey and cart through, and they didn't go outside the farm or the forest without weapons or on their own any more. It was also made of vertical shafts, like spears, and you could see between them. And if you took care to stay kind of to the side of the wall as you looked, no one could see you.

The three men outside the gate were definitely strangers, all of them on horses. Good horses too, which to Ree were horses no one in the region could possibly afford—tall of leg and sturdy. The man at the front wore fancy armor, the kind Ree remembered Imperial officers wearing, and had what looked like a brand new red cloak over his shoulders. He looked about forty, blond and bearded, with that hardened look all soldiers got sooner or later, and he looked angry.

"Who is it, Ree?" Jem whispered. He'd come running from where he'd been, near the chicken coop, and skidded to a stop near Ree. He'd gotten a bit taller since last summer, but mostly he'd put on muscle, filling out to match his height. Sometimes Ree felt like a child beside him, even though Ree was older.

But then, no one knew how Ree was supposed to

grow. He was a hobgoblin after all, part cat, part rat and part human, changed by the magic storms. Jem might treat him like a human, and Garrad, the old man whose farm this was and who'd become a kind of grandfather to both of them and who looked enough like Jem to be his real grandfather. Even little Amelie, whom Ree had found after soldiers burned Three Rivers last summer and whose parents had been killed treated Ree like a human, but no one else did.

They accepted him, even were grateful for the way he'd scared off the soldiers, but his fur, and the tail he kept tucked in his pants, and his claws and cat-eyes made him different. Too different to be one of them.

"Three soldiers. They don't look like the other ones that came last year." Ree whispered back as Jem leaned into him, partly trying to see around him and partly probably instinctive protection against the bitter cold. He indicated the gate. "But they're not happy, and blondie out there is getting ready to break things if he doesn't get an answer soon."

Jem nodded. He narrowed his eyes at the gate, listened to the way the big man was bellowing and got what Ree thought of as his Garrad look. It was the stubborn, *no one makes me do anything* look, and it usually meant trouble. Ree had seen it a lot while they helped keep people fed and rebuilt Three Rivers and put a wall around the village so soldiers couldn't easily burn it out again.

Jem had been a scared little thing when Ree had saved his life on the streets of Jacona, just about three years ago, but he was almost a man now, and while he would help those who needed it, he did it on his own terms and refused to be pushed around no matter how much bigger or older those doing the pushing might be.

"Granddad's plucking the old rooster," Jem said his voice slightly louder. "He'll be out as soon as he's done.

Meanwhile, I'll deal with them." He walked up to the gate as calm as if he were going to talk to young men from the village.

The blond fellow didn't wait for Jem to speak. The moment he could see someone, he demanded, "Where is Garrad? And who are you?"

Jem folded his arms on his chest, tilted his head up, and gave the blond a frosty look. "Until you tell me who you are, it's none of your damn business who I am or where he is, stranger."

Ree heard the sharp catch of breath and the creak of leather that meant the man's massive fists were clenched tight enough to strain his gloves. "Get this thing open now, before I break it down."

Jem smiled a little. The blacksmith had put special care into the lock and into the forging of that gate and had told them that it would withstand a small group of soldiers. "Go right ahead and try."

"Jem! Ree!" Garrad's came from behind them, with the short breath that meant he'd been running.

Ree turned to see the old man hurrying toward them, his walking stick, the one Jem had carved for him two years back, thumping into the ground with every step. He really didn't need the stick most of the time, but the cold made the ground slippery, and Garrad was all too aware of what falls could do at his age. When they'd met him, he'd been rendered helpless by one such fall. "What's going on out here?"

Ree had been looking at the blond and thought he noticed a startled jump at their names, but it was nothing to the way Blondie's face seemed to melt out of its harsh lines and his voice softened at the sight of Garrad. "Father?"

Father? It could be. The old man's son had been conscripted by the Emperor's army years ago.

Garrad rocked on his feet, and Ree raced to steady

him while Jem kept on giving the blond man his coldest glare.

"Lenar?" Garrad waved Ree off—with the walking stick, so Ree had to jump out of the way—and scurried to the gate. "Gods be praised, it *is* you!" He fumbled with the lock that held the locking bar down and nodded to Jem. "Get the gate open, and let him in, lad."

Ree helped Jem with the gate, lifting the heavy bar while Jem hauled it open. The blond man, Lenar, gave them a disdainful look, and the other two men got closer to the blond and started to draw their swords when they saw Ree. But they looked at Lenar before they drew them out all the way.

Lenar didn't even see them look. He jumped off his horse and hugged Garrad so hard he lifted the old man off his feet. If Garrad's eyes were a bit too bright, well, Ree didn't have to say he'd seen it. Not that Garrad would ever admit to it, anyhow.

Jem caught the horse's reins while Ree closed the gate behind the other two men. Having his back to them made his skin itch and his fur try to rise, but if this was Garrad's son, then this farm was his. It wasn't up to Ree to be inhospitable to Lenar or his guards.

"Not so close now, you'll break something," Garrad protested, and he disguised his wavering voice with a cough. "Now come on inside and tell me what's brought you back home and all that happened to you all these years."

Lenar sounded grim when he said, "Not so fast, Father. What are you doing with a hobgoblin and some other brat here? Who are they?"

Ree got the gate barred and turned in time to see Lenar posed just as Jem had been shortly before, trading glares with Garrad.

Garrad grinned grimly, as though this were a game he was used to. "Boys, you get them horses looked after, you hear? The rest of you come on inside out of the cold, and then we'll talk."

Taking all the gear off the horses and stacking it neatly near the barn door took a while, and rubbing the horses down and getting them fed and watered took longer. Jem didn't say anything, and Ree couldn't think of anything to say. They'd never talked about it, but Ree had always figured Garrad assumed his son had died. He'd never expected anyone to come back, and Jem made a kind of a replacement.

He wondered where the son's return left them. Oh, Jem looked enough like Garrad to really be his grandson, but they didn't know, and Ree wasn't anything anyone would want. He was useful, maybe, but that was all. A tame pet, *Garrad's goblin*.

And little Amelie was just another one of their group of waifs that Garrad looked after and tolerated. She'd lightened up some since Ree had brought her here, but men scared her, and a harsh word from anyone except Garrad got her tearing up and clutching at her skirts as though someone were going to do something horrible to her any time. Ree had only ever seen her smile around the Damn Young Cats—they were too big now to be Damn Kittens, although he suspected next spring there'd be more Damn Kittens to make Garrad grumble. Were all of them surplus now that Garrad's lost heir was back?

As if thinking about them was a cue, Ree felt a brush of air, then a solid thump on his shoulder. He winced and bit down on a yelp when claws dug in. The Young Damn Cats never could remember that his fur wasn't as thick as theirs.

The horse he was brushing down didn't seem to care that it now shared its stall with a hobgoblin and a cat, or that the cat was complaining to Ree in a thoroughly put out tone. "Yes, yes," Ree said, hurriedly. "Your mama doesn't catch enough rabbits, and mice are boring. That doesn't mean you have to complain so much."

The Damn Young Cat added Ree's indifference to the list of complaints, and Ree paused long enough to pluck it from his shoulder and set it on the floor of the barn. It was the gray and white one he'd rescued from a tree last summer. Of all the Damn Young Cats, this one was the one that got into the most trouble and had to be rescued most often.

Jem came into the stall, grinning. "Damn cats," he said. "Anyone would think you enjoyed having them climb all over you."

Ree finished with the horse and gave the animal a friendly pat before he left the stall. "Yeah, I know. Portable tree for damn cats, that's me."

Jem was worried, for all he tried to hide it, and Ree didn't think he was hiding things any better. "We'd better go protect Amelie."

Jem caught Ree's hand for a moment in his now larger, calloused hand. "Don't worry, Ree. Whatever happens, we've always got each other. And when have we ever needed anyone else?"

It seemed to Ree the house was colder inside than it was out in the snow, what with Lenar's two companions—guards, actually, since he was an officer and he'd been given a title and enough Imperial gold to buy an estate anywhere he liked—watching Ree as if they expected him to try to eat someone, and Lenar glaring at Jem, Ree, and Amelie.

Ree didn't understand why the Damn Cats made it worse, but they did, and Lenar practically accused Garrad of having gone soft in the head, letting those damn cats have the run of the house. To which Garrad—who complained about the cats all the time—had responded that the cats were homey and friendly and got rid of vermin a treat.

Even the fact that Jem was doing the cooking, quietly getting smoked meat from the cellar to supplement what had been planned as a simple meal of bread and vegetable soup, seemed to set Lenar off. It appeared that cooking was woman's work, and Garrad should have hired a wench from the village and not have this boy do such things. To which Garrad had boomed that Jem cooked better than any wench he'd ever met. It was true, but hardly a point to argue over. Stubborn and loud sure did run in that family.

"C'mon, Amelie. Let's get beds made up for our guests," Ree said. Poor kid had been sitting in the corner clutching a Damn Cat and was white and terrified. She ran to him, putting a sweaty hand in his and sniffling back tears. Might as well get her away from what would be a huge fight.

Garrad's lips were set and thin, and he had the full stubborn on him. Without the beard, Lenar would have been just like him only younger, and Jem was as bad as both of them together, cutting into the smoked meat and glaring at Lenar as if he wished he were hacking into the soldier.

Amelie clutched Ree's hand until they were out in the main room, and she needed both hands to climb up the ladder to the loft. Her room was up there, tucked in under the eaves, but Ree figured he'd make up the other bed in the room he shared with Jem anyway. Amelie would feel safer downstairs with Lenar and his guards in the house.

He pulled out quilts and sheets and blankets from the chests in the bedrooms, enough to make up three beds, and tossed them up to Amelie, then climbed up after her. "What do you think, Mama 'Melie? Should we give them straw beds or make them sleep on the floor?"

She brightened a little, showing the prettiness her mother had tried to protect when she'd shoved her in the cellar to escape the raid of the soldiers. At six she should have been too young to be in danger, but they'd learned no one was too young. "They should have proper beds, Ree." Amelie wagged a finger at him. "It wouldn't be right to make them sleep cold."

He grinned and winked. " 'Sides, if we make them nice, comfy beds, they'll sleep all night, and they'll only wake you up when they curse about having to go to the outhouse."

She covered her mouth with her hands, almost as if she were scared to smile. "Don't we have a spare pot?"

"For three of them? We don't have one big enough."

There was always fresh straw up here; keeping it fresh was one of the jobs that was never finished. The straw in the loft kept winter cold from seeping in through the roof and stuffed the mattresses and cushions. It got used for kindling as well. They kept what they weren't using at either end of the house, farthest from the chimney in the middle of the loft, and since Amelie's arrival Ree and Garrad had partitioned off a room for her near the chimney.

Ree saw no reason not to put the men's beds as far from Amelie's room as they could, even if Amelie wouldn't be sleeping there, though it meant bringing a lantern around so they could see to pull the straw together and tuck sheets around it so each man had a more or less comfortable bed. The thick sheets would stop any straw poking through, and with blankets and quilts they should sleep warm. The room was Amelie's, and he didn't want them wandering into it by accident. Not that she had much there. Just a couple of cloth dolls and the few shifts they'd found in the ruins of her once prosperous home.

"Good enough, do you think?" he asked when he and

Amelie were done. She nodded, but she looked scared, and her hands were plaiting her little pinafore.

"Tell you what," Ree said. "You sleep in our room tonight, all right? In the other bed. I'll make it up for you." With strangers in the house and the way Jem was looking, nothing untoward was going to happen in that room tonight, anyway. Ree saw the relief in her eyes and wondered. She had told him she spied through the cellar lock onto the destruction of her home, but he didn't know what had happened. Her father and brothers had been killed. Her mother had been killed too . . . but it probably hadn't been that simple.

Amelie might carry the scars her whole life. He felt toward her as to a little sister or perhaps a daughter, though that was an abomination, of course, as he could never have children and certainly not human children.

Hobgoblins didn't. They lived wild until someone or something killed them. Most of the ones Ree had seen were alone, the only things like them. Except for the snow bears, of course. Maybe several bears got caught in the same magic circle and then bred, but there seemed to be lots of those.

There was a kind of wolf creature that bred, too and hunted in packs. Ree hoped they'd never see any of those again. They were nastier than the snow bears, and there were more of them. But most of the hobgoblins were the only ones and couldn't breed with anything even if they wanted to. He didn't want to. All he wanted was Jem. And they already had Amelie to look after.

After a dinner eaten in silence, while Garrad, Lenar, and Jem traded cold looks, Ree excused himself and left to put Amelie to bed. He made up the spare bed with fresh sheets and obligingly turned his back while she changed out of her day clothes into a nightdress of soft wool that Jem had bought her. Once she was tucked in, he folded her clothes for her and set her boots at the foot of the bed, then blew out the lantern. He and Jem knew the room well enough to come in here without any light at all, and it wasn't that dark. Ree's cat-eyes could see everything from the patched plaster to the chests of bedding.

He closed the door softly and padded toward the kitchen. He'd just tell Garrad good night and go to bed.

But halfway through the great room he heard Jem's voice. "Not going to 'put it down.' 'It' is Ree, and he's saved all our lives."

Ree froze as Lenar growled back—sounding like Garrad when he was angry or hurt. "That thing isn't safe, damn it! None of them are. They turn on their owners, or you find dead men in alleys with their throats torn out."

For a moment, Ree couldn't breathe. Dead men in alleys with their throats torn out.... The memory returned to him. Gods above, he'd only been trying to protect himself! And then he'd found Jem and realized what the bastard had been doing. He couldn't regret killing that man. It had brought Jem into his life, and Jem had called back the human part of him and stopped him from being all animal.

"Some *men* hurt and kill other men for fun." Jem said in that cold voice that meant he was so angry he was shaking. "You don't kill every man because of it. You don't kill every dog because someone tormented or starved one until he turned."

"It's not a man and it's not an animal," Lenar said stubbornly. "It's a magic-made unnatural thing!"

"So's that lamp up there, son," Garrad said. "You going to destroy it, too?"

Lenar made a sound of disgust. "Sure. It hoodwinked you too. No wonder they're talking about hobgoblins ruling here and making the people their slaves."

Ree didn't know whether to laugh or cry. The trick he'd used to scare the soldiers away, using everyone's fear of hobgoblins to make them think he was a terrible creature who was ready to eat them right there, *had* stopped other people trying to bring soldiers in. And it made Garrad's son think hobgoblins were secret lords here.

"I ain't hoodwinked, boy. Ree has lived here for two years. He's as human as you and I, fur face or not."

Lenar didn't get a chance to answer, because Jem started, his voice tight with fury. "You think your father's an idiot? You think he'd let something dangerous stay with him?" He was on a right tear, and he was going to say what he thought, no matter what. "Gods above. I love Ree. Ree and I . . . we're closer than brothers and always will be. He's *never* hurt me, and he's gotten hurt for me. I'm no idiot, and I don't think anyone could be that close to someone for more than two years and not know who they really are and if animal or man."

Ree's throat tightened, and his chest hurt. His eyes burned so much he had to blink to keep them clear. Jem couldn't know what he was saying or how a man like Lenar would react. He couldn't. His pride in their love made his heart want to burst, but he was afraid now they'd both be thrown out into the cold night.

Lenar made a choked sound, then a disgusted one. "What do you know about love, boy? That is not only male, it's not even human."

"You'd better believe Ree's human," Jem snarled. "He's better than damn near all men I've ever seen."

Jem stomped from the kitchen in full high and mighty temper, very pointedly not slamming the kitchen door and walked past him, not seeing him in the dark of the great room, after the light of the lantern in the kitchen. Before Ree could speak, Jem opened the door to their bedroom and went inside, closing the door softly behind him.

Ree closed his eyes. He should go to bed too. The

chores would still be there tomorrow, and no matter what Garrad's son thought about him, stalls still needed mucking out and cattle needed milking. Garrad would probably be kept busy with his son, so it would be Ree doing the milking. And he doubted Lenar or his fancy guards would do any of it, so they'd better think twice about throwing him or Jem out. Or Amelie, for that matter.

Garrad's voice echoed, calmer and full of dry amusement. "You ain't making a good showing of yourself, son."

Lenar sounded as though he felt a bit guilty when he said, "I know, Father. I shouldn't . . ." He cleared his throat. "The thing is . . . I think . . . your Jem might be my son."

"I thought he might be," Garrad said. "Your by-blow or my brother's, only my brother was never that much interested in women, you know."

Ree raised his eyebrows, wondering how Lenar would respond to that, but Lenar just sounded resigned. "I got married in Jacona, nearly seventeen years ago now. I thought I was going to be posted there until I was old enough to retire. I was already an officer. I was going to bring her to see you as soon as I got leave. Pretty little merchant's daughter. Myrrine." He made a sound half sob, half laugh. "She was expecting when my division was sent south to deal with a minor uprising. We were going to call my son Jem, after her late father. We were gone nearly five years, and when I came back I couldn't find her." There was real pain in his voice, real anguish. "Nothing I did . . . I thought she must have died, and the baby. It was a miracle for him to get here, somehow . . . And he's attached himself to that *thing*. How can he be happy with that? How can he not want a family, children of his own?" He paused. "Do they . . . do they *sleep* together?"

"There's two beds in that room," Garrad said. "And they use one. But it ain't none of my business, and it's not yours either, son, leastways unless they tell you." Garrad just sounded matter-of-fact when he said, "They ain't said much about it, but I reckon Ree saved Jem from a lot worse than just dying back in that city. There's a look Jem gets sometimes, and when he's sick, he talks in his sleep, and some of what he says would curdle your blood." A short silence, as though Garrad shrugged. "And when Jem talks in his sleep and calls his mama, sometimes he says Myrrine."

"Then he *is* mine," Lenar said. "He's all I got. He can't live with that—that—I'll never have grandchildren."

"And you're all I got, and I thought you were dead." Garrad's dry amusement came back. "Did you have him because you wanted to have grandchildren?"

"No, I was young, I—"

"You're still young, son. And even if you weren't, it don't justify making Jem into something he ain't. 'Sides, Ree and Jem … Ree brought Jem in, and Jem was dying of consumption. Ree risked getting killed so he could bring Jem in to get help. And then he helped me too. I'd tripped and fallen on that damn rug your mother made, and Ree nursed me and Jem both. Then they both worked hard as any ten men to get the farm back working again. Fact is, if you were to kick them out tonight, I'd have to sell most of my animals and give them the money. They bought those animals with the furs of the creatures they killed in the forest. And they never asked for anything."

"It's not right, Father," Lenar insisted. "It's just not. I mean, it's not like I didn't see enough of it in the army, but … with an animal?"

"Ree ain't an animal."

Ree couldn't listen any more. There was too much, and all it made him think was that Lenar was right. Who knew when the animal would take over?

He padded across to the bedroom and slipped inside. Jem sounded like he was asleep, and Amelie too. The old painting on the wall, of Garrad and his brother when they'd been young, made Ree think about families and how he couldn't have one, not of his body. Nor would Jem as long as they were together. The two young men in the old picture looked happy and relaxed, and so like Jem it hurt.

Ree felt as if something inside him had frozen. Carefully he removed his clothes, all of them, even the boots with their warm felted lining. Jem belonged here. It was Ree who was in the way, Ree who would be a problem for them all the time. Ree who would make Jem's life difficult. He touched Jem's face, where it curved in the moonlight, and felt the close-shaved blond beard. The idea of never touching Jem again, never seeing Jem again made him hurt deep inside. But it was just him. He was a hobgoblin. They had no real feelings. Not like people.

"Ree, get in bed," Jem said and smiled a little, but he didn't wake up. Not fully. He didn't move as Ree left the room.

Ree had forgotten how miserable cold he could get, even through his fur. He ached with it, and his feet hurt with each step on the frozen ground. Instead of going far into the forest, he curled in one of the abandoned burrows near the farm. He shivered and dozed till first light, and then he thought he should hunt.

A rabbit, he thought. They were sort of a fuzzier smell than cats and not musky like foxes. He was starving. But he remembered how nasty raw rabbit was, and it made his stomach clench and bitter bile come to the back of his throat.

Some wild hobgoblin he was. Hobgoblins did not

use fire. They were animals. But his stomach refused to believe him, and he knew better than to force it. Later. When he was hungry enough.

He'd managed before, hadn't he? There wasn't any reason he couldn't do it again. Let Garrad and Lenar and Jem be a family, without him in the way. There were enough places to hide and not be seen if anyone came looking for him.

His feet were so cold they hurt, and he felt every stone and fallen branch underfoot. His toe claws kept catching on frozen ground, until he thought he'd wrenched them. And no matter how hard he told himself it was better for everyone this way, and he'd get used to living wild, he couldn't make himself believe it. He already missed Jem.

It was a relief when the long, lonely day faded to darkness and he could find an empty burrow and try to sleep.

A scream sounded, startling Ree awake.

Someone was in trouble. Ree scrabbled from the burrow and raced toward the scream. He ran blindly through the trees, then stopped.

Lenar was ahead of him fighting something. Something invisible.

A snow bear. Ree approached, carefully. He wouldn't be able to see it unless he was right up close or it got in front of something dark.

Though Lenar knew how to use his sword, the creature was bigger and stronger than he was and would kill him and eat him. It took two people to kill snow bears. He and Jem hunted together. As he thought this, he had launched himself toward the creature's back.

Ree scrambled to climb up, digging his finger and toe claws into the snow bear's fur while it swung wildly, trying to dislodge the annoyance. Blood sprayed over the snow, shockingly red against white.

He wrapped one arm around the creature's head, going by feel to get his claws into its eyes. It howled in agony, rearing to its full height. Lenar struck. His sword went all the way into the snowbear's chest and came out the back, nearly skewering Ree as well.

Ree jumped off and rolled to the side while the creature collapsed. In the time it took him to climb to his feet and shake snow off his fur, Lenar had pulled his sword free and was staring at the snow bear with a grimace. He glared up at Ree. "Damn fool old man was out at first light chasing after you," he said. "If there's more like this, he's probably got himself killed, and that damn stubborn young pup with him."

Lenar wiped his sword on the snow bear. "I came looking for them both." He gave Ree another sharp look. "That thing was waiting for me."

"They do that." Ree looked around, hoping that there would be tracks, something he could use to find Jem and Garrad. "You can't even smell the damn things." It was too confused here, with the snowbear's musk and blood, but a little farther on he saw the rounded hole of Garrad's walking stick and two sets of footsteps. "This way."

Lenar didn't say anything else, but he didn't argue with Ree leading, only gave him more of those long, searching looks. "You're like no hobgoblin I've seen," he said.

"No," Ree said. "You see, Jem thinks I'm human. He . . . I think he made me human, he's so stubborn." It sounded dumb, but Ree didn't really care what Lenar thought. He had to find Jem and Garrad and get them home safe.

When he heard snarls in the distance, he started to run. It didn't sound like snow bears, more like the wolf things. That was bad.

Lenar kept up with him. Ree couldn't run too fast

over the rough ground. Lenar didn't answer when Ree told him about the wolf things and how the best way to stop them was to kill the queen bitch, because she ruled the pack and they'd be lost if she died. The queen bitch was always the biggest one, sometimes twice as big as the others, and she was usually all white, where the rest of the pack were gray and white.

Jem and Garrad were back to back, Jem using a pitchfork and Garrad his walking stick to keep the pack off them. The pack was playing still, wearing them down for the kill.

Ree slammed into the pack, throwing one of the smaller wolf creatures aside. The smaller ones were maybe hip high at the shoulder, long and lean with jaws that could crack bones and wicked curved teeth. The queen was almost as tall as Ree and more muscular than her packmates.

That didn't stop Ree from jumping on her and holding on with his knees and toe claws while he scrambled for her eyes with one hand and her throat with another. He had gotten a good hold when one of the creatures crashed into him, and they all went tumbling. Ree felt flesh tear under his fingers, and at the same time he realized that his back and side hurt. The damn wolf goblin must have clawed him. It wasn't moving now, though.

The pack ran, fast, deep into the woods. They'd be harmless until they found another queen.

It took him a while to pull himself free, what with his claws tangled in the pack queen's fur and flesh and trying not to get the other hobgoblin's claws any deeper into him when he moved.

Ree shuddered. He forced himself to look at Jem and Garrad. They weren't hurt. Garrad stood and leaned on his walking stick, breathing heavily, while Jem and Lenar made sure that the wolf queen was indeed dead.

Garrad glared at him. "What possessed you to run off like that, Ree?"

Ree swallowed. "I don't belong." It was harder than he thought to say that. "I . . . Jem should have children. He doesn't need me."

"You're a stubborn proud young cuss is what you are. Seems to me that kind of stubborn is right at home in my family." Garrad sounded more like his normal self now. "What about Jem, then? Do you know how much he missed you, just one day? Did you ask him if he needed you?"

"But . . . you've got your family now. Why would you want me?" Why would anyone want him, really? He might turn bad, forget being human even though he didn't want to.

"You're going to tell me who my family is now, boy?" Garrad asked looking stubborn. "You're family if I say you are."

And now Lenar was glaring at him. He still looked furious, but somehow it was all different. "Family's people who look after each other and fight for each other, too." He shook his head. "And I guess love each other." He pushed Jem toward Ree. "Help your young man, son. He needs to get those wounds seen to."

As Jem's arm came around him, supporting him, Ree could swear Jem said under his breath, "My damn stubborn young man."

It was the best thing he'd ever been called.

Nothing Better to Do
by Tanya Huff

Tanya Huff lives and writes in rural Ontario with her
partner, Fiona Patton and nine cats. One more and
they officially qualify as crazy cat ladies. Her twenty-
fifth novel, *The Enchantment Emporium*, a stand-alone
urban fantasy, was recently published by DAW Books.
In her spare time she practices barre chords instead of
painting the bathroom.

Jors stiffened in the saddle, head cocked. He could hear
bird song. The wind humming in the upper canopy,
leaves and twigs rubbing together as percussion. Small
animals moving in the underbrush.

:Chosen?: Gervais turned to stare back over his
shoulder with one sapphire eye.

:I thought I heard a baby crying.:

:Out here?:

It was a good question. They were more than a day's
ride from Harbert on a path that would lead, by the end
of the day, to a new settlement set up by three foresting
families who'd been given a royal charter to harvest this
section of the wood. Besides the usual responsibilities
of a Herald on circuit, Jors had specific instructions to
make sure they weren't exceeding their charter.

Jors had never met one of the near legendary Hawk-brothers, wouldn't actually mind meeting a Hawkbrother, and had less than no desire to meet a Hawkbrother because a forester had gotten greedy and begun cutting outside the territory they'd been granted. He'd grown up in such a settlement, his family still lived in one, and he knew exactly how tempting it could be to harvest that perfect tree just on the edge of the grant. And then the tree just beyond that.

Go far enough *just beyond* in this particular corner of Valdemar, and problems became a lot more serious than reestablishing the boundaries between feuding families.

An infuriated shriek pulled Jors from his reflections and sent a small flock of birds up through the canopy, wings drumming against the air.

:There! Did you hear it?:

:Given that I haven't gone deaf in the last ten paces, yes, Chosen, I heard it. But that didn't sound like an infant.:

:No.: Jors had to admit it did not. *:Whatever it is, it sounds furious. And if there's also a baby . . . :*

As Gervais picked up his pace, Jors readied his bow. He was reasonably proficient with a sword—he wouldn't be riding courier if he weren't—but even the Weapons Master agreed there were few currently in Whites who could match his skills as an archer. It came from wanting to eat while growing up, as foresters depended on the woods for most of their meat. Small game, large; by the time Gervais had appeared outside the palisade with twigs tangled in his mane and an extraordinarily annoyed expression on his face, Jors had learned to place his arrows where they'd do the most good.

But there were predators in the woods as well, and it wasn't unusual for the hunters to find themselves hunted by something just as interested in a meal.

:I smell smoke.:

Jors flattened against the pommel as Gervais took them off the main track onto what might have been a path, might have been a dry water channel. Either way, branches had not been cleared for a man on horseback.

He could smell the smoke now too, but it wasn't the heart-stopping scent of leaves and twigs and deadfall going up, it was more pungent. Slower. Familiar . . .

"Charcoal burner!" he said just as they emerged into a clearing.

There, the expected cone of logs over the firepit. There, the expected small . . . well, in all honestly, hut was probably the kindest description. A little unexpected to see three scruffy chickens in a twig corral by the hut, but eggs were always welcome. Completely unexpected to see the half-naked toddler straining to reach the firepit, held back by a leather harness around his plump little body and a rope tied to a cedar stake.

The toddler turned to face the Herald and his Companion; tiny dark brows drew in, muddy fists rose, and he shrieked.

In rage.

:Well?: Gervais said after a long moment.

:It's a baby. I'm not . . . I don't . . . : He sighed and swung out of the saddle.

The toddler stared at him in what could only be considered a highly suspicious manner and shrieked again.

"Hey there, little fellow." Jors kept his voice low and nonthreatening, as he would when approaching a strange dog. And he'd *rather* be approaching a strange dog. Two strange dogs. A pack of strange dogs. He'd know exactly what he had to do to rescue this child from a pack of dogs; he just wasn't sure what he was supposed to do with a child alone.

:I doubt he's going to bite.:

Jors realized the fingers on his outstretched hand were curled safely in. *:But you don't know that for sure,:* he muttered as he uncurled them. "It's okay little guy. We're not going to hurt you. We're here to help."

Blue eyes widened as the toddler stared past him. Leaning against the support of the harness, he scrambled around about twenty degrees of the circle the rope allowed him until he faced Jors, hands reaching out and grabbing at the air. "Ossy!"

"Ossy?" Glancing back, Jors thought Gervais looked as confused as he felt. "Ossy . . . horsey! He thinks you're a horse." The shrieking picked up a distinctly proprietary sound, interspersed with something that could have been *me* or could have been random *eee* noises, Jors wasn't sure. *:Come a little closer and see if he'll quiet down.:*

The noises changed to happy chortling as Gervais moved slowly and carefully close enough for the toddler to throw himself around one of the Companion's front legs. It wasn't exactly quiet, but it was definitely *quieter*.

:He's sticky.:

:Is that normal?: Jors wondered, heading for the hut.

:How should I know?: The young stallion sounded slightly put out. And then a little panicked. *:Chosen? Where are you going?:*

:To look for his parents. They can't be far.: If they were, Jors intended to have a few *official* words with the sort of people who'd wander off leaving their child tethered to a stake in the deep woods. Might as well tether out a sacrificial goat.

And speaking of goats, as he came up to the hut, he could see a bored-looking nanny staring at him from the back of the chicken corral, jaws moving thoughtfully around a mouthful of greenery. The fodder in the pen, still green and unwilted, suggested the parents were . . .

He froze, one hand on the stretched hide that covered the opening to the hut.

:Chosen?:

:I heard.:

Moaning.

He found the charcoal burner no more than ten feet out from the clearing, pinned to the ground by the jagged end of a branch through his chest. Jors could do a field dressing as well as any Herald, maybe better than a few as he spent so much time out on the road, but not even a full Healer, present when the accident happened, could have changed the outcome. With the branch in the wound, the charcoal burner died slowly. Pulled free, he'd bleed out instantly.

Looking up, Jors could see the new scar where the deadfall had finally separated from the tree. The charcoal burner had probably passed under it a hundred times, forgot it was up there if he'd even noticed it at all. It wasn't easy to see a branch hung up in the high canopy—Jors had lost an uncle to a similar accident when he was eight. Could remember the tears on his father's face as he carried his brother's body back in through the palisade.

The charcoal burner was older than Jors expected, midthirties maybe, allowing for the rough edges of a hard life—although it couldn't have helped that he'd been slowly dying since the branch had pinned him. When Jors knelt by his side, he opened startlingly blue eyes.

The knowledge of his imminent death was evident in the gaze he locked onto Jors' face as he fought to drag air into ruined lungs. "Torbin?" he wheezed. "My son?"

"He's fine."

"Take . . . to sister. Rab . . . bit Hole." A callused hand batted weakly at Jors' knee, leaving smears of red-brown against the white. "Prom . . . ise."

"My word as a Herald. I will put your son in your sister's arms."

He held Jors' gaze for a long moment, then closed his eyes and sighed.

He didn't breathe in again.

*   *   *

The only evidence of a woman inside the hut was a faded ribbon curled up on a rough shelf. Jors set it on the pile of the charcoal burner's possessions, wrapped them in the more worn of the two blankets on the pallet, and tied the bundle off. Without a mule—and mules were more trouble than they were worth in the deep woods— he couldn't carry much more than his own gear, but Torbin's inheritance from his dead father and his missing mother was so tiny he didn't feel right leaving any of it behind.

While Jors buried his father—the soft, deep loam making an unpleasant job significantly easier than it might have been—Torbin had fallen asleep curled up against Gervais' side, still secured by the rope for safety's sake. Herald and Companion both had agreed he was too young to get any sort of closure from seeing the body. Although given that their combined experience with small children could be inscribed on a bridle bell with plenty of room left over for the lyrics to *Sun and Shadow*, Jors could only hope they'd made the right decision.

As he stepped out of the hut, Torbin's head popped up from under the other blanket. He blinked sleepily and screamed.

:He's hungry.:

:How can you tell?:

:He sounds hungry.:

He sounded furious as far as Jors could tell. *:What do I feed him?:*

:The goat needs milking.:

He looked from the goat, who continued to chew on the last few bits of fodder, to his Companion. *:How do you know?:*

:She's leaking.:

Jors had never milked a goat, but he'd been around,

and he'd seen goats milked, and how hard could it be? After all, goats producing milk *wanted* to be milked.

Although he couldn't prove that by this particular goat.

As Torbin's screams increased in both volume and duration, Jors finally managed to tie the goat to a hook on the side of the hut and get the small pail he'd found hanging from the hook more or less in position under the leaking udder, but it wasn't until Gervais moved close enough to catch the nanny's gaze and hold it that he actually managed to get his hand around a teat.

:I'm beginning to think the Collegium needs to add a few more practical courses,: the Companion said thoughtfully as Jors decanted the frothy milk into a mug with a carved wooden spout.

:I'd have been willing to lose an hour of instruction in court etiquette,: Jors admitted, handing the mug to Torbin. He'd found the mug in the hut and had to unpack it from the blanket bundle.

The child clutched it with both hands, sat down on his bare bottom, and began to drink.

With Torbin occupied—and blessedly quiet—Jors dealt with the fire pit and released the livestock.

:Will they be safe?:

:I'd put that chicken up against a Change-lion.: Sucking at a bleeding, triangular wound pecked into his left thumb, Jors dug a travel biscuit from his saddle bags and handed it to Torbin just as the child put down the now empty mug and opened his mouth to scream. *:I think I'm getting the hang of this.:*

:We need to bring the goat with us.:

:We what?:

:We were a day from the settlement when we rose this morning, and it is now past midday. The child will need to be fed again before you can give him over to his aunt.:

:*I was figuring I'd tuck him up in front of me and we'd
concentrate on speed rather than . . . :*

:*Safety?:*

Torbin's possessions having been secured with his behind the high cantle, Jors took a moment to beat his head
gently against the saddle. Gervais was right. Alone, he
might risk a gallop in poor lighting along a rough track
bracketed with branches ready to slam the unwary to
the ground, but he couldn't risk it while holding a child.
If it were later in the day, he'd suggest they stay the
night, but it was high summer, and he hated the thought
of wasting the five, maybe six hours of daylight remaining. :*If we move as quickly as possible and make no stops,
we should get there before full dark. I really don't want to
camp while responsible for this child.:*

:*Agreed. Chosen? The child is leaking.:*

Still gnawing happily on the travel biscuit, Torbin
now sat in a spreading puddle.

There had been two square pieces of cotton spread
out on bushes behind the hut. Jors hadn't realized what
they were for until it became obvious that, as practical
as it was to allow Torbin to run half naked around the
clearing—or more specially around the part of the clearing his lead line gave him access to—it was significantly
less practical to have him up on the saddle in that condition. Releasing him from his harness, Jors carried the
child over to the half full water barrel and scooped some
of the sun-warmed water over his muddy bottom.

Torbin stared at him for a moment in shock, let loose
a sound that would have shattered glass, had there been
any glass in the immediate neighborhood, and made a
run for it. Given the length of his legs, he was surprisingly fast.

Once caught, he objected, loudly, to having his bottom covered.

"This is ridiculous," Jors muttered, holding the struggling child down with one hand and securing the folded cloth with the other. "I mean it's not that I have an inflated idea of my own importance but there has got to be someone better qualified to do this than me."

:You are the only one here.:

Torbin screamed, "Ossy!" again, and with both arms up and reaching for the Companion, he actually lay still long enough for Jors to tie off the last piece of rope.

:Chosen, that looks . . . :

"Yeah, I know. There must be a trick to it." But as unusual as it looked, it seemed to be holding, so Jors lifted Torbin up into his arms, then tried not to drop him as one flailing foot caught him squarely in a delicate place.

Getting into the saddle while holding a squirming child away from further contact with that delicate—and bruised—place ranked right up there as one of the more difficult things Jors had ever accomplished.

Tucked securely between the Herald and the saddle horn, legs sticking straight out, Torbin bounced once and twisted around to look back behind them as Gervais moved out of the clearing.

Jors barely managed to catch him as he tried to fling himself from the saddle.

"Pa-Ah!"

Your papa is dead, but his last thought was of you, and I promised him I'd take you safely to your aunt, was a bit complex for a child of Torbin's age. *:What do I say to him?:* Jors demanded holding the struggling child close, his ears ringing.

:He does not want to leave his father.:

:Yeah, I got that.:

:You cannot explain, you can only comfort.:

One hand rubbing small circles on Torbin's back, the other hanging on for dear life, Jors murmured a steady stream of nonsense into the soft cap of tangled curls until Torbin reared back and, still screaming, slammed his forehead against Jors' mouth.

:I don't think this is working.: Jors admitted, leaning out to spit a mouthful of blood down onto the trail.

:Try a lullaby.:

:He'll never hear me.:

:Not with his ears; he'll hear you with his heart.:

After twenty-one repetitions of the only lullaby Jors knew, Torbin finally cried himself to sleep, his eyelashes tiny damp triangles against his flushed cheeks.

Jors sent up a silent prayer to whatever gods might be listening that the exhausted child would sleep until they reached the settlement, and, as he stayed asleep while Gervais' steady pace ate up the distance, Jors half thought his prayers might actually have been answered.

"What is that smell?" Head up, Jors turned his nose into the breeze which, weirdly, seemed to lessen the impact. "Okay, that's strange."

Torbin squirmed and giggled, nearly pitching forward as he reached out to grab a double handful of Gervais' mane. The odor got distinctly stronger.

The Companion stopped walking. *:I think,:* he began but Jors cut him off.

"Yeah, I know." The smear of yellow brown on the thigh of his Whites was a definite clue. "I bet that's going to stain."

It was amazing how much poop one small body had managed to produce. Jors distracted Torbin through the extensive clean up—involving most of their water, half a dozen handfuls of leaves, saddle soap, and his only other shirt—by feeding him slices of dried apple every time he opened his mouth. He buried the soiled cloth by the side of the trail.

:You know, if we carried this with us, we could probably use it to keep predators away from the camp at night.:

Gervais snorted. *:It would keep predators away from this whole part of the country, but I'm not carrying it.:*

Smiling, in spite of everything at the tone of his Companion's mental voice, Jors patted down the final shovel of dirt and turned to see ...

"Where's Torbin?" He'd left the child tucked between Gervais front feet, chewing on a biscuit.

:He's right . . . : Gervais turned in place, his hooves stirring up little puffs of dirt. *:He was right here!:*

:You were supposed to be watching him!:

:I was *watching him!:*

Jors swore and dove for his sword as a patch of dog willow by the side of the trail shook and cracked and Torbin shrieked. Gervais used his weight to force the thin branches apart, then Jors charged past him and nearly skewered the goat who had followed them from the clearing and was currently being fed the remains of a slobbery biscuit by a shrieking toddler.

Apparently, sometimes the shrieking was happy shrieking.

It became distinctly less happy when Jors attempted to remove Torbin's arms from around the goat's neck. Only Gervais' intervention kept him from being bitten—by the goat, although Torbin had teeth he wasn't afraid to use.

:Are you hurting him?:

:No, I'm not hurting him.: He managed to pry one handful of goat hair out of the grubby fingers, but it was almost impossible to hold that hand and pry open the other.

"Ossy!"

"That's right, Torbin. Horsey."

:Is is wise to lie to the child, Chosen?:

:It's not a lie, it's a simplification.: "Torbin, do you want to ride on the horsey?"

"Ide ossy!"

"Then you have to let go of the goat." The goat aimed a cloven hoof at Jors' ankle as he bounced the toddler and made clucking noises that didn't sound remotely like a Companion's hooves against hard packed dirt, but the combination was enough to convince Torbin.

"Ossy!" Releasing the goat, he squirmed out of Jors' grip and wrapped himself around Gervais' front leg.

:He's still sticky.:

Practice made getting up into the saddle this second time a little easier.

:Fast as you can, Heartbrother. We're down to half a canteen of water, one cloth, and . . . : "Ow!" *:Why does he keep hitting me there?:*

:Perhaps he wants to make certain you never have children of your own,: Gervais sighed as he lengthened his stride.

They reached the settlement just as dusk was deepening into dark. Like all family compounds in the deep woods, it was surrounded by a strong palisade designed to protect against both wild animals and bandits who might consider that isolation meant easy pickings. The gate was already closed, but Jors wasn't too concerned.

He was not only a Herald, he was a Herald holding a small child.

Followed by a goat.

Steadying Torbin with one hand, he rose in the stirrups and hailed the settlement. He caught a quick glimpse of a blond head over the wall by the gate, then his entire attention was taken up by the sudden need to stop Torbin from crawling up Gervais' neck to chew on his ears. At least he assumed that was the intended destination as "Ears!" seemed to be one of the words being shrieked during the struggle.

By the time he managed to pay a little more attention to his surroundings, Gervais had entered through the palisade, the gate was swinging shut behind them, and a middle-aged woman was plucking Torbin from the saddle saying, "Oh, the poor wee mite! No wonder he's unhappy, he's wet."

"Usually," Jors muttered, dismounting.

Besides the dried blood left on his knee by Torbin's father, he had yellow-brown smears on one thigh, various fluids drying on his shoulder, vomited-up apple on one boot, and his lap was distinctly damp and unpleasant smelling.

He felt weirdly smug when Torbin, still shrieking and now clearly furious, tried to launch himself out of the woman's arms and back to his. He felt understandably relieved when the woman competently prevented the launch and said, "I'll just get him straightened out and quiet, and you can explain what's happening when you're all clean and fed."

There was, apparently, a trick to making oneself heard over a screaming child.

"I assume," she continued, "that there's no emergency requiring more immediate attention?"

When Jors assured her that there was not—mostly with a combination of sign language and facial expressions—she left him to the care of her brothers, who just as competently showed him where he could tend to Gervais, wash, and change into his other, distinctly cleaner uniform. He had to borrow a shirt.

The deep woods settlements didn't have Waystations, as sleeping outside the palisades ranged from being a bad to a suicidal idea depending on how long the settlement had been in place. Since most were single-family dwellings spread over a number of buildings, it was difficult for anyone to claim favor if Heralds bunked down with their Companions either in the communal barn if the weather was bad or outside it if not. Some of the older settlements had built a Herald's Corner that offered a little privacy, but this one, young enough that some of the logs in the palisade were still leaking sap, was still concentrating on getting a secure roof over everyone's head before the cold weather came.

With Gervais unsaddled, brushed down, and settled with water, food, and three little girls who stared at him in adoration, Jors headed off to the male side of the communal showers, dumped a hide bag of sunwarmed water over his head, scrubbed himself down with a bar of soap and a soft brush, and felt a lot better. His ears had almost stopped ringing.

"Ah, Dylan, he got broke a bit when he lost Tiria." Allin, the older of the brothers, leaned back against the wall and scratched at the edge of his beard. "Was a fine fellow before, 's why we agreed to let him set up on the edge of our grant. Got to say, I'm not surprised he ended like you found him though, Herald, all alone out there like he was, heartbroken, no one to watch his back."

"Loved his boy, though," Helena added, glancing over to the pallet where Torbin lay asleep with a child close to his own age and a large orange cat. "I expect he'd have come back to people when the boy got a bit older. It's one thing to mourn while rocking a baby, it's another thing entirely when that baby's running you ragged."

"Then he should've been heading for people a couple of months ago," Jors sighed.

"I'm sure you did your best, Herald." Helena smiled as she refilled his mug. "But what do you know about babies, a young man like you. And your Companion's a stallion too, isn't he? Never mind, my grandson's near enough to Torbin's age as to make no difference, and we'd be happy to take him in."

All his instincts said these were good people, and Jors knew Torbin would be happy here. He could get on with doing what he'd been trained to do.

Except . . .

"I promised his father that I'd take Torbin to his aunt in Rabbit Hole."

"Dylan wanted him sent to Mirril, did he? Makes sense, she was as near broke up when Tiria passed as he was. Girls grew up together."

It occurred to Jors as he finished his bowl of stew that it was good thing these foresters knew Torbin's aunt. Had they not, he could have spent days trying to find her, wandering around Rabbit Hole looking for a woman related to a dead charcoal burner with very blue eyes. Well, maybe not days, Rabbit Hole wasn't that big, but it was still going to be a lot easier going in with a name. And facing another two days on the trail with Torbin, Jors was looking for all the easier he could get.

"There's a spring where you'll be stopping, so chill any milk you have left in it overnight, and it should be good until he drinks it all. There's six hard boiled eggs in the pack; as long as the shells don't crack, they'll be fine for two days, but it probably wouldn't hurt to chill them in the spring as well. Let's see, what else . . ." Helena frowned, bouncing Torbin on one hip. "Oh, yes. I've put six cloths in the pack, but let him spend as much time without anything on his bottom as possible. It's just baby poop," she snickered, as Jors failed to prevent a reaction. "After he goes, take the cloth off him and pay attention. If he starts to pee, dismount."

"Or point him out over the trail," Allin added.

That got a laugh from most of the gathered adults and a delighted shriek from Torbin, although he couldn't have understood he was the subject of the discussion.

After checking the girth one last time—any further checking of his tack would start to look like a deliberate delay—Jors swung up into the saddle. "I'll return when I've placed him safely with his aunt."

"There's no hurry, Herald. Do what you have to."

　　:*Ready?*:

　　Gervais shook his head. He'd had his mane braided the night before, and the early morning sunlight painted ripples into some of the strands. :*As ready as I am capable of being.*:

　　"Ossy!"

　　"All right." Deep breath. "Hand him up.

　　Jors spread the sixth cloths out over the bushes and hoped at least one of them would be dry by morning. He'd done his best, but there was a limit to how much he could get out with spring water and a stick.

　　"Point him over the trail," he muttered heading back to the camp—he'd moved downhill to do Torbin's laundry in the hope of avoiding contamination. It might be, as Helena had said, just baby poop, but as far as he was concerned, there was no *just* about it. :*How is it possible for him to expel more than he's taken in?*:

　　:*Are you counting vomiting?*:

　　During one of their stops, Torbin had eaten a handful of leaves he'd ripped from a bush by the trail. And some dirt. And a bug. A little further down the trail, he'd brought them all back up again. Jors had been happy—by certain specific definitions of the word happy—that he'd changed back into his stained uniform. Gervais had insisted they stop immediately and clean his mane.

　　:*Chosen!*:

　　He'd have never heard an actual verbal call over the shrieking.

　　Arriving at the campsite at a dead run, Jors found Torbin straining against Gervais' hold on the back of his smock, the Companion's teeth gripping a fold of the fabric as the child fought to get to the spring.

　　:*He ate another bug.*:

　　"Ossy!"

Jors scratched at a welt across his bare chest and sighed. :*At least he's not a fussy eater.*:

Wrapped up in the fluffier of the two blankets Jors had taken from the charcoal burner's hut, thumb tucked deep in his mouth, eyelashes a dark smudge against the upper curve of chubby cheeks, Torbin looked as though he would never consider trying to throw himself off a Companion's back causing that Companion's Herald to temporarily stop breathing. As though he'd never try to poke his own eye out with a stick. As though he'd never drop a half-dead cricket into someone else's supper.

Jors settled another log on the fire and leaned back against Gervais' shoulder to watch Torbin sleep. :*Why are we doing this again?*: he sighed.

:*You gave your word to his father.*:

:*I know but . . . .*: He dug another bit of mashed egg out of his ear. :*This isn't exactly what Heralds do, is it?*:

:*Yes.*:

:*Yes?*: Jors repeated, wondering if he'd heard correctly. Given the egg, he might not have.

:*Yes, it is exactly what Heralds do.*:

:*How do you figure?*: he asked, stroking one hand along the Companion's silky side.

:*The Heralds not only protect Valdemar as it is but, by their actions, Valdemar as it will be. This child is the future of Valdemar. It doesn't matter if he is Chosen or he becomes a charcoal burner like his father; here and now, he is not only himself, he is the potential for everything he could be. Without him there will be no future in Valdemar, so yes, you are doing exactly what it is Heralds do. There is nothing more important you could be doing.*:

:*That helps.*:

:*I thought it might.*:

:*You have to admit, though, he certainly puts something like a* diplomatic *mission to Karse into perspective.*:

:*It is unlikely that you and I would be sent to Karse.*:
:*Not diplomatic enough?*:
:*Not even close. Still, a mission to Karse would likely involve less vomiting.*:
:*There is that.*:

Rabbit Hole was not exactly a bustling metropolis, and the second person Jors asked was able to direct him to Mirril. The charcoal burner's younger sister had married the son of a wheelwright, and they lived in the family complex surrounding the work yard. She had her brother's bright blue eyes.

Torbin tried to stick a finger into one of them, but he didn't shriek when she cuddled him, her tears falling to gleam against his curls, so maybe, Jors thought, maybe he knew this was home.

"At least Dylan didn't die alone, there's that. He had a Herald with him." Mirril blinked away tears and managed a watery smile. "He used to tell me stories about Heralds when we were growing up." She frowned suddenly at the long white hairs Torbin was clutching in one hand. "Oh, no . . ."

:*Tell her he may keep them, Chosen.*:

When Jors passed on Gervais' remark, she blushed and tucked the hair into her apron pocket. "I could braid them into a bracelet for him. He wouldn't eat them then."

"I wouldn't count on it," Jors told her. "He likes to eat. He likes travel biscuits and egg and goat's milk. Oh, and Helena at the settlement said that the next time they bring a load of lumber out, she'll pay you for Torbin's goat. She followed us to the settlement." Torbin reached out a hand, and Jors pretended to grab it and eat the fingers, making him shriek with laughter. "He likes to run, and he seems to have no idea of self preservation, but he's a tough little guy and a big believer in picking himself up and getting on with things when he falls. He doesn't talk a lot. I don't know if that's usual for his age, but he says *no* and *ride horsey*." And *Papa,* but Jors didn't add that out loud. "He's pretty good at making his wants known."

"Ossy!"

She was smiling now and shaking her head.

"We need to get back on the trail so . . . uh . . ." It was harder to say goodbye than he'd expected. He planted a kiss on the dimpled knuckles and released Torbin's hand. "Be a good boy for your auntie."

"Ossy!"

"Thank you for everything you've done."

Jors thought of Torbin's father. "I wish I could have done more." He turned, then turned again. "Do you think, I mean, would you mind if I stopped by to visit him if I'm in the area? I wouldn't be checking up or anything; I just . . ."

. . . had stains all over his uniform, and the smell might never leave his saddle bags, and it was entirely possible he still had egg in his ear.

"Would I mind if a Herald came by to visit my brother's son? Why would I ever mind that? Why would anyone. But why would you?" Mirril's cheeks were flushed, and she ducked her head in embarrassment. "I mean, you have so much more important things to do."

"Ossy!"

With an ease that came from three days of intensive training, Jors caught the future of Valdemar as he threw himself out of his auntie's arms shrieking, "Ossy!"

"Actually," he said, letting Torbin slide to the ground and wrap himself around one of the Companion's legs, "I don't. Not really."

:*He's still sticky*,: Gervais sighed.

The Thief of Anvil's Close

By Fiona Patton

Fiona Patton was born in Calgary, Alberta, Canada, and grew up in the United States. In 1975 she returned to Canada and now lives in rural Ontario with her partner and nine cats. She has six books out from DAW, including her latest, *The Golden Tower*, the second in the Warriors of Estavia series and is currently working on the third and final book, tentatively entitled *The Shining City*. She has over thirty short stories with Tekno Books and DAW. "The Thief of Anvil's Close" is the second Valdemar story featuring Haven's Dann family.

It was a beautiful, autumn afternoon in Haven, the kind you remembered long afterward: warm and brightly sunny, with just enough breeze to sweeten the air with the heady aromas of baking bread and . . .

Standing on the crowded threshold of the Iron Street Watch House, Sergeant Hektor Dann took a deep breath, his eye tightly closed . . .

And . . . meat pies.

He smiled. Every year, from the very first day his mother had allowed him to bring his father and grandfather their dinners at age six to the day he was named, first watchhouse sweeper, then runner, then finally constable, the autumn breeze had carried the same scents on the breeze. He could almost feel the cloth-wrapped pot of warm stew against his chest, the worn, wooden broom handle in his hands, the cold cobblestones against his bare feet, the scratch of the brand new uniform tunic against his wrists.

"Hek! Hektor! I mean, Sergeant!"

Almost, but not quite. He opened his eyes.

His youngest brother, eleven-year-old Padreic, newly made watchhouse runner, rocked to a halt in front of him, breathing like a forge bellows. His face was red with exertion, but his eyes shone with importance and just a hint of mischief that Hektor instantly mistrusted.

"Runner."

"You're wanted on . . . Anvil's Close," his brother panted, ignoring his older brother's attempt at a stern expression. "At *Edzel's* shop," he added in a meaningful voice.

"Who's wantin' me, Edzel or one of his neighbors?"

"Edzel."

"Well that's somethin' anyway. Leastways, there won't be a public nuisance complaint or an assault charge." Last month, Master Blacksmith Edzel Smith had thrown an andiron at a farrier who'd though his concerns were "funny." Edzel was a lot of things, but he was never funny.

"There might still be," Padreic disagreed, his breath back and the look of importance growing on his face as he savored the information he possessed that his older brother didn't. "He's throwin' a right barny this time," he embellished. "Rantin' and ravin' like a fit's on him. Says someone's been thievin' his goods."

"Edzel always thinks someone's been thievin' his goods."

Hektor turned to see their oldest brother, Corporal Aiden Dann, standing behind him, an unimpressed expression on his face.

"This time he's worse, Aiden," Padreic assured him. "'Cause this time he might be right."

"Hm." Aiden glanced at Hektor. "Well, *Sergeant*," he said, giving the brand new stripes on Hektor's sleeve a sharp prod. "You goin', or you gonna stand there actin' like you're still afraid of a crazy old blacksmith?"

"I'm goin' . . ."

"Only?"

"Only . . ." Hektor gave his older brother a helpless look, and Aiden shook his head in disgust.

"Fine, I'll go with you."

"Thanks, Aiden."

"Thanks, Corporal," his brother prompted.

"Yeah, thanks Corporal."

Anvil's Close lay just off the Iron Market entrance gates. A narrow, neatly cobblestoned street, it was made up of small forges and iron shops where the city's blacksmiths and their families sold everything from wrought iron railings and window grills to surgical tools and musical instruments: anything that could be fashioned out of metal. An older woman, dressed in a stout leather apron, leaned out the door of the first shop as they passed by.

"Well, well, Sergeant Dann," she said with a wicked smile. "Haven't you just gotten all grown up an' promoted. Ismy wouldn't know you to look at you now."

Hektor kept his expression as neutral as possible although he could feel his neck turning red above the collar of his blue and gray watchman's uniform. "Hello, Judee," he replied.

"Crazy old fool'll bring on a fit if he's not careful," she noted, jerking her head down the Close. "Best get yourself over there double quick afore he does his heart a mischief."

Hektor nodded and carried on at once, but Aiden paused for a moment.

"I've a buckle that needs mendin', Judee. You got time?"

She nodded. "Send it over with Paddy. I'll have it done by your shift's end."

"Thanks."

As he made to follow his younger brother, her expression turned serious. "Really, Aiden, get that old fool sorted out, will you? His rantin's bad for business, an' not just for him; for the whole Close."

"We will."

"You tell him he's scarin' his grandbaby. That might do it."

He nodded, catching up with Hektor as he made—with some reluctance—for the small iron shop across the street and three doors down. Like most businesses in this part of Haven, it was little more than eight feet wide, with two horizontal shutters at the front. The top was supported on tall posts to provide an awning for the bottom, which, supported on two shorter posts, acted as a display counter for tools, nails, hinges, handles, and whatever other bits of ironwork the proprietor thought might lure a customer inside. The brightly painted sign depicting a bell flanked by two ornate candlesticks above a decorative anvil declared the owner to be a master smith capable of crafting more refined objects than mere horseshoes and hammers. But what had always set Edzel's shop apart from the others and what had kept Hektor, Aiden, and many of the boys their age coming in and braving the smith's legendary temper was that in his prime, Edzel Smith had made toys of extraordinary skill: tops and jacks, metal whistles, tin flutes, and polished iron marbles, lead guardsmen with arms and legs that actually moved, and tiny, beautifully crafted Heralds and their Companions, painted a heavy, enameled white. Hektor remembered saving his pennybits for months just to be able to afford a single articulated watchman no bigger than his forefinger when he'd been nine years old. Edzel's daughter, Ismy, had given him another when he was twelve.

He glanced down to the end of the Close where it opened up onto Saddler's Street before loud shouting issuing from Edzel's shop jerked him forcibly from the memory.

"I tell you, I'm bein' thieved from!"

Edzel Smith stood in the middle of the shop shaking his fists in rage. A squat, heavyset man in his late sixties, his gray hair thinning on top and gray beard covering a jutting and belligerent chin; years of forge work had bent his back and twisted his hands, but his arms and shoulders were still covered with thick, corded muscle, and his temper was as volatile as ever.

"Don't you try an' shush me, boy!" he continued, his face turning a dangerous purple. "I know when I'm being thieved from, don't you try an' tell me otherwise! I had thirteen thimbles, thirteen, on that there back worktable and not a one less! I had a full box of lath nails, that's twenty-four exactly, an' now there be naught but nineteen!"

The *boy* he was shouting at, his son Tay, a tall, broad man of almost thirty-five and a full smith in his own right, did his best to look if not believing then at least respectful as Edzel stomped about, shaking his fists in near apoplectic rage. Usually at work at the forge behind the shop, Tay entered this world of crammed shelving and angry fathers as seldom as possible, but with the rage on him, Edzel was more than Tay's long suffering wife, Trisha, who helped him run the shop, could handle.

"Boggles maybe?" Tay suggested, trying, without success, to lighten his father's mood.

"Bollocks it's boggles!" Edzel shouted back. "I know boggles! I seen a boggle when I was a little, walkin' home from the forge at twilight one summer, an' it ain't them.

It's her, I tell you!" He spun about to shake one fist out the open doorway. "That's who it is, that heartless, thievin' stepmother of yourn! An' I'll have the Watch on her! See if I don't!"

"Now, Da," Tay said, trying to keep his voice reasonable. "You know Judee h'aint been near the shop since she moved out two years ago."

His father's face darkened still further. "You mean since she took half my hard-earned brass an' opened that spiteful rat-infested trap she dares call an iron shop with your ungrateful half-wit of a brother, you mean, is that what you mean!?" Edzel demanded, his voice turning even more shrill.

Tay sighed. In the nearly twenty years since his mother's death, his father'd had three other women in his . . . in their . . . lives, and each one had finally been driven away by Edzel's unpredictable temper, made worse now since age and arthritis had driven him from the forge and into the shop full time. Judee'd lasted longer than most, long enough to give Tay and his younger sister, Ismy, a half-brother before she too had left them. But this time she'd gone no farther than along Anvil's Close to open up a rival iron shop of her own with their brother Ben, who'd just gotten his blacksmith's papers.

And whose business was doing much better than theirs, if truth be told, Tay admitted.

He glanced around the shop. It wasn't that it was small or cramped or dirty. It was roughly the same size as any other shop in the Close with a tiny back room for small repair jobs and a front room laid out neatly with a long sandalwood table in the center and sturdy iron shelving on three of four walls, with the larger goods on the bottom and the smaller on the upper. The more valuable were locked in an actual glass and iron-barred case behind a wide, golden oak counter that Edzel polished every morning with ferris oil until it shone.

And it wasn't that their goods were particularly expensive; their prices were comparable to any other shop in Haven. No, Tay told himself for the hundredth time as he watched a customer step just inside the door, listen for a few moments to his father's language, then carefully back out again. It was the shop owner himself. They had to do something about Edzel before the business failed entirely, and a few misplaced thimbles were the least of their worries. But he had no idea what the something should be.

Tay turned as Trisha came in from the tiny back kitchen alcove, her expression exasperated.

"I tried to get him to go in for some tea," she said in a strained voice. "But he won't have it."

Tay nodded. "We need to fetch Zo-zo," he said, trying to hide the strain in his own voice. "She's the only one that can calm him down now."

She frowned. "Meegan brought her by first thing this mornin'," she said doubtfully. "She'll be at Judee's for the rest of the day now."

"I know, but he'll rant himself into a fever if he keeps on like this. Ask Judee, will you, just for a few minutes, for me, please? Ask her?"

"I've sent for the Watch!" his father continued to no one in particular. "An' don't you think I won't call the Guard too if that shiftless lot up at the Iron Street Station House don't get here soon. I told that Dann boy to fetch Sergeant Thomar, he'll get her sorted out in a hurry!"

Tay turned. "Thomar Dann's retired, Da," he said gently.

"Then he'll fetch Egan instead."

"Egan's dead. He died in the Iron Market fire last month, remember? He'll probably get Egan's son, Hektor. He just made sergeant. You remember Hektor, Da?"

Edzel glared at his son with a malevolent expression. "Course I remember him," he shouted. "I chased him away from Ismy when he were thirteen, an' gave him a damn good thrashin' to boot. I don't care if that boy fetches Hektor Dann or the Monarch's Own Herald. I want someone here, and I want 'em here now!"

"Mornin', Edzel."

As one, both smiths whirled about to see Hektor and Aiden standing in the shop doorway. Edzel's expression never changed. "Bout time you two showed up," he snarled as Trisha made her way past them with a sympathetic expression. "Get in here an' do your job! I could be missin' half my shop for all the protection I get! I'll call the actual Guard an' have them do your job for you if you don't give me satisfaction right this very minute!" He fixed Hektor with a rheumy-eyed glare. "See if I don't!"

Hektor nodded, struggling to remember that he was twenty-one and not thirteen and trying to keep as neutral an expression on his face as possible. "So, what exactly are you missing . . . sir," he said, using the non-committal but respectful tone he'd learned from generations of Danns in the Iron Street Watch.

It did not mollify Edzel. "I told that brother of yourn when I sent him!" he snarled back. "I had twelve silver spoons in that there locked cabinet," he said, thrusting a gnarled thumb behind him. "I was giving 'em a good cleanin' last night. Now there's naught but eleven! You just go look and see!"

Hektor squeezed behind the counter to peer into the cabinet in question. Three shelves contained a collection of delicate metalwork, including eleven silver spoons. About to ask if Edzel was sure he'd put all twelve away last night—a question that would certainly have caused another round of shouting—he was interrupted by Aiden.

"Didn't know you worked in silver, Edzel," his older brother said absently, studying a long-handled toasting fork with a discerning eye.

"I don't," Edzel snapped, snatching it away from him. "Tay's makin' 'em a locked case to protect 'em against fire. But there's more what's gone walkin' too: thimbles, nails, one stylus, two boat hooks," he said, counting each one off on his fingers, "a diagonal, a rounded bill, an anvil swage, two hot punches, a driver, an adze blade, an awl, an edge shave, three whole palm irons, a seat wheel, a cleave, an' nine pair of arms and legs!"

The long list of unfamiliar words, ending in arms and legs, caused both Hektor and Aiden to stare at him, and Edzel spat at the floor in disgust. "For lead soldiers, you idiots, what else would they be for? An' don't you go lookin' at me like I lost my wits neither, I done a full inventory just last week, an' I know my stock! All them things is missin'!"

At that moment, Trisha returned with a small girl of around three years old in her arms. The child caught sight of Edzel and threw her own arms out, nearly hurling herself from Trisha's in the process.

"Ganther!"

The smith's entire demeanor changed. His wrinkled face split into a huge grin, and he snatched her up at once, twisting her around until she sat precariously perched upon one bent shoulder. "Here, now, what's all this then, my little Zo-zo bird?" he chortled, his recent ill temper completely forgotten. "Thort you was at your granny's for your afternoon nap?

"My grandbaby, Zoe," he explained almost pleasantly in answer to the watchmen's questioning expressions. "Now, where was I? Oh, yeah." He waved a warning finger at Hektor. "You do sommat about this thievin', or I'll be up to your own granther's myself. Retired or no, he'll light a fire under your . . ." he paused as the child began to bounce up and down on his shoulder. "Well, you just mind you do," he finished.

He glanced over at Aiden with a withering expression. "An' you've got a buckle there what needs mendin'. What's the Watch comin' to? It wouldn't a been allowed in Thomar's day." He turned, the child still on his shoulder. "Tay, you've a moment to fix yon buckle?"

"Sure, Da."

As his son came forward, Aiden shook his head. "It's nothin'. It can wait."

"No need to wait," Edzel said, waving a dismissive hand at him. "The boy can manage that kinda work at least. It's not like it's *fine* work. You have that off an' he'll fix it up a twinklin'."

"But . . ."

Tay just gave him a strained smile. "S'all right Aiden, just come on in the back. I'll be naught but a moment."

They all made for the workroom. As Aiden struggled to remove the buckle, Zoe threw her hands out toward an ornate iron cage on a shelf beside the worktable.

"Lillbit!"

Edzel chuckled. "Lillbit's right there, all safe an' sound, jus' like you left him earlier," he assured her. Reaching over, he unlocked the door, and a small, gray creature dove from the cage and clambered up the old man's arm towards her.

Aiden started in surprise. "That's a rat!"

Both Edzel and Zoe turned equally indignant expressions on him as the child caught the creature up, cupping it protectively in her hands.

"My Lillbit!" she shouted.

"Lillbit's her pet!" Edzel snarled. "Zo-zo tamed him up her own self just this summer, an' he's still a little himself, so don't you dare think about doin' him any mischief, Aiden Dann!"

"A rat? You let your granddaughter play with a rat?"

Aiden looked so horrified that Zoe immediately began to cry.

"Yes, a rat!" Edzel shouted. "Not that it's any of your business!" As Zoe continued to cry, he caught up a leaf hammer, brandishing it at Aiden with one hand while he frantically patted Zoe's hair with the other. "Now get out, you're upsettin' my grandbaby. Get out, get out, get out!"

"Out, out, out!" Zoe echoed.

As Aiden retreated, shaking his head, Edzel whirled on Hektor. "An' you find that thief, you hear me!" he shouted, his earlier rage returning. "I pay my guild fees, an' I have the right to protection. If I don't get it, I'll call the Guard! I'll call the Heralds! They've a proper court, an' that truth spell of theirs'll sort you all out good an' proper!"

He almost slammed the shop door on them both as they left.

Across the Close, Judee gave them an ironic salute with a ceramic tea cup before disappearing into her own shop as well.

"You want us to guard Edzel Smith's iron shop all night?"

Hektor's two middle brothers, Jakon, nineteen, and Raik, seventeen, had served as night watchmen since being taken on as full constables. It worked well for the Danns since they could use the smallest of the family's bedrooms during the day, and Hektor and Padreic could use it at night. But it also meant that neither of them were used to taking orders from their new sergeant. Now, they both just stared at him.

"You're joking," Jakon protested.

"No, I'm not."

"What does the captain say about it?"

Hektor's expression hardened. "The captain's left it up to me. I'm the Sergeant."

"You're the *Day* Sergeant, Hek," Raik replied.

"Yeah, an' the *Day* Sergeant posts the shifts," Hektor reminded him. "So here's your shifts: one at the entrance to Anvil's Close, one at Edzel's shop door. Take it in turns if you like, but you're takin' it."

"For how long?"

"A few nights likely."

"How many's a few?"

"As many as I say it is. Get seen, let any possible thieves know we're on the job. There'll be a couple posted durin' the day too."

Jakon shook his head in disgust. "You don't really think someone's been thievin' off Edzel, do you, Hek? I mean, he's always been a suspicious old bugger, glarin' at everyone who comes near his place. It's a wonder he has any customers at all."

"He's off his head," Raik agreed.

"Maybe, but it makes no matter. He's paid his guild fees like he said, so you're for Edzel's shop until I say different. Get used to it, *Constables*."

"Yes, *Sergeant*."

Hektor chose to ignore both the tone of voice and the sarcastic salutes of his younger brothers, merely turning and stalking away.

The next morning, they made their report with equally sour expressions. It had rained all night, and they'd spent a cold, wet, and uneventful shift guarding nothing. No one had come near the Close, never mind the shop. As far as they were concerned no one was going to.

Padreic, however, had a different report to make.

"An' you're sure the settin's were right here, moonstones an' all?"

"No, the moonstones weren't here; moonstones are rare," Edzel said angrily, thumping his fist on his work table behind the main shop. "The moonstones got locked up good and proper when I was finished with 'em. The iron settin's were fine work twenty year ago, but they ain't so rare they have to be locked up too. They was right here on this very table, and now two of 'em's gone!"

Hektor peered down at the three clawed bits of metal, used, Edzel had told him stiffly, to affix gems to sword and dagger hilts, then turned to Trisha, standing just inside the door. "Did you see 'em?" he asked hopefully.

She shook her head. "Sorry, Hek. Edzel was bent over 'em till long past when Tay an' me went to bed," she answered. "I didn't see how many he had then nor later."

"I had *five*," Edzel sputtered. "I already told you, five!" Only the presence of Zoe, playing happily in the corner with Lillbit, kept his voice down to a dull roar, but Hektor could see a vein in his forehead throbbing dangerously.

"Could someone have come in the back way, through the forge," he asked. "Or through one of the windows above, maybe?"

"The forge is closed up tighter'n a drum at night, an' my window locks are the best in Haven; I cast 'em myself!"

"The roof?"

"Paw! My granther build that roof, an' it's a sound as the day it went up! 'Sides, this one's a right light sleeper," Edzel said, jerking a thumb at Trisha, "She's up half the night. She'd have heard if anyone was creepin' about up there."

Trisha nodded. "Tay snores," she explained.

"I tell you who it t'was; it was that woman!" Edzel continued. "She had that ungrateful son of ours make a shop key afore she left, that's what she did, an' she snuck over here in the dead of night. Your lot must have fallen asleep on duty!"

Hektor felt his face flush angrily, but he refused to rise to the accusation. "I'll talk to Judee," he said stiffly.

"So, lemme get this straight ..." Crossing her arms over her amble bosom, Judee looked more amused than indignant. "Your askin' me if I have a key to Edzel's shop?"

Hektor just nodded.

She chuckled. "No, boy, I don't. An' even if I did, do you really think I could sneak about at night, at my age, with my girth, *in the rain*, so as to hide from two grown constables what spent the entire night moanin' an' complainin' about the weather till the wee hours?"

Hands on hips, she almost dared Hektor to say something, then turned as Trisha crossed the street with Zoe in her arms. "C'mere, darlin'," she crooned. "Come'n see your Granny." Catching the child up in her arms, she chucked her under the chin. "Now, you left Lillbit behind, yeah? To keep your granther company? Cause you know your granny's not fond of rats in her shop, an' Ginger'd just as likely eat him as look at him."

Zoe nodded happily, bouncing up and down in her grandmother's arms much as she'd done in her grandfather's. "Ganther'll keep him safe," she said happily.

"That's good." Judee turned back to Hektor. "Edzel's losing what's left of his wits," she pronounced. "Nobody's thievin' from him at all. He's either imaginin' he's got more stock'n he has, or he's misplacin' it all himself. It's a waste of a constable's time, if you ask me, but you go right ahead an' post your brothers on my very own door if that make you happy, *Sergeant* Dann. But I should warn you," she said with a snicker, "it's gonna rain again."

"I don't think we need to do that," he replied gravely, refusing to rise to the bait. "But one on Edzel's door an' one inside his shop might calm him down some."

*   *   *

Neither Jakon nor Raik took the order at all well. Aiden finally had to step in and threaten to knock their heads together, and it was with some acrimony that the two of them headed off for their shift after supper that evening. As the rest of the family settled into the small sitting room, Hektor threw himself down next to his sister and grandfather. Tucked up next to the flat's small coal stove, he glanced down at the pigeon cupped in thirteen-year-old Kasiath's hands with a questioning look.

"Peachwing's ailin' again?" he asked, struggling to keep his tone of voice light.

"Some," she admitted.

"Mites again," his grandfather sniffed.

"And she's sad 'cause the autumn's endin'," Kasiath added solemnly, listening to the sound of rain pelting against the sitting room window. "There won't be such nice flyin' when the snow comes."

"That won't be for a while yet, though, will it?"

"Peachwing figures it'll be afore the end of the month."

Hektor peered down at the bird, who peered myopically back up at him from the protection of his sister's fingers. "Don't know how you can know what she's thinkin'," he said with a touch of admiration in his voice.

"The girl's always been right smart when it comes to feathered creatures," their grandfather agreed. "But I think she a bit batty, myself."

"Thomar," their mother admonished, looking up from where she and Aiden's wife, Sulia, were stitching a piece of embroidered cloth together.

Kasiath just shrugged. "S'all right, Ma. Granther's just teasin'." She stroked the bird's head with one fingertip. "Don't know that she is thinkin' exactly," she admitted to Hektor, ignoring their grandfather's wink. "It's more

like a feelin', really. She gets all pouty, layin' down in her
feathers, an' I just know it's cause she can feel the snow
comin', an' she hates it on her wings. But I just sit with
her a while, and then she feels better."

"Kassie's always known how to do that ever since she
were a little," their grandfather added proudly as Kasiath gently tucked Peachwing into a small wooden box
at their feet. "Best birder I ever knew, my granddaughter. It's a gift, she has with 'em. They takes to her right
outta the egg. Tamed up her first one when she were no
more'n three years old. You remember, Jemmee?"

Their mother nodded. "I remember bird droppings all
over my table," she said with a smile that belied the sour
tone in her voice. "And I remember tellin' you both that
my kitchen was no place to tame up a wild creature."

"Huh. Sounds like Zoe and her pet rat," Aiden said
from the other side of the room where he was playing
with his own children, three-year-old Egan and six-
month-old Leila, before they went to bed.

"I'm amazed Meegan lets her keep such an animal at
all," Sulia noted with a frown.

"Zoe keeps it at Edzel's," Hektor replied. "But that's
even stranger, what with him dotin' on her so much.
You'd think he'd be scared it would bite her."

"Age's addled his wits," Aiden pronounced.

"Just 'cause a man's gettin' on in years don't mean
any such a thing," their grandfather said sternly, pulling
the ends of a well-patched shawl more tightly about his
shoulders.

"He thinks Judee's creepin' in an' stealin' his goods,
Granther," Padreic said, looking up from the pig's blad-
der ball he was perpetually mending.

"An' I asked along the whole Close," Hektor added.
"No one's seen anyone suspicious about or lost anythin'
themselves."

"'Sides, who steals one silver spoon from a set of

twelve, or five iron lath nails?" Aiden added. Rising, he scooped up both children under his arms and headed out the sitting room door amidst shrieks of laughter.

"He's right, Granther," Hektor said. "I think Edzel's' losin' his wits. His temper's gettin' worse an' worse. The whole Close's gettin' sick of it."

Thomar just sniffed. "Edzel was a fine craftsman in his day," he answered. "One of the best for small, delicate goods as I ever saw. He might a made a fine jeweler or even an artist if he'd come from a different family. The arthritis is what made him so sour. It robbed him of his craft, that's enough to turn anyone ugly."

He fell silent, staring at the stove until Jemmee glanced up. "You'd best be off to bed now, Paddy," she said. "You too, Kassie. Take Peachwing back to the coop now."

"Yes, Ma. G'night, Granther."

"Night, darlin's." Thomar accepted a kiss each from his youngest grandchildren. A few moments later, Jemmee and Sulia headed off as well with a warning to Thomas and Hektor not to sit up too late.

"Mornin' shift comes early, Hektor Dann," his mother admonished as she snuffed out the room's few candles. "An' you need your sleep."

"I'll be along soon, Ma," he promised. But once they were alone, he glanced speculatively at his grandfather. "Do you miss watchhouse duty, Granther?" he asked.

Thomar just shrugged. "Sometimes," he admitted. "But I've got my birds, and young Kassie to pass my knowledge on to. You lot as well if it comes to that," he added. "As long as I can pass on what I learned from my watchhouse days I'm happy enough. Problem with Edzel's that he ain't got that. The shop's not for him. He never were too good with folk, just iron. When his own littles were young, he could teach 'em what he knew, but they haven't exactly followed in his footsteps."

"Two of his boys are blacksmiths, Granther," Hektor reminded him gently.

"Sure, but neither one of 'em has the same skill with small things, an' that was what he was always the most proud of. Dunno, maybe when Zoe gets older, he can teach her to make toy soldiers an' whistles or somethin'."

The two of them sat in silence for a long time until Thomar gave his grandson a speculative look of his own. "Asked along the whole Close, did you?" he asked.

Hektor nodded.

"All the way to the end?"

"Yeah. Why?"

"No reason." Thomar stretched his hands towards the fire. "Little Leila'll be walkin' soon, Sulia says. An' you know what that means, don't you?"

"Um, no."

"It mean your Ma'll be anglin' for another grand-baby, soon."

"From who?"

His grandfather just shrugged. "Weren't you sweet on young Ismy Smith once?"

Hektor raised an eyebrow. "You sure, it ain't you an-glin' for another great-grandbaby, Granther?"

"Maybe. But you was sweet on Ismy once, yeah?"

Hektor nodded cautiously.

"And?" Thomas prodded.

"And . . . she married a saddle maker two years ago."

"And?"

"And . . . he died," Hektor admitted reluctantly. "Last winter."

"And?"

"And nothin'."

"Nothin'?"

"Nothin'."

"Hm." Thomar hunkered down into his shawl. "Pity

that. She were a nice girl." He glanced about the flat with an innocent expression. "I hear Lorin Potter an' his family from downstairs are movin' in with his wife's Da next spring."

"Oh?"

"Yep. That leaves a flat empty. Sulia says she an' Aiden might think about takin' it. There's even an extra room for Jakon an' Raik to help 'em out with the rent. We figure that'd give us plenty of room here should someone else maybe get interested in havin' a family, now that he's bringin' in a sergeant's pay an' all."

"Who's we?" Hektor asked, both amused and a bit annoyed at the same time.

"Me an' your Ma," his grandfather answered easily. "An' Sulia. An' Paddy."

"Paddy?"

"Sure, he's bringin' in a proper wage as runner. He figures he can put in some to help out now."

"I s'pose he can." Hektor stared at the tiny flickering flames behind the stove door. "Not sure I'll be bringin' in a sergeant's pay for long, though," he said after a moment. "Don't think I'm suited to it. Aiden woulda made a better choice. I never shoulda been promoted above him. I'm no good at tellin' folk what to do, whatever the captain says."

"Bollocks," his grandfather scoffed. "Aiden's too bad tempered, just like your Uncle Reed. Your da got promoted above him, an' they worked it out just fine."

"It ain't me an' Aiden, Granther, it's me an' Jakon and Raik."

His grandfather snorted unsympathetically. "They'll come around. Keep doin' what you're doin'; stick 'em out in the rain until they mind you." He pulled his shawl more tightly about his shoulders again. "Now, you best be off to bed afore Paddy gets too comfortable with all them covers. Go on now, I'll head off myself in a bit."

Hektor nodded. "G'night, Granther."

"G'night, boy."

His brothers' report the next morning was much the same as the day before. They'd taken it in turn to guard the shop inside and out, and, once again, no one had come near. Jakon made it clear that as far as he was concerned, any more time spent on Anvil's Close was a waste of time.

As the day wore on and there was no word from Edzel, Hektor began to believe they were right.

Just before his shift's end, he pushed aside the mountain of reports that being a sergeant seemed to involve and headed out to see for himself.

The shop seemed strangely quiet when he arrived. Trisha was wrapping a piece of string around a set of fire tongs for a customer, and Zoe was playing happily with Lillbit behind the counter when he stepped inside.

"Where is everyone?" he asked.

Trisha shrugged. "Tay an' Edzel are at a guild meetin'," she said in a resigned tone of voice. "Edzel wants 'em to hire a force of private guards for the Close since he says he got thieved from again last night."

Hektor blinked. "You're joking?"

She shook her head. "Apparently one of his moonstones is missin' now. Edzel just about went off his head this morning when he found out. But at least he ain't blamin' Judee no more. She an' Ben are at the meetin' too, so it's just me an' Zoe here all by our lonesome today, ain't we, Zo-zo?"

Zoe nodded happily.

"I'll just go an' check on our tea," Trisha continued. "You an' Lillbit watch the shop for me, all right?"

"We will." Zoe glanced up at Hektor with a sunny smile. "Lillbit's glad it's tea time," she pronounced, "Cause 'e say's 'e real hungry."

He grinned down at her. "Is he now?"

She nodded vigorously. "'E wants biscuits an' jam wif 'is tea. I tol' Auntie Trisa."

"Biscuits an' jam? Really?"

"An' butter. It's inna cupboard inna kitchen." She pointed towards the back. "Lillbit can get inside if I ask 'im too, but Auntie Trisa don't like 'im in there 'cause 'e gets 'is feet inna butter 'cause 'e knocks the lid off."

"He's that smart, is he?"

She nodded. "Lillbit can get inta all sorts a cupboards an' cases."

"You talk to him, then?"

"Yeah, an' 'e talks back."

A chuckle made Hektor glance up to see Trisha standing in the kitchen doorway holding a tray. "Lillbit's Zo-zo's *special* friend," she said emphasizing the word special. "Isn't he, Zo-zo?"

"Yeah."

"I kinda had one of 'em too," Hektor admitted. "When I was a little, only no one else could see him except me."

"No one else can hear Lillbit except Zoe," Trisha agreed. "Will you stay for tea, Hek? We're havin' biscuits an' jam."

"An' butter," Zoe prompted.

"An' butter, a course."

Hektor shook his head. "I should be gettin' back. I got reports to file," he said woefully, watching as Zoe set Lillbit carefully onto her shoulder before lifting a loose floorboard up with practiced ease and depositing something shiny beneath it. He frowned.

"Zoe, whatcha doin' there?" he asked lightly.

"Tidyin' up shop," she answered. "Granther say's ye should always tidy up shop when ye close. Even for tea."

"Is that your shop, then?"

She nodded. "Lillbit's an' mine. When we get big, we're gonna run Granther's shop; maybe Granny's too."

"Can I see your shop?"

She nodded. Setting the floorboard to one side, she pointed into the cavity below. "We gots goods an' tools jus' like Granther," she explained. "But we don't gots a sign yet. We will though, real soon. The tools're um . . ." she screwed her face up in concentration " . . . hundred pennybits, an' the good're . . . four hundred."

Hektor leaned over the counter to see a number of small, unfamiliar tools lined up neatly beside two boat hooks, one thimble, a silver spoon, two iron settings, five nails, a handful of lead arms and legs, and a moonstone cradled in a piece of cloth. Beside him, Trisha's eyes widened in exasperated surprise.

"So it was his own grandbaby thievin' his goods?"

Back at the watchhouse, Jakon gave a loud guffaw. "Bet Edzel felt like a right fool when he found that out."

Hektor just shrugged. "Seemed to make him happy, actually," he replied. "When I left 'em, they were talkin' about what kind a sign her shop should have."

"A rat an' a anvil, maybe?"

"Maybe. Seems like Zoe's got the same talent with animals as Kassie has with birds. Don't know how that'll help her run her own iron shop, but it should help Edzel come to terms with runnin' his."

Raik leaned against Hektor's desk, threatening to send the pile of reports to the floor. "So that's the end of rain-soaked shifts on Anvil's Close then, yeah?" he said, with a triumphant grin.

Hektor nodded. "An' the start of rain-soaked shifts on Tannery Row, so get your waterproof cloaks out."

"What?" Both younger brothers stared at him, and he turned a frown worthy of Aiden back at them.

"That's what I said, *Constables.*"

"Aw, c'mon, Hek."

"C'mon, *Sergeant.*"

"For how long?"

"That depends."

"On what?"

"On how long I figure it needs doin', so get home to your suppers. An' tell Ma I'll be home later."

"Where're you goin'?" Raik asked sullenly.

"Saddler's Street."

His younger brothers' expressions immediately changed from aggrieved to interested, but when he simply jerked his chin toward the door, they obeyed him with minimal grumbling.

Once they were gone, he carefully straightened the pile of reports, then his uniform tunic, then the reports again, then, finally left the tiny sergeant's office. As he headed down Iron Street, he took in a deep breath of the crisp autumn air, tasting the familiar aromas of baking bread and meat pies, before heading down Anvil's Close. At the door to Edzel's shop, both Zoe and her grandfather totally ignored him, but both Judee and Lillbit gave him equally knowing expressions before Trisha called them all inside to their own supper.

Twice Blessed

by *Judith Tarr*

Judith Tarr has written many novels and several Friends of Valdemar stories under her own name. As Caitlin Brennan she writes novels about horses, especially the Lipizzan horses she breeds and trains on her farm in Arizona.

Nerys and Kelyn were born on the same day, in the same town, to mothers who were cousins as well as the best and closest of friends. Their fathers were partners; Nerys' father bred and raised sheep that were famous for the softness and richness of their wool, and Kelyn's father turned the fleeces to a fine and subtly dyed fabric that had even clothed the queen in Haven.

Everyone had hoped one of the children would be a boy so that the two families could unite in marriage as well as in business and friendship. When both turned out to be girls, they were universally expected to be companions in childhood and friends and allies when they grew to womanhood.

That was a lovely dream. The reality manifested when they were barely old enough to sit up: Nerys challenged Kelyn for a doll that happened to be identical to the one she herself had, and Kelyn fought back with single-minded ferocity. They had to be separated by force and carried off to their respective nurseries.

"Ah, well," Nerys' mother said. "They're only babies. They'll grow out of it."

Kelyn's mother wondered about that, but then she chided herself. All these children had ever known was love. What could either of them know of its opposite?

However they had learned it, Nerys and Kelyn disliked each other on sight. Age and maturity did nothing to improve their mutual antipathy. It was one of the very few things they ever agreed on: that they could not stand one another.

Everything, with them, was rivalry. They vied with each other for friends, for prizes in contests, even for marks in school. If Nerys wore the latest fashion, Kelyn had to set a completely new one; if one entered a race at the fair, the other had to enter it too, and fight for every stride.

It was like a curse, but no one in Emmerdale could imagine what or who might have laid it. Their families had enemies, of course; prosperity always attracted envy. But none of those had the resources or the knowledge to cast a spell of perpetual discord on a pair of children. Some tried to blame it on the Wizard's Wood that touched the western edge of the town, but nothing had come out of that in time out of mind, except truffles and the occasional wild boar.

For Nerys and Kelyn, it was simply the way things were. Their families tried everything from gentle remonstrance to outright whipping with complete lack of success. They never stopped trying, and Nerys and Kelyn never stopped detesting one another. It was an epic battle in its way, as much a part of life in Emmerdale as the sheepfolds and the woolen mill.

Nerys and Kelyn shared one other thing besides mutual loathing: a lifelong fascination with the Queen's Heralds

and their magical Companions. From the time they were
old enough to understand, they never tired of hearing
about Companions.

"When I am grown," Nerys said, "I shall be Chosen."

"Oh, no, you won't," said Kelyn. "*I* will. And you will
see me riding my Companion, all bright and shining in
my Whites, and tear out your hair in rage."

Nerys laughed at her, but with an edge of unease.
Nerys had beautiful hair, long and shining, so black it
shone blue, and she was very vain of it. Kelyn, whose
hair was slightly less straight but otherwise exactly like
it, had no reason for envy, but it made a useful weapon
in their endless war.

When Nerys was old enough to ride, her father gave
her a beautiful white pony with a long silken mane. Nat-
urally Kelyn had to have one, too, but hers had blue eyes.
Though they were not the deep clear blue of a Companion's, they were close enough to keep a child happy—
until Nerys mocked them. "Glass eyes! How ugly. She
looks as if she's been dead in the water for days."

Kelyn reared back, knotted her fist, and knocked
Nerys flat. It was the one and only time in all their en-
mity that either struck a blow against the other.

Kelyn stood over Nerys where she lay sprawling and
said perfectly calmly, "Leave my horse alone."

To everyone's amazement, Nerys did. Their war went
on, but people and animals were exempt. It was entirely
and exclusively personal.

One splendid summer morning, a few days after her thir-
teenth birthday, Nerys galloped her pony up the steep
track to the highest sheep pasture. It was not a track to
be galloping on, and her errand was only mildly urgent,
but Nerys was out of patience with the world.

In honor of their unfortunately mutual birthday, Kelyn had received her first silk gown and had been al-

lowed to put her hair up. Nerys' mother had given her a necklace of amber beads, a fine wool cloak, and a new saddlecloth for her pony.

Those were excellent gifts, and under any other circumstances Nerys would have been delighted. But Kelyn had outdone her, and Nerys' parents would not hear a word about it. "There's time enough for you to play at being a woman," her mother said.

It was small consolation that Kelyn spilled barley beer on her dress before she had been in it an hour, and it was not even Nerys' fault. The dress was still silk, and fit for a woman grown. Nerys was still being treated like a baby.

In the back of her mind, Nerys knew she was being unreasonable. That was hardly enough to stop her. So she pushed her pony hard up the steep and rocky track, and trusted him not break either of their necks.

The pony might be small, and growing smaller for Nerys by the year, but he was surefooted and quick. He brought them both safely to the high pasture.

The sheep were grazing peacefully in the clear morning sunlight. The shepherd's big white dogs stood guard, looking like sheep themselves unless they moved. The shepherd was not in her hut or anywhere on the mountaintop.

She could not have gone far. Nerys had brought fresh bread and honey sweets and the first small hard apples of the season as gifts from her mother; she left them in the hut where the shepherd could see them. The message she had to deliver, that some of the ewes had been sold and should come down off the mountain within the tenday, could wait all day if it had to—and so could Nerys.

A whole day to herself was a rare and wonderful thing, now she was almost a woman. The *almost* barely

stung up here, where the air was thin and clear and the
world seemed far away.

Nerys pulled the saddle and bridle off the pony, rubbed
him down and turned him loose among the sheep. He
paused to drink long and deeply from the stream that
ran through the pasture and then set to grazing on the
rough, scrubby grass.

Nerys thought briefly about swimming in the stream,
but it was as cold as snow even in the dead of summer.
She walked along it instead, hunting for the sweet scarlet berries that hid in the grass and eating those that she
found.

The stream wound into a grove of wind-stunted trees.
They stood in a circle, almost as if planted; the space
inside had always seemed to Nerys to be larger than the
space without.

When she was younger, she had played games in and
around the grove, pretending that it was the Companions' Grove and that magic grew there by moonlight or
starlight. Once when a ewe give birth to a late lamb in the
shelter of the trees, Nerys called the little ram "Grove-
Born" until Willa the shepherd boxed her ears to teach
her respect.

Nerys had kept her dreams to herself after that, but
to her the grove had always had a certain sacredness
about it. When she could, she visited it just to sit and be,
to listen to the wind in the leaves and breathe the sweet-
ness of the flowers that bloomed in the grass.

Today she had grievances to nurse. She was not sure
she wanted the calm the grove could give. Still, the day
had grown warm, and the shade under the trees would
be blessedly cool.

She wandered in, nibbling a handful of sweet berries.
The cool green smell and the soft shade wrapped around
her. She yawned, suddenly and powerfully sleepy.

Under her drooping eyelids, in sight blurred by

warmth and sleepiness, she saw that some of the sheep had taken refuge in the grove: a moving cloud of whiteness. It drifted toward her; she braced for the jostle of woolly bodies around her knees.

Warm breath blew in her face, sweet with the scents of grass and flowers. She looked down at silver hooves—single, not cloven—and up into the deepest, bluest, most breathtakingly beautiful eyes that had ever been.

:Hello,: the shimmering white creature said.

The voice Nerys heard in her head was warm and deep, with a faint, musical lilt. It was the most beautiful voice she had ever heard, with her ears or otherwise.

"Hello," she answered politely, as her mother had taught her. "My name is Nerys."

:Mine is Coryn,: the Companion said. Of course that was what he was. He could not possibly have been anything else.

Part of Nerys was dancing wildly, and part was telling itself to calm down, stop being an idiot, she was only dreaming. But it felt as real as it could possibly be.

She stretched out a hand. She was prepared for the vision to vanish, or for her fingers to tangle in sheep's wool.

His neck was as smooth as water. His mane was long and waving and as fine and soft as the fringe of her mother's prized silk shawl. He was warm and solid and very much alive. He had a smell, sweet like his breath, but with a hint underneath of the horse smell she loved.

He *was* real. He was talking to her. She was Chosen. She looked at him, asking permission. He dipped his beautiful white head.

He was much taller than her pony, but he lowered himself to his knees for her. She gripped that silken mane and swung her leg over his broad back.

When she was settled and comfortable, he rose smoothly erect, tossed his mane and pawed. Her heart

fluttered a little. Companion or no, Chosen or no, he was
a tall and powerful stallion, and she was used to riding
an opinionated but thoroughly safe pony gelding.

She felt as much as heard his snort of amusement. *:At
least you can ride,:* he said, *:more or less.:*

That stung her pride. She forgot her fear and dug her
heels into his sides—remembering just a fraction too
late that a Companion was not, all appearances to the
contrary, a horse.

He was kind. He bucked her into a bush instead of
hard ground or stony creek or the thicket of brambles
that was covered with green fruit.

The second time she mounted, she was moving stiffly,
but she was not about to back off. "Please," she said.
"Will you walk?"

:Simple intention will do,: he replied, *:and a little en-
couragement from your seat.:*

He had not moved while he spoke to her. It dawned
on her that she was supposed to follow instructions.

"Companions, nothing," she muttered. "They ought
to call you Tyrants."

His amusement was all the answer she got. She glow-
ered at him. Then she willed him to walk and bumped
with her backside.

:Not exactly,: he said, *:but just this once, I'll accept it.:*

His walk was huge. It was as big and swooping as her
pony's best canter. It made her clutch his mane and try
her best not to clutch his sides. It was alarming, and exhil-
arating, and more than she could ever have imagined.

She would never have dared to ask him to trot. He
gave it to her of his own will, and that was even bigger
and almost as smooth. When he flowed into a canter, in
spite of all her fear and fret, she was grinning like a fool.
It was glassy smooth, yet deeply and subtly powerful.

He circled the whole of the high pasture, catching her

pony on the way and sweeping him in their wake. It was better than any dream she had ever had.

When he stopped, she burst into tears. He waited out the storm and offered no commentary as she wiped her eyes in fierce embarrassment. When she was as composed as she was going to be, he said, *:I have to go now, for a while. Be patient; go on about your tasks. Tell no one that I came to you. I promise I will come back.:*

All her high joy collapsed into bafflement and something like grief. "You're going away? How can you do that? I thought—"

:Just for a while,: he said. *:That is a promise.:*

She tried to argue, but he deposited her neatly on the grass beside her pony, ruffled her hair with his breath, turned and vanished into the dazzle of sunlight and sudden tears.

Kelyn had won this round of her long battle with Nerys, and she was proud of it. But her hair felt odd and tight in its pins and braids, and her long skirts were heavy and made it difficult to stride out. As for riding her blue-eyed pony, that was hardly a womanly thing to do.

A woman had more than enough to occupy her, between keeping the house, overseeing the servants, and making sure that the menfolk were fed, clothed, clean, and content. And, now that she was a woman, Kelyn had to consider her duty to the family and the business: to find a husband who would help them both to prosper.

"It is a pity Margit's child was a girl," her mother sighed—as she did almost every day. She never added the other thing, the thing that mattered so much to so many people in the town: that Margit's child and Alis' daughter hated each other with such single-minded intensity.

Kelyn felt guilty about it as often as not. But she sim-

ply could not stand the girl. Just being near her made
Kelyn want to hit something—preferably Nerys.

On that particular day of summer, while her womanhood was still fresh and uncomfortable, like a new pair
of shoes, Kelyn finished all her tasks early and won an
hour to herself.

In this new life, she was expected to fill it with needle-
work or study, or else with dreaming about her future
husband—if she had had any candidates, which she did
not. The face that came to her when she closed her eyes
was long and white, with glassy pale eyes, and it was buried in the grass of its paddock.

Her pony was growing fat already with lack of exer-
cise. He needed to get out—and so did she.

Her old, childish clothes were still in the press, tucked
under the stiff new skirts and petticoats. She put them on
with a kind of shamed relief. They were so much more
familiar than the gowns she wore now, so much softer
and more comfortable.

They were freer, too. She could move in them: raid
the kitchen for provisions, groom and saddle a pony,
mount and slip out through the gate in the back garden
and ride up the hill toward Wizard's Wood.

No one in Emmerdale remembered why the forest of
pine and fir was called that. It had the magic that all forests have, of sweet scents and dappled shade and green
silences. But no wizard had ever come out of it, and
while the Mage Storms raged, none had touched either
Emmerdale or the Wood.

Kelyn's mother, who sometimes startled people with
the things she said, had observed once that maybe the
Storms passed the town by because of the Wood. No one
had paid any mind. Emmerdale was a perfectly ordinary,
perfectly unmagical place.

Sometimes Kelyn regretted that. No one from Emmerdale had ever been Chosen, and no Mage had ever

come from there. Her dreams of magic and of Companions were only dreams.

As she rode under the trees, following a path that led to the heart of the Wood, she rejected that thought—fiercely, almost angrily. Even if she was a woman now, she was *not* done with dreams. There *was* magic in the world. She would see it, feel it, even touch it—someday.

The Wood's heart was a low hill with a ring of stones on the summit. Whatever or whoever had put them there was long gone, and whatever power the builders had had or meant to raise was gone with them. Grass grew there now, and flowers that the children of Emmerdale plaited into chains and strung from stone to stone.

Why they did it or what purpose it might serve, none of them could have said. It was just what one did if one was in the circle.

No one else was there on this warm, bright afternoon, though there must have been at least one visitor earlier: a string of daisies fluttered in the breeze, wound around and around the tallest stone. The flowers were barely wilted, their yellow centers bright against the pitted grey rock.

Kelyn's pony snorted, then did the most embarrassing thing she knew how to do: she flipped her tail over her back and squatted. Kelyn slapped her neck hard. "You idiot! There's no stallion here."

Kelyn was wrong. As it happened, there was.

He had not been there an instant ago, standing between two of the tall gray stones. He was as white as snow, and his eyes were pure and luminous blue. His long mane rippled in the breeze that played around the hilltop.

His nostrils flared at the sharp scent of the mare's longing, but he was a great deal more than a stallion. He dipped his head to her, respectfully, yet made no move to claim what she offered. There was a hint of regret and apology that he must disappoint her—all in the glint of an eye and the turn of an ear.

Kelyn loved him for that, suddenly and completely. "Thank you," she said.

:You are welcome,: he answered.

"Everyone thinks she's just a pony," Kelyn said, "but she's a person. I suppose you get a lot of that, too?"

:Occasionally,: he said. His voice in her head was dryly amused.

"Your Herald must get tired of setting people straight," she said.

:I can see that you do,: said the Companion.

Kelyn started to answer, but then she stopped. It had dawned on her, belatedly, that there was no one in Whites standing near him. Then she realized what exactly he had said.

She went perfectly still, inside and out. The world around her was supernaturally clear. She could hear every rustle of the wind in the grass, and see every glint of sunlight on the stones, and count each flower that sprang around the Companion's silver hooves.

She wanted to remember everything, every breath, every fraction of this moment.

:You are Kelyn,: he said, *:and I am Coryn, and I've come for you. Will you sit on my back?:*

The pony offered no objection when Kelyn slid out of the familiar saddle and tied up the reins so that she could graze if she chose. For all the stallion's attractions, the grass to her mind was sweeter.

Kelyn patted her neck a little sadly, because a woman's clothes had changed little after all, but this changed everything. The pony tilted an ear, otherwise ignoring her. The grass was delicious, and she was hungry.

Ponies were as unsentimental as living creatures could be. Kelyn turned away from her toward the being she had dreamed of since she was small.

He was waiting for her. For *her*, and no one else.

She sprang onto his back. It was a long way up, but she was agile and strong. Her only regret was that there was no human there to see it.

Nerys would die of jealousy. That brightened Kelyn's mood beyond measure.

Coryn carried her from one end of the Wood to the other, striding long and smooth, with power that made her heart sing. He was wide through the back and barrel, too, which she would have to get used to. But she would. She had the rest of her life to do it.

She had expected to gallop into Emmerdale in a blaze of glory, but his circle took him back to the ring of stones and her pony dozing peacefully in the light of the westering sun. There he halted and made it clear that she should dismount. "But," she said, "I thought—"

:I know,: Coryn said. *:And you will, I promise. Go home now; keep this as our secret. In a little while the world will know that I have Chosen you; and then you'll have your dream.:*

"That's not what any of the stories say," Kelyn said. She should not have been so stubborn, but she could not help herself.

:Every story is different,: the Companion said. *:This is yours, and it is wonderful.:*

"Not if I have to go home without you," she said.

:It's not for very long,: he said, gentle but firm. *:Now hurry. Your mother is looking for you.:*

That was a shrewd blow. Kelyn glared, but she gave way. "You'd better come back soon," she said. "Tomorrow. Promise."

:Soon,: the Companion said. Her Companion, who had Chosen her.

That would keep her warm inside, even if she could not tell anyone. Except maybe—

:Not even your mother,: said Coryn.

"You're worse than she is," Kelyn muttered. "*She* doesn't read my mind."

His laughter filled the circle and melted into sunlight. When the dazzle faded from her eyes, he was gone. She was alone with her pony and her temper and the best secret she had ever had or hoped to have.

The next day was market day in Emmerdale. Kelyn and Nerys had duties there: Kelyn in her father's shop among the bolts of wool, and Nerys in the livestock market, where she kept the records of the sheep as they were bought and sold. It was pure coincidence that the sheepfolds and the cloth market were at opposite ends of the square, but it had served their families well over the years.

The white horse came trotting down the middle of the market at the stroke of noon. His coat was dazzling in the sun. His mane and tail streamed in the wind of his passage.

More than one young and not so young person reached out to catch hold of his bridle or tried to bar his way. He never seemed to veer from his path, nor did he slow or stop. He simply was not there for those who hoped to make him Choose them.

The center of the market was a fountain that had not run in living memory. The well that fed it was dry.

As the Companion came to a halt in front of it, water bubbled up in the bowl, filled it and spilled over into the basin below. He lowered his chiseled white head and drank, while the market watched in spreading silence.

Two voices at once broke that silence, from opposite ends of the square: "Coryn!"

Nerys and Kelyn ran toward him. Neither saw anything or anyone but the Companion, until they reached to embrace him in front of everyone and found themselves face to face instead.

The shock was as sharp as a slap. It struck the words out of them and left them staring, too shocked even for hate.

That came next, so strong and so perfectly matched that no one who watched could have said who sprang first. There would have been blood or worse if the Companion had not set himself quietly and immovably between them.

They climbed up and over him, yowling like forest cats. His head snaked around and plucked first Nerys and then Kelyn off his back, dropping them to the ground and looming over them until their yowling stopped.

It was Kelyn's mother, Alis, who spoke for them both, and for the whole town, too. "They can't both be Chosen."

"We aren't!" Nerys cried. "I was Chosen. He came to me in the high pasture, and he told me—"

"He came to *me*!" Kelyn shouted over her. "I was in the stone circle in the Wood, and he—"

The Companion lifted his head and let out a ringing peal. It sounded like laughter—and from the girls' expressions, that was exactly what it was. "You can't *do* that!" they sang in chorus.

Except, it seemed, he had.

"The trouble with success," Herald Egil said, "is that everyone expects you to succeed all over again."

His Companion ignored him. She had found an unusually succulent patch of grass and was savoring each leisurely mouthful.

She was all too obvious about it. Egil sighed and leaned back against a tree. It had been an easy ride out from Haven, but there were still, according to his map and Herald Bronwen, another two days of it.

Bronwen had ridden ahead. She had little patience with what she called Egil's elderly ways—though he was hardly more than twice her age—and her Companion fussed if he had to walk or trot all day.

They would be back by the time Egil was ready to go. Meanwhile, he was glad of the time to himself.

Egil was a quiet person and a solitary one. He had managed to evade the better-known duties of a Herald for years, until an emergency and a dearth of available Heralds had forced him out at the queen's command.

He had done well on that errand, put an end to a dangerous if inadvertent working of magic and saved a valley from spelling itself into nothingness. Unfortunately, he had done so well that people had noticed. Now he had to go on another and equally peculiar errand, just when he was getting comfortable again in his familiar place and space.

In Egil's perfect world, he would never ride outside the Collegium at all. He would live his life between the classroom and the library and leave the Heralding to those with more of a taste for it.

Bronwen, for example. She came galloping back down the road, mounted on her fiery Companion, like every child's dream of the Queen's Own. She was tall and slim and elegant, her wheat-gold hair plaited down her back, and her sea-blue eyes flashing as Rohanan reared to a halt directly in front of Egil.

Plain brown Egil looked calmly up at the tall Companion and the equally tall Herald. "Already?" he said.

"The message was urgent," Bronwen said. "Also, odd. Aren't you curious?"

"No worlds will end if we arrive an hour later than we planned," Egil said.

"Maybe not," she said, "but a pair of Chosen may have killed each other before we get there."

"So we're led to believe," Egil said. He rose reluctantly and stretched, and brushed at his Whites. There was a grass stain, of course. Or two or three.

Bronwen, who was always immaculate, visibly refrained from commentary. "The message must have been garbled. It can't be one Companion and two Chosen. Somehow two Companions showed up in the same town and Chose a pair of enemies. Now they're at each other's throats, and their families are at wits' end."

"That would be the logical conclusion, wouldn't it?" said Egil.

Bronwen's eyes narrowed. "You don't think—"

"We'll see soon enough," he said.

"It's impossible," she said. "How would it work? Would they ride double? Would they bring a remount? Is one supposed to kill the other, and the survivor gets the Companion? It's preposterous."

Egil let her babble on while he mounted Cynara and set out on the road to Emmerdale. Bronwen was as different from Egil as a human creature could be. He did not particularly like her, nor did she like him. Left to themselves, they would have crossed paths seldom if at all; certainly they would never be friends. And yet somehow, when they worked together, it worked.

:Friction,: Cynara said. *:Like flint and steel. Alone, they're nothing alike, and they have little in common. Together, they spark fire.:*

There was truth in that. Egil was dull gray flint. Bronwen was sharp and shining steel.

:Do you think . . . ?: he asked Cynara.

He had no need to finish the thought. She snorted softly. *:You'll see,:* she said.

For the first day or two after Coryn showed himself in the market, Kelyn could hardly see or think or even breathe, she was so furious. She alternated between storms of tears and fits of icy rage.

She so alarmed her family that they locked her in her room and put her under guard. When she could shape

a coherent thought, which was not often, she saw the
wisdom in it. If she got out, if she had even the slightest
chance, she would hunt Nerys down and kill her.

Shut inside familiar walls, under the unrelenting
stare of her mother or her father or one of her many
burly cousins, she calmed slowly. Her anger was no less
strong, but her thoughts were clear again. She began to
feel other things besides rage. Shock. Disappointment.
And, as the hours stretched into days, a sensation that
she could only recognize as grief.

He was always there. She was too angry to speak to
him, but she felt him, white and shining in the back of
her mind. She looked, when she could stand to, for the
taint of Nerys that must be on him, but there was nothing. Only the whiteness and the warmth and the sense of
rightness that stung like salt in an open wound.

By the fifth day, Kelyn knew what she had to do. Her
watchdogs were as vigilant as ever, but she saw a way
around that. She only had to wait a little longer, and
then she could act.

A Herald was coming from Haven to sort the confusion.
Nerys was not supposed to know, but her ears were keen
and people were talking.

She knew that Kelyn was locked in her house. Nerys
could not go anywhere without a pair of her father's apprentices in tow, but she was allowed out. She reckoned
she had won this contest, for what good it did either of
them.

She could even have visited the Companion if she
had wanted to. He was stabled in the best inn in Emmerdale, in the best stall, and by all accounts was getting
the very best of care.

She wished him well of it. It hurt inside to keep her
mind and body closed off from him, but it hurt worse to
think of sharing him with Kelyn. Better for everybody if

she pretended he had never come, let alone pretended to Choose her.

:It's not a pretense,: he said.

She shut him out so ferociously that she gave herself a crashing headache. The pain was worth it, she told herself. He was gone. She hoped his head was pounding as badly as hers.

The Herald was due to arrive tomorrow, people said. They were all expecting him to decide which of the Chosen was the real one, then take her off to the Collegium to earn her Whites.

In her calmer moments, Nerys was sure she would be the one. Kelyn had put her hair up and submitted to the tyranny of skirts. She could find herself a husband and get to work making heirs for both families.

It was logical and elegant and perfectly practical. It also meant that Nerys need never set eyes on Kelyn again. It should have felt wonderful, and yet it did no such thing. It felt like a blow to the gut.

"This is wrong," Nerys said. She was alone for once, shut in her room like Kelyn, only she had locked herself in and could go out if she chose.

She had left dinner early, pleading an indisposition that was only half feigned. A Choosing should have been a wonderful and joyous occasion. Not this stomach-wrenching confusion.

The Herald would resolve it. But what if he did not? What if he decided that Kelyn was his Chosen? What then?

Nerys would have to live with it. Except that she was not sure she could. Never to see Coryn again, never to hear his warm deep voice in her head or feel his warmth in her heart—she would die. She would not want to live.

Maybe that was the answer. It was a terrible thing, but she had never shrunk from anything that frightened her.

She had to think about it. The Herald was coming to-morrow. Whatever she did, she should do it before he came. That left her with little time—but it ought to be enough.

Egil and Bronwen rode into Emmerdale in good time, in spite of her fretting. It was a little after noon on a beautiful summer day, neither too hot nor too cold. A few clouds drifted in the sky, but none of them carried a burden of rain.

Emmerdale was an unexpectedly pretty town. It nestled amid green fields at the foot of a mountain range so small it barely rated a name. To the west of it was a stretch of forest; it reminded Egil somehow of the Pelagirs, and yet it seemed as peaceful and empty of fear as a forest could be.

Egil's senses came to the alert. The last such place had turned out to be under a dangerous and deadly spell. But this one lacked a certain something. Foreboding, maybe. The deep hum of magic running underneath it all. There was no ill magic in Emmerdale: Egil would have laid a wager on it if he had been a wagering man.

The only strangeness here was basking in the sun in the field that belonged to the best inn. The Companion was a stallion, and while he was not as tall as Rohanan, he was more substantially built.

His Chosen should have been hanging on him, unable to let him out of her sight. Or their sight, if the message from Emmerdale told the truth. He was alone, and he seemed content.

"Maybe he hasn't Chosen anyone yet?" Egil wondered aloud.

:Oh, he has,: Cynara said. Egil could not tell what she thought of it, or of the stallion, either. Her tone was unusually bland, as if she had no opinion at all.

That Egil could not believe. Cynara always had an opinion.

He glanced at Bronwen. She stood with her Companion in a crowd of townspeople, basking in their admiration. They seemed to have forgotten that Egil was there, in spite of his Whites and the shining coat of his Companion.

That suited him admirably, but Bronwen was too hemmed in with people to either catch his glance or hear him if he asked the question that was in his mind. He asked Cynara instead. :*And Rohanan? Is he as non-committal as you?*:

Cynara did not trouble to answer. Egil had known she would do that. He drew his breath in sharply, as close to a fit of pique as he ever came.

Fortunately for his peace of mind, Bronwen asked the other question, the one that had brought them here. "Pardon my impatience, but your message was urgent. There is a problem with the Companion's Chosen?"

The man who answered was no older than Egil, but he carried himself with an air of easy authority. "There is," he said. "It seems he's been unable to make up his mind. He's Chosen two of our young women: my daughter and Hanse's daughter."

"I gather they're not friends," Bronwen said.

Both fathers rolled their eyes. That they were friends was unmistakable, which made it odder that their daughters were not. "They hate each other," Hanse said.

The other nodded. "There's no sense or reason to it. It just is."

"Nothing ever just is," Bronwen said.

"Then maybe you can find out why they were born like that," said Hanse. He sounded more tired than skeptical.

Egil was in full sympathy with the man. When Bronwen did not ask the next and essential question, Egil did it for her. "Where are they, then, sirs?"

They started a little at the voice that to them must seem to come from nowhere. Hanse recovered first, enough to answer. "Secure under lock and key," he said grimly.

"Well," said the other, "more or less."

"Pitar," Hanse said. "By the Powers. You trust her?"

"I trust my daughter," said Pitar somewhat stiffly, "to do nothing foolish while under the watchful eyes of my apprentices."

"So you hope," said Hanse.

People started to rumble around them. Some spoke for one, some for the other: a low growl of division that made Egil's nape prickle. He had felt something like it before, long ago, while he was still a Trainee. Within the hour there had been a riot.

Egil interjected politely but firmly. "I think we'd best begin our inquiry. Which of them would be closer?"

"That would be Kelyn," said Hanse. His voice and face were tight.

With a last glance at the Companion who had done this baffling thing, Egil followed both Pitar and Hanse down through the town.

Kelyn was not in her room. The cousin who had been guarding her was almost in tears, which was disconcerting: He was head and shoulders taller than Egil's middle height and as broad as a barn door. The tiny woman who had reduced him to a quivering wreck whirled on Hanse in such a fire of fury that even Egil fell back a step.

"She went to the privy," the woman said, biting off each word. "Two hours ago. Rickard only began to worry, he tells me, after an hour. Because every girl takes forever to do what she will do. And then," she said, "he was afraid to tell anyone."

"I can hardly blame him for that," said Egil mildly.

The woman bridled, then transparently remembered what his white uniform meant. "Herald," she said with prickly respect. "Thank the Powers you've come. The girl has bolted. If she's not with the Companion, someone had better make sure Nerys is still home and safe."

Pitar muttered something that sounded like a curse, spun in the doorway and ran.

Nerys was nowhere to be found either. The apprentices who should have been shadowing her had fallen for the same ruse as Kelyn's cousin.

Egil was not quite ready yet to find a pattern there, but from what he was seeing and hearing, he was inching toward a conclusion.

:Cynara: he said in his mind, since she was still out by the fields, taking the opportunity to dine on sweet grass and be adored by a gaggle of children. *:Their Companion must know where they are:*

Her reply was somewhat delayed and redolent of grass. *:He says they're not choosing to enlighten him. He also says they're not together.:*

:How can he not—: Egil broke off. Companions had a notorious habit of not telling their Chosen everything they knew. It could drive a Herald mad.

Egil did not intend to lose his sanity. Nor was he about to lose these two children—not, at least, until he knew why one Companion had Chosen them both.

"Bronwen," he said in the middle of the milling and expostulating that had taken over this part of the town. He spoke softly, but his Herald-intern heard him. "They won't have gone far. Enlist some of the locals and go after Nerys. I'll find Kelyn."

Time was when Bronwen would have argued simply for the sake of arguing. In this long, warm summer afternoon, she nodded and set about doing the sensible thing.

Mind you, Egil thought, *if she decided my orders weren't sensible, she'd perfectly well disobey them.*

:We are surrounded by obstreperous youth,: Cynara said.

It was all Egil could do not to break out in painful laughter. As it was, one or two townspeople looked at him oddly.

He pressed them into service. "Tell me where Kelyn would most likely go."

There were many opinions as to that, but Kelyn's mother glared them all down. "There is one place where she goes when she needs to think. She doesn't know anyone knows about it."

"I won't betray your secret," Egil assured her.

The woman nodded brusquely, called over one of the boys who had been hanging about, staring at the Herald's Whites, and said, "Take him to the Wizard's Wood, to the stone circle."

"Maybe it would be best if you simply told me where to go," Egil said, "since she's likely to run if she sees anyone she knows."

"She might," her mother conceded. "Well enough, then. Galtier will take you to the edge of the Wood. Stay on the track and don't let yourself be tempted to wander off it. It will lead you to the circle."

"That's clear enough," Egil said, "and I thank you." He added a brief bow, because she was worthy of respect.

That flustered her into a scowl. "Go on," she said. "Before she gets all her thinking done and runs off the Powers know where."

Escape was almost too easy. Kelyn kept looking for pursuit, but she had made it as far as the Wizard's Wood without anyone seeing her. They were all off gawping at the Heralds—for there were two of them; Coryn made sure she knew.

Two Heralds, two Companions. Kelyn hoped he felt the full force of her bitterness over that.

It seemed to trouble him not at all. She shut him out once more, diving into the solitude of her own mind.

That was not the most pleasant place to be. Such plan as she had was to ride her pony through the Wood, then keep on riding as far and fast as she could, until Coryn was no more than a memory.

A large part of her would rather stay and fight for him. But Kelyn had been raised to be practical. It simply did not make sense for a Companion to Choose two Heralds-to-be.

She should be that one. Not Nerys. By the Powers, never Nerys.

And yet as she endured the days of waiting for the Herald to come, Kelyn had seen and felt what this unprecedented Choosing was doing to Emmerdale. All her life she had done her best to outrun and outride and outsmart her rival. This was the greatest contest of all—and she was running away from it.

She hated Nerys, but she loved Emmerdale more. At last, after so many years, people were choosing between them. Lines were being drawn. Emmerdale was splitting down the middle, half of its people convinced that Nerys should be the Chosen, and half contending that Kelyn deserved it more.

Kelyn had never wanted that. Watching it happen tore at her heart.

Coryn was a dream. Emmerdale was real. Whatever grief or pain it cost to her to rip herself away from the Companion, the thought of Emmerdale splitting apart over it was worse.

It was the hardest thing she had ever done, and the most necessary. She kicked her pony into a canter down the familiar track, in the whisper of pine boughs and the dusk-and-dazzle light of the Wood.

Nerys had no time for anything but to throw a bridle on her pony and turn his head toward the mountain. The pony had been pent up for days; he was more than glad to burst out of the gate at a flat run.

Nerys was not running away exactly. She needed to think. There was no chance of doing it in town, with everyone in such an uproar and not just one but two Heralds come to muddle what little sense anyone had left.

The last people she ever wanted to see were Heralds who were truly Chosen, who had not been mocked with a false and bitter Choosing.

:It's not false,: Coryn said.

She refused to hear him. He might be lurking in the hidden corners of her heart, but she did not want him there or anywhere. If a Companion wanted her, let him choose *her*—not force her to share with her worst enemy.

She more than half expected him to take issue with that, but he seemed to have gone. She refused to be disappointed, let alone sad. *Good,* she thought. *Good riddance.*

The track up to the high pasture seemed unusually long and arduous today. Nerys realized as she rode that she never had given Willa her mother's message when she was there last. Coryn's appearance had driven it straight out of her head.

That gave her an excuse. "At least I'll get some use out of the whole sorry mess," she said. Her pony slanted an ear at her, bunched his hindquarters and sprang up the last and steepest part of the trail.

He paused on the pasture's edge, blowing hard. Nerys was breathing a little fast herself. She slid off his sweaty back and led him the rest of the way, taking her time, until his breathing slowed and his body cooled.

She took her time rubbing him down, too, then washed him off and rubbed him again until he was respectably cool. By that time Willa should have come out of the hut, or else come toward her from the edge of the pasture where the sheep were grazing.

But there was no sign of the shepherd. That might not have meant anything—Willa did like to wander on occasion—but she had been gone half a tenday ago, too, and it felt odd.

The hut was cold inside, with an air about its emptiness that said it had been abandoned for days. The hearth was swept clean, and Willa's few belongings were neatly stowed, except for a half-filled water jar on the table and the last quarter of a loaf of bread gone rock-hard and stale beside it.

Willa never wasted food. If she had left the bread there, she had meant to eat it while it was fresh.

Nerys started off running toward the sheep, but she remembered just in time that neither the sheep nor their guardian dogs would respond well to human panic. She made herself take a deep breath, relax her body as much as she could, and walk slowly and easily toward the cluster of woolly white bodies.

They were all well, and all accounted for as far as Nerys could tell. The dogs did their own hunting; they could survive a whole season on their own if they had to.

But Willa was gone. Nerys told herself it had to be nothing, the shepherd was out hunting or visiting her daughter over the mountain. Except she would never leave the sheep for more than a day, and she would have taken the bread with her to eat.

Nerys knew a little bit about tracking, much of which

she had learned from Willa. It was not much good on grass and after half a tenday.

She did not want to think about what that meant. If Willa had had a fall or been attacked or taken ill, she would have been alone and abandoned for days. It was all too likely she had not survived it.

"No," Nerys said. "I'm not going to think like that. She's somewhere she can't get out of, but she's alive. I'll find her. I'll bring her back."

The sheep ignored her. One of the dogs pricked its ears at the sound of her voice, but she was neither a sheep nor a predator. She did not matter in its world.

She stood still, taking long, calming breaths. Willa could be anywhere on the mountain. But there were hunting runs she favored, and Nerys knew the way to Willa's daughter's village; she had gone there with the shepherd more than once.

That might be the easy and therefore the wrong way, but it was a start. If something had happened, with luck Willa's daughter had been expecting her mother, and when she did not appear, had gone searching herself— and Willa was safe in Highrock, maybe with an ague, or a sprain, or at worst a broken leg.

Nerys paused to fill a waterskin and carve off a wedge of strong sheep's cheese from the wheel that hung in the hut. She found a net bag of fruit, too, that were soft but still good.

With water and provisions and a firm refusal to panic, Nerys set out on the path to the village. She left her pony behind. He was tired, and the path was narrow and steep. She could search it better and faster on foot.

Under the best conditions, it took most of a morning to climb and scramble and occasionally stroll to High-rock. Usually Willa stayed the day and the night and came back the next morning, though when Nerys had been with her, she had gone both ways in a day.

Nerys concentrated on finding the path and then keeping her feet on it. With no little guilt, she realized she was glad to do this. It was a distraction. It kept her from having to think about what waited for her in Emmerdale.

Maybe she should spend the rest of her life hunting down the missing. The world must be full of them. It was like being a Herald, in a way.

She could still be a Herald. Somehow. If she wanted.

"I *don't* want it," she said.

She had come to the summit of the first of three ridges. The track was narrow here and slippery with gravel and scree. A little ahead, the cliff dropped away sheer, plunging down to a narrow valley and a ribbon of river.

There was no sign of Willa here—not on the track and not broken on the rocks below. Nerys did not know whether to be relieved. The rest of the way was less perilous, but it was steep and stony, and parts of it tended to wash away in storms.

A little way past the cliff, Nerys paused to rest and breathe and sip from the waterskin. The leathery taste of the water made her think of other times she had traveled this way; somehow, without quite understanding why, she felt tears running down her cheeks.

Willa would say she had filled her cup of troubles, and now it was running over. If she closed her eyes, she could hear the warm rough voice and feel the shepherd's presence close by her, just a little warmer on her skin than the sun.

Nerys had always been able to feel things and people when they were nearby or when they were thinking about her. She had never thought of it as magic, especially since Kelyn had it, too. It was just a thing they could do.

Up on top of the world she knew, all torn with confusion over Coryn and Kelyn and Willa's disappearance,

Nerys felt as if she had walked right out of her skin. She *knew* where Willa was. She could feel it, smell it, taste it. It was stone and running water and the whisper of wind in leaves.

There was nowhere like that on this track, and yet it felt as close as the next turn. When Nerys tried to focus on it, the thought that came to her was like a fold in fabric, but the fabric was the world.

Maybe the Mage Storms had touched her part of the world after all. If they had, and if Willa had fallen into the strangeness that they left, Nerys was no mage. She knew nothing of magic.

She would panic when she knew for certain. She needed her eyes for the path, but she focused her mind as much as she could, following the sense and the memory of Willa.

It could be a trap. Her gut insisted it was not. It was hard to travel in two worlds, to keep from tripping and falling on her face, even while she held fast to the thread of sensation that was all she had to guide her.

Another presence slid beneath her, lifted her up and held her steady. It was Coryn, and he neither asked nor expected permission.

The simple arrogance of it made her breath catch. But she was not a complete idiot—she needed all the help she could get.

Then something else came into focus in and through him, something clear and bright and clean that sharpened all her senses and made her immeasurably stronger. It was as if she had lived in a fog all her life and now, suddenly, she could see the sun.

She could not afford to go all giddy—or to realize what and who must be doing this. Willa was trapped in a slant of sunlight, in a bend of the path that did not exist in the world she had thought she knew. The key was in Nerys' hand and heart, but the way was only open while the sun was in the sky.

Among these tumbled ridges and sudden cliffs, night came fast and early. It had been after noon when Nerys left the pasture; the sun had sunk visibly since. She had to hurry, which on that track was no easy thing.

She found the place where the trap had closed. It looked like nothing: a sharp bend among many on the steep path and a sudden drop where the track had washed away. A trickle of water seemed to run there, out of nowhere and into nowhere. The sun sparkled on it.

:Steady,: Coryn said, with that echo behind him. *:Hold fast to me. Don't let go.:*

She knew he was not physically there, but he was present in every way that mattered. The other beyond him made a chain, and that chain bound her to the world.

She stepped through the sun's door into madness.

Egil's guide left him as instructed, with a clear track ahead of him and Alis' admonitions still ringing in his ears. A small needling voice kept insisting that he had followed the wrong one, but Bronwen was well capable of handling whatever she found in the sheep pasture. Egil needed to be here.

The path was well traveled. Egil occupied himself and entertained Cynara by inviting her to dance down it. She did love the dance of horse and rider, and under the trees, in and out of sun and dappled shade, it was a wonderfully pleasant way to spend an afternoon.

It cleared his head splendidly. When the sunlight spread wide over the hill with its crown of stones, he was calm and focused and ready for whatever he might find.

It seemed at first to be nothing remarkable. A slim, dark-haired girl sat on a white pony inside the circle. The pony grazed peacefully. The girl's eyes were closed, and her face was turned to the sky.

She looked like her mother. Even at rest she had a hint of Alis' fierce edge.

As Cynara halted in front of the pony, Kelyn's eyes snapped open. Her Companion—for he was that, Egil could not mistake it—stepped delicately past Egil and presented himself for mounting.

"No," she said. "I don't want you."

He tossed his splendid white head and stamped. Kelyn's face set in adamant refusal.

The pony bucked her off. On that thick turf, the damage must have been more to her pride than her backside. She stared up at the traitor in utter disbelief.

"They always side with Companions," Egil said in wry sympathy. "Get up now and do as he tells you."

"Do you know what he's asking?" she demanded.

"Not specifically," he said. "Will you enlighten me?"

"Ask *her*," the girl snapped, jutting her chin at Cynara.

Egil had to admit that her complete lack of awe was refreshing. It was also not unheard of in the newly Chosen. In those first heady days, it was hard to see or hear or think about anyone but the magical white being who had come only and purely for them.

In this case, of course, that was not true. Egil did not need to ask Cynara; it was in every line of the girl's body. "Nerys is in trouble. He wants you to help."

"Worse," said Kelyn. She looked ready to spit. "He wants me to stop hating her and start facing the reason why."

"Because you're exactly alike," Egil said. "Everything you hate in her is everything you hate in yourself. Everything you love about yourself—in someone else, it grates horribly. That makes you wonder, and then it makes you twitch. It's enough to drive a person out of her mind. Is that where she is? Gone mad?"

"Not yet," she said. "He says there's a rift in the fabric of the world, another of those plague-begotten Storm remnants, and she's gone through it to save a life. Or maybe a mind. He's not exactly clear."

Egil's lightness of mood, such as it was, evaporated. He held on to his calm, because he was going to need it. "Ah," he said. "I see." He bent his gaze on the girl's Companion.

:Coryn,: Cynara said.

"Coryn," said Egil with an inclination of the head, which the Companion returned. "If you will, take us to her."

"No time," said Kelyn. "It's leagues away and the sun is going down. The sun keeps it open. Once it's gone ..."

Egil eyed her narrowly. "Cynara," he said aloud with the courtesy of Heralds, "is that true?"

:It is true,: Cynara said.

Egil nodded, oblivious to Kelyn's glare. "I did wonder. If my worst enemy were about to wink into nothingness, I might not be terribly inclined to do something about it."

"She is not my enemy!" Kelyn burst out. "I just can't stand her. I don't want her dead, either." She turned on Coryn. "I get your point—all of you. I'll help get her out of there. But I'm not your Chosen. I won't be anybody's second best."

:She is not,: Cynara said. From Kelyn's expression, Coryn had said the same.

Kelyn did not look ready to believe it. But she pulled herself from her pony's back to Coryn's, and for all her resistance, she could not keep herself from running her hand down his neck.

She drew herself up with a visible effort. "He needs you to help," she said to Egil. "She's on the other side of the—wall, I think he means. Rift. Something. He can guide her out, but he wants to open the rift here in order to do it. It's a stronger place, he says, and safer to stand on. With you and the other Herald and your Companions, he thinks he'll almost have enough strength."

Egil opened his mouth to point out that Bronwen and Rohanan had gone the other way, but before he could speak, they cantered into the circle. Bronwen looked ruffled and out of sorts, the way she always did after she had lost an argument. "Rohanan says we need to be here," she said.

"You do," said Egil. "He's told you what happened?"

She nodded. "Are we doing another dance?"

They had helped a quadrille of riders to close a much larger rift, not so long ago, by performing a spell that was framed in the movements of the equestrian art. But this was different. "We'll follow his lead," Egil said, tilting his head toward Coryn.

Bronwen sighed faintly, as if she would have preferred the quadrille. Egil most certainly would. Her Companion came to stand on the other side of Coryn, gently nudging the pony out of the way.

Coryn raised his head. On his back, Kelyn had closed her eyes again. She held out her hands.

Bronwen took one. Egil took the other. It was thin but strong, and it trembled slightly.

The child was either furious or terrified. Egil would have wagered on both. "We're ready," he said.

:They're ready,: said Coryn in the midst of howling nothingness.

The only solid thing in all that incomprehensible place was an honest miracle. Nerys had fallen on top of a warm and yielding object that protested in Willa's voice.

The shepherd was alive, apparently sane, and profanely glad to be found. Nerys wrapped her arms around the tall and substantial body. Willa stiffened, then closed the embrace.

If Nerys closed her eyes, she could almost stand to be here. The screaming that was not wind and not voices—

at least, not human or animal or anything of earth—still battered at her, but she could focus on the soft voice in her mind and almost, after a fashion, shut out the ungodly clamor.

Coryn's voice led to something else. It was like an image in a mirror, or another part of herself.

She and Kelyn were cousins. People said they could be sisters—twins, even, what with having been born on the same day.

What if they were more than that?

They could not be the same person. That was impossible. If each had half a soul, she certainly did not feel the lack. Maybe it was that they were meant to be something new, something larger than either of them: something that fit perfectly through a Companion.

Washed in the white light that was Coryn, Kelyn did not grate on her nearly as badly. He softened the raw edges. He muted the dissonance that had always clanged between them.

The fragment of it that was left gave her a foothold in this hideous not-place. The stabbing of irritation helped her focus. Coryn's presence was a light and a guide. Through it she saw the world she belonged in, and the person she belonged with—kicking, screaming, protesting, but in the end, neither of them could escape it.

There was a wrenching, a tearing, a rending of mind and soul and substance, all the way down to the core of her. She had never felt such pain—nor had the Companion, nor Kelyn whose will and strength were all that kept Nerys' mind and body from shattering.

The nothingness tore asunder. Nerys fell forever, down and down into endless light.

The rays of the setting sun slanted through the standing stones. Out of one fell a large and amorphous shape that resolved into a slim girl with a glossy black braid and a

broad-shouldered, massive woman who levered herself
to her feet, looked about her, and said, "Thank the Powers. I was afraid we'd end up in a sorcerer's lair."

"Would I lead you that far astray?" Nerys demanded,
but there was no mistaking the affection in her tone.
She faced the Heralds and the Companions, and last but
never least, her rival. "Thank you," she said, "for both
of us."

Egil moved to respond, but Kelyn was already speaking. "You're welcome," she said stiffly. "You're not hurt?
Either of you?"

"We're well, now we're out of that place," Nerys said.
She shuddered. "What *was* it?"

:*Gone,:* Coryn answered.

"You really do think like a horse," said Kelyn.

"He does," Nerys agreed.

That felt strange. Kelyn was not sure she liked it.
"Listen," she said. "I've made up my mind. You can have
him. Go. Be a Herald. I don't need the glory, and my
family needs me here."

"And mine doesn't?" said Nerys. "Go ahead, keep
him. You know that's all you've ever wanted."

"What we think we want isn't always what we ought
to get," Kelyn said. She had always thought her mother
was a sour and cynical woman for saying so, but in that
moment, in that place, she understood perfectly.

She slid down off Coryn's back, though it was brutally hard, even harder than closing a rift in the fabric
of the world. "Goodbye," she said. "I don't know why
you did this, but we're done now. It's one Chosen to one
Companion. We all know that."

:*Not here,:* Coryn said.

"Think!" said Nerys. "What will we do? Ride double?
We'll kill each other. Take turns on patrol? What's the
point in that? Just Choose one of us and be done with it.
I won't die if it's not me. I might want to, but I won't."

:No,: Coryn said.

"Why?" Kelyn demanded. "Why are you so stubborn?"

:Why do you hate her so much?:

"I just do," Kelyn said.

That was not exactly true. It used to be, but now, instead of the itching and crawling that had always beset her when she was near Nerys, she felt nothing. She looked at her old enemy and through habit wanted to hate her, but it was as if the rift had swallowed up all the hate.

"No," said Nerys, following her thoughts through Coryn—arguing as always; that was still the same. "It's him,: Coryn. He's doing it."

"I still don't like you," Kelyn said. "But I can stand to look at you."

"Heralds don't have to like each other," Herald Bronwen said. Her eyes were on Egil; their expression made perfect sense to Kelyn. "They just have to be able to work together."

"With the same Companion?" asked Kelyn. "How are we supposed to do that?"

It was Nerys who answered. "I don't know, but I think we're supposed to try."

"I think so, too," Egil said. "Look at what you did, the three of you. You saved a life and disposed of a powerful threat. That's what Heralds do. You did it as it's never been done before: two together with the Companion between. It wouldn't have been possible if there had been just one of you."

He was right. Kelyn had to admit it. "It's allowed, then? If we can stand it?"

"I'm not riding double," Nerys said. "I'd rather walk."

"We can take turns," said Kelyn, "and take our ponies for the rest of the time. At least I will. I'm not leaving Brighteyes behind."

"You think I'd abandon Cloud?"

"No," Kelyn said. "I don't think you would."

"It's settled, then," said Egil. He shook his head. "Gods and Powers help us all."

:That they will,: said Coryn.

The other Companions nodded, dipping their beautiful white heads. It was a blessing and a promise—with a spark of mirth. Whatever the humans might think of it all, the Companions were inordinately pleased with it.

Kelyn would not go that far. Her heart was beating hard, and she was dizzy, caught between joy and terror. But mostly what she felt, in spite of everything, was joy.

Be Careful What
You Wish For

by Nancy Asire

Nancy Asire is the author of four novels, *Twilight's King-
doms, Tears of Time, To Fall Like Stars,* and *Wizard
Spawn. Wizard Spawn* was edited by C.J. Cherryh and
became part of the *Sword of Knowledge* series. She has
also written short stories for the series anthologies *Heroes in Hell* and *Merovingen Nights*; a short story for Mercedes Lackey's *Flights of Fantasy;* as well as tales for the
Valdemar anthologies *Sun in Glory* and *Crossroads.* She
has lived in Africa and traveled the world, but she now re-
sides in Missouri with her cats and two vintage Corvairs.

"They still followin' us?"

Doron rose in his stirrups and looked. "Don't see nobody," he said, settling down into his saddle and letting
his winded horse rest. "Maybe they gave up, Ferrin."

Ferrin snorted. "Likely."

He was a big man, was Ferrin. Tough as they come.
As leader of this small band, he radiated authority ... an
authority accompanied by a big right fist if necessary.

Doron turned to the man at his left and grimaced.
Jergen was pretty much the opposite in all ways from
Ferrin. Slender, sandy hair always falling in his eyes, he
never had much to say, but when he did, the rest of them
tended to listen.

303

"Damn pack horses slow us down," Jergen grumbled, letting their lead ropes go slack. "Only got two, and we'd be farther away if'n we didn't have 'em."

"Ain't no cure for that." Chardo, another big man, rode to Doron's right.

Doron nodded. No cure for that, for sure. Behind them they'd left a merchant's caravan in disarray, two of its guards dead or wounded enough they'd hardly pose a problem. The other three were the danger. The chase hadn't lasted long, Vomehl's skill with the bow keeping their pursuers at bay.

Maybe we bit us off a little bit more'n we could chew, Doron thought. Gerran lay dead behind them, taken in the neck by a lucky swordstroke. He offered a brief prayer to Vkandis Sunlord that Gerran might find a better life in the hereafter. So now they were only five: Ferrin, Jergen, Chardo, Vomehl, and himself. With the element of surprise on their side, it had seemed a fairly sure thing: five of the merchant's guards and six of them. Didn't turn out that way. Truth be told, the caravan guards were obviously better fighters.

And now that the Son of the Sun (a female Son of the Sun!) had repealed many of the laws that had governed Karse for generations and had reined in the worst of the offending priests, things were changing here on the border between Valdemar and Karse. They'd even heard rumors Solaris had hired mercenaries from the Guild to hunt down bandit bands, and had plans to arm villagers. If that was true, their future could turn out to be a very bleak one.

"So," Chardo asked, "what d'we do next?"

Ferrin was silent. Doron watched his leader from the corners of his eyes. This raid hadn't gone well, and Ferrin was smarting over it. The bandit chief shrugged.

"Guess we ain't got no choice," he responded, lifting his reins. "Make for yonder grove, and we can see what these packhorses carry." He glanced at Doron. "Don't think those caravan guards will keep after us now. Only three of 'em, and we outnumber 'em, *and* we know the land 'round here. They don't."

Doron relaxed somewhat. Now that Ferrin was making decisions again, things were righting themselves. The grove was a resting place for the band, somewhere they could make camp before returning to their stronghold in the hills. If fortune smiled, the contents of the packs they'd snatched from the caravan would prove enough to keep them in food, clothing and supplies for some time to come. Unless, of course, the rumors *were* true and the Guild came looking for them.

Tomar had been this way before, only going in the opposite direction.

Yet the land he rode through looked the same, smelled the same. Brought back memories in a rush. The setting sun seemed right to him; it had always seemed a bit out of place in Haven . . . too far to the south. It had taken some getting used to after he and his family had fled Karse years back for the safety of Valdemar. And all because of his "witch powers," which would have doomed him to the Fires.

Yet his Gift was slight, and he knew it. A small power of Empathy, the ability to put folk at ease, to lower mental barriers and encourage them talk to him when otherwise they would have been reticent to say much of anything.

:A Gift nonetheless, Chosen,: Mindspoke Keesha. *:One cannot change what one is born with. And your Gift has proven itself numerous times. Don't sell yourself short.:*

Tomar leaned forward and stroked his Companion's neck, warmth filling him as always when sharing thoughts with her.

:I'm not dismissing it, Keesha. It's just that—:

He let the thought die. Sometimes it was hard to watch those other Heralds who had Gifts far more powerful than his. Yet, he knew he would not have been Chosen unless he had something of value to offer the world. Companions did not make mistakes in their Choosing.

:And lest you think yourself all that unimportant,: Keesha continued, *:a Herald who was born in Karse, who knows the land, the language and the customs, can be invaluable in the coming days.:*

Truth. If what had recently happened in Karse with the election of a new Son of the Sun, whose very existence as a woman ruler was earthshaking, and if the potential alliance between Valdemar and Karse solidified, there would be need of Heralds who spoke fluent Karsite. Even more valuable, those who had been born in Karse.

Keesha snorted softly, not needing Mindspeech to tell him he was thinking straight.

:Well, I suppose you're right, as usual,: Tomar admitted. He glanced to the west, at the sun sinking closer to the horizon. *:We're going to have to find a place to camp for the night. If I remember, there's a sheltered grove with a clearing in it not all that far ahead. Has a stream for water, and the trees offer some protection. Let's make for it, Keesha, and let tomorrow take care of itself.:*

Once they'd reached the grove, Doron and Jergen had hobbled the horses and now stood watching Ferrin sift through the packs they'd stolen from the merchant's caravan. Doron hunched his shoulders, feeling unease in the group rising. What they'd hoped would be goods they could barter in return for food and clothing turned out to be books. Books! As if any one in this area of Karse cared for books, even if they could read. He could read and cipher some; his parents had sent him to what passed for a village school in these parts. Not that he was all that interested in sitting down and plowing his way through a thicket of words or numbers. His parents had held lofty expectations for their only son: perhaps he could become a scribe who traveled from village to village, writing down various agreements between villagers, to be sanctioned later by local priests.

So much for that wish. His parents had died of a winter flux, and he, at the awkward age of twelve, became an orphan. All that schooling and he didn't know a damned thing about farming. His aunt and uncle had taken over the little farm with the intent of keeping it in the family. Their attitude toward Doron had been much the same as if they'd been caught out in a violent storm with no cover handy. For several years, they'd tried their best to make a go of it but, having little experience farming, they'd finally sold the land to a neighbor. Now sixteen and finding himself cast adrift, he'd tried to live on what little money his aunt and uncle had granted him from the sale. He'd done odd jobs here and there, but when his money ran out and no one seemed likely to hire him, he'd joined Ferrin's band of outlaws, choosing that life over starving to death.

They had become his family. Been so for nigh on five years.

Books.

"Damn it to all the hells!" Ferrin exploded. "Who be interested in books?"

"We could always use 'em for fuel," Chardo ventured. "Burn right nice, I think."

Ferrin growled something. "Won't get us no food, Chardo, or d'you think you can eat words?"

Chardo subsided. Doron shifted uneasily as Ferrin opened the packs from the second horse.

"Well, now. What we got here?" Ferrin lifted something and held it up for inspection. His big hands tore open the bindings. "By all the demons below!" he bellowed. "Paper! Books and paper!"

Doron cringed. And for this Gerran lay dead behind them?

"Could be worse," Jergen said, "village priests *always* need paper. They might even find somethin' to use in them books there."

Ferrin angrily jammed the paper in the pack. "You best hope that be so," he snapped, "or we may go hungry real soon!"

"Least we got waybread to eat tonight," Chardo said.

"Gettin' sick of that stuff myself," Doron offered in a conversational tone. "Glad we got some supplies waitin' for us when we get home."

Ferrin muttered something vile under his breath. At least he hadn't lashed out at Doron's comment. It was just bad luck. Real bad luck. How was anyone to guess the merchant would be carrying items that weren't in demand out here on the border? Nothing anyone could do about bad luck.

"Wish things been different," Chardo said. "Wish we could've got *somethin'* worth while."

Sudden noise made them all turn. They'd left Vomehl at the edge of the grove, bow in hand, to serve as sentry in case the caravan guards had followed. Or, Vkandis forbid, some of the Guild had turned up. Vomehl rode into the clearing by the stream, his face hard to read in the dusk.

"Someone comin'," he said, tethering his horse to a tree. "Seen 'im a ways off."

Doron stiffened, his hand automatically going to his sword.

"Recognize 'im?" Ferrin asked.

"No. Light not the best, but I could see enough. White horse and white rider."

A chill ran down Doron's spine. White horse? White rider? That could only be a Herald. A Herald from Valdemar! What in Vkandis' name was a Herald doing out in this part of the borderlands?

"A demon-rider on a hell-horse?" Chardo shuddered in an automatic response to fear. "You sure?"

"Trust my own eyes," Vomehl said. "Be headed our way."

Ferrin straightened, a look of anticipation crossing his face. "Our luck's turned. Comin' in from behind you?"

Vomehl nodded.

"Then we be less'n charitable not to welcome 'im to our fire," Ferrin said with a nasty grin. "Doron, you and Jergen hide left of the trail. Chardo, me and you wait to the right. Vomehl, you and that bow of yours make this demon-rider and his hell-horse wish they'd never come this way. Now, move!"

Tomar rode toward the grove, deep in thought. Though fairly new to his Whites, he had asked for, and been granted, leave of absence to seek out kin in Karse. As far as he knew, he still had aunts, uncles, and cousins living near the edge of the border between Valdemar and Karse, and for years he had wanted to seek them out. Tomar always wondered what had happened to the relatives they had left behind when he and his family fled.

His father, mother, and sister had settled into a fairly normal existence in Valdemar, made all the more secure because of Tomar's Gift. Now, after attaining a position none of them had ever dreamed of, his heart had turned to the rest of his family. With the possible normalization between Karse and Valdemar, it seemed a good time to make the journey.

:You don't think this is a stupid idea, do you, Keesha?: he asked.

:Why should I think that, Chosen? Family is always

*important. And this gives you a chance to see your home-
land again.:*

Tomar smiled. He looked ahead at the large stand
of trees, just about where he remembered it from his
earlier days in Karse. The light was fading fast, and the
sooner he and Keesha found a place to camp, the better he would feel. He had seen no one on his journey
through the borderlands thus far, only a remote farm or
two. Aside from that, he imagined they would encoun-
ter few people. He still felt it a bit risky to be riding as
a Herald into a country that had been an enemy for so
long, despite all the reforms of the Son of the Sun.

And yet, given the choice of venturing into his native
land disguised and riding a horse of no distinction, he had
been unwilling to leave Keesha behind. Oh, Keesha could
ghost after him, but the physical closeness of Companion
and rider was one thing Tomar did not want to lose.

:Nor do I,: Keesha said. *:It would have been lonely
without you on my back.:*

The warmth of their bond filled Tomar's heart with
joy. How could anyone be more fortunate than to have
been Chosen by such a being as Keesha? Wise—so very,
very wise—elder partner in all he did, she filled an inner
space he had not realized lay empty.

Reaching the edge of the trees, he rode a bit to his
left, then cautiously urged Keesha forward down the
trail he found. The light was getting chancy enough that
he did not want to risk a fall on uneven ground. It grew
darker under the trees, and he radiated his concern to
his Companion.

:Do you think—:

:Chosen!: Keesha's Mindspeech was suddenly urgent.
*:Horses ahead. We need to get out of this place. This could
be very bad for us!:*

Tomar came alert in an instant. He reined Keesha
around. *:Where?:*

Keesha screamed.

It was a scream of both a horse and the mental cry of a Companion. Tomar grabbed for the saddle as Keesha reared. A heavy weight tore him from her back. He landed hard on the ground, partially smothered by two large men who pinned him down. His last view of Keesha was of his Companion racing off toward the edge of the grove. He heard the thrum of an arrow being released as a searing blow of pain ripped across his consciousness.

Blackness filled his mind.

Doron stared at the bound Herald who lay unconscious by the fire. Vomehl had returned, his head hanging and a sour look on his face. He'd loosed several arrows, but he knew he'd hit the hell-horse only once.

Hell-horse. Doron grimaced. The Son of the Sun had said there were no hell-horses, no demon-riders. Most everyone in Karse would be slow to change long-standing beliefs about the Heralds of Valdemar and their unnatural mounts. But change they must, because it was the will of Vkandis, spoken through the Son of the Sun.

Ferrin sat next to the Herald, a calculating expression in his dark eyes. Chardo and Jergen had passed out waybread, and everyone had settled down to eat. Doron kept glancing at the Herald. There was something familiar about the man, but Doron couldn't place it. Chewing the last bit of waybread, he washed it down with a cup of water from the stream. Damn! What was it? Why was this Herald so familiar?

"What you goin' t'do with 'im?" Vomehl asked.

"What d'you think?" Ferrin answered. "Ransom 'im. 'Magine his folk will pay a pretty price to get 'im back again."

Doron wiped his nose to keep his expression hidden. Oh, yes. A pretty price. And just who could they find who'd negotiate that?

The Herald groaned slightly and stirred as best he could, bound as he was with stout ropes. Ferrin leaned over, grasped the man by his hair, and lifted his face to the firelight.

"What you be doin' here?" he demanded.

"Think he understands you?" asked Jergen.

"Don't know," Ferrin growled, throwing an icy look in Jergen's direction. "Maybe."

* "And maybe not."

Ferrin hissed something under his breath and let the Herald's head fall back. But in that short time, Doron suddenly realized why the Herald seemed so familiar. It was his face, the set of his eyes, his chin, his cheek bones. Take away the passage of time that changed the features of anyone who survived childhood and what was left? He could swear he'd seen this man before, years back, when both of them were young.

When he'd escaped the Fires himself because his own witch-powers hadn't grown strong enough for the priests to notice.

The small birthmark over the Herald's right eye convinced him.

Vkandis protect! This man was his cousin!

Tomar opened his eyes and winced in pain from the blow to the back of his head. Firelight flickered across the features of those who had ambushed him. Sitting directly next to him was a big man whose face was unforgiving as a slab of rock. The other men were of all sorts: tall, short, light-haired and dark. One and all, they went clad in rough-spun clothes, their boots scuffed and worn, but their weapons were clean and appeared well cared for.

He closed his eyes again, tried to ignore his headache and the anxiety twisting his heart.

:Keesha! You're hurt! Did they—:

The response he received from his Companion melted the ice in his soul.

:I'll be fine, Chosen. I'm in a little pain, but all right. The arrow grazed the top of my neck. I was very lucky that the archer's aim was a little off. And you?:

:Bound. Head hurts. There are five of them, but you know that. Bandits, I suppose. Where are you?:

Wry amusement filled Keesha's reply. *:Close. Sneaking around in the trees. Unfortunately, there are too many of them for me to be of much help getting you out of there. The man who wounded me is no mean shot. We'll have to think of something else.:*

The big man sitting next to Tomar said something in Karsite.

:Don't let them know you speak the language,: Keesha said. *:Play ignorant. That could aid us in the long run.:*

Tomar nodded inwardly. Easy enough. Maybe, just maybe, he could change their attitude toward one they had always considered an enemy. Perhaps they had yet to hear the words of the Son of the Sun that Heralds were not demons. Or they had, and their ingrained superstitions still held them fast. Yet he might be able to use his Gift to ease them from their hatred and fear, to make them comfortable in his presence.

:I'm going to try it, Keesha. I'm going to project what Gift I have. It could turn things around enough for them to let me go.:

:I'll be watching, Dear Heart. And I'll never be far away. That's not a bad idea. I wish you luck with it.:

Ferrin gave up trying to get a response from the Herald. Doron frowned. Ferrin's reaction wasn't what he was used to seeing. In the past, he would have tried to beat his victim into talking, sometimes merely to take out his frustrations. But Ferrin only sat staring at the Herald, a somewhat puzzled expression on his face.

"Now what we goin' to do?" asked Jergen. "He don't speak our language."

"I'll think of somethin'," Ferrin said.

Doron sat frozen, shaken by the knowledge his cousin lay tightly bound by the campfire. When he'd seen the birthmark, that was all he needed to be convinced the Herald was Tomar. It had been a sad day for Doron when he'd learned Tomar and his family had fled Karse all those years ago. Not that they were all that close, though they had become friends. Farms hereabouts lay far enough apart that folk seldom got together unless it was to help each other during harvest. But those days still remained fresh in his memory. He and Tomar had played together, had wound up in the trouble young boys could so easily find. When Tomar began to exhibit his witch-powers, Doron had first reacted in fear. He wasn't afraid of Tomar—well, not exactly. No, he was more fearful Tomar would be given up to the Fires if any priest recognized what he might become.

And now Doron faced a terrible conflict. He couldn't let his long-lost cousin be harmed, yet his loyalty to his companions was all he had left in the world. They were what passed for family, had been for years.

An odd feeling of ease stole through his mind. He glanced at Jergen and Chardo and saw they'd relaxed some, weren't as edgy as before. Even Vomehl had set his bow aside, no longer keeping it trained on the Herald. Doron's own inner power reacted to something he couldn't place a name to. He felt certain, however, Tomar was its source.

"You said our luck's changed," Vomehl said. "How be that, Ferrin? We got ourselves a demon-rider with nowhere to take 'im."

"I said I'd think of somethin'," Ferrin said, rubbing his stubbled chin.

"Who we goin' to take 'im to?" Chardo asked.

"Maybe one of the priests could arrange for ransom," Jergen suggested.

"Don't think so, Jergen," Vomehl said. "Likely his fellow demon-riders will come lookin' for 'im, and then where will we be?"

"I *said* I'd think of somethin'," Ferrin repeated.

Doron blinked in amazement. Not even a moon-turn before, Ferrin would have backhanded the man foolish enough to question him. Now, all Ferrin could say was he'd think of something.

"It been *your* idea," Chardo complained. "We could've just brought 'im down and left. He wouldn't have knowed what hit 'im."

"*My* idea?" Now some heat entered Ferrin's voice. "Damned right, Chardo. Ain't none of the rest of you had any bright ideas lately."

Doron shook his head. No group of men living close as they did could go day after day, week after week, without some minor quarrels. But this reminded him of times when he'd seen strong drink lower inhibitions, when men would say things they'd normally keep locked behind their teeth.

"Our luck's turned, you said." Vomehl stared into the fire. "So what we got ourselves now? Got us a demon-rider and nowhere to take 'im. Since you be the one with all the ideas, Ferrin, come up with one for *this* situation."

Doron cleared his throat. "Calm down, everyone. We ain't got no choice. We got 'im, and we got to figure out what to do with 'im. Vomehl, you think maybe you killed the Herald's horse?"

"No, dammit. And I be a better shot than that! Cursed hell-horse must've dodged at the last moment."

Doron tried to sound utterly reasonable. "Then how 'bout we leave 'im bound here and ride out at first light."

"Why d'you say that?" Ferrin demanded, growing more belligerent than ever.

"Because," Doron said, keeping his voice level, "if his horse ran off, hard tellin' where it went to. Perhaps to get help. You want to face down a group of angry Heralds?"

"Doron's right." Jergen sat up straighter. "Been a mistake to capture 'im to begin with."

"Whole damned bunch of you gettin' weak-willed," Ferrin snapped. "We got 'im and I'm goin' to make somethin' of it. We got nothin' but books and paper, and it ain't sure we can barter that. Least we can try to get a ransom out of 'im!"

Doron looked away. So much for his attempt to help his cousin. Now Ferrin would be calling all the shots.

At least that was normal.

It was not easy, projecting his Gift while suffering from a splitting headache. What was nearly second nature now became an effort. Tomar tried to concentrate harder, but that only made his head hurt worse. However, from what he could tell, the bandits were responding, their mental defenses lowered enough for them to start arguing among themselves. He could only hope this was not normal behavior. If he could just keep trying, he might be able to convince them nothing would be served by keeping him captive.

He looked at each man in an attempt to see who his Gift had affected the most. Certainly not Ferrin, obviously chief of this band. The bowman who had wounded Keesha had grown peevish, as had the two men named Chardo and Jergen. Tomar thought he had the best chance of influencing the fifth man, who had suggested leaving him behind.

The fifth man. The one who seemed oddly familiar, but whose name was quite common in Karse.

He listened to the bandits snipe at each other, aware he had loosened control over their tongues. They probably never confronted their leader this way. Even outlaws needed discipline, especially when away from their stronghold.

:*It's hard, Keesha,*: he Mindspoke, aware without looking that his Companion lurked unseen somewhere in the trees and brush. :*My head feels like it's splitting open.*:

:*I know, Chosen. I can feel it. Keep trying.*:

:*They'll have to sleep sometime. Maybe then you—*:

:*I doubt it. They'll take turns watching through the night. They're away from their base, and they won't rest easy until they get home.*:

Tomar sighed. Even if all of them slept, Keesha would be hard pressed to take down the entire group. And he was bound tightly, of no help whatsoever. He glanced around the fire at the outlaws who still argued among themselves. The fifth man kept silent, eyes glinting in the firelight. Who was he? Nothing about him stood out to Tomar. He could have been any number of men from this area of Karse. But, aside from being familiar, it was as if he had power of his own, though it lay banked, hidden from all but the most intrusive probes.

:*Keesha, I think I've got an idea. These outlaws possess a lot of buried animosity. Instead of making them trust me, as I've been able to do with people in the past, I've lessened their inhibitions to the stage they're quarreling. What would happen if my Gift was stronger? If I could lay bare the injustices they feel, their anger at each other over slights in the past?*:

:*Then what, Chosen? You're hoping they'd come to blows and possibly wound each other?*:

:*If I could do it, that's a possibility. And if I succeeded, there might be fewer of them for you to immobilize.*: He swallowed heavily. :*But my Gift isn't that strong, and I can't stand to see you hurt again.*:

:Then let's try this,: Keesha responded.*:I'll add power to yours and, between us, we could be more than one alone.:*

Tomar inwardly nodded in assent. He felt the touch of Keesha's mind intensify on his own, added to the familiar warmth that came with the connection. And then, as if he had taken some stimulant, strength poured into him from Keesha, augmenting his Gift.

:Let's see how they deal with this,: he said to Keesha. *:It's worth a try and it* could *work.:*

Doron felt tension mounting again, only this time on the verge of explosion. His own thoughts clamored in a jumble. He remembered times when he'd been pushed aside, when his opinions had been overlooked. Just because he was the youngest didn't mean he should be—

He shoved his anger aside. Not that what he remembered was untrue, but he'd always had better control over himself than this. He glanced at Tomar, at the odd expression on the Herald's face. Maybe that came from the blow to his head, or something else entirely.

"And why'd you decide to attack that particular caravan?" Jergen asked, staring at Ferrin. "Five men guarded it. You be the one who always said we only go after forces much smaller'n us. Six ain't all that much of an advantage."

"Greedy," Chardo muttered. "Always wantin' more and more and more."

Ferrin's eyes nearly popped from his head. "Shut your mouth, you useless piece of—"

"Call me a useless piece—"

"Hey, Ferrin, 'member the time you left me behind in our last raid?" Vomehl's chin jutted out. "Oh, you'll be all right, you said. Got that damned bow of yours."

"And what 'bout *you,* Chardo?" Jergen growled. "Always runnin' your mouth. Nearly got us in trouble last village we stopped in."

"Who elected *you* captain?" Chardo's hand drifted to the hilt of his dagger. "You be more insultin' than Ferrin betimes."

"Insultin'?" Ferrin stood. "I'll show you insultin', Chardo." He glared at the men around the fire. "Only reason I put up with you is we be stronger together than alone. I be better'n the whole lot of you. Smarter, faster, and—"

Chardo jumped to his feet. "Think you be so tough, Ferrin? I could take you down and not breathe hard after. You treat me like I be stupid or somethin'!"

"Stupid? You be more'n that! Twice stupid, most like!"

Doron buried his head in his hands. Everyone seemed to be losing control. He glanced up in time to see Ferrin and Chardo stalking each other, knees slightly bent, circling the fire. The dagger in Chardo's hand glittered in the firelight.

Jergen turned to Vomehl. "And keep your hands off that bow. Don't want to end up with an arrow in my gut."

"S'pose I ain't thought of that many a time?" Vomehl snapped. "You act like you be the only voice of reason in the whole wide world. Like none of us got sense the God gave a goat to figure things out."

Doron felt sweat start on his forehead. A fight between Ferrin and Chardo could leave one of them wounded or dead. The anger he sensed between Jergen and Vomehl could also spark into violence in no time at all. He needed to do something, but he was afraid of what he *could* do. His witch-powers gave him a solution, but he was half afraid of using them.

Chardo struck out, nearly knifing Ferrin in the side. That settled it. Doron stood, backed off into the darkness, clamped his jaw tight, and concentrated.

The grove suddenly filled with the sound of neighing

horses—many horses. Their own mounts snorted and shifted nervously. Vomehl and Jergen glanced around, their faces gone tight in fear. Distant shapes appeared off in the gloom, eyes gleaming in the darkness.

"Hell-horses!" Jergen shouted. "They be comin' for us!"

Ferrin's hand snaked out and grabbed Chardo's knife hand. "Stop, you idiot! That damned horse gone and got himself friends!"

Jergen and Vomehl scrambled to their feet.

"I ain't waitin' around to find out!" Jergen yelled. "Stay here if'n you want!"

"Too many to shoot! Run for it!"

Chardo looked off into the night. "Oh, crap!" He sheathed his dagger and crashed off into the brush and trees, following Jergen and Vomehl.

For a long moment, Ferrin stood rooted by the fire. The sound of the approaching horses grew even louder. He aimed a kick at the bound Herald, missed, and sprinted off after Chardo.

Hidden in the brush, Doron sought to keep the illusion as real as he could possibly make it. When he could no longer hear his outlaw companions, he crept forward, circling around so he approached Tomar from behind. He drew his dagger and began sawing at the ropes binding Tomar fast.

"Your horse be waiting for you somewhere close," he said. "You ain't got much time. Now get out of here, Tomar. They'll be back soon as I lower the illusion."

The Herald's eyes grew round as an owl's.

"Go, dammit! I can't keep this up forever!"

Tomar struggled to a kneeling position, sensation flooding back into his arms as the ropes fell away. The face of the man before him settled at last into recognizable features. He blinked in the firelight, not trusting what he was seeing.

"Doron?" he said, his voice cracking. "Cousin? Is that really you?"

"It be me."

:*Keesha!*:

:*I'm here, Chosen.*:

Tomar glanced over his shoulder as his Companion edged into the clearing. Dried blood stained the utter whiteness of her neck, but aside from that she appeared untouched. He looked at Doron, who slowly backed away, unease in every move he made.

"Keesha won't hurt you," Tomar said. "In fact, she's fallen in love with you."

"What?"

"You saved me, and she thinks you're wonderful."

"I won't be if'n you don't get on that horse and leave! Ferrin and the rest of 'em won't stay off in the woods 'til morning. And I can't maintain my illusion forever."

Sure enough, the sound of uncanny creatures shrilling their anger still filled the grove, only now seeming to follow the fleeing outlaws.

"But how did you escape the Fires?" Tomar asked, scrambling to his feet. He rubbed his stiff arms and ankles to get the circulation flowing again.

"Came late to my witch-powers. And managed to avoid the priests."

Tomar threw both arms around Keesha's neck in a brief hug, then gently traced the bloody track the arrow had left behind. "Come back to Valdemar with me, Doron. You'll be safe there."

Doron shook his head.

"Can't."

:*Don't force what cannot be,*: Keesha said, her Mind-speech tinged with regret. :*It's his decision, Chosen. Maybe in the future . . . .*:

Tomar retrieved his sword and dagger from where Ferrin had dropped them. He met and held Doron's eyes.

"Aunt Chalva? Uncle Lomis? Where are they?"

His parents? Doron winced slightly. "Dead. Winter flux. Nearly died myself. Uncle Branno and Aunt Savia took me in. Tried to keep the farm goin'. Couldn't, so they sold it. Left me with next to nothin'. Joined Ferrin and the rest when I was starvin'." He spread his hands. "Don't you see, Tomar? They be all I got. They be my family now. Can't leave 'em." He licked his lips. "Not yet, least wise."

"But—"

"Tomar . . . please! Get out of here. I be losing my hold on the illusion. Can't keep it going much longer!"

:*He's right,*: Keesha interposed. :*I'm amazed he can divide his attention like this, but his strength is weakening. You don't want to throw away the help he's given you, do you?*:

A flood of sorrow washed over Tomar. He reached out and clasped hands with the cousin he had set off to visit in a world he had erected in his own mind, a world that could never be save in memory.

"All right. But remember this, Doron. There's a place in Valdemar waiting for you. And for what you did . . . I can't find enough words to thank you." He set foot in stirrup and mounted Keesha. "If you ever tire of life as a bandit, come to Valdemar. When you get there, ask for me. They'll find me, and I'll do anything to get you settled in a new home."

"Go, Tomar!"

"Promise me!" He watched Doron closely. "By the God!"

"By Vkandis Sunlord, I promise. Now get out of here!"

Tomar touched hand to forehead in a salute, reined Keesha around, and rode out of the grove. Looking back over his shoulder one last time, he saw his cousin standing by the fire, his own hand lifted in farewell.

* * *

Totally drained, Doron fell to his knees, his body feeling as though he'd been badly beaten, his mind stretched to a thinness he'd never experienced before. It had been a long time since he'd used his powers, and he was amazed he still knew how to cast and hold an illusion that strong.

The grove lay silent now. No neighing horses, no crashing in the brush and trees. Ferrin and the rest of the band would be returning before long. He stood, knees shaking, and slipped off into the darkness. Wouldn't be good if they found him sitting by the fire as if nothing had happened.

He sat down beneath a tree, crossed arms on knees, and stared into the darkness. Tomar. The cousin he thought he'd lost all those years ago. Could be, if life proved different from what it was now, he just might take a journey north. He'd heard about Valdemar . . . how couldn't he, living so close to the border.

Life was change.

And Tomar had given him good reason to think about a different existence. His bandit companions . . . well, they'd survive somehow. Right now, so would he, with them in place of the mother and father he'd lost.

But he had family in Valdemar. *Real* family.

Life was not only change, it was choices to be made.

He heard rustling in the brush and stood. Ferrin and the three others were cautiously returning to the clearing now that the "danger" had passed. He drew a deep breath, squared his shoulders, and slipped back into the clearing to wait for them.

Interview with a Companion

by Benjamin Ohlander

Ben Ohlander was born in South Dakota and grew up in Colorado and North Carolina. After completing high school, he enlisted in the Marines before attending college in Ohio. Upon graduation, he was commissioned as an officer in the Army Reserve. He has been mobilized three times and is currently serving in Afghanistan. In the intervals between deployments he works as a software consultant for IBM and writes as time permits. He lives in southwest Ohio with his wife, three stepsons, two cats, and a mechanical parrot named Max. The cats are generally tolerant of his writing and encourage all of their "staff" to have outside interests.

Dave Matthews (no relation) pulled his aging Chrysler off the two-lane road to consult his map. Kentucky was full of twisty roads anyway, and Lexington more so. Horse farms predated roads here, and cutting up perfectly good bluegrass to put in a straight right-of-way was not only pedestrian, it was downright tacky.

The Google map was pretty clear, five miles north on 88th, across four miles, left turn at Mountebank, one and half miles past the bridge, near the old barn. Come alone. Okay, he was there.

He dug into the aging knapsack that combined computer bag and lunch sack and pulled out the digital recorder. It took him a few seconds to figure out where the batteries went and another several minutes to read the instructions. That, of course, was only after trial and error failed.

"June 12th. Here at Tri-Bridge to meet a source with inside information on purging techniques used by jockey to make weight." He played it back and listened to himself. Not newsy enough.. He turned the recorder back on. "Here at Tri-Bridge to get the skinny on the jockey-purging scandal." Snap. Much better.

The meeting out here in the middle of nowhere seemed perfectly rational for a source with inside information . . . even if "middle of nowhere" was maybe twenty-five minutes from downtown Lexington. The scene fit . . . but no one who looked like a source. No one at all, in fact.

He looked back toward the old barn, some fifty yards away, and on the far side of the white rail fences that were required in horse country. There was a girl working in the barn, but no sign of anyone who fit the profile of a source.

He checked her out. She looked slim enough, with the youngish-colt look of so many of the women in this part of Kentucky. He tried to guess how many millihelens she was, but from the distance he could tell little other than she was slim and lithe. Given his last date had been sometime last year, that was enough to launch a navy of six or seven hundred ships right there.

Still no source.

He checked his watch. He was still a minute or so early, but he thought there ought to be some sign. This was his first source, but he was pretty sure they were supposed to be on time.

He looked back the way he'd come. Nothing there and nothing on the opposite side of the road except a shiny white horse. The horse was heavier than the whippetlike thoroughbreds they were breeding up these days, not a racer at all . . . maybe a show-horse done all in white.

A show horse standing on the far side beside a split rail fence in central Kentucky. Not odd. A show horse standing next to a golf bag in central Kentucky. Very odd.

The horse stared at him, ears perked forward, brown eyes on his. Their eyes met through the streaky windshield.

He took a second look at the golf bag. Okay, definitely odd. A horse and a golf bag standing by the side of the road. Sounded like the lead in for a joke.

He opened the car door and looked down. The driver's side swung over a small drainage ditch that ran alongside the road. He stepped across the ditch and walked around to the front of the car to peer up and down the road. He glanced at his watch, then tipped his baseball cap back on his head.

In the distance, a crop duster puttered, biplane momentarily silhouetted against the sky.

The horse stood calmly looking at him, then dipped his head into the golf bag, and nosed his way between the woods sticking out, each with its own embossed horseshoe cover. When his head came up Dave saw a golden apple between solid, shiny white teeth. Dave blinked. Horses with big yellow choppers, he had seen. These were the sort of teeth usually bought on credit.

The horse crunched the apple thoughtfully, still looking at Dave. It was, he thought, an uncommonly odd feeling, being stared at by a horse.

He looked back at the barn. The girl, obviously mucking out, had a large wheelbarrow full of fun that she pushed around the side of the barn and out of sight. He glanced back at the road, then stared at the horse as it dipped its head into the bag again, rooted between some irons, then came up with a carrot, which it chewed like a cigar. The green stalk flopped back and forth.

A cricket chirped. He flexed his feet, listening to his tennis shoes squeak.

He stared at the horse.

The horse stared at him.

The biplane puttered just on the horizon, dropping a long cloud of pesticide.

"Hot day," he said to the horse.

:Middlin' hot,: said a voice.

"What the f . . .", Dave spun around. "Who said that?"

:Over here, by the golf bag,: said the voice.

Dave whipped his head around. The horse stared at him . . . then slowly and deliberately winked. The eyes, the ones he had thought were brown, now shone a bright, sapphire blue.

Dave took two shuffle steps backward, startled beyond thought. The second ended in profanity as he stepped into the little ditch alongside the road and went down knee deep. His new recorder, bought for the occasion, went "glunk" in the only water for thirty feet in any direction.

"What the f . . ." he repeated, stepping out of the ditch and into the road. Had there been any traffic, he would have been in someone's on-coming lane.

:You came here to get inside information from a source,: said the voice. *:You don't get more inside than this.:*

"What the . . ."

:Gotta say it . . . straight from the horse's mouth.: The horse did something with its hooves, and the sound was a mix of rim-shot and silver bells.

Dave shook his head and began looking for a portable loudspeaker, feeling now that he'd been badly put on. Some jerk out there with a camera, filming him for a sucker, and conning him into talking to a horse.

"So, you're a talking horse? Like the one on TV. Name's Ed? Or that mule?" Dave milked it as best he could, playing along until he could find the speaker system. He zeroed in on the golf bag. He was such a putz. So obvious.

:Don't be an ass, Dave,: said the voice. *:Are my lips moving? In fact, are you really hearing it?:*

That stopped him cold. The horselips not moving, no sound issuing. It was the voice in his head that disturbed him. It wasn't his inner monologue . . . the sort that slipped up when he'd been drinking and checking out pretty girls, and got him into trouble. It was a deeper, masculine voice, the sort that sounded as though it ought to be coming from outside his head. Except it wasn't outside.

"Maybe it's cancer," he said. "Maybe I'm just hearing things."

:Did you read the books I sent?: The horse replied, changing the subject.

"My sister used to read those as a kid. I tried a couple. Chick fic."

The horse rolled his eyes, really rolled them, the whole head tossing.

:Okay, Mr. Pulitzer, just how many stories have you published?:

"Umm, well, I'm working this angle . . ."

:Jockey drinking milk with ipecac chasers ain't exactly news, monkey boy. Next you'll be doing an expose that models are anorexic.:

"Umm . . ."

:How about a real story?:

"Okay, I may be losing it, but I'm talking to a horse."

:Telepathy.:

"What?"

:Telepathy. You are speaking to me, and I am answering you telepathically:.

"Oh, I thought it was called something else."

:So, you have read the books?:

"Okay, one or two. When I was in college. I was broke."

:I won't tell the other guys you were reading pastel pony stories.: The horse actually grinned. *:I know it would get you thrown out of the club. It's called Mindspeaking by the way.:*

"Why not telepathy?"

:Well, we talked to our publicist about it and agreed that calling it telepathy . . . was too science-fictiony. Miiiiiiiiiiiiiiiiind-speeeeeach conveys the same idea, and keeps it in the fantasy canon.:

Dave grasped the only part that made sense. "Horses have a publicist?"

:Yes. A woman in Oklahoma takes our history, dresses it up a bit, and resells it. Makes an okay living at it.: The horse looked long and hard at him. *: What you call chick fic pays pretty well. Not as well as romance, of course, but better than puking jockeys or space guns. Look. We need to get down to business, here. Got your notebook?:*

Dave looked back at his voice recorder, continuing to do its U-boat impression. No way Best Buy was going to take that back. He dug out his analog recorder—a notepad and pen. Somewhere in the back of his mind he realized he had accepted that he was talking to a real live horse. Talking to, maybe not totally unusual . . . but one talking back in slightly accented English was way, way out there.

"Okay, lessee where to start. You are a Companion from Valdemar."

:Yes. And you've misspelled it. It's not Comapnian.:

"Sorry, I'm a little out of my league here. And you are here in Kentucky?"

:Obviously.

"But, why?

*:Vacation. Don't they call this 'horse heaven'? Maybe
this is where we rest up between gigs.:* The Companion
shifted a Number 1 wood a little to take another apple
from the golf bag.

Dave stepped closer. "Is that a . . . a Nicorette
patch?"

:Don't worry about it:. The horse . . . the Companion
sounded genuinely peeved. *:What goes to Kentucky stays
in Kentucky, okay?:*

"Okay, okay. Sorry, I'm a reporter."

:Then, do you want a story or not?:

"Umm, sure. Once I figure out how I'm going to sell
my editor that I've had a conversation with a horse . . .
sorry, Companion, that I communicate with telepathically who has given me news that is fit to print."

*:That's a bit cynical. Why don't you just let it play out
and see where it takes us? Maybe something will suggest
itself that you can use. Let's start on background, and
we'll work up from there.:*

The Companion looked up and down the road, then
crossed one hoof in front of the other.

It was the hoof that sold Dave, once and for all. It
wasn't silverish, or silver painted. It was real silver, real
solid silver, with the deep luster that only the best had
and that he'd spent many hours polishing as a child. He
didn't know much, but he did know his silver.

"No, sh . . . this is for real. You're a real Companion?"

*:Again. Obviously. Ask some questions. Pretend you're
a reporter.:*

Dave fumbled for a place to start. "On background.
Good idea. What's magic?"

The Companion took a deep breath. *:That was original. OK, stock question deserves a stock answer. We are*

surrounded by energy; everyone is all the time. Sun, heat, light, magnetic . . . called leylines for magnetic flux lines, easiest to see and tap. Most of it is ambient, but it's like catching a cup full of drizzle. Easier to grab magnetic flows as they go past. Some people can tap that energy, adapt it to their needs, and alter it by force of will. Please don't say "just like the Force." Because it isn't.:

"Then, who can use this energy?"

:Not sure. At least part is genetic . . . a mutation in the hippocampus or hypothalamus. One of those "H" words. Happy?:

"Yeah, I guess." Dave paused. "Okay, then, the timeline spans two thousand years. So why don't things progress much?"

:Well, you have to understand that magic and technology are fundamentally incompatible. The focus in Valdemar early on was to expand and improve magic . . . which is fine for small tasks, but it fails miserably at the big stuff. Easier to take a crew and pave a road than to magic the dirt to repel water. So, instead of learning physics and how to make things, the mages focused more and more on magic. It's no accident that all of these books have just enough technology to string a sword together or mash up some armor. There is some effort in Selenay's time to go the other way, but it's a late start.:

That made some sense to Dave, but the publicist bit had him going.

"Okay, then what about the stories about the elves making the aluminum cars down in Daytona. That's magic *and* technology."

:Savannah, actually. They're all friends of mine.:

"Okay . . . so now there are elves?"

:Sure, why not? Straight-up Darwin. Adapt or die, even for the fey. Some haul pizza, others carry messages, a few make racecars:. The Companion saw Dave's incredulous expression. *:Look, until twenty minutes ago you'd never*

*had a conversation with a telepathic avatar horse with
nifty silver hooves either, had you? So, why not elves in
LA?:*

Dave had the sense this was all getting way ahead of
him.

"So, if that's true . . . then what about the ones about
the witch . . . the one who hunts ghosts and stuff?"

:Naw. That's pure fiction.:

"Why does that have to be fiction when the rest of it
isn't?"

*:I mean, come on. Ghosts and demons? Prepos-
terous.:*

Dave shook his head, glanced at his notebook. It gave
him a moment to steady himself.

"That seems a bit arbitrary."

:So's life. Next question.:

"So, then just what happened to the Herald Mages?"

*:Two factors came together. Magery was a distrac-
tion. It's hard enough to be a good Herald. Heraldry is
a full-time job by itself. Magecraft is a full-time job as
well, one that doesn't tolerate very many mistakes. Most
of the Heralds who tried both were either not very good
at either or had serious control problems. More than a
couple blew themselves up, or lost control at the wrong
moment. In your world it would be like having a nuke,
incredibly powerful, but one that you were pretty sure the
safety worked. Mostly sure.:*

"What about Vanyel? Oh, I see. Never mind."

*:Magery was going away anyway . . . in Valdemar, at
least. Vanyel was the hot mash after the rubdown, as we
Companions say.:*

He tossed his head at Dave's obvious confusion.

*:For a guy who writes about horses, you don't know
very much. The cherry on the sundae, then.:*

"I write about horse racing. I'm an investigative
reporter."

The Companion looked at his POS car. :*So, how's that working out for you, then?*:

"You were talking about Vanyel?"

:*He was wired tighter than a banjo, and losing it on all sides. He lasted as long as was needful, but only just. His Companion was all that was holding him together at the end. The magic requires a wildness inside that just doesn't mesh well with the discipline that is required to be a really good Herald. Most Herald Mages never mastered the level of discipline needed to be good Heralds but got too much to really embrace the wildness . . . they were the battle cruisers of our world, a compromise design that didn't work very well.*:

"That's from World War II. Firepower of a battleship, speed of a cruiser. Looked great on paper. German sub killed one with one shot."

:*It was the* Bismark, *actually, sank the* Hood. *British battle cruisers got roughly handled at Jutland in the first go, but the Brits didn't learn the lesson for another war. Figured that just because the idea hadn't worked didn't mean it wasn't still a good idea.*:

"Hmmm, that might be a bit obscure for my readers . . . Maybe the Windows ME of Valdemar?"

:*No, that's not right, either. The HM's worked . . . it was the internal contradictions that they couldn't resolve.*:

"OK, how about like a spork . . . compromise design that works okay, but not outstandingly, and does two mutually contradictory things."

:*Hmmm . . . let me think about that one. Van's going to be spinning like high-speed lathe in his grave to be compared to an eating utensil, but I guess it does sort of capture the essence of the idea. Vanyel, the most powerful Herald Mage to ever come down the pike . . . as a spork.*: The Companion considered it a moment. :*Okay. Spork it is.*:

It was the obvious question, so Dave asked it. "How do you know so much about our world?"

:I read a lot.:

"How. I mean how do you turn the pages?"

The Companion gave him a very long look. *:E-book. Next question?:*

Dave looked at his notes, momentarily off stride. "Umm, yeah. Lessee. Okay. But magic eventually came back, right?"

:It never really left. We just sort of locked it out of Valdemar until we were ready... until our hands were tipped anyway. Magic had grown more wild and more dominant among people who were wild anyway and didn't care about consequences. So, we brought it back... in a way that shaped it as a tool we could use. It was a tool, a weapon, but secondary to the Herald/Companion team. That remains the core of what we bring to the fight. The wildness of the magic brought under the control of the Herald, under discipline, not competing with it.:

"You said there were two reasons."

:Yes, with the Herald Mages underfoot, we had an internal elite ... it got to the point where being a Herald wasn't quite good enough. There was something a notch higher, a Herald Mage, that you were either born with or not. A lot of people thought it was descended from the male line, so every HM who peed standing up was hip deep in noblewomen ready to breed their own mageling on the spot... and not a few noble husbands looking the other way.

:It created real problems within the Heralds, and not the least when the sovereigns saw their magecraft dim, those that had them. There were even whispers among the nobility that not only should heraldry be a condition of sovereignty, that magery should be as well. We were well shut of it.

:Now, it's good enough to just be a Herald. Those that have magecraft now have an extra weapon, but that's all.:

"Umm, Okay, then. Internal elites. Let me write that one down." Dave tapped his pencil against his jaw, the way he had seen reporters do when they were going to ask a thoughtful question. "Okay, then. What about all of the bratty nobles. Every book has at least one. Aren't they an elite?"

:Same deal, really. Valdemar is an old-fashioned monarchy, common people, nobles, honcho. Garden variety. None of that "constitutional" business. The sovereign's is absolute but is subject to outside interests. The nobility forms the foundation of the power of the sovereign . . . and that foundation can shift when interests diverge.:

"Oh, that's crass." Dave said.

:It's pragmatic. The Companions are the mortar that holds the foundation of the kingdom together . . . there isn't a noble family that can't count exactly the number of Heralds in their ancestry and exactly how many the other noble families have had.:

"So, if someone gets crosswise with the monarchy, then no more Heralds?" *:Not exactly, more to say that if you stray too far from the ideals of Baron Valdemar . . . but it's sufficient that the major Houses are unlikely to take the chance. So, it amounts to the same thing.:*

"Wow. Good old fashioned interest politics."

:Is there any other kind?:

"Now who's being cynical?"

:Think it through . . . where does succession lie?:

Dave considered a moment, walked back to the car and opened the trunk. He pulled out a marked-up DAW copy out of the cardboard box that served as his filing cabinet. He tucked his notepad into his pants pocket. He riffled through pages. "Sovereign and consort are both Heralds?"

:And?:

"The only way your family gets a shot at being in the royal bed is to be a Herald."

:Yes. The system is very stable, Sovereign to Heir, to Sovereign to Heir. All in neat succession . . . with the distaff side coming usually from the noble houses, so each major family has an equal shot. No pun intended.:

"Okay, so much for the heroics, then. It's all about maintaining social order."

:That's one reason why is called "Being Chosen," Dave, and not "Being Random." Every Choosing serves a larger purpose.:

"Okay, then, I'll bite. What's with all the orphans, sneak thieves, and wretched refuse that get pretty ponies?"

:Well, Dave, it's one part literary convention . . . who wants to read about a bunch of rich kids who get all the prizes? You can get that on the news.:

"I thought you said it was history?"

:Of course, Dave. The woman has to eat, and pure history is pretty dry. Why not sex it up a bit? Doesn't take much. Some literary conventions are pretty darned universal. Noble falling on his fundament and getting his comeuppance, usually at the hands of poor but proud girl, who flummoxes him all before they fall in love and get married . . . snooty rich girl meets poor guy with heart of gold. Same tale, reverse the genitalia for equality's sake. Half of all the stories ever sold used it as a theme. This is being sold as fiction, you know.:

Dave refused to be knocked off stride and plowed ahead.

"So, then, every scullery maid, every farmer's daughter, every (he flipped the book a few more pages) Holderkin girl of a certain age has to be dreaming that a white horse is going to sweep in and take her away from her Cinderella-ashes and to a life of Cinderella-princess. How do they fit in?" Dave trailed off. The Companion actually managed to look a little embarrassed.

:Umm, well, there is also a practical side. The orphaned,

the poor kids aren't conflicted, you see. They are typically so happy to be there ... and just so darned lucky ... that they don't count the cost and are just happy to be in Haven. The rich kids know they are important. Sometimes the nobles are divided, loyal to both House and Sovereign. In the moment of truth, sometimes Heralds have to lay it all on the line ... easier in that moment for it to be someone whose only care is to Sovereign and Crown.:

Dave blinked. "So, the lower classes are cannon fodder?"

The Companion shook his head, silvery mane flying.

:Not at all. Companions are too great an investment to spend willy-nilly, but the hardest missions often go to those with the least to lose. It's never phrased that way, but the sovereign has to balance considerations. Losing a key connection that diminishes a major House may hurt the realm. It good to have some people around where you don't have to balance those considerations. One is whether a moment's hesitation, a moment's pause, means failure and death. It's better to send someone who's already chosen. Pun intended.:

"That's a harsh pun."

:It's a harsh business. To be fair and answer your question ... it's mostly the commoners who excel at the spying. Our noble Heralds do better at the raids and up-close combat, or riding circuit and meting judgment. Most are superb circuit riders. They understand and care about law and work with their Companions to mete justice. Many have too strong a sense of themselves to make good sneaks, however. It just isn't in them.

:The confidence, the sureness ... soldiers turn to it in battle. HUP HUP! Head to the Front! Follow the shiny white coat! But for a spy, you need a street rat.

:The poorer kids have had their lives torn up and have had to adapt themselves, make themselves over to survive, become someone, something else to survive. They

get hazed once they hit the Academy. It's a harsh change for them, harsher than it seems, but it is necessary. Once they are broken down, a mentor comes and lifts them up. That mentor is close to the state, linked to the sovereign. The mentor will take the newer Herald, and will become teacher, confessor, and sometimes, yes, even lover. But the purpose is to attach the loyalty of that Herald to that group who is bound only to the sovereign, no conflict with lineage, or House Honor.:

Dave blinked, taking it in. "I remember a war correspondent telling me a similar thing about how commandos are trained. Just how many Heralds make it to retirement?"

The Companion shuffle-stepped.

:Most times, most. Now, with the Wars, maybe a third get sent out to pasture. The ranks got thinned during the Tedrel Wars, a few for Hardorn, but now that it's gotten worse, there is some serious attrition. Training standards have slipped, as bodies are needed in the field, so losses go up. For those loyal only to crown, it's higher. The queen has to measure carefully how many of the noble Heralds she spends.:

"Still in the white coats?"

:Mostly, yes. The heraldry is a symbol, and the symbol is White. A few get into mufti, but for most, the heraldry is what we are. Skulking about is all very good for Alberich, and it works for those who came from outside the system, but surrendering the Whites is surrendering who we are. Going to grays is a surrender of sorts, that we have to hide who we are, what we represent. We'll do it, of course, but its really hard. Even for the street kids. Sometimes they out White the nobles.:

"Out White?"

:Play the orthodox Herald more vigorously than the nobles. Then their Companion has to find a creek somewhere and drop them in it, to shrink their heads.:

"Why? So far you've described it as a prop for an oligarchy with some pretty hard-nosed ideas about who gets killed in the line of duty."

:Baron Valdemar's Bargain was to create someplace special, a rallying point, a beacon in the night. He was an idealist, of course, but a realist as well. He realized that you can create something special, but sustaining it would need help, so he committed himself, his children, and his children's children to standing against the forces that threaten all free peoples everywhere always. The agreement was simple: to provide a Haven against the dark, to stand as a beacon, to succor all in need, and to rise in defense when no one else would. The Companions are the visible, tangible sign that the Bargain is being honored. Valdemar delivers up idealists, some noble, some common . . . none of whom ride cheerfully into the cannon's mouth, but who will ride nonetheless if there is no other choice.:

Dave dropped the book back in the cardboard box. He closed the trunk hard, using the heel of his hand to get it going. The latch stuck, of course, bouncing the lid back an inch or two. He leaned his hand down on the trunk, trying to hold it closed while he fumbled for the piece of wire that was his backup for when the trunk latch failed, which was most of the time. It took two tries to get it threaded through the trunk latch. He released it and watched the trunk open again and stop about an inch free. He pulled his notepad out of his pocket.

"Now we get to it. So, then, what exactly are the Companions then? Angels sent by God?"

:Hrmmm . . . human concepts are so limited. Let's try this. In my universe there is a Manifestation, a great Creator, a Great Maker, if you will. Humanity can only touch a portion of that concept, and then only imperfectly . . . so that flawed understanding is what gets interpreted locally, in different ways, shaped by different cultures and differ-

ent experiences. In Karse, Vkandis is a very real god, very male, oft given to showmanship, and with a blisteringly large ego. He is definitely his own man . . . err, god. But he is also, at the same time, a part of the Manifestation.:

:We are also part of that Manifestation, not unlike the fire-cats, who are of Vkandis' shaping. But as part of the Bargain we represent all the gods and so are truer to being the agents, the avatars of the Manifestation itself.:

"So, kind of like an angel then?" asked Dave.

The Companion tossed his head, impatient now.

:There is no way I'm going to take a stab at that. Your world is caught in enough killing over whose version of "peace and love" is the right one. I'm not going to toss any more theological fuel on the fire.

:What we are works for Valdemar. Translating it into your world isn't going to help you understand. Let's just stick with avatars—damned stylish avatars, if you will. Let's move on, shall we? Got enough background?:

"Okay. I think so. I still don't see a story."

:Then ask the right question.:

"All right, then. Why are you here? I get that you like the grass, but I'm not buying the vacation bit."

If a horse could smile, the Companion conveyed the sense.

:It's not an accident that many heroes, even in your world, have ridden on white steeds. Your George Washington, of course, a paragon among men, who willingly handed over the reins of power lest he be thought a king. Do you have any idea how rare that is? How astonishingly, vanishingly rare that is? How often does anyone today in your world willingly, voluntarily relinquish power . . . much less when there was no precedent for it?:

"You're saying he had a Companion?"

:He had a conscience to help him be who he already was. A voice to steady him in the darkest watches of the

night, when he was afraid or most in doubt. A friend when he was most alone.:

"There were others?"

:A few. A man in Spain who set the conditions for the world to change, to break through and become when it was, ready to be born in modernity. Much tragedy and millions of lives would be lost in the birthing.:

"Spain . . . ummm, Spain. White horse. El Cid?"

:Very good.

"Thanks. Liberal arts education. Any others?"

:Girl in France. Thought she was talking to God. Rode a white horse.:

"The Maid of Orleans. Joan of Arc."

:Yes. Her inspiration created the idea of the nation of France, set the stage for the rise of the modern state . . . and began the end of the idea that land and king were one.:

"Others?"

:General in your Civil War. Led the southern armies in the east, and whose graciousness in defeat set the tone for knitting the country back together once it was done. And his nemesis, because the rebel had to lose. Both were needed in their essential roles. That war made the country that followed possible, brutally hard for those at the time."

"Lee and Grant . . . But neither of their horses were white. Traveler was a chestnut."

:Was he? Are you sure? Interesting choice of names, isn't it?:

"No. I'm not sure, now that I think on it. I'll have to look it up."

:Wikipedia has a good entry. Try that. And like our Chosen, we can go in mufti, when needful.:

"Good to know. Any others?"

:Hrmm . . . Okay. General in Greece, opened up the east and west. Great tragedy in his wake but made pos-

sible the rise of the west and the linking of the world, the Silk Road.:

"Alexander. But he wasn't Greek, he was Macedonian."

:Whatever.:

"So, just how many Companions in this world?"

:A few. For critical people at a nexus in time, where one person's single choice will decide the fate of millions, for those few, we are a quiet voice, a nudge here, a suggestion there. We are Companions to our Chosen. We suggest, we recommend, we aid.:

"But, compared with here, Valdemar is lousy with them."

The Companion drew himself closer to the fence. The voice in Dave's mind lost its humorous edge and became all business.

:The Chosen are Chosen by Fate, David. We become their Companions to help them fulfill that fate. We're an expensive line item, silver hooves and all, so we go where the need is most.:

"So, then you're here to Choose someone?"

:Yes, David.:

He looked up and down the road. No one was in sight. He began to get an odd, warm feeling in the of his stomach.

:No, David. That role is not yours. There is always a bard, to record the history, to document the story of the Chosen for all ages. It will be your story, if you choose to write it.:

He felt a surge of bitter disappointment. In an instant, he'd seen, he'd read, the flash of sublime joy at being Chosen, and it was gone. "So, then. A job as a sidekick. Great." He made no effort to hide the hurt. "What about the woman in Oklahoma?"

:This is beneath you, Dave. She can tell our story as fiction, but I will not be in this story, except as steed. My

story is told elsewhere. This will be the Chosen's story. The one who changes the future.:

The Companion glanced towards the golf bag. *:Would you get my clubs? The woods are Calloways, but even good clubs can't fix a tendency to slice. I have an appointment.:*

The Companion turned toward the barn.

"The girl?"

:The girl who changes the world. Want to write the story?:

Dave thought about it for almost a minute.

"Sure."

MERCEDES LACKEY

Gwenhwyfar

The White Spirit

A classic tale of King Arthur's legendary queen.
Gwenhwyfar moves in a world where gods walk
among their pagan worshipers, where nebulous
visions warn of future perils, and where there are
two paths for a woman: the path of the Blessing,
or the rarer path of the Warrior. Gwenhwyfar
chosses the latter, giving up the power she is born
to. But the daugther of a king is never truly free
to follow her own calling...

978-0-7564-0585-4
hardcover

To Order Call: 1-800-788-6262
www.dawbooks.com